*Praise* ⸺

"Ms. Hart is a maste
and she remains on n ... add her to
yours!"
—*Ecataromance*

"Megan Hart is one of my favorite authors . . . The sex is hot and steamy, the emotions are real, and the characters easy to identify with. I highly recommend all of Megan Hart's books!"
—*The Best Reviews*

"Terrific erotic romance."
—*Midwest Book Review*

"Unique . . . Fantastic."
—*Sensual Romance*

"Megan Hart is easily one of the more mature, talented voices I've encountered in the recent erotica boom. Deep, thought provoking, and heart wrenching."
—*The Romance Reader*

"Probably the most realistic erotic romance I've ever read . . . I wasn't ready for the story to end."
—*A Romance Review*

"Sexy, romantic."
—*Road to Romance*

"Megan Hart completely wowed me! I never read an erotic book that, aside from the explicit sex, is [also] an emotionally powerful story."
—*Romance Reader at Heart*

"Uplifting . . . Fascinating worldbuilding."
—*Dear Author*

"Enjoyable erotic romances . . . Strong characters and intriguing . . . plots."
—*Genre Go Round Reviews*

*Berkley Sensation titles by Megan Hart*

PLEASURE AND PURPOSE

NO GREATER PLEASURE

SELFISH IS THE HEART

VIRTUE AND VICE

# Virtue
## and
# Vice

## MEGAN HART

BERKLEY SENSATION, NEW YORK

**THE BERKLEY PUBLISHING GROUP**
**Published by the Penguin Group**
**Penguin Group (USA) Inc.**
**375 Hudson Street, New York, New York 10014, USA**
Penguin Group (Canada), 90 Eglinton Avenue East, Suite 700, Toronto, Ontario M4P 2Y3, Canada
(a division of Pearson Penguin Canada Inc.)
Penguin Books Ltd., 80 Strand, London WC2R 0RL, England
Penguin Group Ireland, 25 St. Stephen's Green, Dublin 2, Ireland (a division of Penguin Books Ltd.)
Penguin Group (Australia), 250 Camberwell Road, Camberwell, Victoria 3124, Australia
(a division of Pearson Australia Group Pty. Ltd.)
Penguin Books India Pvt. Ltd., 11 Community Centre, Panchsheel Park, New Delhi—110 017, India
Penguin Group (NZ), 67 Apollo Drive, Rosedale, Auckland 0632, New Zealand
(a division of Pearson New Zealand Ltd.)
Penguin Books (South Africa) (Pty.) Ltd., 24 Sturdee Avenue, Rosebank, Johannesburg 2196,
South Africa

Penguin Books Ltd., Registered Offices: 80 Strand, London WC2R 0RL, England

This book is an original publication of The Berkley Publishing Group.

This is a work of fiction. Names, characters, places, and incidents either are the product of the author's imagination or are used fictitiously, and any resemblance to actual persons, living or dead, business establishments, events, or locales is entirely coincidental. The publisher does not have any control over and does not assume any responsibility for author or third-party websites or their content.

PRINTING HISTORY
Berkley Sensation trade paperback edition / September 2011

Library of Congress Cataloging-in-Publication Data

Hart, Megan.
    Virtue and vice / Megan Hart.
        p. cm.—(Order of solace ; 4)
    ISBN 978-0-425-24298-8 (pbk.)
    I. Title.
    PS3608.A7865V57 2011
    813'.6—dc22
                                                                2011019256

PRINTED IN THE UNITED STATES OF AMERICA

10  9  8  7  6  5  4  3  2  1

*This book is dedicated to the readers—each and every one of you. Without you, there'd be no point in writing. Thank you for your support.*

*Also, as always, to Superman. To my children. To my family. To friends. I love you all, and I'm so glad you're in my life.*

*To the model on this cover, whoever he may be, I couldn't imagine a better set of pecs to represent my hero.*

# Acknowledgments

I could write without music, but I'm so glad I don't have to. Below is a partial playlist of what I listened to while writing *Virtue and Vice*. Please support the artists through legal means.

"Come Here Boy" by Imogen Heap

"Fair" by Remy Zero

"Lost Forever" by The Guggenheim Grotto

"The Promise" by Tracy Chapman

"Swans" by Unkle Bob

"Whataya Want From Me" by Adam Lambert

"Untitled" by Jason Manns

"Ghosts" by Christopher Dallman

"Brand New Lover" by Christopher Dallman

*Five Principles of the Order of Solace*

1. *There is no greater pleasure than providing absolute solace.*

2. *True patience is its own reward.*

3. *A flower is made more beautiful by its thorns.*

4. *Selfish is the heart that thinks first of itself.*

5. *Women we begin and women we shall end.*

# Chapter 1

Run.

It was the only word in Notsah Mevoot's brain. Her feet moved, one in front of the other, bare flesh slapping on polished marble. She ignored the pain in her ankle from where she'd twisted it leaping the stairs and the different sting across her shoulder blades from the cook's switch. She clutched the loaf of bread to her chest beneath the fluttering tatters of her blouse.

Her father, Invisible Mother watch over him, had always said if you're going to do somewhat, do it well. It was clear Notsah lacked her father's evasive skills, her mother's light-fingered talents, else she'd not be running this way with the Shomer Melek as hot on her heels as hounds after a hare. Apparently, she couldn't thieve worth a damn, but she could run faster than the king's guard, at least for the moment. Favoring her wounded ankle, she dodged a few pillars and took a sharp turn down a small hallway half hidden by a tapestry. She leaped the faded carpet that threatened to trip her and stumbled on the other side. She skidded on the marble, not quite as polished in this corridor, and rolled.

Hands and knees, skinned. Bread, squashed. Head, spinning. Notsah got to her feet. Her heart pounded but she paused, breathing hard, listening for the sound of boots on marble. Shouts. Maybe they'd passed by this hallway, gone another way.

"Down here! The chit's gone this way!"

A waft of air pushed ahead of them warned her of the soldiers' approach. Notsah gulped at the air, trying to fill her lungs but only giving herself a dizzy head. She had to run. Harder, faster, longer, dodge and weave or stay still and silent as a statue in the shadows until they passed. Whatever she had to do, she needed to do it well.

And now!

"She won't get away." She recognized that voice.

Erekon Kosem, the Aryon Melek. The King's Lion, leader of the Shomer Melek.

She knew him overwell. The smell of him. The taste, too. A man who'd taken her up against a wall without even bothering to kiss her first couldn't be expected to show her any sympathy now, no matter what they'd once shared between them. Notsah tested her hurt ankle, which after a few moments' rest had stiffened and ached even more.

*Run,* she thought, and pushed herself as the bang and thump of boots came closer. The shouts. They had weapons, those soldiers, but they needed no spears, no swords to wound her. They had their laughter and anger, and most of all, they had their righteousness.

Ahead of her, tucked into an alcove, was another floor-to-ceiling tapestry. Notsah knew what that meant—you couldn't be a kitchen slag or a thief without recognizing that here in House Bydelay such hangings disguised doors not meant to be opened. Not secret, exactly, just unused rooms or back passages between state rooms for the purpose of smuggling lovers in and out.

The soldiers would know it, too, of course, and look inside, but if the Invisible Mother was smiling on Notsah she'd find a place to hide. Maybe even another door to another corridor. Make her escape, though the possibility of this seemed less and less likely the closer the Shomer Melek came.

"All of this for the sake of a pie," she muttered, rolling the shoulders the cook had switched upon the discovery Notsah'd had a taste of what she wasn't meant to savor.

The theft of the bread had been an afterthought, somewhat to nourish her on the road as she ran away from this place, the only home she'd known for the past five seasons since both her parents had been imprisoned and she'd been sold at auction to serve here. Now she was likely to join them and for what? A half-burned crust and a fingerful of fruit pie.

The thought of facing her pursuers, of begging for mercy, passed through her mind swifter than a flash of silver in the sky. There'd be no mercy for the likes of her. The thought of taking her own life came next, but she had no knife to stab herself and the windows here were all barred. She couldn't even jump.

"She's this way!"

"After her, lads, the first to catch her shall have a ten-arro coin from my own purse!"

Her ankle hurt too much to run for long, but she put on a burst of speed and headed for the door behind the tapestry. For one awful moment Notsah thought it was locked, but then the wood creaked and gave as she yanked, and she hurtled herself through it, closing it behind her without a slam to alert the soldiers. It was a small room, a closet almost, set up with a wee fireplace burning scented logs. A chair, a footstool, a pair of bookshelves. A ewer and basin. This was a sanctuary, somewhat like a chapel. A refuge.

But she wasn't the only one in it.

The young man sprawled on the chair, thighs spread, trousers open, startled when she flew through the door. His feet pushed at the floor, tipping the chair but not sending it over backward. He let out a hoarse cry of alarm.

Her mind whirling, Notsah took in the scene and wanted to laugh.

Some young lord had snuck in here to indulge in what was known in the kitchens as the cleric's vice, though Notsah had always wondered how anyone could ever consider celibacy a virtue and self-pleasure a vice. Here she was, interrupting. His fist was still closed around his prick, though he was no longer pumping it, and his eyes glittered with bright passion.

"What the—who by the Void are you?" His face had flushed crimson, a color that did not suit him, as his face was marred by a series of small, blistery pustules that now stood out all the more against his cheeks and forehead.

Notsah knew this man, too, not by the cut of his waistcoat or color of his hair, but by that face. Only one man in House Bydelay suffered so blatantly from Trystan's Pox.

Jarron Bydelay, prince and heir to the throne of the Second Province.

"I plead your mercy," Notsah said.

From the corridor, the shouts grew louder. She stared straight into the prince's eyes. In all her dreams of him, and she'd had many, Notsah had imagined herself in this place many times, though never in this situation. Without thinking twice, she dropped to her knees in front of him.

He didn't resist when she replaced his hand with hers, but when she covered him with her mouth, he cried out again. Low and hoarse. Surprised. His hand came down to grip at her hair. He was very hard, thick and throbbing on her tongue, and Notsah closed her eyes as she sent up another prayer to the Invisible Mother that she might be granted mercy.

*Let the soldiers come and see only the prince and his whore, let them be shamed of their intrusion. Let them go away without bothering overmuch to check. Please.*

He groaned, a familiar noise of male pleasure she knew would soon culminate in his climax. He'd been almost there before she even began, and though it was far from the first time Notsah'd ever had a cock in her mouth, and nor was it the first time her skills had brought the act to a swift conclusion, she needed him to hold off a while longer. Just a little. She slowed the pace, adding a hand to the base of his cock, the other cupping his sac. She sucked gently, but not fast.

His fingers in her hair twisted, tangled. Pulled. Not hard enough to force her to release him, and she couldn't tell if that was his intent or if, like so many men, he was simply so lost in his own pleasure he had no idea he might be causing her pain. She didn't really care. She was not his lover. Not even a mistress. She was simply a thief, stealing even this act for her own purposes and reasons.

Jarron cried out again in the same low, hoarse voice. His cock throbbed and in the next moment he released inside her mouth. Notsah shook, not with her own climax though he might've thought so—men often did—but with resignation. He was finished. So was she.

She swallowed and took her mouth from his cock. She sat back on her heel, careful to keep the pressure off her injured ankle. She wiped her mouth with the back of her hand and looked up at the man from whose kitchen she had so recently fled. He'd never missed a meal in his life, that one. He dressed himself in silks and satins and wiped his ass with lace.

His eyes fluttered as he looked down at her, then opened wide. She'd never been this close to him before, though she'd mooned over his portrait often enough from the shadows. Erekon had hated it when he saw her staring with wide eyes at the pictures of the prince, whose formal portraits never showed the blisters. Jarron Bydelay had blue eyes beneath the shock of thick, dark hair tumbled over his forehead. The blisters, some clear, some white, stood out against the blush on his cheeks.

"Who are you?" he breathed.

The door flew open hard enough to slam into the wall and rattle the books on the shelf. Two of the Shomer Melek burst in, tangling the tapestry as they came and pulling it from its hooks. Erekon came just after them, his dark eyes flat and assessing as he looked around the room.

Too late. If her face had still been buried in Prince Jarron's crotch, Notsah might've had a chance, but as it was, Erekon was already crossing the room to snatch her up by the back of her collar. Notsah dangled in his grip, her breath catching as the shredded throat of her blouse cut into her skin. Her wounded ankle connected with Erekon's shin and hurt her worse than it ever could've hurt him.

"Steady, little *kalbah*," Erekon said, lip curled, the pet name cruel but murmured in a voice like a caress. "Watch yourself, else I feel forced to punish you further."

"What . . . what is . . . ?" The prince hastily arranged his clothes to cover himself and got to his feet. He wasn't nearly as tall as Erekon, but then he was hardly a man grown. He lifted his chin, looking at the King's Lion and ignoring Notsah, who hung like a puppet between them. "What is the meaning of this?"

"This"—Erekon shook Notsah—"is a thief, my lord. She thieved a pie from the kitchen and when she was caught and punished for it, she attacked the cook, stole some bread, and fled."

The world was graying, lack of air sending Notsah into the dream-world. Maybe the Void, she thought with a hint of gratitude. Maybe Erekon would simply choke her into death right now and spare her the rest.

"Put her down," she heard the prince say. "Can't you see she can't breathe?"

Sweet air whistled into her lungs on a gasp, though when she hit the floor at Erekon's feet, every bone in her body seemed to break at once. Notsah whimpered and curled into a ball next to Erekon's polished black boots. No more running. No use.

"My lord prince, she is a thief. Stole right from your kitchen; it's the same as if she'd pranced into your bedchamber and lifted one of your jewels."

Notsah gripped the floor, cold under her fingers. "I was hungry."

Erekon nudged her overhard with his boot, right in the tender spot near her ribs. "Shut up."

"Hunger can move even the most righteous to unnoble acts," the prince said.

Was he . . . defending her? Notsah lifted her head to look up at him, but Erekon pushed it back down. Weary, bruised, nevertheless she drew in a breath of hope.

"My lord, she comes from a long line of thieves and vagabonds. The girl needs no reason to steal, it's in her nature. She can scarce help it."

"And yet she was employed in my kitchens?"

Erekon hesitated before answering. He turned to his two companions. "You two. Out."

He waited until they'd gone before saying, "I had naught to do with such a decision, but aye, she was so employed."

"And it was common knowledge she was inclined to thievery, aye?"

Notsah pressed her forehead to her palms, the backs of her hands flat on the floor. She bit back a smile, though Erekon couldn't possibly see her face. He'd only have to suspect, and he'd kick her again.

"Her service was purchased at auction, so . . . aye, I suppose it was well known." Erekon shifted, his boot coming dangerously close to Notsah's fingers but not crushing them.

Yet.

"If it was well known, if her service was purchased knowing this was what she was, why then the surprise? Why the outrage I hear in your voice, Kosem? You chased her in here as though you meant to kill her for stealing what . . . a loaf of bread? My kitchen bakes a dozen such loaves every day to feed us. Surely one could be spared."

"You don't understand, my lord. It's not what she stole, it's that she stole at all. It's that she attacked the cook. It's that she ran, thinking she could get away with it. . . ." Erekon's voice trailed off and Notsah felt the weight of his attention on her. "It's that she's an uppity, foul-mouthed little kitchen slag who finds it to her pleasure to make herself as better than the rest, who breaks the rules and thinks she can get away with it."

"Let me ask you this, Aryon Kosem. If you stumble upon a nest of wasps and kick it open, do you expect the wasps to sting you?"

"Of course!"

Notsah felt firm but gentle hands on the back of her blouse, pulling her to her feet. She stood, unsteadily, favoring her ankle. The prince was staring at her with an expression she couldn't determine—not pity. Not compassion. Not lust.

"And what do you do when that happens, Aryon?"

"I kill them, of course. Dead as I can."

The prince blinked and shook his head just slightly. "You kill them for doing what is in their nature, and what you yourself brought on. Why?"

"Because I can, my lord," said Erekon sternly. He put a hand on Notsah's arm and pulled her a limping step toward him. "Just as I can punish this little bitch, this *kalbah*, for stealing from your kitchen. It's within the dictates of my duty. And pleading your mercy, if you've an idea otherwise, it's your father I'll answer to. Not you."

The prince's eyes narrowed. So did his mouth. He straightened his shoulders and gave Erekon a looking-over that made Notsah wince.

"Are you saying I have no authority in this matter?"

Erekon nodded. "Aye."

The prince looked her over. "I'll speak to my father, then."

"As it pleases you," Erekon said and yanked Notsah along with him as he backed up. "Come along, you. We've somewhat to discuss."

"Aryon," the prince said.

Erekon stopped. "Aye, my lord."

"Take her to my father."

"Now?" Erekon sounded astounded, and his grip on Notsah tightened.

"Now," said Prince Jarron. "I would speak on her behalf right now."

"King Zevon would hardly want to be bothered on this account right now. . . ."

The prince fixed the King's Lion with a look so regal it made it possible to ignore his ravaged face. "My lord father will hear me, whether it be in plea on behalf of this girl or in condemnation of your service."

Sweet, fierce joy rose up from Notsah's toes and all through her at the way Erekon was then forced to duck his head, to give in. To obey. His grip twisted her blouse, and she didn't even mind the sting against the welts on her shoulders. She was held between the two men, one who'd loved her in the past and one who seemed bent on saving her.

"My lord prince," Erekon said in a low voice. "Your mercy, but this is not the battle you wish to fight."

"Is it a battle, Aryon?"

Erekon hesitated again before answering. "It would seem so."

"It needn't be," said Prince Jarron. "I would not have it be so. Come with me to my father's room now, and he'll hear me out and tell you the course to take. I'll abide by his word."

"My lord prince would do well to remember that I've been his father's Lion since the prince was in nappies," Erekon said.

Prince Jarron smiled, and if his earlier look made it possible to look beyond the scars and blisters, that smile transformed him into somewhat beautiful. "And you'd do well to remember that when my father passes his throne to me, I shall be in charge of the Shomer Melek. You shall be my Lion then."

"But not yet." A familiar anger layered Erekon's tone. Notsah had heard it often, had been spared it on occasion.

Prince Jarron's gaze slid over her, and she understood somewhat. This was not about her. Not about the pleasure she'd given him moments ago, nor about her crime. This was somewhat between the two men between whom she was caught.

"Take her to my father," the prince said in a soft, steady voice.

And Erekon, having no choice, did as he was ordered.

# Chapter 2

*TEN SEASONS LATER*

And the sky blue, I think. Satin, for the breeches. With the cream hose." Adam held up two swatches of fabric, neither of which Jarron gave the simplest damn about, then shook his head. "Not the white. White would be too harsh."

"Have I reminded you today I am considering removing the position of King's Dresser?" Jarron said mildly, looking at his reflection.

Adam rolled his eyes and held up the fabric next to Jarron's face. "As you've done every day for the past sixmonth. This one, I think. It will bring out your eyes."

Jarron turned from the sight of his own face and Adam's in the mirror. "And if I don't want my eyes brought out?"

Adam Delano, Jarron's distant cousin and dearest friend since childhood, put aside the fabric and stood behind him to look at their reflection. "Listen to me, love. You're the Melek Gadol Shetaya, true?"

Jarron glanced at him, eyebrows lifting at the use of the old term. "It surprises me to see you so old-fashioned."

"See?" Adam grinned. "You do care about fashion."

"It has naught to do with fashion, but custom."

"Fashion is custom," Adam said. "King, then, of the Second Province. It doesn't matter how you name yourself, everyone will be looking at your face whether you like it or not. Unless you demand they all stare only at your boots, in which case it's equally as important you choose the right leather."

"I know overwell the sight of my own face."

"Look harder." Adam put a finger to Jarron's chin, turned his face from side to side. "You see that face? It's a handsome face. It's a face the ladies would give up their honor to ride."

Jarron's frown didn't change, but he didn't look away. He saw his own features. Blue eyes, dark brows, long nose, thick lips. Clear skin faintly patterned with the remnants of the pox that could and did break out without reason or warning.

Adam frowned, too. "Ah, such a look! 'Ware, it'll freeze that way."

"Could that be worse?" Jarron said solidly, turning again from his reflection and refusing to allow his friend to pull him back to it. "Make the suit in any color you like, in whatever fabric. I don't care."

Adam sighed and put away the scraps into his voluminous bag bulging with similar samples. "Jarron. Talk to me. You've been in a state for a quiverful of days. It's becoming tedious."

Jarron poured himself a draught of worm and savored the sharp bite of the liquor, the sting of the mild drug diffused inside it. "So go. Leave me."

"You know I won't." Adam took a glass and poured himself a drink, too. "It's because of that whore Lady Trudy, aye? I know it, there's no point in playing coy with me."

"Lady Trudy is hardly a whore."

Adam snorted. "Only because whores charge a reasonable sum for their affections, and Trudy's costs encompass far more than what most men can easily pull from their purse."

"She's a well-respected and much-beloved member of this court," Jarron said with the slightest curl of his lip, thinking of Trudy's simpering laugh, the sweep of her skirts and scent of her perfume.

"Ah, and I suppose the fact she used to call you Prince Prickleface has naught to do with your distaste for the lady's company?"

Jarron wanted to laugh at the old nickname, which Lady Trudy had indeed invented. He wanted to scoff that a childhood wound could still burn and sting. Instead, he shrugged and sipped at his worm. "Her opinion of me has changed a bit since then."

"Of course it has. You're the king now."

"I was a prince, then," Jarron pointed out. The worm worked its way through him, warming and soothing tight muscles. "She had to know I'd eventually take the throne."

"You were children, then. And she was a little runt-faced brat, now grown into a ferret-faced whore who'd like to get her teeth into you." Adam said this with full authority.

He wasn't wrong.

Jarron shrugged and took a seat on the low, plush couch he'd had for so long he felt no compunctions about putting his feet up on it, though Adam rolled his eyes at Jarron's lack of manners. "Her place in this court is determined by her birth and her father's relationship with mine, not by my whim."

Most of the court had, in fact, been in place or at least had been suggested to him by the old man before Jarron took his father's seat on the throne. The advisors, too. Though Jarron had trained and studied for his entire life in order to replace his father, he'd wanted to respect the former king and not turn everything topsy-turvy just because of old resentments.

"You should put her out," Adam suggested. "Right out. She's got money, she's got a passable face if you like that snub-nosed, tiny-lipped look. She'd find a husband right away; it's not as though you'd be sending her onto the street to beg for crusts."

"Oh, she's looking for a husband." The lady in question had made that quite clear.

"You?" Adam burst into raw laughter. "After the time she spent teasing you, now she wants to marry you? But of course, of course she does. I told you, love, you're fair gorgeous."

"And the crown and throne have naught to do with it, true?" Jarron said, amused by his friend's response. "Nor do they matter to any of the ladies who've shown an interest in keeping my company in a rather more intimate manner than I've been used to."

"As if you've ever lacked for such intimate company since you grew hair on your balls."

This was true. The difference was that in the past it had been kitchen drabs and whores who'd spread their legs for him, glad to take his coin in exchange for a few hours' pleasure, and now his potential bedmates were of much loftier lineage.

"Envy doesn't suit you, Adam."

"Nor does self-pity suit you." Adam shrugged and tossed back the last of his worm, then bent to the bag at his feet. "I understand you care little for frippery and fashion, but it's not really about the color or length of your cravat. It's about an appearance. If you care enough to call yourself king instead of melek, you care enough about your responsibility to look like one. Which includes the leather of your boots and the fabric of your suits. Really, Jarron, I'm only trying to make life easier for you, not more difficult."

"I know you are. And I do appreciate it." The worm loosened Jarron's tongue, and he yawned, stretching. "It would seem everyone's set on making my life easier these days. Asking my thoughts on this or that or the other, catering to my tastes in ale, in bread, in the fowl they place on the table. I just want to eat, Adam. Sit at the table and eat, so that I might be away to other pursuits. I don't care for idle conversation, I don't wish to discuss the tax on hose or even dance the latest gavotte."

"You're spoiled. You spent your youth in hiding, and you'd like to keep living all to yourself, tucked away here in your rooms with your books and papers. Well, you can't."

"I can do my work here as well as, if not better than, in any War Room with a bunch of advisors hovering over me, breathing down my neck and trying to curry my favor so that I take their counsel over another's. I don't need the playacting of court to amuse me. In fact, it only distracts." Jarron finished his glass and considered pouring another, but didn't. Overindulgence could lead to breakouts.

Adam rifled through the bag and pulled out a handful of silks he laid against each other, head tilted to study the color combinations. "You need to play the social role as well as the regal. If we were at war, you could seclude yourself in your War Room with your Lion and his cubs and play at strategy all day. If we were in financial difficulty, you could get away with wearing last season's jacket and refusing to host any parties. Thank Sinder that the Second is in neither situation."

"Not at the moment, no. Nor do I intend it should ever be, which is why instead of focusing my attentions on fashion and whimsy I turn my efforts to important matters."

Jarron yawned again, eyes closing. He should go to bed. The sun rose early, even for a king. His courtiers might lay abed until the noon chime, but he had to get up and tend to whatever needed tending.

"Jarron," Adam said. "If you don't open your eyes, I'm going to choose for you, and you'll have to wear what I design."

"I trust you."

Adam sighed and shook Jarron's shoulder until he opened his eyes. "The tenchime has not yet rung, and you're dozing. For shame!"

"Should I stay awake that I might go and lose at a hand of cards? Or so I can flirt with a gaggle of ladies dressed in their best who think beauty can replace wit or even charm? Gorge myself on sweets and get drunk, just because I can?" Jarron yawned again and fended off Adam's grip with a swift jab to the other man's side.

Adam danced out of reach. He might act the part of prancing

posy, but he could hold his own in a real fight, Jarron knew from experience. That poke was the last he'd land against his friend—tonight, at any rate.

"And what would be wrong with that if you did?" Adam demanded.

Jarron sighed and pushed himself up higher on the couch, then scrubbed at his face. Though the skin was clear, his palm still skidded over his cheeks and forehead and he felt the phantom pain of blisters that hadn't plagued him in near a twelvemonth. "I need sleep, not late-night indulgence. For my health."

"Jarron . . ." Adam said, then sighed. "Your father did you a great disservice. Do you know that?"

Jarron's eyes narrowed. Adam had been his boon companion since boyhood, their mothers cousins via marriage. Though he and Adam weren't blood-related, he was the closest Jarron had to a brother.

"Dare you to speak against my father?"

"Only out of love and fondness for the old man, and you know it. He doted on you. Still does. More even than on your sisters, much to their dismay and the amusement of most everyone else."

"It's not wrong for my father to make me his favorite, as I'm the one who's succeeded him. And he loves my sisters, as I do. If you're suggesting my father's love for me was a disservice, I might be persuaded to hit you."

Adam rolled his eyes. "Love, if you were going to hit me over somewhat as simple as my opinion, you'd have laid me flat with your fists a dozen times over in the last few chimes, alone."

"True." Jarron gave the other man a slight smile.

"And I say it was his love for you that has done you wrong. He gave you everything, there's no lie about that. He taught you well, too, made certain you'd be able to take over for him when he decided it was time. But he also never forced you to face society, and now that it's time for you to do so, look at you."

Jarron frowned. "My father was concerned for me. My health."

"Your mind's health. There's naught to say your physical condition would be aggravated or made dangerous by social contact." Adam shook his head and took a seat next to Jarron. "He didn't want you to suffer from mockery."

"Or pity," Jarron said coldly. "Think you he was wrong to so protect me? I'm his son."

"Only those who don't know you would pity you."

Jarron's lip curled at this. He knew this to be untrue. Many who knew him pitied him when the pox were fresh and oozing on his flesh. Even when the blisters healed and disappeared, as they always did, he saw them reflected in the gaze of those who'd seen him at their worst.

"Only fools, then," Adam amended.

"But fools with whom you insist I socialize? Take as my bosom comrades? Flirt with, knowing that behind that fan of lace the lady is likely smirking in disgust at the thought of kissing me?"

"You overthink this."

Jarron shook his head. "You have no idea, Adam. None."

"Not from my own experience, true, but you forget how long I've known you. Your father let you hide away as though it were all right for you to be ashamed, Jarron. So you are."

"I'm not . . . ashamed," Jarron growled and stood. Paced. "I'm practical! I'm honest! Nobody likes to look at disfigurement. It makes them uncomfortable. Awkward. Disgusted. Believe me, I know."

"Because when you look in the mirror it makes you so?"

Jarron flicked a dismissive hand toward his friend. "There is naught wrong with me relying on my brain and talents rather than my face to accomplish what must needs be done. I'm the king of the Second Province, not some dandy dancing boy. It matters not if I am fair of face, only that I'm able to rule this kingdom fairly, wisely, and responsibly."

"I don't argue that fact, love," Adam said, not at all put out by Jarron's outburst. "But tell me you don't quake a little inside when you face a crowd. Tell me your stomach doesn't eat itself with anxiety when you must introduce yourself to someone new, or when you've been called out to lead a dance, or sit at the head of the banquet table. Tell me you don't practice every word you ever speak in public a thousand times in your head before you utter a single one, and I'll thrash you for being a liar."

Jarron might be many things, but not a liar. His shoulders slumped. He faced his friend. "There is so much to be done. So many niceties to follow. I become weary from following them all, from fending off the advances of the women setting themselves in my way so that I might notice them. The men courting my friendship is a might easier to handle, for at least they don't wish to get their hands in my trousers."

"Well, not most of them," Adam said.

Jarron found a small smile at that. "I've known my entire life there would always be people cozying up to me to gain my favor for their own reward. But this past sixmonth since I took the throne has been exhausting. And it's different, Adam."

"Because the pox has been dormant?"

"Because women who turned their eyes from me as I passed now step up to greet me. Because they smile and flirt and coo over me. Because I need a wife and I could have my pick of dozens of beautiful women who'd gladly accept my troth, and yet I find myself unable to consider a single one of them."

"Don't tell me you mean to make one of the handsome gentlemen pining for your touch happy," Adam said. "I'll not believe that no matter how you try to convince me!"

Jarron sighed. "No. Not that. Because I know that no matter how long I've been clear, the pox will never be cured. It could come back at any time, stay for any length of time. You're right. My father did do me a disservice by allowing me to hide away. Perhaps if I'd been made to stand in front of the world I'd have grown thick-skinned enough to do it now without anxiety. Perhaps I could take a woman to wife knowing that when the pox breaks out she'll turn away from me, revolted, and be able to love her anyway. But I can't."

Adam put a hand on his shoulder. "Which is worse, a face full of blisters or a mind gone astray?"

Trystan's Pox manifested itself in two ways—either in the random, painful outbreaks of blisters or in eventual madness such as his father was now facing. Jarron shrugged. "I wasn't given the choice, what difference does it make?"

"Without a wife, you'll have no heir."

"My sisters have had many sons. One of them can take my place when it's time."

Adam laughed. "Which one? You'd do better to have a boy of your own rather than set your sisters squabbling over which of theirs will next become king. Not to mention the safety of your own throat if their husbands learn you intend to choose one of their spawn. And don't forget the lives of your nephews, fighting over which becomes your favorite—"

"Enough," Jarron said, but laughed ruefully. "Curse you to the Void and back again, Adam, for being a good enough friend to be honest."

Jarron wasn't surprised when his friend pulled him into an embrace. Adam was ever the more affectionate. He let his friend pat his back and squeeze him before he pulled away.

"In all matters of my duty as king, I am fully comfortable and confident," Jarron said. "All but this one."

Adam put his hand flat over Jarron's heart. "Sadly, my friend, though I might dress you and make sure you know the latest gossip, I can do naught for this burden you bear here. Your solace must needs come from a place within you."

Jarron put his hand over Adam's. "Tell me true. But until then, I shall continue in my old ways, avoiding what is unnecessarily fanciful, and you shall continue to scold me for it."

Adam took his hand away and tilted his head, studying Jarron thoughtfully. "It needn't be such hardship. I know what could help."

"Do you?"

Adam nodded. "Let me tell you."

# Chapter 3

Being treated with respect never became dull, Demi thought as the footman reached for her hand to help her from the carriage that had picked her up at the train station. She'd been driven in luxury for half a day in a coach carved from fine Shetayan wood, seated on cushions stuffed with groshawk feathers, and served sweet wine and fresh rolls at each of the three stops the coachman had made for her convenience. Now, her hand clasped lightly in the footman's, she was guided carefully down the foldout steps and onto a drive of stones, each carved to match the others in shape and size.

"Your bags, mistress," the coachman said. "It's been a pleasure serving you."

"Thank you." She turned to the footman. "I have only the one bag."

"Very good, mistress." The footman bowed his head and took the bag from the coach. "This way, please."

Sometimes, her patrons were so eager to make her acquaintance they met her at the gate. She hadn't expected as much this time. One did not expect a prince to make such an effort, not even for his Handmaiden. Demi was surprised, however, by the line of expensively dressed lords and ladies who were waiting for her. She was not unused to attention, but as the murmurs and blatant stares followed her down the long, marble-floored corridor, the composure she'd gained from her training threatened to crack.

The men and women followed her like a bridal train, keeping some respectful steps behind but making no secret of their presence. Demi kept her chin high. None of them could know that once she'd fled these halls with stolen bread in her fist. None of them would remember and even if they did, they wouldn't recognize her. So why, then, were they staring? Following? Humming with conversation in which she clearly heard the words "Handmaiden" and "Order."

The footman pushed open two large carved wooden doors and ushered her through into a large room with a dais and throne set up on one end, couches and chairs placed comfortably about the rest of it, along with small tables set with tea services and a long sideboard groaning with a bounty of food. The social hall. She'd been in there before, though never as guest. She'd seen it set for parties, had done the work of cleaning it.

A man sat on the throne.

He stood when she came through the doors. He wore dark trousers and a white shirt, a dark blue vest open at the throat. His boots gleamed in the lamplight, she could see that clearly enough, even if the rest of his outfit lacked the display of the men and women filing in after her. He had ribbons on his wrists, tied tightly. No crown, not even a circlet, held back his thick, dark hair, though it was bound at the base of his neck and fell over one shoulder.

Time had changed him. Given him a length of limb, breadth of shoulders. It had cleared his face of the Trystan's Pox that had so plagued him. Yet she knew him at once. He'd been kind to her long ago, when her name had been Notsah. She'd never forgotten his plea to his father on her behalf. Without it she'd likely be dead by now, or maybe back to whoring and thieving on the streets. She would not have found her comfort in service to the Order of Solace.

A prince no longer, though. Now he was king. Demi had never served a king. But beneath the crown, a king was but a man, and she'd been in service to a number of them. She straightened her shoulders and put on her best face, then moved forward. She went to her knees in front of the dais, ignoring the gasps and giggles from all around. Placing one hand inside the other, Demi Waited.

"Sister Redemption," said the man in front of her in a rough, low voice. "Please. Get up."

She did, gracefully, meeting his gaze with her usual forthright stare. It seemed to discomfit him, for he cut his gaze to the side. "My lord. I am here."

"Right, right," he said, then naught more.

They might stay this way for an hour, a day, a moment. For as long as it took. Demi could be patient. This was his moment, for whatever he'd planned. She smiled.

The king stepped off the dais and stood by her side. He made as though to take her elbow but hesitated. He turned, instead, to face the room. Demi turned, too, at once, following his lead.

"Lords and ladies of House Bydelay. Much rumor and speculation has been flying about regarding my procurement of a Handmaiden of the Order of Solace."

More murmurs, some of admiration, some confusion. No few with a bitter undertone, Demi thought, her gaze going 'round the room to find the faces of the ladies most likely to resent her presence. Not that she cared. She was here to provide her patron with solace, should it be possible to do so. Not to make friends.

Her gaze caught on the face of a tall man standing at the back of the room. Dressed in no less splendor than the others, nevertheless somewhat in his bearing made it clear he wasn't here for social reasons. She recognized the dark hair, now shot through with silver. The dark eyes. The strong jaw and thick, dark brows.

Erekon Kosem. The King's Lion. Even from this distance Demi could see the flash in those fierce eyes.

*Women we begin and women we shall end,* she thought. *Invisible Mother, grant me the wisdom to know my past is the bridge to the woman I've become, not a cage trapping me as the woman I was.*

"This," said the king from beside her in a much stronger voice, "is Redemption. She is, indeed, Handmaiden of the Order of Solace, as you can all clearly see."

The murmuring rose. Demi, uncertain of her patron's purpose, said naught. From his place at the back of the room, Erekon straightened, but Demi carefully kept her gaze from him lest he see even a hint of recognition in her eyes. He would never believe she didn't remember him, but she need not give him the satisfaction of her attention.

"It is my intention to avail myself of her services. All of them," added the king sternly. "As such, she will be my constant companion in all matters. I'm sure you'll all make her welcome and accord her the respect due her position."

It was far pleasanter to be presented in such a manner than to be hidden away as somewhat shameful, but Demi did wonder at the king's reasons. Ah, well. She'd discover them soon enough as she learned him. For now, she stayed at his side in silence, as he'd not indicated he desired her to speak to the crowd. Or him, for that matter.

He turned to her, then, one hand on his heart, and gave her a formal half bow. "Welcome to House Bydelay, lady. Thank you for coming."

"I go where I am required," Demi said easily with a nod to acknowledge his respect. "And it pleases me to do so."

He looked at her face for the first time. He had very lovely blue eyes and an unreadable expression—but no matter, she'd learn him soon enough. That was her purpose and possibly, with the Invisible Mother's blessing, her pleasure as well.

"You must be weary from your travels. We could retire."

Demi again nodded. "If it pleases you, my lord, I would be happy to have a chance to rest. Here or someplace rather more quiet, whatever you wish."

A smile quirked one side of his mouth. "Are you hungry? Thirsty? I could arrange for whatever you'd like to be brought from the kitchen, should you find naught to tempt you on the sideboard."

With his attention on her, the king seemed not to notice the chatter of conversation or the weight of curious eyes. Demi, therefore, ignored them as well. She stepped a bit closer and lowered her voice to keep her words between them.

"I am hungry and thirsty, to be certain, for my journey was a fair long distance. Whatever you have available is certain to suit me, for I'm long accustomed to accommodating myself to what's offered. The question is, my lord, would you like to keep me here on display for a while longer, or would you rather retire now so that we might become better acquainted?"

She didn't necessarily mean more intimately acquainted, though of course should her new patron require that sort of soothing she was more than prepared to provide it. King Jarron had been specific in his petition to the Order. He required a companion, as he'd said moments before, in all matters.

He might not remember she'd already served him on her knees once, but as with his kindness to her, Demi did not forget.

"I thought you might like to acclimate more slowly than that," Jarron said softly.

Demi stepped yet closer. "My lord, it is my pleasure to follow your lead in matters such as this."

Emotions warred on his face. Jarron turned, surveying the room, perhaps noticing how every eye that had been upon them turned away at once. Perhaps not. He looked back at her.

"Tell you true, I'd rather be in my rooms with a fire and book and my feet on an ottoman right now."

"Then I suggest we make our exit at once," Demi said firmly, and took his arm.

Jarron's muscles leaped under her fingertips, but he nodded and put his hand over hers. With a step too swift to be fully confident, he led her toward the doors. Lords and ladies bowed or curtsied as they moved out of his way, but though several of them appeared ready to speak, Jarron ignored them. He kept his eyes on the door. Demi, however, made good use of her gaze to take in what the room offered. To understand what it was he ran from.

Just before they reached the door, one woman stepped in front of them. The width of her skirts blocked their way well enough, but the deep curtsy into which she folded herself made it impossible to ignore her. She dipped so low her breasts made effort to surge out of her gown.

"My lord king," she said.

"Trudy." Jarron stopped short.

Demi didn't stumble, of course; she was too aware of her surroundings to be unsteady on her feet. But she did take a step beyond Jarron's before stopping herself. Demi's traveling boots were of fine leather but badly in need of a polish, and when she tread upon the lady Trudy's gown, the lady at Demi's feet looked up with a sneer that faded with obvious effort.

"Your mercy." Demi moved her foot. "I meant no insult."

Trudy swept upward in a froth of lace and satin, her bosom still heaving. "My lord king, I wanted merely to welcome your new companion to House Bydelay."

*Women we begin,* thought Demi without an outward trace of her inner amusement. She'd faced worse than this. Trudy was no threat to her.

"Please excuse us," Jarron said.

Once through the doors and into the empty hallway, Demi felt Jarron relax. He wasn't looking at her, but his stride had slowed to a more reasonable pace. His arm against hers was no longer as stiff, though he twitched at a sudden burst of laughter and noise from inside the room they'd just left.

"They might not go so far as to mock me to my face any longer," he said in a tight voice, "but I'm sure I remain a great source of amusement, just the same."

"Would you prefer they mock you to your face?"

Jarron stopped and looked startled. "I'd prefer they didn't mock me at all."

"Of course," Demi said. "But as you seem convinced they'll do it anyway, would you prefer it be to your face rather than your back?"

He started moving again, leading her up a long flight of curving stairs. "There are few, if any, who'd dare to do so."

"Now that you're king."

"Yes," Jarron said, stopping at the end of another long hallway in front of a simple wooden door without adornment. "Now that I'm king."

He pushed open the door and stepped aside to allow her to enter, a courtesy of which Demi made note. "One might wonder why you'd keep a court so close to you yet trust them so little or enjoy them so scarcely."

Jarron closed the door behind them. "One might. Do you?"

Demi thought she understood but wanted to hear it from his mouth. "I do, if it pleases you to tell me."

Jarron crossed the room, furnished simply but with taste. Floor-to-ceiling bookcases. A desk. A pair of chairs and a sprung-cushioned couch. He poured from a jug of worm and offered her a glass, which she refused.

"They are the children of my parents' courtiers. Or cousins. Or somehow related to my father's court. They are lords and ladies whose families grew up dancing attendance on my parents and to whom it seems natural enough to do the same for me now that I've taken over. It's a lot of politics, frankly. Not affection."

"Still, you could fill their places with your own friends." Demi took a seat in front of the fire and held out her hands to warm them. She was growing weary, her eyes heavy, but would not prepare for sleep until he did.

Jarron barked out laughter. "It would be a very small court, indeed, if I were to do that."

Demi made no comment on that, but merely studied the fireplace to see if it had ample supplies for brewing tea or if she would be required to ring for service. There was a metal hook that could be hung over the flames to support a kettle, but no kettle. She stood and looked around the rest of the room, spotting her trunk in one corner, unopened.

"Redemption."

She turned. "You might call me Demi, if you like."

Jarron's gaze was bright as he finished off the glass of worm and set it on the desk. He moved toward her. He took her in his arms.

"Is this all right, Demi?"

She tipped her face back to look into his. "Of course."

"You don't mind being brought here from so far away to meet a stranger? To . . ." He paused to wet his lips. "To bed a stranger?"

"Jarron, if you were granted my service, then you know full well what can be expected of me. If you need the comfort of my body, I'm bound to provide it."

"But do you want to?"

She supposed it was more evidence of his kindness, his courtesy, that he asked. Some patrons didn't care to ask. Some simply didn't care.

"Is it difficult for you to believe I might?"

He ran a fingertip down her hairline, then along her jaw to cup her chin. "You don't even know me."

This was not the truth, but she kept silent. She stood on her tiptoes to offer her mouth. "I know much about you. The Mothers-in-Service are very thorough in what they ask of potential patrons."

He laughed a bit uncomfortably. "You know all of me, and yet I know naught of you."

"Would it ease you to know me better before you take me to bed?"

Jarron didn't push her from him. His tongue wet his lower lip before he spoke. "It shouldn't. You're a woman, fair of face and form. That should be enough."

She laughed merrily at that and stepped from his arms to turn slowly in a circle to look about the room. "I could use a drink of some-what other than worm. Somewhat to eat. The use of your privy, more immediately than either of those. Then you might show me what arrangements you've made, and we can talk about whatever you like. I believe that will suit you nicely, true?"

He smiled. "You already know how to please me."

"What I don't know, I'll do my best to learn. Jarron," she said, tak-ing the chance of using his name and not some other honorific, "really, this need not cause you anxiety. I'm here to bring you solace, not keep you from it."

"I know that." He sighed and ran a hand through his hair as though forgetting it was tied back at his neck. "And I know the purpose of the Order, of Handmaidens. I thought it would be perfect."

"Very little in this life is perfect, though I'll do my best to be as close as possible." She laughed again. "I fear on an empty stomach and with travel-weary bones, I might be rather less than prepared for the task."

At once, Jarron gave her that odd half bow—not odd in its execu-tion, which was perfect, but strange in his use of it. Kings, not even princes, weren't bound to bow at all. "Your mercy. The privy is through there, and I'll ring for somewhat to eat and drink at once."

"Thank you." She followed his pointing finger into the privy cham-ber, where her smile slipped from her face and she rested both hands on the washbasin, her head bent.

She stayed that way for only half a breath before forcing herself to look in the glass hung over the sink. She didn't look half as exhausted as she felt. Not at all nervous. In truth, Demi had served seven patrons and had never felt this much anxiety. Not even with her first.

But then, none of the others had been the man who'd saved her life.

# Chapter 4

Jarron rang for a basket of bread, a platter of cold sliced meats and cheeses, a jug of spiced wine. The maid laid it out on the table and took her leave at once. Demi had not yet finished in the privy, so Jarron paced.

Back and forth, boots swishing on the rug. Physically, she was everything he'd told the Order he found attractive. Lush figure, pale hair, dark eyes, fine features. Cultured tone. A bright and merry laugh. She was lovely.

She was his.

Jarron's parents hadn't raised him in the Faith, though they celebrated all the holidays. House Bydelay didn't even have a chapel. Yet the moment Adam had told him about the Order of Solace, Jarron had known it was the right choice. A companion trained in every imaginable manner to meet his needs. One who'd do her best to entertain him, soothe him, make him happy. One who'd give him the use of her body without any expectation other than the respect she was due from her position. One who'd never demand to be made a greater part of his life than she was meant to be.

One who could not become pregnant with his child.

Adam's scoffing about the difficulties Jarron would face should he decide against marrying and providing House Bydelay with an heir hadn't changed his mind, even if he had quieted his speech about the idea. His sisters and their husbands had given him a number of nephews. One of them could become king as easily as any son Jarron spawned. Adam hadn't been wrong about the conflicts it could cause. Kingdoms had been torn asunder and lost for less than the naming of an heir. It would require a subtle hand and negotiations, the working of trust, the management of jealousies between his sisters. All tasks of which Jarron felt fully capable.

Jarron Bydelay would never have an heir of his own, because he would never have children. Trystan's Pox was hereditary, passed only from male to male. Never to daughters. Not always from generation to generation. His sons could very well be free of the disease, yet pass it along to their sons, the way Jarron's grandfather had passed it to Jarron's father. Or a man could live his life entire without so much as a single blister and not know he carried it until dementia took him. There was no cure, and though it wasn't fatal, it was painful, disgusting, inconvenient, and destructive of any sane man's self-esteem. It was a nobleman's disease that made its victims far less than noble.

As far as Jarron was concerned, this line ended with him.

A wife might be considered socially necessary, but unlike some of the surrounding provinces that required their regents to be wed within a twelvemonth of taking the throne, there was no such law in the Second. Jarron could remain a bachelor for the rest of his days or take an official, recognized mistress who'd never bear the title queen but whose offspring could lay claim to the throne. He could even, were he so inclined, take a male consort.

Yet even mistresses who claimed they were barren had been known to turn up with their bellies full of kings, and it wouldn't be fair to bind his life to a male consort in name only when Jarron preferred to share his bed with women. Nor did he want to spend the rest of his life alone, without a companion. With nobody beside him.

No, a Handmaiden was the perfect choice, her span of duty as long as it took for him to achieve that fleeting, indefinable moment known as absolute solace. Which would take the rest of his life, as far as he could tell, Jarron thought, turning to face the archway in which Demi had now appeared.

She looked fresh-faced, her hair tidied, the fringes damp. She still wore the dark blue gown, buttoned throat to hem, but the dust had been brushed away. She had, however, taken off her boots and now padded to him on bare toes she wriggled with a sigh into the thick nap of the rug.

"Ah. Much better. Oh, thank you," she said and turned to the food laid out on the table. "I'm fair famished. Shall you join me?"

"I hadn't intended to eat, but aye, now that you mention it, I am hungry." Jarron made to move toward the table, but Demi waved a hand at him.

"Sit, sit. I will serve you."

"You needn't," he said. "I'm not incapable of loading my own plate."

"Of course not," Demi told him. "But if you won't allow me to serve you, why did you send for me?"

For reasons far more complicated than a plate of meat and bread, Jarron didn't say. He studied her. Merry, twinkling dark eyes, a quirked smile. This was easier than he'd even hoped. She seemed much at ease, which put him so, as well.

With a shrug, he took a seat in his favorite chair. "I like—"

She'd already layered his plate just as he'd have done it himself. She smiled again. "You prefer breast of fowl and sharp cheese, rather than roast mutton and soft cheese."

He took the plate with a small laugh. "You would know this already, aye?"

"Indeed, I do, and much appreciated, as it makes this ever so much easier to start off." She turned back to the table and fixed her own plate, then settled into the chair across from him.

"I half expected you to kneel in front of me," Jarron said. "The way you did in the social hall."

Demi's laugh was light and free. It tickled him, made him want to laugh, too. "Oh. Waiting? It's called Waiting. And I will gladly Wait, if that's what you prefer. Though I find it difficult to eat on the floor!"

They laughed together, and he once more marveled at this conversation. Every woman he'd ever met had spent her time either sneering at him or cooing over him, depending on his title and the condition of his face. Whores could be great conversationalists and were often happy to take his coin in exchange for words instead of fucking, but Jarron was ever too aware that their laughter at his jokes had been bought and paid for, and was therefore suspect. In a sense, he'd bought and paid for this, too, but it was different, somehow.

Demi had tilted her head, watching him as she took a dainty bite of her meat and bread. "You are thinking quite fiercely on somewhat."

"You," he said, having no reason to lie.

She laughed again and got up to pour them both glasses of the good wine he'd ordered. She handed him his, then sipped hers. "Ahhh. Lovely! I do so enjoy fine wine, though tell you true, I've satisfied my thirst with sour more often than not. You're thinking of me, and no wonder, as I'm brand new to you. Perhaps you could ask me about myself. I guarantee you'll learn more from my own lips than by trying to imagine."

"It does rather work better that way, usually," he admitted. "Your mercy, Demi, I'm well aware my social niceties are quite lacking. My friend Adam tells me, often enough. And truth be told . . . I find I often care very little for the sort of casual small talk employed by most. The latest gossip of who's bedding whom scarce matters. Nor does what sort of cards a gentleman prefers, or which dance a lady likes best, or their plans for celebrating the Feast of Sinder, or if, in fact, they celebrate at all. Those are all matters of discussion I find tedious and unnecessary; subjects I truly care about only as regards my friends and family, and of which in that case, I already know."

"I would argue it could behoove a king to know who's bedding whom, if for no other reason than bedfellows do tend to have loyalties to one another that might not otherwise be obvious and which might affect politics." She sipped her wine. "I could argue as well that unless you suffer the tedium of discovering details of other people's preferences, it's unlikely they'll ever become your friend enough that you might not need to know them from small talk."

Her response was unexpected but not irritating. "I'd not thought you'd argue with me at all."

Demi leaned forward to say with a wink, "Only if I feel it might lead to solace, my lord. Only then."

He laughed at that. "Ah, absolute solace. The goal, true?"

"Aye, indeed. Mine and yours, as well." She finished her wine and put it on the table along with her empty plate. Then his. "Shall I ring for someone to take this away or would you prefer me to do it?"

"Do you often have patrons who like to watch you doing the work of a serving maid?"

Demi looked at him. "On occasion. Other times I've been assigned to patrons who had no serving maids, and I was happy then to play the part if it meant they needn't do it themselves and could spend their time in pursuits that pleased them rather better."

"No serving maids." Jarron thought on that. "What sort of nobleman has no serving maids?"

"The sort who's not a nobleman. My patrons have been as varied as . . . well, as the colors in this rug." She scuffed at it with her bare toes again.

The patron fee required by the Order of Solace was so prohibitive, Jarron couldn't see how any but a nobleman could pay it. He frowned. "You mean you might be assigned to . . . a shepherd? A merchant?"

"I might be," she said. "But right now, I'm not. I'm assigned to you."

She'd fitted herself onto his lap before he knew what to say, one arm curled around his neck and her other hand toying with the lace at his throat. "And well pleased I am."

Jarron shifted her weight, slight as it was, his hands on her hips. He looked into her face, aware of her scent, fully feminine. Those dark eyes. The sleek hair, more silver than gold. His hands moved upward instinctively, just below the swell of her breasts.

"Are you, Demi?"

"Aye, indeed I am." She didn't kiss him, though her mouth looked as ripe and ready for kissing as any he'd ever seen.

"How so?"

Jarron hadn't been with a woman in a quiverful of days—not from lack of offers but out of some misplaced self-spite he knew Adam abhorred. He'd been waiting for his Handmaiden. His perfect companion. Now that she was here, however, though his body reacted the way any man's might, somewhat held him back from merely lifting her dress and finding out what she wore beneath it.

Demi traced a fingertip across his brows, then down his nose, and so lightly over each of his lips it tickled and he had to lick them. "Should I tell you what you think I might say?"

"Can you guess what I'm thinking?"

"You're thinking I am pleased because you are a king, not a shepherd, first of all, and I can't deny that's true. I serve in a hovel as well as a palace, but there's no doubt the latter is more comfortable."

This close, he could see sparks of gold and green in those dark eyes. She wore her hair in a long, intricate braid down her back to her hips. What would it be like to loose the tie at the end and spread it out with his fingers?

"You're thinking I am well pleased because it's my purpose to tell you so," she added.

"Is that not the truth?"

"Of course. But it is never my purpose to lie. You should know this about me, Jarron."

She kissed him, then, soft and full on the mouth. The sweet pressure surprised him—had a woman ever moved to kiss him first? If she had, he could not recall. His fingers tightened against her as he responded without thinking to the kiss.

She'd begun it; she ended it, too. She kept her mouth close to his, her breath caressing him, so when she spoke each word became another kiss. "You think it impossible for me to want you for yourself on so short an acquaintance, when you forget how greatly I know you already."

"But you don't, not really," he said against her lips. "Only what you read in a bunch of papers I could have easily lied about."

No woman had ever laughed and kissed him at the same time. The sensation was intriguing. So was the way Demi shifted on his lap, pressing her rear against his rapidly filling cock.

"Those who send for a Handmaiden don't lie to the Order of Solace. Or if they do, they're quickly found out, and you can imagine what happens then."

Jarron was having some difficulty imagining anything but what it might be like to be inside her, but he murmured, ". . . They're not granted a Handmaiden?"

"Indeed, they are not."

Her kiss this time was longer. Deeper. Her mouth opened and her tongue stroked his.

"What if the lies aren't discovered until after they've sent one?" He managed to say between kisses.

"The Mothers-in-Service call her home, of course," she murmured into his mouth.

"And the patron?"

"Condemned to the Void," Demi said with a low, sensual chuckle. She cupped his face in her hands and looked into his eyes. "So you see, very few would dare risk such a thing."

"I can't imagine why."

"Jarron," she said. "Please, take me to bed."

He put an arm beneath her knees and stood, lifting her as she giggled and buried her face against his neck. Jarron Bydelay was no fool, no mutton-headed dolt. When a beautiful woman sat upon his lap and offered herself to him, he took her.

# Chapter 5

Jarron carried her to the four-poster bed, large enough for four bodies and appointed with lush bedding and hangings, where he let them both fall into the mound of pillows and blankets so thick there was no possible way for it to hurt. Demi laughed when his kisses found her throat and his hands the curve of her hips. When his fingers inched up her gown, seeking her bare skin beneath. She laughed and it became a low, slow, sigh of pleasure when his fingertips skimmed her knee. Then, her thigh. She looked at him.

He couldn't know how often she'd thought of him. How many men had worn his face when they pushed it between her thighs, how many times she'd closed her eyes and remembered the taste of him when she knelt between a lover's legs. Never when with a patron, oh no, she took her Calling more seriously than that. But during the in between times, when she'd taken her temporary pleasure with the men who worked on the Motherhouse grounds or those she found willing enough in taverns . . . then, ah, then it was all she could ever do to bite back his name when she came.

There was no reason for him to know, even if he ever did think of that long-ago day. As prince of the Second Province and now king, he'd have had opportunity to bed countless women. A random cock-sucking from a straggle-haired whore on the run from the Shomer Melek would hardly have made an impression . . . though truth be told, she couldn't help hoping it had. How many women had he saved from prison, or at the very least the Lion's lash? Could it have been so many he'd not remember her?

"You stare," Jarron said in a low voice. "Am I so remarkable?"

"I would say handsome," Demi said at once, blushing at how he'd caught her.

Jarron pushed onto his hands and knees, the bed dipping as he moved. Then he pushed up farther to look at her. "Tell me somewhat, Demi."

"Anything," she promised.

"I know you're willing to bed me with barely more than a few hours' acquaintance because it's part of your duty, but how do you really feel about the idea?"

"I've been without a patron for a sixmonth, Jarron, and my last one was a very spoiled young woman who never required my services in her bed. I've not had a lover in nigh on a twelvemonth's time. How would you imagine I feel about the prospect of making love to you right now?"

He laughed, ducking his head, and his blush endeared him to her. The young prince had ever been humble. It was good to see he'd not lost that now that he'd taken the throne.

"I don't know, that's why I asked you," he said.

"Then I shall tell you." Demi got up on her knees, too, and gathered her gown about them to puddle on the bedcovers. She put her hands on his shoulders and looked into his eyes. "I look forward to it very much, indeed. In sooth, my lord, I fair to ache with the wanting of your touch."

Jarron shivered beneath her palms; she felt him, though it was so subtle a shake she'd not have noticed from gaze alone. He met her eyes squarely and put his hands on her hips.

"I could be a selfish, unaccomplished lover," he said.

She smiled. "You could, though I find that an unlikely idea."

His fingers twitched, pulling her slightly closer. "Many women pursue me."

"I'm fair certain quite a few have managed to catch you, at least for an hour or two, true?" Demi moved a little closer, their bodies touching but not pressing. "I'm fully aware of your reasons for bringing me here, Jarron. I know what you want, dear one, and please believe me when I tell you it will be my pleasure as well as my purpose to provide you with it."

He dropped his head again. Drew a breath. Then another. He shook again, though not with laughter or tears, but some other emotion Demi couldn't quite determine. Her heart broke a little for this man in front of her who ought to have the world in his grasp—or at least his small piece of it—and yet who struggled so seriously with what he was unable to change.

The Mothers-in-Service had chosen to send her here. Demi had made no petition, no requests to them, and how could she? She'd never have known Jarron would send for a Handmaiden, and even if she had, it would've been impossible for her to force herself into the place the Mothers decided was worthy of filling. She'd prayed to the Invisible Mother and never dreamed her prayer would be granted in this manner.

Yet now it had, and she was here, in his bed. By his side, where she would play the part she'd perfected through hours of training and service and, of course, true faith. Her own desires would play second part to his. For an instant, Demi was shamed. She'd come close to getting lost in her own glee while ignoring the reason she was here.

"Jarron," she murmured until he looked up, and then she cupped her hand over his cheek. "I want naught from you. Moreover, I can take naught. I am here to lead you toward absolute solace, whether it be through the gift of my body or my conversation, or even somewhat as simple as lending you an ear into which you might vent your frustrations. Do you believe I can do that?"

He hesitated. "Absolute solace sounds like a pretty myth to me, I must confess."

"Sweetheart, it sounds that way to most people. Truly. There are actually very few patrons who believe wholeheartedly in what my Sisters and I do our best to provide."

He laughed a little and turned his face to kiss her palm, then put his hand over hers. "It must be frustrating for you. Trying so hard to convince them."

Demi leaned toward him. "The Invisible Mother turns minds and hearts, not me. All I can do is be here for when your mind and heart are so turned."

"I want . . . no. I need someone," Jarron said.

"I know you do."

He kissed her gently. Then deeper. His hands tightened, bunching her gown. His tongue teased at hers until he broke away, gaze bright and mouth wet.

"How long has it been, did you say? An entire twelvemonth?"

"Aye," Demi whispered, her breath catching in her throat.

"Nobody has touched you in all that time?" Jarron's hand slid from her hip to cup her breast through the thick fabric of her traveling gown. "Not like this?"

Her nipple peaked at once. Her breath hitched again, but she managed a smile. "No."

Jarron's thumb passed over her nipple in a way that denied anything he might have claimed as selfishness or lack of experience. "And you would have me be the first in so long?"

There was no point in playing coy. It was not the style employed by Handmaidens. Nor by her. Demi arched into his touch, offering her body to him. "Please."

Emotion flickered in his gaze again, though she wasn't able to determine his feelings from the tiny shift and ripple of his features. That would come in time, she thought as he kissed her again. All of it, in time.

Jarron pushed her gently back. "I would have you undress yourself for me, Demi."

"If it pleases you." The response rose naturally to her tongue. Habit. Yet it was not habit but eagerness that set her hands to trembling as she put them to the first button at her throat.

She loosed it from its slot. Then the next. One by one, down the length of her body, baring her skin and the sheer shift she wore beneath the gown. Her nipples poked, clearly outlined, at the fabric, and she knew that the dark triangle between her thighs would be just as easily glimpsed. She shrugged out of the gown and let it puddle around her thighs, then shifted to push it off entirely.

"The shift, as well. I would see you. All of you."

For that, Demi got slowly off the bed to stand in front of him as Jarron swung his legs over the side. She let first one sleeve and then the other slide from her shoulders. The shift had a ribbon to tie it above her breasts, and she tugged it open. The material fell away to slip down her body. She stepped out of it and stood naked in front of him.

"You are so lovely." Jarron sounded surprised.

She couldn't be offended. She'd had stranger reactions from patrons at the sight of her. And, truth, she knew he'd had at least the opportunity to bed women far more beautiful than she, even if he'd never taken it.

Demi cupped her breasts lightly, passing her own thumbs over the tight nipples. The cool air teased her flesh. She made no move toward him, and no motion to cover herself.

Jarron loosed his cravat and tossed it aside. He took off his vest. Undid the ribbon at his throat and cuffs, all while watching her. He pulled his shirt off over his head. That, too, he tossed to the side, and sat in front of her with his chest bare.

"Indeed, my lord, you are lovely, too."

Jarron passed a hand over his bare skin to press his palm over his heart, fingers slightly curled. The pox had left him unblemished for the most part, at least from this distance. His skin was smooth but for a few curling dark hairs around his nipples and a sleek line of hair running from his navel over a lean, taut belly and into the waistband of his trousers.

"Unlace my trousers." His voice had gone hoarse. Rough. Raw.

Demi knew how that felt. Her own body was full of tremors, shivers, her muscles tight with anticipation. She'd been truthful about how long it had been since she'd had any lover's touch. Her own touch was no replacement for a lover's hand or mouth. His cock.

She surprised him, she could tell by the way he drew in a hissing breath when instead of dropping to her knees to obey, Demi put a hand on his chest and kissed his mouth while the other hand slipped between them to tug at the cords at his waist. She slid the lacing from its grommets and cupped his cock through the sleek fabric of his trousers.

Jarron groaned. She squeezed gently, and stroked, feeling his thickness. She pushed aside the open crotch of his trousers and put her hand inside to find his bare flesh.

She groaned, too, deep into his mouth. She kissed him harder and used both hands to push his trousers over his hips. Down his thighs. She wanted him naked.

She was already slick for him. Wet. The miracle of her body's response to arousal never failed to move her, and she sent a silent prayer of gratitude to the Invisible Mother for granting her the ability to experience such pleasure.

Jarron's kiss deepened. He pulled her onto his lap, his cock trapped between them, grinding against her pelvis. He moved to the edge of the bed, feet flat on the floor, and put his hands beneath her bottom to lift her.

"I want to be inside you." His voice snagged on the words and sent a hot wave of desire coursing through her.

She pushed a hand between them to grip his cock and guide it inside her as she sank slowly, slowly down until he'd filled her. Ah, Land Above, it felt so good. The way he groaned again told her he felt the same, but Jarron didn't move right away.

He'd pressed his face against her, his breath caressing her nipple. His cheek was hot on her skin. His hands still cupped her bottom. Inside her, his cock pulsed as he let out a long, shuddering breath.

"You feel so good," Jarron murmured. "So tight and hot. So wet."

"For you," she whispered into his ear, her eyes closed.

Mouths moved and words came out, stumbling, when bodies were aroused. Demi found silence as pleasing as this sort of conversation and could provide whatever best pleased her patron—but for some reason, that Jarron seemed inclined to talk during lovemaking surprised her.

Truth, so had his command. He didn't speak as a young man eager to live out longtime fantasies once granted the chance, but a man who knew what he wanted. How to get it. Not afraid to make certain she knew how to give it.

"I would have you tell me," Jarron said, "how well this pleases you."

He shifted to press his fingers against her clitoris. The pleasure that had been growing with his every touch now surged abruptly, and Demi gasped a little. He eased the pressure, gently circling her clit with his thumb, still not thrusting inside her.

"Look at me, Demi," Jarron said in a tone that allowed no disobedience. "I would watch you take your pleasure."

"That . . . that well pleases me," she managed to say. "Touching me in that way, it's . . . ah . . ."

He smiled. "This?"

"Aye, that." She arched her back, eyes closed.

It was impossible not to rock against him, but no matter how she moved, Jarron did not speed his pace. Slowly, steadily, he rubbed her in small circles even as he kept himself still. He filled her, but didn't thrust into her.

"I said, look at me."

She did at once. His gaze had gone hot, his brow furrowed. Mouth thin in concentration. A flush crept up his chest to paint his throat, and Demi watched as Jarron swallowed hard. She put her hands on his shoulders, her nails digging into him, but if it caused him pain, Jarron showed no sign. Her thighs pressed at him as her body moved. Pleasure spiraled higher inside her.

"I would have you take your pleasure with me," Jarron said in a low voice. "I would see you break apart with it."

No one had ever spoken to her in such a manner, described a climax in such a way, but Demi knew at once exactly what Jarron meant. She was breaking. Splintering. This pleasure would shatter her in a moment or two, no more than that, so long as the steady pressure of his thumb against her remained unceasing.

She wanted to move on him, to feel him thrust inside her. His grip on her hip eased in silent permission as his tongue crept out to stroke along his lower lip. Demi, helpless to remain still, pushed with her knees to rock against his cock.

Jarron shuddered and bit his lower lip. Only then did his stroking falter, and just for that moment, because in the next he was moving with her. Slowly, pushing deep inside and pulling out. Then faster. Harder. His thumb kept up the delightful pressure where she needed it most, and Demi did, at last, break.

She shuddered with her climax, her head bent, breath hissing out of her as her fingers dug deeper into him. He moved his hand from between them, using it to grip her bottom and move her even faster on his erection. She was so wet, each thrust was effortless. He pushed harder into her, fingers bruising, but she was too filled with ecstasy to care. Her orgasm swept over her, leaving her senseless to anything but the bliss. She hadn't realized she'd closed her eyes until he spoke.

"Look at me, Demi." Jarron's voice had gone impossibly deep, rough.

She opened her eyes again to look deeply into his. The muscles on his arms had gone tight with effort as he fucked upward into her. She'd already broken, as he'd commanded, but when he growled her name in that way, somewhat inside her twisted.

He was close to spilling inside her—she'd been with enough men to see it on his face. She should rock with him, ease him into his own climax. Make it easy for him. She wanted to. She'd intended to.

Yet watching him, what Demi thought of was not the pleasure he'd just given her, not the lovemaking they were sharing just now. Not even his face as it was before her, the man he'd become, but the boy he'd been then. Her vision blurred as she moved faster with him, and this time, when she closed her eyes, Jarron didn't command her to open them.

She'd been running, her heart pounding. She'd opened the door. She'd seen him, the young prince who'd always been so kind without ever even knowing he was. She'd gone to her knees to save herself, thinking to hide . . . but no. Not really. She'd have gone to her knees for him anyway. She knew that now, as she knew the woman she'd become. She'd have gone to her knees to take him in her mouth because she'd wanted him, even then.

And now, she had him.

She said his name as desire built up inside her again. Fast, sharp, strong. A wave of climax so fierce it stole her breath and left her light-headed. She opened her eyes and looked into his as she came. Jarron's lashes fluttered as he filled her, but he was looking at her, too.

Slowly they eased into stillness, both breathing hard, both sweating. She tasted salt when she licked her lips and on his mouth when he kissed her. The kiss didn't surprise her, but his laughter did. Delighted, full-fledged, without reserve. It transformed him.

"This will be everything I wanted," Jarron said. "Everything I need."

She'd come here for just that purpose with no doubts she'd succeed and yet, watching now, for the first time since taking her vows as a Handmaiden, Demi wondered if she was fit for the task before her.

# Chapter 6

She's perfect," Jarron said smugly to Adam. "Utterly, astoundingly perfect."

"Absolutely?" Adam asked coyly.

"Not yet, and frankly, brother, it will be fine with me if we never reach that point. I asked her how we'd know."

Jarron tossed a grape into the air and caught it in his mouth. He'd woken every morn for the past sennight to find Demi waiting for him with open arms and eager mouth. It was the first time he'd ever had a woman in his bed for longer than a few hours and he'd slept better than he ever had. Having her serve his breakfast in the privacy of his quarters had been additionally delightful.

"And what did she say?" Adam snagged a grape from the cluster and popped it into his own mouth, then swiped a slice of cheese. "And did she make this platter for you?"

"She did," Jarron said in a low voice with a glance toward the hall leading to the privy chamber where Demi had gone to have a bath while Adam visited. "Chose the cheese and fruit herself from the kitchens, told me she wanted to make sure it was the best."

"Are you not always served the best?"

"Demi says the most expensive or best in quality isn't always the best to suit an individual's palate." Jarron held up another grape to the light before eating it. "I've never been served this kind before. She says it's the sort they use to make jam, not to be eaten on their own. But I like them."

"And of the rest? What answer did she give to your other question?" Adam settled back in his chair, one leg crossed over the other, and cocked his head to stare at Jarron with bright eyes.

"She said we'll simply . . . know."

Adam's brows rose. "Indeed? What magic is that?"

Jarron shrugged, uncomfortable under his friend's piercing stare. "I don't know. Frankly, I don't care. She's here, and that's all that matters to me."

"You've the glow of a man who's been well and thoroughly bedded, that's fair obvious. And she's certainly made a difference in your attire."

Jarron grinned. "She lays out my clothes for me in the morn."

"My envy knows no bounds," Adam said with a wave of his fingers. "Still, I suppose that so long as she's not actually designing the clothes, I can suffer the fact you allow her to choose them instead of me."

"She's made everything so easy. So simple. She anticipates my every need, provides it sometimes before I even know it myself. I scarce need do more than wake, wash, and eat."

"And fuck," Adam said. "Let's not forget the most important thing."

It was more than that, though Jarron was hard-pressed to explain why. Or how. Yes, Demi was so eager to bed him, so accomplished and varied in her talents, that Jarron could count himself a fortunate man indeed. Yes, she'd rearranged the furniture in his library, ordered new bedding for his bed, and turned his formerly dark and somewhat gloomy quarters into a bright, inviting, and thoroughly cheerful space. And yes, she served him on her knees in that particularly appealing position she called Waiting, which pleased him beyond his expectations. But Jarron might've hired maids to do the same, a designer to accomplish what Demi had done, taken whores to give him sexual release.

"She is everything," he told Adam.

Adam studied Jarron with narrowed eyes. "'Ware, else you'll tell me next you're in love with her."

"No. Not that. Of course not." Jarron shook his head. "She's a Handmaiden, brother, they're not meant for love."

"No? Those aren't the rumors I've heard in times past. But then, who am I, your dearest and longest friend, the brother of your heart, to argue with you?"

Jarron threw a grape at him, and Adam plucked it from the air as easily as if he'd known the path of its flight before it hit the air. "Ah, brother, you're the one who told me about it. Encouraged me to seek a Handmaiden, as I recall. Helped me fill out their stacks of papers. Now you say I should be careful? What kind of brother are you to lead me astray?"

Adam laughed. "Not astray. Surely, love, I didn't think you'd be so . . . taken . . . by her. But she's lovely, I can understand why. It must be a fair pleasant thing, to be served so completely. It's a wonder more people don't take on Handmaidens. I'm fair tempted, myself."

"You?" Jarron said with a snort. "They're women, you know. All of them."

"Just because I don't like to put my cock in one doesn't mean I can't appreciate their qualities. I might like a woman puttering about my quarters, setting things to rights. Tidying. Serving me grapes I'd never had except in jam."

"You might." Jarron leaned back in his chair with a self-satisfied grin. "I didn't know you were in need of solace, though."

"Who isn't?"

Adam sounded so serious that Jarron thought on his answer before making it. "Think you we all are? Every one? Do you not think there are those in this world who've found it, all on their own without the help of a Handmaiden? Surely the world can't rely on the Order of Solace for its happiness."

"Happiness," Adam said bluntly, "is not solace. I'm not saying nobody can be happy on their own without the services of a Handmaiden. But solace is somewhat else altogether. Absolute solace? If it exists, I do believe it's difficult to come by. Aye. And surely they believe it. The priest of the Faith, and the Sisters of the Order. So do lots of people."

"Lots of people think the moon is made of cheese." Jarron lifted a slice from the platter and bit into it. "Thinking such doesn't make it true."

"And how do you know the moon isn't made of cheese?" Adam demanded. "Have you been there?"

"If it were made of cheese, it would wear away."

"It does," Adam said. "Every thirty days or so. And then it grows back. It's made from self-generating cheese."

Jarron threw another grape at him. "No wonder you were such a poor student, with a head full of ideas such as that."

Adam didn't catch it this time. He laughed and looked toward the hall. "And she happily goes away so conveniently. If I were of a softer heart, I'd think it was because of me."

"It was because of me. She'd have stayed if I told her to." A hot thrill shot through him at that, one he was unused to feeling.

"She does whatever you say. Without question, true? Without regard to anything but your whims? What makes you happy? No wonder you look so addled since she arrived."

"I don't," Jarron protested.

"You look happy. Don't think the court hasn't noticed. Your dear mother herself commented upon it just yesterday when I passed her in the gardens."

Jarron frowned at the mention. "One might imagine my lady mother would be gratified to know of her son's happiness."

Adam laughed heartily at that, and no wonder, for he'd known the woman for as long as he'd known Jarron. "Your mother? Grateful for somewhat that does not somehow involve her? Land Above, love, you should know better than that."

Jarron shrugged and toyed with a grape, his stomach gone sour at the thought. "She knows full well about Demi. I'm a man grown. I don't need her permission to marry or to take a mistress; why should I need her permission for this?"

Adam waved a languid hand. "Ah, the fact you don't need her permission to do anywhat is no reason, in her mind, for you not to consult her. You know that. Sinder's Arrow, Jarron, the woman would like to see the handkerchief you sneeze into, so that she might see the color of your snot. Think you she's not been gnashing her teeth at the thought of some woman living in your chambers, at your side, in your bed, for the love of Sinder! A woman to whom she's not been intro-duced, no less—"

"The court met Demi the night she arrived. It's not my fault my parents weren't present."

They were silent on that matter for a moment, contemplating. It was well known that Jarron's mother, Queen Yewdit, now known simply as the lady Yewdit, had not been happy with her husband's decision to pass on the crown even as his increasingly ill health had made it necessary. Ever a difficult woman, she'd grown even more so since Jarron's ascension to the throne.

"She'd have been happier to let the old man die on it than she was to have him give it up so that he might spend the rest of his time here enjoying the life he built," Jarron said after a hesitation, knowing his friend wouldn't argue. "Instead of enjoying this time with him, she's bent on making his life a misery."

A sound from the doorway made them both turn. Demi, fresh-faced, hair still damp though bound into a pretty braid, smiled at them both and came at once on soft-slippered feet to Wait at Jarron's feet. On her knees, bottom resting on her heels, the back of one hand placed against the palm of the other in her lap, she looked so pretty Jarron lost the thread of his conversation for a moment while he admired her.

"I should be going," Adam said, getting to his feet. He inclined his head toward Demi. "My lady."

She nodded, and Jarron was sufficiently pleased to note that while she smiled at his friend, her attention turned back at once to him. He caught Adam's eye at this, and his friend gave a small grimace.

"You needn't leave on my account," Demi said. "Jarron, did the grapes please you?"

"You knew they would."

She smiled. "And the cheese?"

"Delicious, the perfect complement. But you knew that as well," he told her. "You're remarkable. Truly."

Adam made a choking noise and held his stomach as though he meant to be ill. "Enough, by the Arrow, enough! Else I empty my belly onto your extremely expensive but somewhat garish rug, Jarron. The pair of you are enough to make even the most stout-gutted man sick with disgust."

"Or is it envy?" Jarron murmured, gaze still upon his Handmaiden, who so well pleased him.

She looked at Adam with a merry twinkle in her dark eyes. "My lord, if my lord bids you stay, please do. I am happy to stay quiet while you talk, or fetch more refreshments, or even to take myself into a chair yonder and entertain myself with some needlepoint."

"Disgusting!" Adam cried, though Jarron knew the drama came for drama's sake and not from anguish. "I beg your leave, love, and that of your dear lady, because in truth I cannot stomach such a display of contentment."

Laughing, Jarron rose to clap Adam on the shoulder. "Brother, is it so difficult to see me joyous? Was it better when I was disgruntled and sour-faced?"

Adam put both his hands on Jarron's arms and squeezed. "You

know I am as thrilled to see your happiness as I would be to find mine own. Just as the rest of your court and, dare I say it, your lady mother, would like to witness as well. You've kept yourself shut away here for long enough. You should come out tonight."

It was Jarron's turn to make a face. "You know I care not for idle chatter and trifling amusements. . . ."

"I know you used to find them unbearable," Adam said quietly, with a glance at Demi, still Waiting. "And you know I feel, as do many, that the king's position is not entirely of a leader. He must be a comrade, too. Lock yourself away too much and you'll never gain the confidences of your nobles. And what then? You'll find yourself on the wrong end of the arguments, short the votes you need on issues on which you'd wish to make your mark. Kingdoms have been lost for less than their sovereign's ability to make friends."

"Won for rather less," Jarron said, irritated, though, with the entire idea he must strut himself back and forth at court like some prized fowl rather than his friend's words.

Adam shrugged and again glanced at Demi. "She's a lovely companion. At the very least, remove the mystery. Give them a reason to lay rest to the rumors. You might not care what they whisper about her, Jarron, but you might consider that she does."

At last Demi rose, as gracefully as she did everything else. "It's not my place to worry what is said about me, my lord."

Adam pursed his lips. "And yet you can't deny, I'm sure, that you'd not wish your name and character to be the subject of false stories designed to harm your patron, would you? When somewhat so simple as playing a game of Snap Me could lay them to rest?"

Her brow furrowed at that. "Jarron?"

"He's only trying to win his way," Jarron assured her.

"Mayhap." Adam shrugged again and fixed Jarron with a look. "If you were better versed in social niceties, love, you might know this, but as you're not it's up to me to tell you. As I've told you often before. There will always be those who seek to harm you, Jarron. You know that; you've known it since you were dandled on your father's knee. He raised you to rule this country, and he taught you well. But you've never known aught but peace. The politics of trade, the wee machinations of lords and ladies bored with naught to do but cause trouble. Naught serious."

"Think you that will change?" Jarron asked in a low voice with a quick look at Demi, who subtly but quickly turned her attention to somewhat else. "You think we're headed to war? With who? And why, for Sinder's sake?"

Adam shrugged again, gaze going soft. "I only tell you what might happen, not what will. Call me muddle-headed if you like, I know it's true. I know I am but your Dresser and Minister of Fashion, set to determine the price of poplin and length of hems. I know overwell my place and how grateful I am to have it. But people say things in front of silly men they'd keep quiet in front of those they respect."

"People respect you, Adam."

Adam laughed then, shaking his head, and kissed Jarron soundly on both cheeks. "You do. And you've already determined you are not like most other men of our acquaintance, aye?"

"I'll come out tonight," Jarron promised with a glance toward Demi, who'd busied herself with tidying the platter of leftover grapes and cheese. "We both will."

"Good," Adam said, and giving Jarron an insincere half bow, he turned on his heel and left.

When he'd gone, Demi came to pop a grape into Jarron's mouth. She tucked herself against him, then looked up at his face with a small smile. "He's insistent, your friend. But he's not wrong."

Jarron sighed and stroked a hand over her hair, tugging her braid so that her face tipped even farther up. He kissed her. "Do you know that since you've arrived, I've felt more content than ever I can remember?"

Demi smiled up at him. "Good."

"It's because of you," he told her, wanting to make sure she understood.

Her smile didn't fade, didn't falter. "It's my pleasure, Jarron, to content you. You know that."

He kissed her mouth. Her eyes. The tip of her nose.

"Adam wants me to be sociable tonight. I promised him I would, yet I must confess, all I really want to do is stay here and make love to you."

She laughed at that, her eyes shining, and stood on her tiptoes to kiss him. "And I would be happy to stay here with you and be made love to. But you should keep your promise to your friend. After all, he will be your friend forever, and I . . ."

She trailed off with a pretty shrug.

Jarron's heart twisted tight in his chest as though a fist had squeezed it. "You will someday leave me."

She nodded. "Aye. When it's time."

Jarron kissed her instead of answering. If he had his way, he would never find solace. Demi would never leave him.

He meant to make sure of it.

# Chapter 7

Sometimes, the best she could do for a patron was listen, and that's what Demi did now. She Waited while Jarron paced, ranting about how he never should've listened to Adam, and when at last he turned on his heel and glared down at her, she offered him only a smile. He scowled.

"He is no friend," Jarron said at last. "No one who claims to love me would force me to go through such torture!"

She rose. "It's because he loves you so that he suggested you make your appearance in court."

"I thought you were supposed to take my side!"

Demi laughed and went to him. She kissed him. She took his hand. "Come to bed."

"It was a disaster!" Jarron cried and turned from her.

Demi paused. This would not be solved with naked flesh and love talk. She laid a gentle hand on Jarron's shoulder, feeling him stiffen at her touch.

"Jarron. It wasn't a disaster."

"I don't know how to talk to them. Speak to me of taxes and trade,

of borders, of training and uniforms for the Shomer Melek. Discuss
the treasury, or history or politics. But not, by the Void, my favorite
color, my favorite dance, my wager on a game of cards! I do not care!"

"Your favorite color," Demi said calmly, "is green."

Jarron whirled to face her. "You see? You already know! I needn't
simper and prance about, complimenting you on your gown or having you fill my ear with the same!"

She bit back a laugh so as not to further tempt his temper. "So
begin a conversation about somewhat that interests you. Surely not
every lord and lady in your court is a muddle-head. What do you
discuss with Adam?"

Jarron shot her a narrow-eyed look. "We talk of sport. Of politics.
Religion. We talk about a lot of things."

"So what makes you think you can't do so with anyone else?"

Jarron shook his head. Demi knew why, though she wanted him
to say so out loud. He held a lot of pain inside him, from a long time.

"They don't see me. Those who know me. They don't see me," he
said at last. "They see only the illness. The ugliness."

"Oh, sweetheart. You're far from ugly." She put her arms around
him, but Jarron didn't hug her in return.

He went to the looking glass and stared, turning his face from side
to side. "It can come back at any time, you know. And it's not just the
pain, though it can be fair dreadful. The fever. The shakes and sweating before the blisters come. It's that once they do come, there's no
hiding it from anyone. It's all right there on my face for everyone to
see. And pity. I could be the greatest king who ever lived. The most
beneficent, the smartest, the greatest negotiator. And what do they see
when they look at me? A face of scars."

"I don't see that."

He turned to face her. "You see whatever you think I want you to see."

"That's not true."

She could tell him now, she thought. Tell him true. Remind him
of the girl who'd gone to her knees for him so long ago.

But would it help him? Would it lead him toward absolute solace, which was her purpose here, or would it serve only to ease her own conscience? Would he put his faith in her if he knew who she really was?

"A flower is made more beautiful by its thorns, Jarron," Demi said before he could protest further. "Such is one of the five principles of the Order, and I do believe them."

She moved toward him. She touched his face, then turned him with a push to his shoulder so that they both might stare into the mirror. Side by side, Demi in a gown he'd provided her but was little different than the half dozen she'd brought with her. Jarron in his dark trousers, white shirt, the ribbons undone at his throat and wrists. Waistcoat gone, cravat tossed aside in the fit of temper he'd had immediately upon returning to this room.

"Look at yourself," she told him.

He could barely stand it for a few moments without cutting his gaze away. "Vanity is a vice from which I've never suffered."

She put a gentle hand on his shoulder. Turned him again. "And honesty a virtue with which I dare say you're well acquainted. Tell me, Jarron. What you see."

"I see a man."

"A tall man," she said. "Broad shoulders. Flat stomach. Long legs, trim waist. A handsome figure, if any ever was."

He stared, stone-faced, even when she loosed the ribbons at his throat further and opened his shirt. She tugged at the sleeves and pulled the shirt off over his head, letting it fall without regard. Demi drew a finger down his shoulder, along his arm, the taut muscles. Over his chest. His nipples tightened when she circled them, but his expression didn't change.

She kissed his back just below the shoulder blade. There were scars, he was right about that, but they were so faint only the most interrogative eye would see them. She traced a finger over his skin, watching him in the mirror. He was still grim-faced, but his blue eyes had gone dark with desire.

"You have thick, lovely dark hair many men would envy. Women, too, I dare say. And eyes like ice. A mouth made for kissing. And for smiles," she added, though he was far from smiling.

She moved her hand over his back, up one side. Down the other. Drew a finger along the line of his spine. She moved in front of him to sit on the dresser, blocking his reflection and forcing him to look at her. Demi lifted her hem and put his hand beneath her gown, over her heat.

Jarron blinked rapidly, not moving. She spread her legs, allowing him to feel her soft curls. The tight knot of her clitoris. She curled her fingers over his, making him cup her.

She put her other hand on the back of his neck, pulling him to her mouth, though she didn't kiss him. She looked into his eyes, vision blurred at this proximity. "When I look at you, I do not see scars."

He took her mouth hard. Bruising. His fingers slid inside her without preamble, and Demi moaned into Jarron's kiss. His tongue hushed her. He broke the kiss, gaze searching hers.

"I could almost believe you."

"Believe me," she told him. "When I tell you somewhat, I swear it's never a lie."

He put her hand on his crotch, rubbing in the same slow pattern he used to thrust inside her. He curled her fingers on his buttons, and she undid them swiftly, eagerness making her clumsy. He was bare in her fist within a moment. Inside her with his cock the next.

Demi cried out as the dresser rocked. Jarron thrust inside her, his thumb pressing sweetly on her clit. Sweet friction built under his touch, and she hooked her legs around him, pulling him deeper. Pleasure such as this was a gift, and Demi took it. Gave herself up to it. She cried out with it.

Jarron groaned. "Sinder's Arrow, how your cunny clutches at my cock."

The handles on the dresser rattled as he thrust. She let herself move with him, closing her eyes so the sensation could fill her all over.

Another ripple of orgasm teased her flesh and she bit her lip with it as Jarron answered with a low cry and shook with his own release.

Demi opened her eyes, smiling, hoping he looked as sated and contented as she felt, but Jarron wasn't looking at her. As he filled her with his seed and his muscles went rigid with his climax, Jarron was looking at his own reflection over her shoulder. She thought at least maybe she'd see herself reflected in his eyes, but all she saw was his face.

One did not ignore the summons from the queen, especially if she were your mother and even if she no longer held the title. When the note came, written in her familiar hand and even smelling of her perfume, Jarron had pinched the bridge of his nose to fend off the instant headache such a missive brought on. Demi had brewed him an aromatic tea guaranteed, she said, to soothe it—but it had worked only as long as he stayed with his Handmaiden in his rooms.

The headache was back, along with a disturbing tingling sensation just beneath his skin, all over. Like the touch of ladybeetle wings, fluttering. No sting yet, though long experience had told him it could erupt at any time, along with the first cluster of blisters. He'd bitten the inside of his cheek and worried the spot with his tongue, wondering if the pox would begin there.

His mother didn't get up to greet him when her maid showed Jarron into her sitting room. Jarron hadn't expected her to, and when he went to one knee to kiss the hand she offered, he found it no more unpalatable than it had ever been to so greet her—even though now that he was king he was no more required to bend his knee for her than was Sinder himself. He did it because greeting her in that manner meant more to her than his title meant to him, and because though she complained bitterly about everything in her life, she was still his mother.

"Jarron," she said when he'd settled himself across from her in an uncomfortable, spindly legged chair. "How generous of you to attend me. I know how . . . burdened . . . you are."

"You sent for me, Mother." Jarron kept his tone neutral, face without expression. This was the woman who'd carried him in her womb, expelled him in blood and agony. She hadn't nursed him, had left him to be raised mostly my nursemaids, but still, he owed her his life.

"Tell you true, I did have to send for you, did I not? Interesting, that unless I write to you, my own son, living within the very same walls I occupy, you treat my quarters as though they were plague-riddled. Aye, I sent for you. I had to, in order to get more than a glimpse of you from across the room."

"I came at your bidding, Mother. And you know you are always welcome to attend any amusement of the court."

She grimaced. "And have them all whisper behind their hands at how much I've aged since my husband removed me from that which brought me such joy? I think not. And what good would it do me, as it comes to you? You avoid such things entirely."

"Unlike you, Mother, I find spending my time in such pursuits less than entertaining."

She glared. "Which is another reason I simply cannot attend! Unescorted? Unaccompanied? Your father, Sinder bless him, is abed by the time dusk falls and up with the first light. He told me he's finished with court, leaving it to you as the new king as he's left all else. Well, I say, let you take the politics, the deadly dull talk of trade and borders, but for the love of the Land Above, why not avail himself of all the pleasures he worked so hard for so long to put into place? At least while he's still . . . able . . . to enjoy it."

It was the closest she'd ever come to admitting aloud her husband was becoming every day lost in his mind. Her perfume washed over him, and the headache bit him between the eyes. Jarron leaned back, away from her scent and fierce gaze. "Mayhap he only ever attended the evening activities to please you, Mother."

"Disgraceful," she muttered. She flicked the hem of her gown to expose her pointed slippers. She pointed her toes, one after the other, then got to her feet.

Yewdit Bydelay was a tall, broad-shouldered woman with large feet and hands. Even clad in the finest fashion and with the most stylish application of cosmetic, she had a mannish figure and face, made little more feminine by her hairstyle. Dark and thick like Jarron's, the curls made stiff with some sort of hair dressing piled high on her head. She played at being tender and sweet, easily wounded, her pouting and tears legendary, but the fact was, Jarron's mother was coarse and brusque.

Still, she'd mastered the art of manipulation. She thought naught of deceit, should it bring her what she wanted, nor had she any hesitation in using her words to wound anyone who stood in her way. Her husband had been long in the habit of placating her, her daughters had taken up her habits as their own, and her son . . . well, her son had done his best to avoid her in his adulthood.

She turned so swiftly to face him her gown swirled around her feet. She meant to weep. He saw the tears glittering, her mouth trembling. Jarron sighed inwardly.

"And you've not even told me about . . . her!"

"The Handmaiden," Jarron said.

"Aye! Her! You told me naught of your intent to send away for one. You asked me no advice, sought no counsel. . . ."

"I'm not obliged to seek your counsel in such matters," Jarron said. "I spoke to Father on the subject when I'd decided it was the path I wished to pursue. He had no opinion."

"Well, I do!" she cried.

Jarron got up, too, not wishing to be sitting while she towered over him. "I daresay you'd have the same opinion whether I'd asked you before sending for her or after."

"You don't care what I think!"

"Do you protest her presence, Mother, or the fact I secured a helpmate without consulting you? Which is it that so vexes you?"

His mother took a step back, jaw dropping. "How can you speak to me in such a manner? I see how she's turned you against me already!"

He laughed at that bit of ludicrousness. "Oh, for Sinder's sake, Mother. She's done naught of the kind. Demi has no thoughts whatsoever on your existence, much less the intent to somehow wound you."

His mother gasped. "But you do? My own son?"

He softened, trying. Truly. "Mother, that's not so. I plead your mercy, I spoke out of turn. But I'm a grown man. And the king, though I know how that, too, vexes you. It's not my wish that you should be shut up in here with naught to amuse you, but if you don't wish to attend court, I can't make you."

Now she would turn to wheedling, which had ever served her well. "Jarron. My sweet. Aye, in truth I counseled your father against relinquishing his seat, but not because I thought you incapable of succeeding him. I know you'll be a fine leader in his place. I merely want you to taste all of what your crown offers. That's all. And, of course, I want to see you well married, with sons of your own to carry on the name. I want what any mother wants for her son, that's all. Your success."

The thing of it was, Jarron didn't believe his mother was lying. At the least, he didn't believe she thought she was lying. She meant what she said, so long as his success provided hers.

"Think you I've failed in some manner?" he asked, reasonably enough, he thought.

Her eyes narrowed. Mouth pursed. If she knew how old she looked when she did that, Jarron thought, he was sure she'd make sure to never crease her face into that expression again.

"You know I'm always here to offer you my counsel, Jarron."

"I know you are, Mother."

"I'm better versed in the ways of this court than you. The running of this province, as well, for I was ever your father's best counsel. Should you need anything, it's best you come to me. Even in the matter of a wife."

"I'll keep that in mind," Jarron said to appease her, with no intention of ever relying on her for anything.

"I shall write some letters of introduction and invitation. Today," she added. "Your father met with their fathers, but I met with their mothers."

"Whose mothers?"

"Young women of good breeding and noble title, of course. Your future wife, among them. I'll start today."

"Mother," Jarron said so stiffly, she paused. "Don't. I am telling you, don't."

She frowned again. "Why not?"

"I don't need you to do that for me. I'm content for the moment where I am. I have a Handmaiden, bound to bring me absolute solace—should I not achieve that before taking on the responsibility of a wife? Think you any woman would wish to take as husband a man still in need of such?"

"Absolute solace is a crock of stinking dung, and the Order of Solace a set of spinsters bent on washing your mind of anything but their Faith. Your father and I didn't practice, why should you? A wife will bring you all the solace you could need."

"Until Demi leaves me, her purpose complete, I'll not seek a wife," Jarron said evenly. He made a leg, as courteous as his mother could demand, and straightened. "I'll bring her to meet you, if you like."

She didn't merely frown. This time his mother's lip curled, the same as a dog baring its teeth. "You've never introduced me to any of your other whores, why should I wish to see this one simply because she's dressed with a prettier title?"

His mother liked argument if only so that she might always be proven right. Jarron had long ago given up fighting against her, which was probably why she felt she had the continued right to afflict her opinions on him unsolicited. This time, as so many others, he said naught.

"Good day, Mother. I must take my leave, now."

She sniffed, drawing herself up as though he'd mortally wounded her. "To get back to her?"

"Alas, no, for I must confess I'd rather that than meet with Erekon Kosem and his shomerim about increasing security."

"What? Why would they be increasing security? Why? Is there danger?" She clutched at her throat in a terror Jarron believed might be only partially true.

"None so far, but anytime power changes hands there's the chance of unrest. Dissension." He eyed her. "My sisters might wish their boys to take the throne in my stead, aye?"

His mother looked stunned at that, but only for a moment. Then she looked assessing for even a shorter breath before her expression turning castigating. "Hush your mouth. Your sisters would never seek to usurp you."

They might, he thought, if one of their boys was to be given the role of his heir. But Jarron didn't say so. This was his business, not his mother's.

"Good day," he said again and left her behind.

His headache got better the moment he stepped through her doors.

# Chapter 8

Jarron was a different man in front of others. Alone with her, Jarron had proven himself to be sensual, courteous, full of quiet wit and humor. He laughed a lot. Now, here, with her hand firmly tucked against his elbow, Jarron's entire body had gone stiff. His face, stern. He nodded at several people as he and Demi entered the first of the series of interconnected rooms that made up the social hall, but he paused to speak to none.

"Breathe," she murmured.

He looked at her with somewhat like panic in his gaze. "I'm breathing. They're staring, Void take them. Why must they always stare?"

Demi was well accustomed to facing crowds of curious stares. The Order of Solace had a reputation many did not understand. Handmaidens drew attention. Dressed in her plain, unadorned gown amongst the women and men in their finery, Demi might've felt out of place had she not so often been in situations just like this. She met every gaze forthrightly, with a kind smile, even when faced with a scowl or lifted brows.

"You're their king, sweetheart," she said a low voice. "They stare because you are important. Because I'm on your arm and they're curious. They stare for many reasons."

Jarron put a hesitant hand briefly to his face before forcing it to his side. "I don't like it."

"I know you don't. Come, let's have somewhat to drink, aye? Some wine? Perhaps you'll play at Snap Me, though I warn you, I'm a very, very good player and shall take the entire contents of your purse without a moment's mercy."

He laughed, then, just a bit, but the tight muscles of his arm relaxed at least a little. She patted his arm and pressed herself close to him. Jarron looked down at her, gaze soft.

"Wine. And cards. I can do that."

"Of course you can," Demi told him and smiled at the young man to her right. "Good even, my lord."

"Good even," he said, sounding startled. "My lord, how nice to see you!"

Jarron would've kept walking, but Demi slowed her steps so that he might as well. This young man wore fine clothes in the latest fashion but of less expensive fabrics than some. His hair was a little too short for style. He looked eager, though. He had kind eyes.

Jarron said naught.

"And your lady companion," added the young man with a quick glance at her. He gave Demi a half bow and an inquisitive look.

Demi nudged Jarron just a little before she spoke. "Sister Redemption of the Order of Solace, my lord. Though I've asked our lord king to call me Demi, and any friend of his shall have the same courtesy granted."

The young man laughed. "Nigel Witherspoon, my lady, and though I'd be honored to be counted amongst the king's comrades, I'd not dare to assume such a privilege."

"Nigel Witherspoon," Demi murmured to Jarron, urging him a step forward without making it seem so. "One of your trade merchants, I should guess?"

His clothes and the dust of his boots, the length of his hair, told her that. Still, both men looked at her, goggle-eyed. Nigel laughed in delight, while Jarron looked perplexed.

"Indeed I am, my lady Redemption! Just back from a trip to the Third Province. My father is Kaplan Witherspoon, my lord," Nigel said. "Your Minister of Spices?"

"Oh, Kaplan Witherspoon, aye?" Jarron said. "He's your father?"

"He is, and I his son." Nigel laughed merrily at that, and Demi joined him.

Jarron looked at them both and found a smile. It relieved her to see it. He might not be entirely comfortable with the dance of social conversation, but Nigel looked so cheerful it was difficult not to respond in kind.

"You've not been at court for long, then," Jarron said.

All around, curious eyes watched this conversation. Demi knew it. Despite Jarron's distaste for being stared at, she thought he might not be paying much attention. Mayhap he'd grown so used to ignoring the looks he didn't see them now. She knew the importance of them, however, and of whatever Jarron might say to this young man that indicated favor.

"No, my lord. Never, in fact. My mother raised me in the country until I was old enough to start work in my elder brother Richard's business. I've been working for him in the spice trade for several seasons now, and my father at last called me to join him here." Nigel grinned. "I must say, it's quite nice to have a roof over my head and a soft bed, rather than a tent on a dusty road."

"Welcome, then," Jarron said. "Your father is a good man. He served my father well for many seasons and has provided invaluable assistance to me even in so short a time as I've been on the throne. And my court, it would seem, is in need of a few fresh faces to liven it."

Nigel laughed and leaned in to say in a low voice, "I can only agree with you."

Jarron laughed. It was genuine, Demi could tell. He reached to clap Nigel on the shoulder in the way men have who are making friends. This was well and good, she thought, watching them both. Jarron needed friends.

"Mayhap you'll join me and Demi in a game of cards?" Jarron masked his hesitation with a brusque tone, but he needn't have worried.

Nigel beamed. "I'd be delighted! If you've an interest, I can even show you a few new games I've picked up in the Third. I've tried teaching them . . . but sadly, I've few acquaintances here and fewer who seem eager to become such."

At that, Jarron looked around the room. Demi wanted to laugh at how quickly every back turned, how all the eyes that had been watching the king speak to this new young lord found somewhat else to gaze upon. Even the conversations, which had dropped to hushed murmurs, rose to a buzz.

"Aye," Jarron said after a moment. "I would see how it might feel that way."

Nigel, for all his lack of courtly manners, knew enough to understand the attention of the king meant somewhat important. "Right. Well, my lord, if it's all right, I'll join you anon? I'll just nip back to my room and grab up the cards. The deck is different in the Third, you see."

Jarron looked at her. "What say you, Demi?"

She already knew how to play many of the games popular in the Third Province, but that wasn't important. Encouraging Jarron was. So she nodded with a wink for Nigel. "Aye, I'd enjoy that most well, my lord."

"I beg your leave then," Nigel said, appropriately polite, and took it at Jarron's nod.

Jarron watched him go, then turned to her. He leaned to kiss her cheek, murmuring into her ear. "They're all still staring."

"They make note of who you favor," she murmured in return, under cover of the kiss.

Jarron straightened and looked 'round the room. Again, lords and ladies burst into the animated buzz of conversation, with only slant-eyed glances to show their attention upon the king. He snorted softly, but his smile quirked, which was better than his previous reaction.

"Funny how a hat can so change a head," Jarron said, "at least to those who don't wear it."

I'm out." Demi folded her hand of cards to the laughter of both Jarron and Nigel, along with Adam, who'd joined them. "I fear you're all too accomplished for my competition."

"Nonsense," Adam said. "You threw that game. I was watching!"

Laughing, Demi got to her feet. "I shall go and bring refreshment. You boys keep playing."

"Boys," Adam said with a leer toward Jarron, who'd lit a bowl of herb and was waving the smoke toward his face. "Hear you how she describes us, brother?"

Jarron looked up and snagged her wrist, pulling her close for a kiss. The herb and wine had relaxed him further even than the game and companionship of his old friend and the new one. "Stay."

"If it pleases you," she said at once, nuzzling at his cheek. "Though I tell you, a fresh pitcher of wine and some meat pies would please you even better."

Jarron looked at the men across the table from him. "You see? She knows. Always knows. Like magic."

"You're a man, brother," scoffed Adam, passing the cards to Nigel, who shuffled. "She needs no magic to determine what might please you."

This was truer than Demi would ever admit aloud, but Jarron snorted and released her. "You think my gender makes me so easily learned?"

"You've a cock and balls and a stomach. That's what we are. Men. Our pricks and our bellies lead us, always." Adam shrugged and nudged Nigel, who'd partaken of quite a bit of wine already.

"I could eat a meat pie," Nigel said solemnly.

Adam looked at him. "I'm sure you could."

Jarron looked from one to the other, then at her. "Hear you the disrespect my supposed brother of the heart provides me?"

"He loves you," she said into his ear and licked at his lobe so that he shivered. "I'll return in less time than you think, sweetheart."

Jarron nodded, attention already back on the game. Boys, she mused with a small laugh as she took her leave of the table and moved through the library into the larger room where the buffet table had been set up. First, though, she needed to use the privy. The social hall was kept overwarm for her taste, particularly since the temperature was regulated to suit the lords and ladies in lighter dress than she wore. She'd drunk quite a bit of wine, herself.

The small privy chamber featured only a wastechair and a sink, both of which Demi utilized swiftly. She cupped a stream of water and dabbed her face with it, looking at her reflection in the looking glass. She wore little cosmetic, just a hint of lip paint and a touch of liner at the corners of her eyes. She turned her face from side to side, making sure her appearance was suitable and appropriate. People would talk no matter what she wore or how she presented herself, and though the only opinion that ever mattered was her patron's, she was sensitive to Jarron's distaste for stares. It would shame him should she behave in any manner unfitting for a queen, for though that would never be her place, it was the one into which he'd put her in all ways but the crown and the ring upon her finger.

This sobered her suddenly as the world slid a bit beneath her slippers. She was a little drunk, a little blurry from the herb she'd not smoked herself, yet had breathed on Jarron's kisses. Too many vices she'd been perhaps unwise to permit herself. She looked at herself, hard.

"He does not know me," she said aloud.

The words stung. She drew a deep, shaking breath and bent over the basin, thinking she might gag. She breathed, deep and slow. Deep and slow.

*Invisible Mother, if a flower is made more beautiful by its thorns, grant me the ability to make the right choices so that I might be made better by my flaws.*

There were many, Demi knew. She'd been given a second chance—redeemed, and given the name to prove it. She was no longer that thieving kitchen slag running from the King's Lion and his cubs. She'd worked hard to learn kindness, compassion, generosity. To become a Handmaiden, bound to providing solace. That didn't mean she was perfect.

Jarron didn't know her, not really. She was still a pretty doll to him, a blank slate. She was his looking glass, reflecting what he wanted to see. And that was fine and well; it was important, it was her duty and her purpose and her pleasure, too. The Mothers had sent her for a reason, and Demi was fair grateful to have been chosen. But she knew that no matter how much Jarron petted and kissed her, or what sweet names he called her, he did it because of what she represented to him and not who she really was.

It was better than naught. Better than memories built into fantasy so grand no man could ever match them. The Mothers-in-Service had sent her to him for a reason, and though Demi would never be so bold as to assume she could ever know the Mothers' purpose, she knew enough to wonder if their reason had been as much for her sake as for his.

She'd spent too long away from him. He was comforted in the company of Adam and now of Nigel, but Demi thought Jarron might still need her at his side. Besides that, she'd promised refreshments, and Adam had been right: Men were often led by their pricks and their bellies in equal turn. They'd been at cards for a quiverful of chimes, with naught but a light supper before that. Jarron would need to eat.

She didn't make it more than three steps out the privy chamber door before a large masculine body pressed her up against the tapestry-hung wall. Demi gasped, but a long-fingered hand had already pressed over her mouth. She went still, not struggling. No sane man would dare harm a Handmaiden, especially not one in service to the king.

"Hello, sweetheart," said a familiar voice. "It's been a long time."

Erekon. The King's Lion took his hand away and replaced it with his mouth—not kissing. Not quite. His breath moved over her face as his lips moved with his words. When Demi turned her head, his mouth caressed her cheek as he spoke.

"Truth, I never thought to see you again."

"Nor I, you," she said.

Her heart thumped. This time, when the world slipped sideways beneath her toes, it was not from too much drink. When she breathed, deep and slow, his scent filled her nose and mouth. She remembered the taste of him. She shuddered, closing her eyes.

She didn't need to see him to know he was smiling. She could hear it in his voice. Erekon had a cruel smile that cut as often as it caressed.

"You've changed," he whispered.

His body still pressed against her. His hand closed tight on her braid at the base of her neck, holding her from moving though she was too wise to try to flee. His knee nudged between her thighs, pressing her through the layers of their clothes.

"You're beautiful. Who'd ever have guessed it?" Erekon said into her ear.

She opened her eyes, then, grateful for a reminder of the reasons she'd left him. Looked straight at him. "You play at astonishment."

His smile faded. The dark eyes flashed. "The Order has treated you well. *Redemption.*"

She put her hands up, against his chest, pushing, and he stepped away. "You play at insult as well, Erekon? You've naught over me now. You know that."

"Even if I tell your new lover he's pitching woo on a kitchen slag who stole from his family?"

She lifted her chin, staring him down, and watched him assess her reaction. She surprised him, she could see, though any who didn't know him as well might not have seen it. "Jarron sent for a Handmaiden, and he got one. Whatever I might've been before, I am no longer."

"He doesn't know you."

Hearing her own words on Erekon's razor-edged tongue, Demi flinched. "No."

"Think you lying to him is the best way to give our young king his solace? Is that what they teach you in the Order? No wonder you're so accomplished a Handmaiden, if such practices are common."

Demi had faced detractors aplenty, those who didn't understand or approve of the Order and her calling. Erekon was different. His words hit her in all the soft places she'd long ago thought to shield with her training and the conviction of her faith. He'd always known just where to wound her . . . and how to heal her, too.

She studied him. The silver streaks in his dark hair. The lines around his eyes. Time had left its mark and his features were too bold for beauty, but there was no question he was a handsome man. She'd never, even when their love had burned into ashes, been able to make him ugly in her eyes.

"You should let me go," she told him quietly. "I'll not tremble for you anymore."

"No? Not even if I tell your patron the truth about you?"

"I'll tell him myself if I think it will soothe him, Erekon. I'm not keeping it a secret from shame." It wasn't entirely a lie. Not entirely.

Erekon's low, silky laugh had once been able to twist her stomach for a different reason than it did now. "No?"

"He agreed to take who the Mothers sent him. That was me. The fact that I once lived here . . . of who I was . . ."

"Think you he'd care not to know you were the wretch for whom he begged his father's mercy? That he's the reason you ended up in the Order instead of prison or a grave? Think you true, Notsah, that he would not care, if he knew?"

"Nobody's called me that in a very long time. I'm not that girl any longer."

"No," Erekon said softly. "Now you are Redemption. But whose?"

"Not yours," she said and pushed past him with her heart pounding. Palms sweating.

She made it back to Jarron's gaming table with her hands full of meat pies and ale. A smile on her face. Her legs steady. Erekon might think he could threaten her, but there was somewhat he'd forgotten.

He didn't know her any more than Jarron did.

# Chapter 9

The warm, sweetly scented body beside him shifted and pressed bare flesh against his. Jarron, eyes still closed and not quite ready to give up their dreams, smiled. This was the best part of his day. Waking with Demi by his side.

He was happy.

True, it wasn't as though he'd spent his entire life in misery. Even during the pox outbreaks, Jarron had managed to find the humor and joy in life. He hadn't spent his time suffering so completely he couldn't appreciate his blessings. He never lacked for coin or sustenance or anything material. He had friends. His province wasn't at war.

But he felt different now, because of Demi. If this wasn't absolute solace, he couldn't imagine how blissful such a state might be. She anticipated his every need and provided it without him having to ask. If he reached for it, she'd already placed it within his grasp. She listened to him when he spoke and could reply on most any subject he wished to discuss. She knew the merriest of jokes and could tell them so straight-faced he would burst apart with laughter before she could finish. She knew nimble-fingered magic tricks to entertain him, could recite poetry, knew the latest dances, and yet was just as content to sit at his feet in silence while he worked.

Sexually, she responded to whatever he offered. Desires he'd never acknowledged took bloom, nurtured by Demi's complete acceptance of whatever he asked. Tasks he'd have been ashamed to set to a whore she readily accomplished . . . even suggested. And never once had she made him feel deviant in his desires, nor lacking in his talents.

Adam was right, he mused, rolling to press himself along Demi's back. Jarron slid a hand over her soft, rounded belly. Men were led by their cocks.

His fingers slipped down to part her curls and dip inside her heat. Ah, she was always ready for him. Slick and wet and tight. He found her clitoris and pinched it gently between his thumb and forefinger, stroking almost as if her bud were a tiny cock itself.

"Mmmm." Her low murmur of satisfaction stirred his prick as much as the feeling of her body's response.

Demi arched against him, her arm going over her head to seek his hair. Her fingers sank deep, tugging him closer. Jarron nuzzled at the spot below her ear, the one that always made her shiver.

This was power. This ability to make her squirm and writhe. Moan his name. It was headier than any he'd had with the mere signing of his name, the ordering of supplies, the approval of laws. This woman, this beautiful, loyal, intelligent woman gave herself to him anytime he wanted, and when she looked at him with those shining dark eyes, Jarron felt more a man than ever he had in all his life.

He stroked her gently, listening to the rise and fall of her breath. Feeling her move, muscles tensing and releasing as he aroused her. It was her purpose, he knew that. But he also believed her when she said it was her pleasure.

With his other hand, he guided his cock inside her from behind. Engulfed in her heat, he held back his own groan by biting into her shoulder. Sucking on the flesh, salty from her sleep, he tongued the mark he left and thrust deeper into her.

This was a dance he well knew. This a conversation he could make. All the rest might wear at him, no matter how he knew Adam was right about the need to perform all the king's duties, including social. But this . . . this would never cease to amuse and entertain him. Fulfill him.

He moved faster inside her. His cock swelled, his balls heavy. He could come this way, moments after his strumming fingertips sent her into ecstasy. Just now, though, he had a desire for somewhat more. He pulled out, laughing low at Demi's moan of protest.

"On your hands and knees." The sound of his own voice, so rough and hoarse with desire, never failed to increase his pleasure. "Up. Let me see that lovely bottom."

Demi obeyed at once, her fingers digging into the sheets as she pressed her cheek to them. She tilted her sweet little ass into the air, spreading her legs for him. Her tight, pink pucker displayed. Jarron's stomach fell out at the sight of it—her offering. Any part of her he wanted, she'd grant him.

He was intoxicated.

Some time ago, he'd gone with Adam to a market that didn't sell vegetables or baskets but somewhat rather more exciting objects. Adam had pointed out the lidded casket, engraved on the top with writhing figures outlined in paint of gold. Jarron had been uncertain even what to request, but Adam had known him long enough to guess. When first he'd seen this toy chest meant for adults, not children, Jarron's cock had filled just looking at the collection of items inside. Adam had shown him their uses, not laughing as was his wont but serious. And unsurprised. Now it rested below Jarron's side of the bed. He hadn't shared it yet with Demi.

He rubbed the soft mounds of her buttocks with his palm. "Stay here."

He reached for the box. Lifted the lid. Jarron selected one small item from the box. He held it to the light. The length of his thumb and about as thick, flared at the base. Carved of smooth, oiled wood. He brought out a flask of thick oil as well.

"Demi."

She looked at him with a smile over her shoulder, her bottom still tipped tantalizingly in the air. "Yes, sweetheart?"

"I have somewhat I want to try."

She pushed up on her hands, still on her knees, to get a better look. He wondered if she might flinch at the toys he offered. If he was the first to require the use of such with her. At the thought, jealousy stabbed at him. He didn't wish to know if he wasn't.

"Anything," she murmured with no trace of fear. Her smile hinted at anticipation. "Anything you want, Jarron. Anything I can give you."

His hand quavered at that. He was a king with the wealth of a king, the power of a king, and yet it was a woman who could make him shake. He uncorked the flask and dripped thick oil down the plug, then put the flask on the table next to the bed.

Demi's gaze had gone dark, her pupils dilated. She drew in a breath and bit her bottom lip, then pressed her cheek again to the sheets. Jarron ran an oil-slick finger up her thigh and dipped it into her cunny, then up to press against her puckered flesh.

He'd never taken a woman this way, nor been so taken, but Adam had told him of how that back passage could bring much pleasure to a partner. Women and men, both. Jarron had listened in rapt fascination, having no partner at the time, and taken his cock in his hand later to stroke himself to orgasm at the thought. Now, he meant to take fantasy and make it his reality.

The plug was slippery, glistening with oil, when he replaced the touch of his fingers with it. Demi made a noise low in her throat at the pressure. Her anus tightened, then relaxed. Jarron's cock twitched.

He eased the plug inside her slowly, careful not to hurt her. Her fingers clutched tighter at the sheets, but her low mutter of pleasure urged him to continue. When it had seated fully inside her, they both let out sighs. Jarron sat back on his heels, his cock thick and jutting in front of him.

"You are so beautiful," he told her.

Her low, throaty laugh sent a thrill through him. That she could find humor in this meant so much to him. That this was not making her afraid or disgusted. That she might want it as much as he did.

"Tell me how it feels, Demi."

"Full," she murmured. "Tight and full. As though it might slip from me at any moment."

He put his fingertips to it, pressing lightly. "Now?"

She shuddered. "Oh, that is . . . so good."

"I wonder if when I put my cock inside you, how that will feel?"

She laughed again, but it broke into a guttural sigh. "Please."

Gripping his prick at the base, Jarron nudged into her entrance as slowly and carefully as he'd filled her with the plug. He could feel it, he realized. The unyielding pressure of it against his cock through her flesh. He moved slowly, slipping in her wetness, and the plug added a delicious extra friction.

She was already moving against him. Her cunny gripped him as she rocked against him. Jarron held her hips to slow her. He wanted this to last.

She stilled at his touch. This as much as anything else, that she should react to even his unspoken commands, shot desire all through him. He pulled out, his cock bobbing.

He wanted her more than moaning; he wanted her weeping with desire. This, too, was power. Jarron slid onto his back and beneath her, his mouth easily finding her clitoris. He suckled gently, hands on her hips to keep her from moving.

Slow, light, feather strokes of his tongue on her clit. Demi's knees slid on the sheets, opening her sweetness to him further, and Jarron lapped at her cunny, hungry for the taste of her. He slid his tongue inside her, then out, and up again to circle on her pearl.

He had put his mouth to few enough women that this was still new to him. The whores he'd frequented had been more eager to take his coin and finish him off so they might find another customer, and most had seemed surprised he'd wanted even to bother trying to please them. The very few who'd allowed him this pleasure did so with suspicion. Only one had ever welcomed this. She'd been a good teacher, but naught made up for practice.

Using his lips and teeth and tongue was vastly different from employing his hand or cock to make her come. His tongue, more sensitive even than the tip of his finger, played nimbly along her clitoris and through her folds, seeking her sweet, tight hole. She tasted of the Land Above, and he nearly spilled when her honey coated his tongue. He could feel every ripple and twitch of her this way, gauge exactly how close she was to climax in a way impossible to determine with other methods of lovemaking.

She moaned his name and sought to rock her hips, to press her cunny to his mouth. This time, Jarron let her. She moved on his mouth, his tongue flat-pressed to her clit as she ground onto it. Only when the flutter of her inner thigh muscles and the tone of her voice told him she was close to tumbling over the edge did he once again grip her hips and hold her still.

Jarron breathed on her. Soft, light breaths. Teasing. Demi let out a low cry and went still, though her every muscle still strained. Jarron touched the tip of his tongue to her clit, then slid one finger inside her. Another. He spread them slightly as he licked her.

Demi drew a harsh, shuddering breath. She tried to speak, but her voice broke on the words. He didn't care. He wanted her broken and unable to speak, able only to cry out in wordless ecstasy.

He wanted her undone at his touch.

He took her clitoris between his lips and tugged gently. She came, shaking and trembling, her hips bucking. She flooded him with her honey, and he feasted on it. When she'd stilled, he put a hand against her, slicked his fingers, and used it to stroke his aching cock. He could hear the whistle of her breath, in and out.

He moved from beneath her. Demi, still on her hands and knees, didn't move. She'd buried her face in the sheets.

"Demi. Look at me."

She did, with bleary eyes and slack mouth. She licked her mouth and pushed herself upright. She swallowed hard and blinked rapidly.

He'd done that to her. Made her that way. Fuckdrunk. He felt that way himself, the world tipping and spinning like he'd overindulged on worm.

Jarron got to his knees and pushed inside her again. He wasn't going to last long, now, a few strokes at most. The sight of the plug still tucked inside her shot another whirlwind of arousal through him. He fucked into her harder. Deeper. The bed moved with his thrusts and she opened to him, tilting her body to take him in farther than she ever had.

He came with a shout that echoed in the room. Triumphant. Delirious. He spilled inside her, hot and boiling. His fingers left red marks on the pale skin of her behind as he gripped her.

It took him a moment or two to recover. She hadn't moved. Quickly but no less carefully than he'd inserted it, Jarron slipped the plug from her and set it aside, then gathered her into his arms. He tucked her up against him, spooning, and pulled the covers up over both of them.

Her breathing had slowed, but beneath his palm, her heart beat thunderously fast. He closed his eyes, buried his face in her hair. He held her close, waiting in terror for this to be the moment she completed her duty. For absolute solace. To lose her.

It didn't come.

"That was lovely," she said in a lazy voice after another moment or so. She didn't turn to face him but put her hand over his against her chest.

"Was it?"

"I forgot mine own name at the end, true." She laughed, her body shaking.

Sweat glued them, but Jarron pressed harder against her. "True? You didn't . . . mind?"

"Mind what, sweetheart? The . . . toy?"

"Aye. That."

Silence. She sighed. She drew his hand to her mouth and kissed it, lips brushing the knuckles.

"Jarron, whatever you wish from me, I'll provide. You know that."

"I know it."

The answer was meant to satisfy him, and for the first time since she'd arrived, it hadn't sufficed. She knew it, of course, as she knew everything. Demi sat up and turned as Jarron lay back on the pillows.

She smoothed her hand over his hair. "What troubles you?"

He couldn't look at her. "How do you know?"

"How to please you?"

He nodded, silent.

Demi drew her knees to her chest and rested her chin upon them. "The easy answer, the one that would perhaps make you feel the best, is that I trained for a long time in order to understand my patrons. What they want, how to serve them. What to give. When to take. It's a complicated business, solace. It's not the same for any two people."

"Is it even possible?"

"I believe so."

He smiled, then, though it felt false and strained. "You must."

"I suppose I must. Or I could leave the Order and not have to believe anything I don't want to."

Jarron turned onto his side, resting his head upon his arm. He ran a hand up her leg, marveling at the softness of the hair there, so unlike his own. "What would you do if you weren't in the Order?"

She didn't answer.

He looked at her, expecting the same merry smile and twinkling eyes, but Demi looked solemn. More than that. Disturbed. Her brow had furrowed, lips turned down. She opened her mouth as though to speak, then closed it without saying a word.

"Don't you know?" Jarron asked.

"I fear I know all too well what I'd do if I weren't a Handmaiden, Jarron. I simply don't wish to tell you."

"Why not?" He cupped her knee briefly before sliding his hand down to do the same at her ankle. Connecting her to him.

"Because . . . I fear it would make you see me as less than you do, now."

"How could I, ever?" He meant to tease but found no humor in the question. He sat up to face her. "How can you think it?"

Tears glistened in her eyes, and she brushed them away with an impatient gasp. He saw the rise and fall of her shoulders as she drew deep breaths. When she met his gaze again, she'd calmed herself.

"You told me yourself, a flower is made more beautiful by its thorns, Demi. How can you say such a thing to me, yet not apply it to yourself?" Jarron asked her. "Or were the words you said false, meant only to placate me?"

"No." She shook her head so that her hair tumbled about her shoulders.

He liked it that way, free of its braid. He liked her this way, too. Naked in his bed. Soft. In her Handmaiden's uniform there could never be any mistake about who and what she was, but here, now, he could pretend she was simply . . . a woman.

"If you believe it of me, you should believe it of yourself, too."

"You're right. Of course you are. The Mothers-in-Service would not teach us the principles if they were not meant to apply to all of us. It's just that . . . sometimes . . ." She drew in another slow breath. "It's difficult, sometimes, to see beyond my own flaws. My own thorns. What I can do for others is not so easily accomplished for myself."

"What vices could you possibly have that would so turn me from you, when your virtues are so great?" He said this lightly, but she didn't laugh.

"Vices and virtues, sweetheart, back each other on the same coin."

"Perhaps you need a Handmaiden of your own," Jarron said.

That brought forth a laugh, at last. "That would be complicated, true?"

"I must confess somewhat to you," Jarron said.

She tilted her head to study him. "Aye, sweetheart?"

"I have no intention of ever letting you fulfill your duty to me. I brought you here upon false pretense. I knew I didn't believe in what the Order promised, but I sent for you anyway."

Somewhat flickered in her gaze, but he was relieved to have said it aloud. Demi leaned forward to kiss him. It lingered, sweetly.

"You didn't send for *me*," she whispered against his mouth. "You sent for someone."

He kissed her, too, and held her close. They passed some long moments in silence before he said into her ear, "I sent for someone. And you are who they sent."

# Chapter 10

Several of Demi's former patrons had required her constant presence. They'd clung to her like a toddler on its mother's skirts, or a burr tangled in a coat sleeve. They'd needed her more right from the start and had also been the ones with whom she'd stayed the least amount of time. They'd needed her more, and harder, but they'd also found what they needed faster.

There'd only been one patron for whom she'd been unable to provide absolute solace. She'd been with him for a full twelvemonth. She'd done her best. But in the end, he'd simply been unable to take what she gave. She hadn't wept upon leaving him; nor had he. They'd parted on friendly terms with a kiss and an embrace, and she supposed that one day he might send for another of her Sisters to help fulfill him, or he might simply live the rest of his life missing that small piece he'd hoped she might find for him.

Everyone needed absolute solace, which was not quite a moment and not anything physical, but rather an indefinable and ethereal idea. Absolute solace was not a thing but rather the absence of it, somewhat Demi believed in her heart every person needed but nobody had. Some might live their lives entire without feeling the loss of it and others might be crippled with the craving for it; her place was not to judge but to provide.

Of the others, most were happy to have her tidy their rooms, take her to bed, drink and eat what she prepared for their sustenance. Most of them seemed to enjoy her company, to like her, which was to be expected since the Order placed its Handmaidens with patrons most carefully. They took what she gave them with open hearts, which was more the reason they could find their solace than anything she ever did, and they let her go when the time came. Sometimes with tears. Never with woe.

She'd never had a patron she didn't want to leave.

Jarron wasn't of the clinging sort, though he did indeed appear to enjoy her company and sought to keep her by him at most times. Yet there were tasks and duties he needed to perform that had naught to do with her and would've been inappropriate for her to attend. He always left her with a sigh, which pleased her as a woman, but he did leave her, and that pleased her as well, for it meant he wasn't so crippled he needed to rely on her for everything.

Still, without Jarron to escort her, Demi didn't feel quite right about visiting the social hall. It wasn't the stares or the whispers that set her back, but the idea that there'd be many who'd seek to make her acquaintance only for the reason of getting closer to him. He was the first king to whom she'd ever been sent in service, but she understood the basics of political intrigue.

There was another reason, too. Secluded here in Jarron's quarters, she remained a bit of a mystery. None that might've known her from so long before would have the chance to recognize her. Well. None other than Erekon, and he'd known her too well.

When the knock came at Jarron's door, Demi wasn't surprised to open it and find her former lover there. She didn't step aside to let him in, but he pushed past her, anyway.

"You shouldn't be here," she said, knowing that had never stopped him before.

"Your king is locked deep with his advisors in counsel. He'll not be back for some hours, perhaps even until after nightfall. Such is the life of a man of power."

"You have power," she said, watching as he strode in his high black boots across the carpet, leaving marks.

He helped himself from Jarron's jug of worm, swirling the liquid in the glass. He held it to the light from the window. He sipped, watching her.

"I do," Erekon said and put the glass down.

They stared at each other from opposite sides of the room. He was waiting for her to look away first, but Demi was no longer the girl he'd once known, and she didn't. He didn't, either, but at least she'd surprised him.

"Why did you come here?" he asked her.

"Jarron sent for a Handmaiden. The Mothers-in-Service chose me for him." It was the truth but tasted of a lie.

"But why did you come? Surely you're able to refuse. They can't make you serve someone, can they?" Erekon tilted his head, leaning on the dresser, one leg crossed over the other. "Can they force you?"

She smiled, keeping her distance. "It would please you for me to say they can."

"Can they?" Erekon asked in a low voice that was not soft.

"No."

"Would they have chosen you had you told them the truth about this place and how you left it?"

"What makes you think they didn't know?" Demi smoothed the front of her gown, her palms skidding on the buttons.

"Did you tell them?"

"The Mothers-in-Service know all they need to know."

Erekon laughed. "Clever answer to the question I didn't ask. Did you tell them, Notsah, where you came from?"

She hadn't. After Jarron had defended her to his father, Demi had been sent to serve in domestic service instead of prison. She'd met a

Handmaiden in one of the houses to which she was assigned. When her indenturement was complete she'd gone to the Motherhouse, where they turned her away three times before at last allowing her entrance. They'd never asked where she came from, or why she sought a life in the Order. None of the Mothers, nor the Sisters.

"I never asked any of them. Why should they ask me?"

"Do you think it fate they chose you, then? To come and serve the king of the Second Province? Of all the kings in all the world, in every province and country served by the Order, *this* is the man to whom you were assigned."

"And of all the Sisters, true, they chose me to serve him. They know best." Demi kept her voice steady, though facing Erekon was somewhat for which she'd never been trained.

"You've grown up," he told her.

She touched her face, her hair. "Time passes, Erekon. Think you I'd have stayed the same, when you yourself show the passage of the seasons?"

"Your nimble tongue has turned itself to wordplay instead of love-play," Erekon told her. "You speak of the silver in my hair, aye? But have I changed, really, beyond that? How would you know?"

"Because the man I knew back then wouldn't have stopped himself from taking me against the wall, if that's what he wanted. He wouldn't have stood as you do now, across the room from me without ordering me to come forward."

Erekon drained the glass and put it down hard enough to crack it. "I still want to."

Her heart thumped, her stomach twisted at that, the raw honesty in his voice. This time, she did look away. Demi went to the fire, which didn't need poking, but she took the poker from its hook and stirred the flames anyway. Sparks flew and she braced herself for the sting that never came.

She braced herself, too, for his touch. That, too, never came. She felt him behind her. Heard his boots shush-shush on the carpet.

Imagined the brush of his breath against her hair. But Erekon did not touch her.

"Your lord king is in need of solace; this is somewhat that cannot be denied by any who know him. There could be few surprised by his decision to send for a Handmaiden, though fewer who'd believe he did it for any kind of faith. There are some unhappy with your presence here, his lady mother amongst the most vociferously opposed and the least vocal."

She looked at him. "I'm not surprised she doesn't approve, but what do you mean by that?"

"I mean the lady Yewdit will speak to the world with a tongue of honey rather than have any know she could be dissatisfied with her darling son's behavior. She's kept herself away from the social hall, the one place she truly had any joy, and would spite herself rather than face the possibility of being greeted with anything less than her former admiration. What she does not seem to understand is that there will always be those willing to pander to the mother of a king so that they might be granted the benefit of his ear."

"Even if she doesn't have it, herself? Jarron isn't close with his mother and, in fact, avoids her." Demi studied Erekon with different eyes for the first time since seeing him again. This man had once been her teacher, her lover, her confessor, and finally, her pursuer. Now she looked at him as somewhat else she could not define.

Erekon's smile didn't touch even the corners of his dark eyes. "Who'd know such a thing? Jarron avoids everyone, or used to until you came and he began making an effort. The gossip is about the war between you and his beloved Adam, if there is such a battle, which I doubt, but there's naught about Jarron's lack of consideration for his mother."

"But you know it," she whispered, watching him.

"I know it. Of course I know it. I know it all."

She swallowed, hard. "Because . . . you are the Aryon Melek."

"Because it is my business to know it."

She needed a drink, herself, and pushed past him to pour herself a glass of worm. It stung her lips and numbed her tongue at once. What had he said? Her nimble tongue, used for words instead of love. Demi's hand shook until the liquid sloshed, and she made no secret of it.

Erekon watched her. "You and I know his mother doesn't have his ear, but I shall tell you somewhat he doesn't know. Nor you. She, though she might pretend otherwise, also knows, and this she finds so dissatisfactory, she is quite likely to do somewhat about it."

"You speak of intrigue." Demi drank again, relishing the burn as it went down and warmed her belly. "That has naught to do with me."

"You're the king's consort. His companion. His Handmaiden, bound to bring him solace. Think you that standing by to watch as his throne is taken out from under him will bring him anything but grief?" Erekon said in the low, half-sneering voice she'd always hated, even when she'd loved him.

"Think you she'll manage to do such a thing? Jarron has his father's blessing and the support of the court, even if he's not the sort of sun-faced sovereign his father was and his mother would prefer him to be. He's far from the sort to make enemies."

"He need make none and will have them anyway, for the sole reason he was born to the crown and not someone else. That's all it takes, sweetheart."

Her throat tightened at the endearment, which almost sounded like an insult. She searched his face. "Do you stand with his mother?"

"Would I be here telling you this, if I were?"

"You might," Demi said with a step toward him, "if you believed it might somehow hurt me."

At this, Erekon stepped back, swiftly and not with his usual grace. He knocked into a side table, sending it to the floor. Demi moved at once to right it, but she stopped herself. Doing so would put herself within his grasp, and she did not trust him. Mayhap she didn't trust herself.

"You hold yourself in very high esteem," Erekon said, voice rough. "Mayhap, too high."

"Why, then?" She demanded. "Do you stand with Jarron? Do you go against his mother in his support? Why not tell him of her schemes, if indeed she has any but what you've concocted! Why not tell your king, to whom you vow such alleged loyalty, instead of me? Why should I be the one to warn him?"

"I'm not asking you to warn him. I am . . . I am trying to warn you."

She had no words for this. No reply, no protest, not even a gasp of surprise. Somewhat twisted in her chest, true, and she put a hand there as though her touch could quell it.

"She does not like you," Erekon said.

"She's not yet even met me, and truth, Erekon, her regard doesn't concern me." Demi shrugged. "Your mother, as I recall, cared little for me, too."

It was the wrong thing to say. She'd meant to jest, to tease. She'd forgotten he was a man not given much to humor, particularly at his expense. How could she have forgotten? She'd spent too long in the company of men predisposed to finding her charming and lovely and tantalizing.

"My mother, may the Invisible Mother bless her, didn't have the power to have you hung by the neck until you died."

"No," Demi said without thinking, "that was you."

"You were a thief," Erekon said flatly.

He spoke with no emotion in his voice, but how could she believe him to be without feeling? She knew better, but as she'd forgotten not to tease him, so she'd forgotten how to read him. He didn't know her, but nor did she know him any longer.

And this, more than anything else that had happened, made her want to weep.

She didn't, of course. This wasn't the place for tears, which Erekon would misconstrue, at any rate. Take for weakness. And mayhap would be right, in fact, for she'd ever been weak when it came to him. Demi straightened her shoulders, stood up tall. She faced him.

"I was a thief, true. A hungry thief who stole naught but a loaf of stale bread, easily replaced."

"You needn't have gone hungry. I'd have made certain you never would have, and you know it."

"Not here," she agreed, her chin lifted, her gaze unflinching. "Not working in the kitchens, no. But on the road, a woman alone, no coin to ease the path? So I stole a loaf to keep me from starving until I could find a means to support myself. So I took somewhat from those who had much. I had naught!"

"Does that make it any less a crime because your belly was empty than if it had been full? If you'd stolen from the jewel box instead of the oven?"

"You *chased* me!" she cried, at last unable to keep the tears away.

The memories came back. The crust in her hands, the smell of yeast, the heat of the ovens and the sound of the cook, complaining. The ache behind her eyes of tears and the desperation of knowing she could no longer stay, not unless she wanted to keep breaking herself apart against the walls they'd both put up between them. She hadn't thought of anything beyond what was in front of her. Taking what would barely satisfy her for more than a day. Foolish, but he'd called her that, had he not? She meant to prove him wrong and shown him to be right, instead.

"You chased me," Demi repeated in a low and shaking voice.

He didn't speak. He backed up another step without stumbling this time. His back straight, eyes forward. Mouth thin. He looked every inch the soldier he was. He looked a stranger.

At the door he stopped to look at her. "You ran."

"Of course I ran." Her voice was small.

"And I should have let you go, is that it? Left off my duty, or at the very least, sent someone else to do it? What might have happened had

I not been the one to go after you, have you thought of that once in all this time? No. I'd guess you haven't." He shook his head and a single strand of dark hair fell over his forehead. "I couldn't let you go, not with the cook screaming about the crime in my very face. And I couldn't let it be someone else. But you don't see that, do you? You didn't then. You can't, now."

"You . . . when you caught me . . ."

Now his eyes flashed, flat no longer, but full of fire. And, she saw with some alarm, pain. "When I caught you, what had you done? Gone on your knees like the little whore you were, true? Only this time, for the prince. Your beloved prince, the one you'd mooned over all those times, following him with your gaze when he passed you in the gardens. Speaking with such longing of his grace, his glamour, the perfection of his stride. Did you think that would save you?"

"Didn't it?" she asked, hating the sound of her own voice.

"You ran away," Erekon said, "from me."

At last, she bent her head. Handmaidens were trained in how to put the benefit of others before their own esteem, but that never meant they lacked pride. She had none, now. She deserved none.

"Aye. I ran from you."

"And do you not understand why I chased you?"

She shuddered at the memory of angry voices, of the thud of boots on marble. Of feeling like the hare whose heels are nipped by the hound. She'd put aside that memory a long time past but clung to the other part of it, the one in which Jarron put his hand upon her hair and told the Shomer Melek he would speak on her behalf. She swallowed. She could taste him, his flavor unchanged from then to now. She couldn't regret what had happened.

"You could've just let me go, Erekon."

He opened the door. It creaked on the hinges in an unseemly manner. In the back of her mind, Demi thought she should find some oil to ease the squeak, lest it disturb Jarron when he came through it next. It was habit, unbidden, and apparently unhidden as well, for Erekon fixed her with that flat black gaze again. When he spoke, his voice was rusty, cutting, and it left her wounded.

"I should have then, true, but I did not. Mayhap now is the time to start."

And then the creaking door closed behind him.

# Chapter 11

A nd would you believe it," Jarron said as he held out his arms for Demi to pull at the sleeves of his jacket, "the man hadn't even been through the door for but the time it took for us to look that way, and he was already waving his fists like a madman!"

"My gracious, what ever did you do?" she murmured and turned to hang his coat in the armoire where the clothes he'd most recently worn were kept.

"I bade him sit and have a drink of wine, which he readily accepted, and that ceased his tongue from its wagging." Jarron eyed her as she smoothed the fabric of his jacket. "Leave that, Demi, that's what I have maids to do."

She turned to him, her smile bright as any she'd ever given him, though somewhat seemed off. "Ah, sweetheart, it's what you have me for!"

"No, I have you for this." He pulled her close to him and kissed her. And again. "This as well."

She slipped her hands up his chest to link behind his neck. "And what else?"

His hands cupped her buttocks through the sleek fabric of her gown. "This?"

"Mmmm." She pressed against him. "I'm well pleased to leave the jacket to the attentions of someone else, then. Distract me, instead."

He laughed and took his time in kissing her, his mind still whirling from the day spent in what his father had always called the War Room, though in truth the Second hadn't been at war since before Jarron's grandfather had been born. In truth, the events of the day were more a distraction to her kiss than the other way 'round, and after a few moments Demi pushed him gently away.

"Sit," she said. "Let me bring you a glass of worm and ring for somewhat to eat. Somewhat light, aye? You'll be going to supper in the social hall, later?"

Jarron sat but shook his head. "No, I don't think so. I've spent enough of the day away from you."

She laughed and handed him the glass, then went to her knees at his feet. "I would go with you to the social hall, sweetheart. I've no fear of it."

"I know you don't." He touched her hair, then her cheek, and marveled at how every day she grew more lovely to his sight.

"Though if you're weary," she added, "I'm more than happy to stay here with you and see that you go to your bed early."

Jarron sipped the worm and sat back in his chair with a sigh as the liquid burned a trail of fire down to his gullet and the dissolved opiates feathered the edges of his vision. "It was a good day, Demi."

"I'm glad." She rested her cheek on his knee as he stroked her hair.

They sat in silence for a while, but the quiet was good. Jarron was beyond pleased Demi felt no need to chatter constantly. Their silences were never fraught with tension. She sighed, her shoulders lifting and falling. His fingers smoothed over her head.

"They spoke of much. The ministers."

"I suppose that is their duty, aye? To advise you." She looked up at him.

"Aye. But what they had to say . . . for the first time since I took my father's place, I feel they spoke not to his memory, but to me. And they listened, too. Well, most of them did, when they weren't ranting away about the borders and unification."

Her brow furrowed. "What of the borders? What of unification?"

Jarron sipped more worm, then put the glass aside without finishing. He might switch to plain wine, later, mayhap ale. But for now he'd had enough of this drug. "There is talk, apparently, of joining together the Five Provinces under one rule. One king for all of them. Joining the provinces to better utilize their resources."

"Who would decide the king?"

"Ah, well, there's the problem, true? Who would give up his crown in order to allow another to take it? Who would swear fealty to a liege when he's used to being the one being sworn to?"

"Either a foolish man or a very wise one," Demi said.

He studied her, having thought only the former and not the latter. "How so? Wise, I mean. I can clearly see the reason for calling him a fool."

She was silent for a breath or two, and he admired again how she took the time to think true on what she said without merely spouting the first words that came to her lips. She looked at him with those lovely dark eyes, her mouth slightly pursed in a way he wanted to kiss. So he did, pulling her to sit on his lap.

"Tell me now," he said.

Demi settled against him, toying with his collar. "Power is intoxicating."

"So many have said."

"Does the number of those who say it make it true?" she asked with tilt of her head and a smile.

"No more than silence makes somewhat false. But what you said is true."

"Worm is intoxicating, too. And herb. So is oblivion, if you've a mind to settle yourself even deeper into darkness. Ale and wine can make a man just as drunk though it might take longer."

He thought on this as he leaned in to take a long, deep breath of her scent. Gillyflowers, he thought, and made a note to ask her what she wore. "You're saying power is a drug."

"Aye." She rested her head on his shoulder, her fingers still toying with his shirt.

He held her there for a while, enjoying her weight and the contentment of sharing silence with someone whose company so pleased him. "I still can see why a man who gives up his crown could be named a fool, but not the other."

She nuzzled his neck. "Your father gave up his crown to you. Think you he's a fool?"

"That's different."

"Is it?"

He pushed her gently so he could look at her face. "Demi, do you care about politics, or are you seeking to somehow please me by talking about this?"

"Can it be both?"

It could be, but he didn't like that he was unable to discern her reasons. "I didn't bring you here to talk about politics or philosophy."

Some expression moved over her face, but smoothed at once. "Of course, sweetheart. Your mercy. I overstepped. Even Handmaidens aren't perfect."

"No, it's all right. I've had a long day of talking about things that may never come to pass. A day spent putting out fires, aye? I'm weary of it, that's all."

She kissed him, then slipped from his lap. "Then we shall speak no more of it. Come to bed?"

She held out her hand, and he took it, but though he looked toward the hall leading to the bedroom, Jarron didn't rise. Demi gave him an assessing look. She kissed his hand.

"You want somewhat else," she said. "Somewhat you've never had before."

His cock stirred at that, imagining the box of toys they'd yet to try. "Magnificent woman."

She laughed and twirled, her hem sweeping the floor before she stopped so suddenly the skirt kept moving while she stayed still. "Jarron. You don't care for the social hall because you find it useless, aye? Stilted and silly."

"Aye." He sighed. "And if you suggest I do it for my duty alone tonight, I'll argue with you."

"I don't want that," she teased. "No. I meant only that it's not the games and cards you object you, nor the idea of taking a glass or two or smoking a bowl with company. It's not the social part of it you don't like, and not even necessarily the company of your court. It's the setting, tell me true? The expectations. The staring."

He frowned. "I like cards and games. And of course drinking and smoking are pleasant enough pastimes. And I suppose there are one or two lords or ladies whose company I don't find too onerous— young Nigel, for example."

Her eyes gleamed. "You spent the day in meetings, talking of great, important things. You'd like to relax now, but not in the social hall. So let's go somewhere else."

His heart skipped a beat. "Where do you have in mind?"

"How about someplace nobody knows you?"

"Everyone knows me," Jarron said.

"Do they?" Demi was giving him that look again, the assessing one. Looking him up and down. "Do they, really? It's still your father's face on all the coins, aye? And . . . forgive me for saying it, sweetheart, but you've been notoriously opposed to having your portrait hung."

He touched his cheek out of instinct, though the skin there was still as smooth and clear as it had been for the past few months. "You suggest we leave the palace grounds."

"Aye. When's the last time you took yourself into the city for a drink at one of the pubs? Or even to shop in the stores?"

"Never," Jarron told her.

Demi looked surprised. "Never? True?"

"Never." He shook his head.

"Oh, sweetheart," she told him with a purr that had his cock straining at the front of his breeches, "you are in for a delight."

Remind me again why you had to wear my breeches and jacket," Jarron said into her ear as they both surveyed the pub they'd just entered.

His breath made her shiver, and Demi turned her head just slightly. "I couldn't very well come traipsing in here wearing my regular attire, could I? I'd attract attention on my very own, true, but also how many people know the king sent away for a Sister from the Order of Solace? You'd be made in a moment, and though it might do you good to be stood a round of drinks, I thought anonymity was what you preferred."

"Aye," he breathed against her, his hand at the small of her back. "But how did you know I'd find you so tempting in my clothes?"

"It wasn't somewhat I learned from what you sent the Order, if that's what you're thinking. You needn't fear there was somewhat secret, a code, in your answers that led me to think you might like me dressing crossways." She laughed, still low, gaze sweeping the room. "It's simply easier, sweetheart, to pass as male rather than face a place like this as the sort of woman who'd come to a place like this." Demi laughed, keeping her voice pitched low and giving it a thicker accent. "Come, m'lud, wot let's have ourselves a pint or two."

Jarron followed her through the crowd toward a table set toward the back, in the shadows. Just in case. She hadn't brought him to one of the roughest places for the simple fact that he could scarcely help the way he spoke and carried himself—one word too many and he'd give himself away. Not necessarily as the king, of course, but as someone noble. Someone worth robbing in the gutter. She'd settled on the

Laughing Pigeon, frequented by lesser lords who thought they were slumming but didn't know enough about the city to find the real slums. Not that they'd want to be in the real slums. Poverty only looked romantic from the outside.

She didn't think any of Jarron's court were likely to spend their coin in a place like this—not with the pleasure of the social hall at their disposal for naught but an exchange of wit and a profession of loyalty. Still, it wasn't impossible that some of them might have felt the same urges she and Jarron had, so keeping to the shadows was the best idea.

Besides, from here they had a view of the entire room while keeping their privacy. With the bulge he'd been sporting in his breeches since she'd first slipped into his shirt and clubbed her hair at the back of her neck, Demi was hoping Jarron might wish to take advantage of the shadows.

He hadn't asked her how she knew about this place, which meant she hadn't had to lie. She'd once worked the kitchens, not here but two pubs over, at the Drowning Cock. The pubmistress here at the Pigeon left out the half-eaten meatpies at the end of the night, though, and whatever the rats and dogs didn't get first, she'd had no issue with the street urchins taking.

She would tell him, if ever she had to. She'd not lie to keep the secret. Her training in the Order had taught her not to be shamed of her past, and besides that, her faith and devotion to the Order meant she'd tell the truth if asked.

If asked.

This was dangerous, skating on the edge, and Demi knew it, but there was somewhat terribly exciting about it as well. Not so much the clothes, for her, because she was accustomed to dressing in any manner of costume to please her patrons. But being here, with Jarron, both of them courting discovery. It was intrigue, but of the playacting sort.

They took seats at the polished wood table and gave their order to the wispy bit of a lad who squeaked at the thump of a fist at the table next to theirs. Demi avoided the pot of mustard and basket of crackers on the table and shook her head when Jarron made to take one. Her stomach had once been lined with iron, but no longer, and surely his had never had reason to be that stout.

"What shall we order, do you think?" Jarron looked 'round the room.

"Somewhat simple, sweetheart. The kitchens here are not as clean as your own. But the drink is strong and should be enough to cover the taste of anything bad."

Jarron was smart, and he studied her. "You sound as though you know this place."

"This and others like it." Demi shrugged, gaze sweeping the room before looking back at him. "Places where men gather are often much the same. So are those where women gather, mind you. I have to be observant. And remember. I have to take with me what I see, Jarron."

"For other patrons." His lip curled just the slightest bit in a way she'd seen before, in others, but had never made her smile before now.

"Aye."

He outright sneered at that. "How many have you had?"

"Seven." There was no point in lying, and besides, she wasn't ashamed. Nor should he be angry or jealous, though that wouldn't stop him.

"Am I the seventh? Or the eighth?"

"Eighth, sweetheart," she murmured as the table next to them became occupied with a rough pair of lads with loud voices.

"You didn't count me among the number?"

Demi looked at him seriously and put a discreet finger to her lips, then gave a pointed glance at the fact they were no longer alone in the corner. Jarron, frowning, glanced that way. She could see him dismiss the other men with a shrug and had to bite back a smile— men, no matter their station or upbringing, were all so very much alike. Jarron leaned forward to whisper.

"I'm not counted?"

"You," she said, leaning close enough to kiss him, if they but moved half a breath, "are still my patron and, therefore, not counted amongst the others who came before you."

He looked only barely mollified. "I am but one of a number."

"You knew that when you sent for me," Demi said.

In other patrons, this conversation had irritated her, or softened her, but for this man it sent her pulse leaping. It had naught to do with her service to the order, or to him. *Women we begin and women we shall end,* she thought, never feeling it was truer than at that moment.

"I would be the only one who matters," Jarron said in a low, serious voice.

They all wanted the same. Demi gave him the same answer she'd given them all, and as with everything else she'd ever told him, she didn't lie. "You are."

Jarron, once again, was too smart to be teased. "For now, you mean. Just for now. Until you leave and go to someone else."

"I will never leave you until you're ready to have me go," she told him. "And when you're ready to let me leave you, believe me, Jarron, you'll be the one who decides."

"Tell me true?" he asked, tilting his head to look her over with a skeptical eye. "You know this as you know all else? Or because all the others did the same?"

Demi reached to squeeze his fingers, wishing this conversation had come up in a different place where they needn't keep their voices so hushed, where she might've been clothed in the garments that made her better able to act as a Handmaiden. Even naked would've been better than this.

"Because if I fulfill my purpose, you'll no longer have need of me. If I do not, at some point, you and I will both know it is of no use to continue trying, and you'll have me leave you. It's the way it works, Jarron."

He turned his hand in hers so that it lay palm up on the table with hers inside it. "And if I never want you to leave? What, then?"

"Then I shall never go." Even as she spoke, Demi thought the words would at last make a liar of her.

But they seemed to satisfy him, for Jarron sat back in his chair with a grin and waved for the serving wench. "Two pints of your best."

It wasn't likely to be anything like what he was used to, and Demi laughed. "Add a bottle of worm to that, my lord." The quality of that, at least, was likely to be the same.

"And a bottle of worm, aye. And bring a bowl of herb while you're at it." He grinned at Demi. "Might as well take it all, aye?"

"Aye, my lord," she murmured, keeping her voice and her hat tipped low, though she'd have bet a dozen arros the wench knew Demi was a woman. Either that or the woman simply didn't find her attractive, though she insisted on flashing her ample bosom toward Jarron.

"And to eat, m'lud? Wot I could bring youse somewhat from the kitchen. We've a nice egg dish laid by. Or a mutton pie."

"Naught for now." Jarron dismissed her and turned back to Demi. "So . . . what else shall we do, here? Surely you didn't bring me only to intoxicate ourselves. We might've done that at home, with better quality."

"Arrows," Demi told him. "I challenge you to a game."

Jarron grinned, and the brightness of his smile took her breath away. "You're on."

# Chapter 12

Jarron had put away nearly the full bottle of worm, along with several pints, and smoked a full bowl. Demi hadn't even tried keeping up with him—most often if she indulged it was in the safety of a patron's bedroom where she could trust herself to be a little tipsy. He had little enough experience in a place like this. One of them had to stay sober enough to get them home without being set upon in the alley and rolled for their purses.

Still, she'd drunk and smoked enough to be deliciously warm and fuzzy, and to find everything amusing. She watched him now, as he lined up the game arrow with his gaze, one eye squinted. He hefted the fringed wood but didn't throw.

"Afraid I'll win?" she said.

Jarron turned to her with bright eyes, slack mouth wet from where he swiped his tongue. "Should I be?"

"Mayhap."

Jarron shook his head. "Will you let me win to soothe me?"

"No. Of course not. Not unless I think you need me to, and you're not the sort of man who would like that, I think." She leaned against the table, watching the room. Nobody was paying them any attention at all, which was good.

"Good." Jarron nodded this time, the motion making him just the slightest bit unsteady on his feet. He turned. Threw the game arrow. Missed the board and hit the wall. "Void take it!"

She laughed and crept behind him to sneak the game arrow from his hand and take her shot. She had the advantage of slightly better sobriety, and though it had been some long time since she'd played at this game, once she'd been very well skilled, indeed. She didn't get the eye in the center of the board, but it was close.

"We should place a wager," Jarron said and finished the bottle of worm in one swig.

Demi turned to him. "Aye? And what would that be?"

Jarron smirked. "Whoever wins gets to . . . have . . . the other."

When she licked her lips, she tasted worm. She also drew his attention, and the power of that was compelling. Most of the time, Demi was happy to take Jarron's lead. Give him the power he seemed to crave. But this was somewhat else, she thought.

She lifted a brow. "If it pleases you to wager, then we shall."

"You say that because you think you'll win."

"Mayhap," Demi said in a low voice with a grin, "I say it because I hope you will."

"I'll feel bad when I beat you. But not too much."

She laughed at him, and he pulled her closer, mayhap forgetting she wore his clothes. Mayhap not caring. They got a few curious glances at that, but not too many. She pushed him gently away.

"You're on."

She did win the round, and the next, and with hardly an effort. Jarron watched her aim and throw, each time getting close to the eye if not directly in it. His shots went wild. He blinked, put his hands on his hips.

"You're winning."

"I am, my lord." She smiled up at him from beneath the brim of her hat.

"I think we should go home now." Jarron gathered the game arrows and replaced them in the holder by the board. He turned to her. "Are you ready?"

In the alley, just outside, he took her hand. "Demi."

"Yes, sweetheart," she said, using the endearment now that they were out of the pub and alone but for a pair of drunkards weaving their way down the street.

"You beat me."

"I did, Jarron. Indeed."

"You're very good at the game."

"I'm very good at a great many things." She linked her arm through his. "Now. Shall I collect my wager here, or at home?"

She could see House Bydelay from where they were. Lights shining in the distance. It sat on a hill overlooking the town and seemed very far away, though if they walked swiftly they'd reach it before the next chime.

Jarron laughed softly. He was a sweet drunk, at least. When he kissed her, she tasted herb, but it didn't mask his own delicious flavor. She sucked his tongue gently before stepping back.

"We might not make it home," Jarron said.

"You've not even asked me my terms, sweetheart. Mayhap you might wish for the privacy of your bedroom." Demi looked up and down the street, but though many of the pub doors were propped open to take advantage of the cool night's air, the street was empty.

She pushed him toward the dark and silent sweetshop two buildings down from the Laughing Pigeon. The door was set far back into a carved brick entryway, providing shadowed privacy. Jarron went willingly enough, laughing under his breath as he stumbled on the step. She caught him and pushed him up against the brick.

"So what are your terms, love?" He wasn't slurring, but his eyes definitely had a glaze of intoxication.

Demi already had an idea of what she meant to ask for. She pushed the brim of her hat up to show her face, then put a hand at the laces of her borrowed breeches. "I think you should service me the way you would a man. On your knees."

Jarron laughed again and pressed up against her. "You think so? Would it please you to have me on my knees for you?"

Truth, she had no such preference, but the way he'd admired her in his clothes told her Jarron might. "It might do you some good to be the one kneeling for a change."

He grunted lightly and nuzzled at her neck. "Think you I need some humility, is that your game?"

Demi pushed him back a little bit and loosed the first lace. "A man can learn much from being on his knees. See a lot looking up instead of always down."

Jarron stepped back from her. In the shaft of light coming in from the street she could see his throat work as he swallowed. "Is this a lesson you intend to teach me for my own good?"

She finished unlacing the breeches and folded open the thick material, then pushed it over her hips to leave herself bare to him. She leaned back against the brick, tilting her hips, making an offering. When he stayed still, Demi carefully wet her first two fingers with her mouth and slipped them down to circle her clit.

Jarron groaned.

Smiling, she arched her back and sighed, watching him from half-closed eyes. From outside on the street came the noise of shouts and drunken singing. Jarron looked over his shoulder, but Demi didn't stop. When he looked back at her, she made a low noise of pleasure.

Jarron went to his knees.

She'd almost thought he would not—not for any lack of humility but because it was not his pleasure to be the one in that place. In fact, she almost urged him to stand again, but he'd already reached for her. His hands grasped her rear, holding her still while his questing mouth found her clit.

It was Demi's turn to groan. Jarron lifted her leg over his shoulder that he might get closer, feasting on her. He licked and sucked gently on her clit, then slid his tongue along her folds. And oh, by the Arrow, inside her! Her hips bucked. Her fingers found his hair, holding him to her.

It was not the act itself—he'd often used his tongue on her cunt this way. It was the position. Her standing, him at her feet, his head bent and mouth working against her flesh. When he focused again on her clit and replaced his tongue with a finger, she thought her knees would buckle from the pleasure of it. The wall at her back kept her standing, as did the support of her leg over his shoulder.

Breathing hard, he paused to look up at her. Lightly, gently, he kissed her clit. He smiled wickedly and flicked it with his tongue. He knew exactly what he was doing.

If she'd thought to have the power with him at her feet, she was wrong.

Jarron had her completely. It didn't matter what she wore or what she said or whether she was on top or bottom. It didn't even matter that he didn't know it.

"Jarron," she breathed on a ragged sigh.

Both his hands went back to her bare bottom, cupping it and holding her still though she yearned to shift against him. He smiled and licked his mouth while her clit pulsed at how close his tongue crept to her without actually touching. He breathed on her, the heat of it a stroke too delicate to do anything but tease.

"This is how you wanted me, aye? On my knees. Does it satisfy you?"

Demi let her head fall back against the brick as she arched her back, but to no avail. She could feel his closeness and the heat of him, but he was deliberately not touching her where she most needed his caress. She gave a low cry when he brushed his mouth, without lingering, over her.

"You were right, Demi. I do see much from this vantage. The question is, what shall I learn?" At last he bent again to press a firmer kiss to her flesh. "Shall I learn how to make you scream? Or should we learn to be more subtle than that, so we might not draw the attention of the gentlemen I hear just beyond?"

She heard them, too. The rustle of fabric, the patter of piss on the stone. The rumble of their laughter. The soft sigh of desire and the moistness of kissing.

"I think they're doing much the same as we are," Jarron said against her cunt. His tongue flicked out again, stroking along her folds and dipping inside quickly before moving up again to circle her clit. "Hush now, lest they hear you."

She could scarcely remain silent when his mouth was working on her in such a way, but she did her best. Jarron's lips and tongue danced on her cunt. He once more added the play of his fingers, pushing two inside her to thrust deep. Then a third while he sucked at her flesh.

She bit the heel of her hand and still a cry leaked out. Jarron looked up at her, and the loss of his dancing tongue made her cry out again. Louder this time.

He laughed against her, which did naught to soothe the pleasure but instead made it all the greater. She tried to rock against his mouth, but he pulled away when she did. Once, twice, and Demi laughed, too, though hers became a sigh.

From outside the doorway came the louder sounds of passion. Grunts. Groans. The slap of flesh on flesh.

When Jarron moved again between her legs, Demi put both hands over her mouth to keep herself quiet. Oh, by the Arrow, it was difficult. She wanted to cry out her ecstasy. She wanted to brag with it. The only thing keeping her from shouting was his murmured "hush."

Again, Jarron pulled his mouth away. His fingers slid inside her, slightly curling. In and out, until great, deep shudders of climax began rippling through her. He pressed his mouth to her clit and pulled her toward him. She came on his tongue in great waves, mindless for the moment.

Shaking, weak, she hadn't yet caught her breath when Jarron slipped her leg from over his shoulder and stood. He gripped her hips.

He kissed her, and tasting her own arousal on his mouth sent a slow, rolling surge of desire through her.

"Hush," he whispered into her ear.

She didn't know when he'd loosed his own breeches, but a moment after he spoke she felt the press of his cock against her. Demi bit down on Jarron's shoulder at the pressure. His hands went back to her rear, lifting her as he filled her. He pinned her against the wall, neither of them moving except for the rise and fall of their shoulders from their panting. Guttural shouts and hoarse gasps came from only a short distance away.

"What do you suppose they look like?" he murmured in her ear as he began to slowly thrust. "Is one on his knees for the other, do you think? Or is one bent over, taking his lover's cock up his ass? Maybe they're kissing, each with his fist pumping the other's prick. . . ."

All the pictures he was painting were pretty enough, but Jarron wasn't finished.

"Maybe it's not two men at all, but two whores, coupling. Think you it could be that? One with her skirts lifted so the other might press her face between her legs, licking and sucking her until she explodes, just as you did? Mayhap one has her fingers buried deep inside the other's tight, sweet cunny, stroking and fucking her the way I'm fucking you right now. Think of that, Demi."

More pretty pictures. She had no answer for him, and Jarron seemed to expect none, for he sealed her mouth with his. His tongue thrust inside in rhythm with his cock into her. His fingers slipped on her behind, gone slippery with their mingled sweat and her slickness. He pushed her harder against the bricks, and she clung to him.

"No matter who it is," Jarron said against her mouth, "no matter what pleasure they bring each other, they do not have what you have, Demi. No matter how they scream and grunt and cry out with their desire, they can never have what you have."

He fucked into her harder, his expression hard, too. She didn't think she'd tip into orgasm again, but somewhat in that look sent her spiraling again into climax. Jarron's brow furrowed, his eyes closed, his mouth went tight. He shuddered his release as hers swept over her, too.

Jarron pressed his forehead to Demi's and drew a breath. "They didn't have me at their feet, Demi. No matter who they are and what they've done, they'll never have that."

She kissed him as he let her settle onto the ground again. Her thighs and back ached from the pressure she hadn't noticed during their lovemaking. She didn't care. Nor did she mind the slow, hot trickle of his seed down her thighs as she pulled up her breeches and laced them.

From outside the doorway came silence. Jarron kissed her. He nuzzled against her. And into her ear, he said, "I did learn much from that position. You were right, as always."

She didn't have time to ask him what he'd learned, because out on the street came a loud cry and the sound of feet on the stones. Jarron put an arm out to keep her from sticking her head out while he checked.

"Bloody bunch of ruffians," he murmured. "Putting up signs or somewhat, sticking them to the fronts of shop windows. Some shop owner must've been inside."

Demi moved to peek, and he let her this time. The street, lit by tall gas lamps, wasn't bright, but she could still see the full length of it. The pub doors, propped open to take advantage of the cool night air, helped, too, with their golden light spilling out. She could see the signs clinging to the glass windows but not read what they said. She could also see the group of young men dressed all in black who were hanging them, and the less discreetly dressed group following with jeers and threats.

"What are they doing?" she asked.

"It would appear the shop owner's rallying his friends. Or mayhap only a group drunk enough to find the cause of someone rallying them enjoyable enough to rally."

She watched as a shop owner clad in a long nightrail and matching cap snatched one of the signs off the window and ran after the group in black, calling for their heads. "Surely he could simply take down the sign."

"Unification!" came the faint cry from the group disappearing down the street, and Jarron turned to her with a frown. He rearranged his clothes. There was no sign of the drunken, lust-filled lover of moments ago. He looked every inch the king when he went out of the doorway and grabbed up one of the signs from the street.

"Some bastards wot put those there," said a grinning man, hat askew and trousers baggy. "Fools is wot they are, m'luds, aye? Talkin 'bout signing up the Second as part of another province. The day that happens is the day I march on yonder palace meself and piss in the face of Jarron Bydelay."

Jarron made a low sound, suspiciously like a laugh. "Will you?"

"Tell you true." The man swaggered around to snatch up another of the signs, spitting on it before giving his rear end an exaggerated swipe. "One king for all, wot? What fools would want such a thing?"

"The sort who dress in black and run down the streets at night instead of facing those whose property wot they defaced," shouted the disgruntled shop owner with a shake of his fist.

"Come, love, let's go home." Jarron took Demi's arm. "The night is waning, and I fear I've had too much drink and smoke to last much longer."

"Aye," she murmured, looking down the street to where the men had gone. She thought of what Erekon had said. She thought about games of power. "Let's go home."

# Chapter 13

I wish you could go with me." Jarron said this from behind a yawn as he tossed off the blankets in which they'd both been solidly entwined.

"I could. I would, if you wanted me to. But I fear I'd be a distraction. Not only to you."

"To the others, you mean." He propped himself on his elbow to look at her.

She smiled and kissed him. "If you think otherwise, I'm happy to oblige you. . . ."

Jarron shook his head and sighed. He swung his legs over the edge of the bed and stretched. "No. I know you're right. As usual. They'd save themselves from giggling behind their hands like schoolgirls, I think, but they'd be distracted. But what good, I ask you, is being king if I cannot lay abed all day should I wish?"

"I think you could change the meeting," said his bewitching Handmaiden with a sultry smile that had his cock twitching. She crooked a finger at him and laughed when he snared her hand and kissed it. Then nibbled it. She pulled it away. "Be gentle, Jarron. I'm still sore from last night."

He grinned at the memory. He swore he could still taste her. Jarron thought he might always have her flavor with him. He leaned to kiss her, taking his time.

But alas, he did have to pull away. No matter how he might wish to stay abed and sleep the day away, or spend it in the arms of a willing and beautiful woman, he did have duties. Demi was up and out of bed before he finished scrubbing at his face with his hands. She held out a dressing gown for him and tickled his sides mercilessly as he belted it.

He captured her hands. "This does not bring me solace."

She gave him a saucy wink. "So you say."

Then she sauntered off, naked, to brew her special blend of morning tea for him. She ran his bath, too, though she didn't attend him in it. She would've, had he asked her to, but Jarron didn't like to linger overlong. He could easily scrub himself and rinse while she laid out his clothes and took care of all the details she'd taken over. Sending for her was the best decision he'd ever made, and he meant to thank Adam again for it today when he saw him.

Washed and not yet dressed, he sauntered into the library to find Demi with a hot mug of tea ready for him. "You're amazing, you do know that."

She laughed. "It's easy enough to time the kettle when I know how long you take at your ablutions. Here. I've made some simplebread, too. I didn't ring for anything else; you'll be having food served at the meetings, aye?"

He nodded and took the hot cup from her to sip. She looked him up and down. She'd dressed while he was in the bath, bound her hair back in the braid to her waist. He couldn't stop remembering how she'd looked in his clothes.

"Would you like somewhat else to wear, Demi?"

"Hmmm?" She looked up at him, and he wondered what she'd been pondering.

"Other clothes. I'm bound to provide you with clothes appropriate for what, the season and occasion, is that it?" He'd had half a dozen gowns made for her based on the measurements the Order had sent in advance, but they were all in the same style. He hadn't thought she might prefer another kind. "The season I've managed, and the occasion . . ."

"You've done well enough. You haven't asked me to attend a formal ball, and these gowns are of lovely quality and fit well. I'm comfortable in them. They show everyone my place beside you. It's easier that way." She ran a fingertip down his bare chest and toyed briefly with the hair below his naval before dropping her touch. "You, on the other hand, ought to put on rather more than this before you leave here."

He laughed and set the cup aside. Just those few sips had wakened him, made his head more clear. Whatever she put in there, it was magic. "I shall. But you. What should we do about you?"

Demi tilted her head in that way she had, her smile secret and slow. "If it pleases you to clothe me in a different manner, Jarron, I'll be happy to wear whatever you like. Or naught, it matters not to me. Only that it be appropriate and fit for the season."

"Don't you long for pretty clothes? Most women do. What is that you say sometimes under your breath when you think I can't hear? 'Women we begin and women we shall end?' Women like clothes."

"I know a fair number of men who do, too. Your friend Adam."

"He should dress you," Jarron decided. "He'd love the chance, and I'd like to see you in somewhat he creates."

"And will you take me to the social hall and parade me about?" she asked him quietly. Not judging. Just asking.

Jarron stopped. He didn't think she meant to trick him; *could* she trick him? Was that allowed? "Would you like me to take you there wearing a pretty new gown and new slippers?"

"If it pleases you," Demi said mildly. "I'm just as happy to stay here."

Her consistent geniality most often did please him, but just now he wanted a different sort of answer. "Would you feel better if I dressed you more like my mistress and not a Handmaiden?"

Her lips parted and she made as though to speak. Somewhat shifted in her gaze. She stepped closer to him. "It pleases me for you to dress me however you like."

"You have an opinion, Demi. Don't act as though you don't." The worst of it was, he knew she was no simpering poppet giving in to his every whim simply to curry his favor.

"I'm not your mistress. Or your wife."

"That's no sort of answer."

She smiled slightly. "It's the true answer, Jarron. When I wear this gown, everyone knows who I am. It's who I am. It makes it impossible for anyone to forget I'm a Handmaiden, bound to the Order of Solace."

"Even yourself, true?" he said, irritated and uncertain of why.

"Most especially myself."

His eyes narrowed as he looked her over. She was right, as always. She wasn't his mistress, nor his wife, and he'd brought her here for that very reason. So that she might never be. He reached to take hold of her braid, hung so casually over her shoulder. He didn't pull it, though her eyes fluttered briefly as though she expected he might.

"If you'd rather not have pretty gowns and paint your face, if you'd rather stand out than blend . . ." He shrugged. "Then I won't ask it of you. Even if you would do it to please me."

"Let me help you get dressed," she suggested.

"I used to have a valet for that. Maids to clean up after me."

"And now you have me."

Jarron tugged her closer. Slanted his mouth over hers. He kissed her, but carefully, not letting himself get lost in the sensation of her soft mouth the way he'd done so often in so short a time. She opened for him the way she always did. Always would, so long as he kept her.

So long as he was in need of solace.

* * *

In the War Room, Jarron paced as he talked. His father had sat on a throne at the head of the table to listen to his Ministers of Advice, but Jarron was too restless. Some of the ministers, the older ones, had taken their places at the long table, while the younger ones lounged in softer chairs in front of the fireplace. Jarron could reach them all as he walked, facing one and then the other when he needed to make a point. When he wanted to judge by each man's face what he was thinking. It was more effective, he thought, as one of the Ministers of Trade stood to face him while he spoke.

"We've had trade routes established for quiverfuls of seasons. We take our goods there, they bring theirs here. We sell what we've an excess of and buy what we lack. It's the way trade works." His name was Kenvin Arukay and he'd taken over for his father, who'd passed away just before Jarron's father stepped down. "But it's not necessarily going to continue that way."

"Why shouldn't it?" barked another minister. Badger Barony oversaw trade with the Fifth Province, the one bordering the sea. "I've built relationships with my fellows in the Fifth. They rely on my men bringing them flaxene and shipments of herb, just as we need them to provide the dyes we use."

Adam piped up at this. Previously, he'd been lounging, silent, feet up on a footstool, and sipping at a glass of wine. "We could make our own dyes."

Barony shot him an arch look. "Funny thing for the Minister of Fashion to say, considering the order you just placed with me for a vat of carmelian."

Adam shrugged. "If it's available, of course I'll use it. But what I'm saying is, we can make our own dyes. We can use other products. Carmelian is not even the cheapest dye, and it ruins fabric as often as it colors it. We grow plenty of gillyflower here in the Second, and I have a man working on the process of refining it right now to create a dye very similar to carmelian. Cheaper, too. And right here within our borders."

Barony sputtered. "That crosses the line of your duties!"

Adam smiled. Jarron knew that look. If Barony wasn't careful, or if Jarron didn't intervene, there'd be a fight starting. Adam claimed he didn't care to sully his hands with physical confrontation, but he had no qualms about using the skill of his extremely sharp tongue.

"There's naught to say Adam is forbidden from such experimentation," Jarron said.

Barony huffed and slammed back a long swallow of wine. "Of course you'd say so."

Jarron gave Barony a long, thorough look that had the man cutting his gaze. "Do you suggest I favor Adam because he's my friend?"

"Of course he does." Adam stood and crossed the room with even more of a swish than usual to refill his cup from the pitcher set right in front of Barony. "Dear Badger here is convinced you and I are lovers, Jarron. Isn't that so, Badge? Isn't that what you've been hush-hushing about?"

"Would it matter," Jarron said evenly, looking around the room, "if that were true?"

To some it might, but others had formed liasions with their own lovers right there in that room. It might be currently more fashionable to take a wife and keep a male lover on the side than the other way 'round, but that wasn't the issue. Jarron solidly met the gaze of his ministers, at least the ones who'd look at him.

"Adam and I have been longtime boon companions. I value his opinion, as would any of you, should you deign to give the position he holds the scrap of respect you give to your own."

"The length of trousers," huffed Barony. "The color of waistcoats!"

"The expense of linen and profit in wool," Adam shot back. "The money to be made in bolts of fabric is far more than you gain with your trade to the Fifth, Badge, my love. And you know it. The fact is, the Second lacks the mines of the Fourth, the quarries of the Third.

We don't have the ocean to give us the fish and access to faraway trade that the Fifth does. We don't have the forests of the First to give us wood, or the mountains of the First to give us stone. We have fields of gillyflowers for oils, fields of flaxene for thread, pastures of sheep for wool, and we have fresh ponds of eels for leather. So tell me again, what products the Second produces for trade that do not, somehow in the end, relate to fashion?"

Jarron studied the room. Some of the men were nodding. Others looked irritated or downright annoyed. This was the way of every meeting he'd ever had, naught new or strange about it. There'd be argument and discussion, mayhap some hard feelings that might become a feud with the taking of sides, but political alliances tended to fade and grow here the way they did in the schoolyard, too. Swiftly and without longevity.

"If you truly wish to discuss how to grow this province and make it the best it can be," Adam said loudly, "it might be best to consider what they're shouting about in the streets."

Silence so thick Jarron felt the weight of it covered the entire room. Every eye turned to Adam. A slick sweat broke out along Jarron's spine.

"What say you?"

Adam turned, looking at him steadily. "They all won't say it, Jarron, because none of them want to be the one to bring it up. But I've heard what they're saying in the town, and out in the fields, too. I've traveled this province back and forth, and let me say that the farmers and shepherds who work themselves to death and still live in squalor are talking. A lot."

"About what?" sputtered Barony, though the cut of his gaze told Jarron the man well knew.

"Unification," Adam said flatly. "The Fourth Province borders us to the east. They've already set it into motion, rallying in the streets and even gaining audience with their premier."

"Deporter? He's granted them audience?" Jarron hadn't heard this.

By the Void, he'd been hearing rumors of this unification movement for a long time, but to learn one of his peers was actually promoting it . . . "He's a fool, at any rate, who never could make his own decisions without the vote of a dozen others."

"Deporter has granted them audience, indeed, and has sent delegates to the Third and First, who border him, though you know better than I what a madman Bander Mezzinghast is. He'll never go for it. Word has it he's building a wall surrounding the entire province to keep out any who try to get him to join up."

"The Third's borders are vast and in the worst country possible. It's the largest but poorest province. But Adam's right, I've heard the same thing." This came from Nigel. "They're building a wall. He's got every able-bodied subject at work. Works them until they die, if necessary."

Jarron poured himself a cup of wine and quaffed it. "Why is this the first I've heard of it?"

He looked at Pinter Bevins, Minister of Information, who looked pained. "My lord king, these are all rumors. And not affecting the Second in the least. It's not as though the Third's declaring war on us. Or anyone. Their efforts at defense have naught to do with us, unless we have intention of attacking them."

"Deporter approached the other provinces, but not the Second? Why?" Jarron demanded.

Bevins looked uncomfortable. "He met with your father and was turned away."

Jarron gritted his teeth. His father was slipping daily deeper into madness, forgetting his own name and certainly that of his son. It would be impossible to get from him any context of conversation he'd had with Deporter even a short time ago.

"They're not rumors," said Nigel. "I had two trade parties turned away in the past sennight by Bander's soldiers. They didn't see a wall, but they heard enough stories about the building of it to believe it. It's the first time they've been turned away from the Third's borders, by the way. We've had a great trade relationship with them in the past."

"What good is this unification supposed to be?" Jarron demanded. He thought of the black-masked men running through the streets. "Joining the provinces under one ruler? What is meant to happen to the rest of us?"

"Unification would make trade easier if we're all under one roof, so to speak. If we're all of the same household, with goods and services to be shared more equally——" Adam began.

"At reduced profit," cut in Barony. "With more taxes to go to the central seat. I've heard the plan, tell you true. I didn't want to believe anyone could possibly be considering it."

"I want to know more." Jarron shot a glare at Bevins. "I want to know who's for this. How it should work. Who proposed it. Most important, who's set himself as the one to rule the rest? And what does he expect us all to do, step aside and give up our thrones?"

"It's Caramin," Adam said.

Jarron stopped his pacing. "Caramin Ahavat of the First? Has she gone as mad as her father?"

Caramin, daughter to Carakin, had taken the throne from her father by force.

"That would be the obvious conclusion, aye? The first place Mezzinghast began the wall was on the border of the Third and First." Adam took his seat again, long legs stretched out, the picture of indolence. A false picture, Jarron knew.

"A woman, ruling over the Five Provinces?" Jarron's laugh sounded false, even to himself. "She must be mad. It is just the Five, tell me true? She's not set her mind to conquer the ones past the sea or across the mountains?"

"I daresay she has no intention of conquering any of us," said Nigel as he took a seat next to Adam and handed him a full cup of wine.

Jarron noted this exchange for a later time. "She wants us all to kneel at her feet—how is that not conquering?"

"She has an entire program outlined for how it would work. How each province would maintain a . . . governor, she calls them. Answer-

ing directly to her, and with equal vote in all matters of the central
government, much the way our own government is structured. Each
governor would have his own lieutenants, I think. I must confess, I've
heard only bits and pieces gathered from the gossip rags," Nigel said.
"Outside of the city, my lord, there has been much talk of this over the
past few months, but it's a new concept. New idea. There are some
who fancy it so fiercely they make every attempt to promote it. Others
care naught for the idea and declare they'll fight it every chance they
have."

Jarron's stomach turned, sick. He looked around the room. "How
many of you have heard more of this unification business than what's
been discussed in here?"

Fewer than half of his twenty ministers raised their hands. Adam,
Nigel, and Barony were of those who had. After too long a moment,
Bevins raised his hand, looking guilty. Erekon Kosem, who had no
vote but attended the meetings just the same, detached himself from
the shadows.

"I've been strongly hearing of it for the past twelvemonth, with
several seasons of rumors before that. I made report to Bevins, but the
threat was determined to be such that no action had to be taken."

Jarron turned on his heel to stalk to the window and look out. The
lawn was turning green. He could see the gardens from here, not yet
in bloom. "This is my land. Mine."

From behind him, silence.

"Are there any here who think this idea of unification makes any
sort of sense?"

A cough. A clearing of a throat. Jarron didn't turn.

Not, at least, until someone spoke.

"I think that whether we like the idea of it or not, it's somewhat we
must needs consider as the future. Somewhat for which we should
prepare ourselves," said a familiar voice, and Jarron turned.

It was Adam.

# Chapter 14

Demi was no fool. When the queen ordered her attendance in her personal quarters, Demi went. She made an effort at smoothing her hair and putting on a fresh gown, the one she'd worn from the Motherhouse, which was her favorite and suited her best. She wore new slippers with it, not the leather traveling boots, and she'd rebraided her hair in a rather more intricate style. All these subtle efforts she didn't quite expect Jarron's mother to notice, though she was certain the woman would notice had she made no effort at all.

"Malkah Shelee." Demi made a perfect curtsy as she spoke in a low murmur.

Jarron's mother had made her high-backed chair as much a throne as if it sat upon a dais, and though Demi still stood, she managed to look down on her. "How quaint. Nobody who's anybody still uses those old terms."

Demi let a smile tweak the corner of her mouth and didn't point out that the Shomer Melek was still referred to by its old name. "Forgive me. Should I address you somehow differently?"

"I thought you'd be kneeling by now. Doing that thing, whatever it is you women do. What do you call it?"

"Waiting," Demi said.

The former queen sniffed and unfolded her fan with a flick of her wrist to furiously flick it, though the room was not overwarm to Demi's mind. "Why don't you do it, then?"

"You're not my patron, my lady. Nor am I in meditation. As such, I am happy to show you the proper respect any lady would."

"But not on your knees, aye?" The older woman fixed Demi with a narrow-eyed glare. "Sit, then. You're making my neck hurt."

Demi took the chair across from her. She sat straight, ankles crossed, skirt hung just so. She folded her hands in her lap. The woman was sure to find enough fault with her, and she meant to offer no additional reasons for criticism.

"So. You're the Handmaiden."

"I am, indeed."

"What is your name? I heard it was somewhat ridiculous."

"I am called Redemption, though your son calls me Demi."

"Ridiculous!" Jarron's mother cried. "Redemption? What is that? How arrogant."

"I didn't name myself but was given the name by the Mothers-in-Service." It was a perfect name for her, Demi thought, but would never have shared with the woman in front of her.

The former queen fanned herself even faster. "You look . . . clean."

Of all the insults Demi had anticipated, this veiled one struck her funny. She laughed. "I bathe daily."

"That's not what I mean, and I daresay you know it. You know what I mean. Oh, I know all about your kind, I do. Your witchery." Jarron's mother slapped the fan closed and put it on her ample lap. "My son, they say, is besotted with you!"

"That may be the case, but I assure you it's no magic." Demi bit back another laugh. "And it's the first time I've ever been accused of such, I must say."

The former queen let out an indelicate and unflattering snort. "So you say."

"I've no reason for lies."

"Your Order," said Yewdit with a curl of her lip, "is naught but lies."

"Your son doesn't seem to think so."

"So! You've seduced him into the Faith, have you? Got him praying at all the chimes? What next, will you have him shave his head and dress in those silly red robes? Take a position in the temple?"

"I'd not have your son become a priest, madam, unless it suited him to do so. I certainly have no stake in that game." Demi studied Jarron's mother. "He looks like you."

"Of course he does. I carried him within my womb, did I not? I birthed him, did I not? He's mine, and he'll be mine, always, no matter what you do."

"My lady, I've no quarrel with the circumstances of your son's birth. I've no need to steal him from your side. If your son chooses to spend his time elsewhere, I am not the cause." Demi had, on two occasions, faced jealous wives. This was the first time she'd faced a jealous mother.

Yewdit sniffed again and turned her face. "You are not who I'd have chosen for him."

"Fortunately, he didn't ask you to choose for him."

Again, the curled lip, the disdainful sniff. "No, he had strangers do it for him. He doesn't love you, you know. He might say he does. He might act like he does. He might even think he does, but he doesn't. How could he? You're not a woman, you're substitute for one."

This stung, but Demi refused to show it. "I'm not here for love."

"Tell me true, you and your solace. More lies. If my son is discontent, a pot of tea won't solve that. You might soothe him in his bed, but that won't last. Will it? No. For that he ought to have a wife, have some children. Have a family and a life. For that he should get himself into the social hall and be a man, not a recluse!"

Ah. So there it was. Demi had heard murmurs—slipping as she did amongst the maids in the kitchen but mostly ignored by them, she gathered much gossip. Disregarded most of it. She'd heard, though, of the former queen's distaste for her son's lack of social interaction. How she craved it herself and wanted him to set up the court the way his father had, that naught would satisfy her until she had what she wanted.

Silence often said more than any words, and Demi kept hers while Jarron's mother fumed and shifted in her chair. Red-faced, Yewdit flicked her fan again, then shouted for some chilled wine. She pointed the fan at Demi.

"Don't think I'm not wise to your scheme."

"I've no scheme, I can assure you. I am here to provide a service to your son, one that he's requested. That's my purpose. I'll stay until I've fulfilled it. That's all."

"My son is special," the former queen said. "He's not well, you know. He was born that way. Sensitive. The first time the pox came out, it nearly killed him, do you know that? The fever struck him, and he nearly died. Do you know what it's like to lose a child?"

Demi shook her head. "No."

"I almost lost him as a baby, then again as he grew. The damned pox! I won't lose him to some foolish Faith, nor to some woman who thinks spreading her legs will keep him satisfied. No," the other woman said with another shake of her fan in Demi's direction. "I know what's best for my son. You do not. And how dare you think so!"

Demi wouldn't argue with the woman. It would be futile. She'd never convince her and at any rate, had no need to prove herself right. Jarron's mother would only fight all the harder to have her way.

"Answer me! Don't just sit there like a moron, your mouth half open!"

Demi's lips weren't even parted, but now she pressed her mouth ever tighter closed. "You've not asked a question I can answer."

"Miserable, miserable girl!"

"Your mercy," Demi said and stood. "I'll leave, since my very presence so upsets you."

"I haven't dismissed you. I could have you sent to the stocks, you know. For being disrespectful. Sent to gaol. Oh, I could have your head chopped off!"

"No, I don't think you could," Demi said, careful to keep her tone neutral but firm. "I belong to the Order of Solace, not to you. Should you harm me for your own pleasure, you'll have to face them."

"They hold no dominion here, not over me."

"Do you want to test that?" Demi asked. "Even in places where the people don't follow the Faith, the Order still has sway. Would you like to test the loyalty of those who'd protect you, should the Order come to my defense?"

Yewdit's gaze flickered, and her mouth thinned. "Intolerable. Get out."

Demi inclined her head and gave another curtsy. At the door, opened for her by a manservant whose face was creased in what looked suspiciously like a grin, Demi bumped into a tall young man with hair the color of wheat, dressed in the height of fashion and smelling so strongly of gillyflower oil her eyes watered.

"Your mercy," he said, stepping aside just in time to avoid treading on her toes.

"Watch where you're going, Redemption," the former queen snapped. "You've nearly knocked over my grandson! Adzo, darling, come give me a kiss."

Adzo, who was looking Demi up and down with a confused expression, looked toward the queen. He nodded briefly at Demi before heading over to dutifully plant a kiss upon the queen's cheek. She patted his arm and threw a triumphant smile at Demi.

"My eldest grandson. My eldest daughter's boy. He's only a season or two behind Jarron, aren't you, my darling? The pair of you were almost raised as brothers."

Adzo's brow creased. "Ah . . . Jarron and I have ever been fond of one another, to be sure, Grandmother. But brothers . . ."

He laughed and shrugged. The former queen simpered and swatted him with her fan, looking for all the world like a woman entertaining a suitor and not one talking to her daughter's son. Adzo looked confused again.

"You must be my uncle's Handmaiden."

Demi smiled at him, for she had no reason to be impolite. "I'm just leaving."

"She's just leaving," put in Jarron's mother. "Pay her no attention, Adzo. She's Jarron's folly, not ours."

But Adzo wasn't paying as much attention to his grandmother as she wished. He took a step toward Demi. "I'm pleased to make your acquaintance. I've a friend from school who spoke often of the Order of Solace and declared he meant to acquire a Handmaiden—though I fear he never did. Or if he has, he's not seen fit to share the details with me. But he always spoke so highly of your purpose, I must confess, I found myself quite intrigued—"

"Adzo!" His grandmother snapped and hit him with her fan rather more sharply than he must've been expecting, for he winced and rubbed the spot. "She's leaving. Give your grandmother a kiss."

He bent with a frown to kiss her cheek again and gave Demi a nod. "Please give my regards to my uncle. I've not seen him in a long time."

"Like brothers," Yewdit said sharply. "As children, you were like brothers."

Mayhap as children, Demi thought as the door swung shut behind her with a click. But not now.

She didn't expect Jarron to be in his rooms when she returned some time later, after taking a tour through the gardens and stopping in the kitchen to replenish the supplies she needed to make the simplebread for him in the morning. Therefore, when a rough hand grasped her by the upper arm as soon as she came through the door, spilling the contents of her basket, she did what had long been natural for her.

She twisted, ducking, and hit her assailant in the face as hard as she could. The smack of her hand on flesh was loud and harsh, and cast her back more fully to her youth than anything else had. Without waiting even half a breath, she turned and used the other hand to punch out as well.

Jarron's head jerked back at the blow. She'd already left a red mark on his cheek. Before she could recover and take back her hand, he'd grabbed her wrist and twisted her arm behind her, pulling her back flush against him.

"Your mercy," Demi gasped, her heart pounding. "You frightened me, Jarron, I didn't know—"

"Hush." His voice was low and stern.

They were both breathing hard. She softened against him, not fighting though his grip on her was hurting. Jarron pressed his face against her cheek and only half loosed his grip.

"Where were you, Demi? I came back and I needed you, and you were gone."

"Your mercy, sweetheart—"

"Don't call me that. You don't call me by that pet name after you've so sorely disappointed me."

"Your mercy," she repeated, mind awhirl at what sin she'd unwittingly committed. "I wasn't expecting you to return so soon. You never have before."

"Aren't you supposed to know this? When I come and when I go, when I might return early and need you? I thought you were supposed to know me so well I never had to ask for what I needed, that you'd provide it for me before I could ask."

She closed her eyes against a sting of tears. "I plead your mercy, Jarron."

His grip loosened a bit more but didn't let go. "I came back, and you were gone. I thought you'd left without telling me."

"I would never do that. Never."

He drew in a low, hitching breath. The hand not holding her wrist pulled at her skirt, lifting it over her knees and thighs, then sought her flesh beneath it. He cupped her cunt, pressing with the heel of his hand against her. His fingers curled, dipping inside her, then up to circle on her clit.

He walked her a few steps toward the desk. "Put your hands on it. Both of them. Flat."

She did, her palms smacking the polished wood. Jarron bent her with a hand on her shoulder, so that her cheek pressed the wood. He lifted her gown to her hips and ran a hand over her bare ass.

"Spread your legs."

She did, pulse pounding. She didn't have to let him do this. She never had to let a patron abuse her . . . but this didn't feel like abuse. His touch was not kind, not gentle, but nor was it cruel. She heard some hidden anguish in his tone that had somewhat, but not everything, to do with his fear she'd left him. Somewhat had happened today that was upsetting him.

"Do you like this, Demi?"

She thought hard on how to answer, but fast, knowing to remain silent for too long would displease him. "I don't know."

"Ah, that's right. You don't lie." He put his hands on her ass, cupping her buttocks before sliding between her legs to stroke and tickle.

She looked over her shoulder at him. "Would you like it better if I didn't like it?"

"No." He rubbed at her clit slowly, the other hand stroking her bare thigh. "I wouldn't like that at all."

Jarron stepped to the side, taking up the bottle of worm and pouring a glass. Demi didn't move, uncertain if he'd released her. Her fingers slipped a little on the wood.

Jarron dipped his fingers in the worm and slid them along her folds, centering on her clit. Warmth spread through her. Demi drew in a breath. Again, he dipped his fingers and painted her cunt with the sweet liquor laced with herb. It stung, but deliciously. Into the cup he dipped, then trickled it down the crack of her ass.

"Do you like that, Demi?"

She shivered. "I do."

"Has any man done that to you before?"

"None."

"Stay there."

She did, until he returned with a small pot. He unscrewed the lid and set it aside. He showed her the open pot, filled with a soft, color-less, and odorless cream.

"Do you know what this is?"

"No," she admitted. "Though I can guess."

Jarron laughed with little humor. "Tell me true, can you?"

"It's an aphrodisiac cream."

He leaned close to murmur in her ear, "You are always so right. And what do you think I intend to do with it?"

"Put it on me." She licked her lips. Her clit was already tingling from the worm, making her want to shift her hips.

"Do you want me to put it on you?"

"If it—"

"It pleases me," Jarron said in a low voice. "It would please me very greatly to have you so aroused for me that you cannot stand straight. That just the merest touch of my fingertip sends you screaming into orgasm. I would have you attend me for the rest of the evening with this adorning you, Demi."

She swallowed, hard. These games . . . she'd been trained for them in the Order, though naught had prepared her for the reality of them. Nor her response, which was so fierce as to nearly overwhelm her. She turned her face just barely against his mouth.

"Please," she whispered. "Do it."

# Chapter 15

To anyone watching, Jarron would be playing at cards with the seriousness of a man bent on winning every coin from his neighbor's purses. He made conversation, casual and simple conversation about the game. His clothes. His preference for the hunt, his taste in wine. He was gracious and talkative and made sure to give every lord and lady dancing attendance upon him his best and brightest smile.

It was easier than ever he'd expected, this wooing of an entire court. He made himself open to the men and women who'd known him his whole life and also to those who were new. He listened to them carefully and gave them conscientious answers, and he didn't worry overmuch about the whispers and looks he knew were still going on.

He was their Melek Gadol, their king, and he meant to make sure they remembered that.

Unification. The ridiculousness of it tugged and snagged at him, even as he wondered who amongst his court thought the idea a good one. Surely some of them did. A goodly number of them would follow whatever someone presented to them as shiny and pretty and bright.

He didn't speak to Adam, though he was there, settled in a corner in deep conversation with Nigel. They were lovers or would be, soon enough. Jarron knew his so-called brother of the heart well enough to see that. That his best and longest friend had not outright denounced the idea of unification grated at him.

This meant Jarron had to think very carefully on the concept, for he'd ever taken Adam's advice to heart. This time could be no different, even as much as it disturbed him. Still, he was irritated enough to avoid him, not that the bastard even noticed, so caught up in his flirting.

Somewhat else made all this tolerable. The unrelenting knowledge that Demi was at his side and growing ever more frantic for him. He'd bade her attend him, as surprised as she was that he chose to visit the social hall without prompting. He liked surprising her. She knew him overwell, but she did not know him entirely. She sat beside him now, not playing at the game but sitting quietly and ready to get him a drink, or food, or whatever he might wish.

It unsettled his card-playing companions, he knew, but Jarron didn't care. It might mark him as eccentric; let them think so. What use was being king if he couldn't indulge in his own whims?

"I've heard Neaku is a lovely province," spoke up a young woman with red hair whose name had escaped him. She spoke to Demi, Sinder bless her, trying to be polite. "Is that where you're from?"

"The Motherhouse is there, tell you true, but I'm not . . . I am not originally . . . from there."

Her hesitation, the breathy catch in her voice, stiffened his cock. Jarron looked at his cards, thinking of sinking into her heat. Hearing her cry out his name as her cunny clutched at him. He tossed a coin into the pile and took a card.

"Where are you originally from?" the redhead asked brightly.

"I was born—" Demi began, her eyes a bit glazed.

Jarron pressed his thigh to hers beneath the table. "Demi, I would have another biscuit with some jam."

"Aye, sweetheart, I'll get it for you." She stood, swaying just a bit, her hand on the back of her chair as she steadied herself.

He watched her walk, the careful gait giving away the effects of the cream on her. He smiled. His cock throbbed. He would put away these cards, soon. And then he would take her back to his rooms and—

"She's quite interesting." The redhead plucked a card from the pile. Annie, her name was. Anakka. Somewhat like that. "My father had a Handmaiden."

"Did he?" This drew Jarron's attention for the moment.

"I never knew that." This came from the young lord next to the redhead. His name was Harbert and he'd been in Jarron's class at school, though they'd never been friendly. Until now.

Anakka looked at him. "Why would you, Har? You never knew my father."

Harbert laughed and tossed a card on the pile to draw another. "No, but I know your mother quite well, and she never mentioned it."

Anakka laughed. "Who do you think was his Handmaiden, you fool?"

"Your father married her?" Jarron paused in looking at his hand.

"Tell you true. Quite the romance." Anakka nodded. "She told me the story many times. How he sent for her. How he found his solace and she left him, and he hunted her down at her next patron's house and demanded she come back to him."

"And she did." This fascinated him.

"Oh, no. She didn't leave her patron. She finished out that assignment, then went back to the Motherhouse and told them she was leaving the Order. Five seasons later, I might add. He'd never married. She went to him, and nine months later I was born!" Anakka laughed merrily.

"I thought Handmaidens couldn't bear children," poked in Harbert as he tossed his hand down. "I'm out."

"She wasn't a Handmaiden any longer, fool."

"She left the Order for him," Jarron said thoughtfully. "And they're not supposed to be able."

He'd made certain of that before sending for her. His gaze sought her, now, expecting to see her by the sideboard. She wasn't there. Eyes narrowed, he swept the room for sight of her and found her in the corner, deep in conversation with . . . Erekon? What could that man want with the king's Handmaiden?

"Are you in, sir?" Anakka asked. "The wager's been raised three arros."

Jarron didn't even look at his cards but tossed them down and stood. He made the barest effort at politeness. "I'm out. Take the pot."

Her surprised laughter followed him, but he didn't care if he made a scene. He left the game table and ignored the tugs on his sleeve as he passed men and women seeking his attention. He focused only on Demi, who'd turned her face from Erekon and was making as though to leave but could not, for the man had her by the wrist.

". . . Convincing," Erekon muttered as Jarron moved closer. He looked up to see the king and let go of Demi's wrist at once. "Sir."

"Aryon." Jarron looked from the man's hand to Demi's wrist, an unspoken question.

She moved between them, that pretty mouth parted. "Aryon Kosem was bidding me to use my influence upon you to stay longer, as he wished to join your game. I told him . . . I told him we were retiring early, as you were tired."

Her gaze dropped briefly to the front of his trousers, then up again. The pink tip of her tongue slipped out to touch the top of her lip. Her cheeks had colored. Jarron imagined her face twisted in ecstasy as he came inside her.

"She's right, Erekon, I'll have to beg off for tonight. I must needs get myself to bed."

Erekon smiled thinly. "Mayhap another night, then."

"Tell you true, another night. Sweetheart, shall we go?" Jarron held out his arm, and Demi took it.

"I shall hold you to it," Erekon said.

Jarron was already moving past him, out the door, and into the hall. Thinking of getting her to his rooms as fast as possible. What had been meant as sweet torture for her had become more so for him.

It wasn't until they reached his rooms and he scooped her into his arms to take her to the bed that he realized somewhat.

"You lied."

The evening had passed in a blur for her. The cream with which Jarron had anointed her smoothed on cool but heated in moments to a pleasantly torturous tickle that grew to a sting with every shift and movement. It was like the persistent stroke of a tongue against her, yet never strong enough to tip her into climax. It was the way he'd wanted it, she knew, her arousal growing until all she could think about was having him inside her.

Now, though, she gasped at his words. He laid her on the bed and knelt beside her. His gaze burned.

She *had* lied.

It had been a long time since she'd felt shame for anything she'd done, and it stung her heavily. Once she'd been able to turn her tongue to falsehood as easily as truth, moreso, in fact, for lies had often saved her when truth would've harmed. There was no precept in the Order against lying, just the understanding it most often didn't lead to any sort of solace. Yet she'd lied to him about what Erekon had wanted her to do. She could blame her lust-fuzzed brain, but Demi knew the truth.

She didn't want to play at politics, didn't want to be the go-between for Erekon or those who supported him. She didn't want to encourage Jarron to give up his throne and take a lesser role. Unification might or might not be the future of the Five Provinces, but Demi didn't care. She had no pleasure or purpose in promoting the whims of her former lover to her current.

"I suppose I can forgive you for it, as I did no longer wish to stay, certainly not to play at cards. Not when I could have you here." Jarron ran a hand up her thigh beneath her skirt.

Demi shivered when his touch brushed her curls. Arched when his thumb flicked expertly against her clit. She'd ever been fond of the pleasures a man could provide her, but with Jarron, everything was different. With him, she gave herself to thrills she'd never thought could move her.

"Tell me, love, how it is for you now," he murmured as he pushed her gown up slowly, baring her.

"Torture," Demi breathed. "All I can think about is release."

Again, he stroked across her clit with his fingertips. When he tweaked it gently, she couldn't bite back the gasp. He didn't want her to, anyway. Demi knew Jarron liked hearing her cries of ecstasy. He liked proof of what his touch did to her. Again, that was power, but she had to confess, she liked it, too.

"Get up. Off the bed. Take off your gown."

Jarron stood as she did. He watched her as she slowly undid each button from her throat to her hips, then stepped out of the gown, wearing only her thin shift. When she gathered the soft material, bunching it slowly to her hips to expose herself to him, Jarron's gaze grew hot. He licked his mouth. He moved, cupping her cunt with his hand while the other went to grab her braid at the base of her neck and tip her head back.

"Sit on that chair." He nodded toward the one by the bed. "Take off your shift. Spread your legs. I want to see all of you."

He let her go and Demi pulled her shift off over her head, tossing it aside. She sat on the chair. The smooth satin upholstery was slippery beneath her bare flesh. Heart pounding, she spread her legs and gripped the chair's carved wooden arms.

Jarron, then, took his time undressing in front of her. Slowly, eyes never leaving hers, he loosened his cravat, undid the buttons of his jacket and vest, unlaced his trousers. He took off his clothes and threw them to the ground as if they were made of rags. He stood in front of her naked, his body lean and fit, his cock erect.

He stroked it, watching her. "See what you do to me? Spread your legs wider, I would see you."

She did, tipping her hips a little. Jarron smiled. Demi flushed, not with embarrassment but longing.

"Such a pretty cunny," Jarron said in a low voice. "It fits me just right. I can see from here that you're slick inside. You'll be hot, too, and tight. Land Above, Demi, I love fucking you."

"I'm glad to so please you." Her voice rasped. He'd not told her to let go of the chair's arms, so she didn't, gripping.

Jarron looked at her face. "You'll do anything I ask of you, true?"

"Within reason." It was another lie. She would do anything he asked of her.

"I know you'll lie for me, I've seen it tonight." Jarron stroked his prick a little faster, then stepped back and sat on the edge of the bed across from her. "Every inch of you is on fire, aye? You ache for my touch."

"I do," she breathed.

"I wonder," Jarron mused, "how little it would take to set you off."

"Very little, sweetheart. I fear I've spent the night craving you so fiercely already."

Indeed, naked this way, spread open for his gaze, her clit throbbed and pulsed with every beat of her heart. Her cunt clenched. Even her back passage tightened under Jarron's stern look. If only he would touch her . . .

Jarron reached to the casket of toys he kept by the bed and pulled out a vial of oil—not the cream with which he'd anointed her earlier, but a shimmering glass bottle. He poured a palmful into his hand and set the bottle back, then stroked his cock until it glistened.

"I never need such help with you, Demi. You always accommodate me so well. But I would watch you, now, watching me." Jarron made a guttural noise as he pumped his prick into his fist. "This is how

I spent so many long hours before I met you. Do you believe it? That the Melek Gadol Shetaya, king of the Second Province, and even when I was a prince before that, should need to find his own satisfaction with his fist?"

Demi knew that all too well, as she'd borne witness to his loneliness. She couldn't look away from the thick shaft, appearing and disappearing in Jarron's closed fingers. She knew well the length and thickness of it, the flavor. How it felt in her mouth and in her cunt. Between her breasts. He'd not yet taken her rear passage in that way, though she didn't doubt his preparations with the plug meant he'd thought of it. And she would let him, not because he was her patron and to give him that would lead him to any sort of solace, but because the thought of giving herself to him in any way he desired made her body shake and quake and her mouth dry, her throat close, her mind go blank with an addictive kind of peace.

"Do you take your own pleasure when you haven't a lover?" Jarron asked.

Demi blinked, at first unable to form words. "Tell you true, I've done so."

"It's never quite as satisfying as when it's someone else, aye?"

She shook her head the slightest bit. "No. I don't think so."

He twisted his wrist to palm the head of his cock, and his eyes closed briefly as he bit down on his lower lip. "Yet we know ourselves better than any lover ever could. Land Above, Demi, I have my own hand on my cock and imagine it's your cunny, and the thought is what makes me want to spill."

She didn't let go of the chair. Her internal muscles clenched again, her hips moved of their own accord, though she could touch naught, reach naught, fill herself with naught but thought.

Jarron stroked faster, looking at her. "You sit so close to me I can smell you, and I want to get on my knees and bury myself between your legs. I want to suck that sweet little clit until you explode on my tongue, and then I want . . . by the Arrow, that's so good . . ." He shuddered and slowed his pace. He swallowed. He fixed her with another burning gaze. "I want to fuck inside you so slowly I can feel every inch of you taking me. Feel every squeeze of you on my cock. I want you to shudder against me, crying out my name. Say it, now."

"Jarron," Demi replied at once.

"Can you imagine that, Demi? How I might fuck you?"

"Aye, I can imagine very well." She drew in a breath and spread her legs just a little wider. She felt the trickle of her arousal down her thigh and into the crack of her ass as she tilted her hips again. One touch. One breath, and she thought she would tip over.

"You want to touch yourself now, aye? But you won't let go of the chair because I've not bid you to do so. I could. You'd come right away. I see it in your face." Jarron's fist moved slowly, slowly. His face and throat had flushed, and the muscles stood out, corded, in his chest and arm as he stroked himself. "Do you know how beautiful that makes you, to me? That you will not loose your grip without my say?"

She couldn't speak. Her fingers gripped tighter. She rocked her hips in tiny, almost invisible movements, but each motion pulled another thread of desire tight and tighter into the tangled ball of sensation building inside her.

"You might come without even a touch," Jarron said. "Think of my mouth on you, Demi."

She let out a low cry. Jarron pumped his prick a little faster, his breath sharp and loud. She imagined him kneeling in front of her, his tongue flicking at her swollen clit. His fingers inside her, thrusting. She thought of him filling her with that lovely thick cock until she . . . oh, Land Above . . .

"I love to watch the way your face twists when you climax. I love how you shake and shudder and claw at my back, helpless against your pleasure. I love that you will sit there across from me and watch me stroke my own prick, and that such a sight can push you into orgasm. . . ."

She was going. Slowly but inevitably. It was not like when she came beneath her own fingers, not like when he made her climax with his mouth or hand or thrusting cock. This built inside her, brought on by the cream and Jarron's words, by her own imagination. The climax built as much in her mind as in her body. She shivered, her gaze fixed on Jarron's stroking hand.

"I'm going to spill," he whispered harshly. "I want to watch you join me. Come with me, Demi."

She did. Exquisitely slowly. Rolling waves of climax rippled through her and lasted forever, each one not fading completely before the next shook her. Her hands gripped the chair so hard the wood slipped under her hands as her buttocks slid on the upholstery. She pushed with her toes, tilting her hips, barely moving even as her body twitched and leaped.

Jarron cried out as he jetted at last, the musky, delicious smell of him sending another slow wave of pleasure through her. Breathing hard, he gave his cock another few strokes before he fell back on the bed with a loud sigh. Demi blinked, noting the ache in her hands and thighs from the position she'd been holding.

On the bed, Jarron laughed.

He looked up at her. "Come here."

She did on stiff legs and crawled onto the bed next to him, where he kissed her mouth thoroughly. He held her close, his body warm though the air was cool. He kissed her temple.

"You're amazing, do you know that?"

She smiled against his neck. "Am I?"

Jarron pushed away to look at her face. "More than anything I could've imagined. Adam told me a Handmaiden was the best choice for me, would make me the happiest, and I wasn't sure I believed him. How could that be? But, Demi . . . you are a marvel. A wonder. Perfection."

He kissed her again and pushed off the bed, away from her. "No matter what I need, no matter if I know it or not, you provide it. You submit to my every whim and take as much pleasure as I in doing it. You are everything the Order promises and so much more I didn't expect."

He was laughing, eyes dancing with glee, and she did her best to match his mood, but somehow Jarron's praise fell flat to her. From other patrons she'd been well pleased to have been so complimented, but as with everything else, it was different with him.

"I told you, it's my joy to provide for you."

Jarron laughed again and smacked one fist into his other palm, still aglisten with oil. His belly gleamed with the evidence of his pleasure, but he didn't seem to notice. Demi got off the bed, meaning to go to the privy chamber for a basin and cloth to clean them both before they went to bed.

Jarron stopped her, both his hands on her upper arms, to look into her eyes. "I mean it, Demi. You've made me a very happy man. You're a perfect Handmaiden."

"I'm glad."

He let her go, and she went to fill the basin. She gripped the sink, her fingers still aching as a reminder of what she'd done at his command. She faced herself in the looking glass. Jarron was beyond pleased with her as a Handmaiden, and that was everything he saw her as, and it should've been enough, but it wasn't.

She wanted him to see her as a woman, too.

# Chapter 16

"Are you going to stop pouting at me some time within the next sennight? Because if you're not, I've a mind to take some travel," Adam said in a languid tone that made it sound as though he cared about a hundred things better than Jarron's answer.

"I'm not pouting," Jarron said. "But you might've told me you and Nigel had become lovers."

Adam's brows rose. "Was it somewhat that needed an announcement? Mayhap I should've had it written in calligraphy on scented notecards and passed them out to all the lords and ladies who abide here in House Bydelay? Oh, I know, I might've put up a banner and had a parade down the center lane of town."

"Sarcasm gives you wrinkles, you know."

Adam pursed his lips. "My love life has never been much of a concern to you before, as I've never made a show of prying into yours."

"You know all about mine. You're the one who encouraged me to send for her. Thanks for that, by the way." Jarron pulled the bowl toward him to draw in a breath of the fragrant smoke.

"I already told you, you're welcome. I told you it would be the right decision for you." Adam tilted his head to stare down at Jarron, then with a sigh folded his long body onto the couch and took his own toke from the bowl before putting his feet up on the table. "Though I'm not certain you can continue on much longer."

"If you start spouting off about unification again, Adam, I'll have to challenge you to some sort of duel, and we both know I'd win if only to prevent you from ending up in gaol, so please . . . don't."

Adam snorted laughter. "You have to face it, Jarron, whether you like it or not. It's coming. You can either face it and be prepared and come out ahead, or you can let others make the choices and end up with whatever they do."

"I told you not to talk about it. Not here. Tomorrow in the War Room we can go 'round and 'round about it." Jarron frowned.

Adam leaned forward seriously. "I know you think I went against you. I can't tell you how it feels to know you think I could ever betray you."

Jarron was silent in the face of that. He'd known Adam since childhood, when their mothers had spent hours giggling and gossiping and their fathers hunted or fished together. At age four, Adam had colored his face with spots drawn with his mother's cosmetic, that he might "match" his friend, who'd been lying abed with an outbreak of Trystan's Pox. Jarron had made other friends, but Adam had been his best and longest.

"You did betray me."

"I didn't." Adam closed the cover on the bowl to put it out. "And stop smoking so much, for Sinder's sake. You need a clear head, now more than ever."

Jarron frowned again. "What, is your new lover an abstainer?"

"It has naught to do with Nigel," Adam said, "but no. This has to do with you. You need a clear head at all times, Jarron. You can't be addled by worm or herb, not even by cunny. Which is why I'm not sure I was right, after all, about the wiseness of your taking a Handmaiden."

"What are you talking about? Demi is everything I wanted and needed. That's the whole point of her existence, Adam."

"She addles you as much as the drugs."

Jarron crossed one leg over the other and leaned back in his chair. "You're mad."

"Not mad. Observant. You walk around with your prick half hard all the time, thinking about the next time you can fuck her."

"What man wouldn't?" Jarron asked evenly, though he wanted to scowl.

Adam rolled his eyes. "Me, for one."

"Only because she's not the flavor you prefer. What about you and Nigel. Tell me you don't spend one moment out of every five imagining what you'll do the next time you're in bed."

"First," Adam said archly, "if you really must know, we haven't been to bed yet. Second—"

"What? Hold a moment, tell me you're not serious?" Jarron laughed.

Adam had ever been a seducer, working his way through lovers as casually as a farmer scything wheat. He took what he wanted, and to Jarron's knowledge, there'd never been one who'd turned him down. Even women who knew better than to try made fools of themselves had upon occasion attempted to gain his attentions.

"Second, I'm not the bedamned king, Jarron, and you are. I can afford to have my mind addled by lust. You, my dear one, cannot."

"Bollocks. First," Jarron imitated him, "I'm not addled. If anything, I'm so fully sated I can scarcely think of what to try next, she's accommodated me so fully in all ways. I barely have a fantasy left. Second, how can it be that you've not bedded him yet? The pair of you have been canoodling for a sennight."

Adam's mouth thinned. He toyed with the lid to the bowl but didn't lift it to relight. The quiverful of past confidences won over whatever had been keeping him from confession, and he sighed. "Nigel has never been with a man."

"Neither have I."

Adam looked at him. "I've never tried to bed you, either."

"So . . ." Jarron was confused. "He doesn't want you?"

Adam sighed again and scrubbed at his eyes, smearing the lines of cosmetic. "He does want me."

"And you . . . want him?"

"Tell you true. Like fire."

"I don't understand," Jarron said.

Adam looked at him. "I don't guess you would."

"What do you mean by that?" Jarron asked, exasperated. "Stop speaking in riddles, Adam. It's me, Jarron, remember? Your brother of the heart? Your longest friend?"

"I think . . . I could love him."

Stunned, Jarron could say naught. Adam looked uncomfortable. He toyed with the bowl and shrugged, not meeting Jarron's eyes.

"Love?" Jarron laughed, though it sounded weak and humorless. "What on earth could you possibly want with love?"

"You might ask yourself that same question."

Again, this unexpected answer set Jarron into silence. He thought of several answers, but none suited. Adam watched him, then shrugged and stood.

"Find your solace and send her back. Then you might be able to focus on what needs your attention."

"Curse you to the Void, Adam. That's ridiculous. You're the one who said I ought to send for her, and I don't see what's changed about my reasons for wanting her. Unification? Whether we bend to it or fight it, the fact remains, I am king of this province and I shall ever remain so unless I choose otherwise. Choose," Jarron emphasized. "And I shall be the one who does so."

"If you're not careful, you might find the choice made for you."

"By whom?" Jarron demanded, angry now. "You say you don't betray me, yet you toss around comments in that matter that tell me naught! Who is against me?"

"I think . . . mayhap Erekon."

"The King's Lion plots against me?" Jarron said flatly in disbelief.
"You *are* mad."

Adam shook his head. "Who closer to you than he, at least in the
matter of his supposed loyalty? Who would you suspect least?"

"The man's no friend of mine, no companion, but he's ever served
my father and has so served me with naught but attention to his duty.
Besides, of what benefit could this be to him? Should I lose my throne,
he'll lose his position, as well. He can't very well be the Aryon Melek
if there is no melek to protect."

Jarron meant to make light—he well knew there never needed to be
a sensible reason for intrigue against a monarch. The Five Provinces, of
course, had once been one vast land, long ago, with different customs
and even languages before an invading army had torn it apart and par-
celed it out into the Five. His own ancestors had been part of the inva-
sion. Since then in the Second Province's history there'd never been a
change in the government, but the Fourth's premier had been over-
thrown in Jarron's grandfather's time in favor of a peasant revolt, leading to the utter destruction of their government and anarchy for close
to twenty seasons before the people again recognized a premier. The
province was still in debt and had suffered so much destitution that
charity groups from all the surrounding provinces still made it their
project to fund missions there. In the province of Sergo, just over the
mountains beyond the First Province, two brothers had fought for
the inheritance, both of them dying by the other's hand and leaving
the throne to their sister who still ruled. Rumor had it she'd never
married so there'd be no quarrel as to her place on the throne, but now
as she got older, the question of whom she meant to name as her
successor had become more heated.

"I'll name an heir," Jarron said, thinking of that.

Adam looked up. "It won't stop those who are in favor of unification from moving toward it."

"It will cement the Bydelay name as ruler of the Second. Show them that even though I might not have taken a wife, have a son of mine own—"

"Inheritance isn't the issue." Adam sighed and scrubbed again at his face, a sign of true exhaustion, since he was ever so careful with his appearance. "It's all about trade, Jarron. Money. The Second is rich in luxuries, but not in necessities. The men and women who toil in the fields to provide what we trade for aren't wealthy enough to afford luxuries, but do they not deserve necessities?"

"Of course they do."

"We've had three hard winters. Three bad summers. And your father, may the Invisible Mother bless him, had fallen away from his duties even before stepping down. He was tired. He allowed himself to be talked into some things he previously might've considered unfair. Taxes and the like."

Jarron scowled. "You know I'm dealing with those, but they can't just be abolished with a finger snap. Too much depends on the revenue at this point—poor planning on my father's part, true, but the blame lies equally with the Ministers of Finance."

"I don't deny that's true, but you forget, Jarron . . . or else you simply don't realize. It's not the lords of your court or you yourself who suffers while these taxes are in the process of repeal. It is your citizens. We are not a province of dullards. They hear the tales of how unification will benefit all of us, not simply the already wealthy. And . . . my friend, my dear one, I believe that to be true."

Again, Jarron felt sick at his friend's words. "You believe I should give up my heritage? My rule? My entire kingdom, for the sake of . . . what? Trade? Cash flow? Or is it history you seek to regain, turning us back into one province the way it was so long ago?"

"You are so focused on what you'd be giving up, you've no concept of what you could gain. Jarron, for the love of the Land Above, if you feel so maniacally attached to the crown you never even wear, why not put forth your efforts to be the king of all? Someone has to."

"So, you would have me not only merge the Second with all the other of the Five Provinces, but you'd have me set myself up as the one who'd bring it about? You want me to go to war?"

Adam sighed once more. "I can't pretend to understand everything about politics, or the effects this will have on us and everyone around us. But . . . the Second doesn't have easily defendable borders. Our army, despite the exuberant leadership of Kosem, is next to nonexistent. And your funds to create one even less. We are teetering on the edge of financial disaster, which I have every faith you mean to correct, but the fact is, whether you move with it or against it, the unification movement is growing. Amongst your own people. Amongst the other provinces, I have no doubt. Queen Caramin is calling for a symposium to discuss matters."

"Tell me somewhat, Adam."

"Anything."

"What think you of my ego?"

Adam looked confused. "I wouldn't call you humble."

Jarron laughed harshly. "No, and I can tell you the same of all the other leaders of all the other four. Some are even less humble than I. So what do you think is going to happen when we all gather to discuss who is going to take over the rule of everyone else's province? You're talking about lands that have been in families for generations. Passed from parent to child. You think anyone, anyone at all, is going to so readily hand that over to someone else? And what of the people in every province, Adam? How on earth do you think anyone means to get them to agree? You'll have those, as you said, who are in favor because it seems like a change would benefit them. They don't know anything for sure. What of those who are happy with their lives, how things are? Do they not deserve to keep their way of life intact?"

"Change is not a bad thing," Adam said seriously. "And to answer your question, I don't know. I decide the length of hems and color of dyes for fashionable fabrics, for the love of Sinder's Blessed Balls."

"Yet you presume to counsel me on this matter." Jarron bent to the bowl and lit it again, waiting for the smoke to curl before taking a long, deep breath.

"I'm your friend."

Jarron let the smoke drift over him for a few moments before answering. "I know you are."

"Erekon is not your friend."

"Can you say for sure he acts against me?"

"I can say for sure he keeps the company of those who are in favor of unification. If they've been his longtime comrades and their new views don't affect him, I cannot say. If he keeps their company because he means to keep an eye out for your safety, I cannot say that, either. All I can say is that he watches you when you don't pay attention to him, and it's not with love in his eyes."

"I don't expect even the King's Lion to love me, Adam. Loyalty doesn't have to be love."

Adam snorted softly. "He looks at her with love."

"Who?" Jarron waved the smoke toward his face but looked up without taking another draw.

"Your Redemption."

Jarron frowned, thinking of the night Erekon had cornered her in the social hall. "She's a lovely woman. Many men look at her with envy in their gaze."

"I didn't say envy, though you're not wrong. I said he looks at her with love."

"Love? What is it with you and love all of a sudden? You never used to speak of such a thing, now you act the part of a moon-eyed swain, sick with it. Or the lack of it. Seeing it in everyone around you." Jarron shook his head.

"Men have done worse than betrayed their loyalties for it. You should be careful, that's all."

"And send her away? So that what, I might be without a companion, a helpmate, so that I might go back to the way I was before? I told you, Adam, and I mean it. I'll not risk the chance of a child who carries the pox. Would you have me be . . . alone?" Jarron stood to face his friend. "Would you wish that for me, to ever be by myself, when with Demi I have the chance, at least, to be made at least somewhat content?"

"How long is it going to last? Until you get your solace? What then?"

"I'll never get it," Jarron said.

"Then . . . why bother?" Adam shook his head and, relenting, bent to wave the smoke toward him for a deep, long breath. His eyes watered when he stood, and he coughed.

"Because I want to keep her with me. And she doesn't want to go. I know she doesn't."

Adam laughed. "And yet you curl your lip when I say love."

"I'm fucking her in every way it's possible to imagine and a few I never thought existed. What are you doing with your lover who's not a lover?"

"It's different with him."

"Of course it is. But I'm not judging you for it."

"You are," Adam said in a low voice. "The difference is, you won't admit it."

For the first time in all their friendship, Jarron stared at Adam as though he were a stranger. He couldn't read his friend's face; couldn't understand his reasons. Somewhat twisted, sharp and cutting inside him. He didn't show it, or at least he tried. He'd be a stranger to Adam, too.

"She's everything I need, and that will be enough. If ever she needs to leave me, I'll worry about it then. But for now, she belongs to me."

Adam laughed, the sound as familiar to Jarron as his own but somehow peculiar. "She doesn't belong to you. If anything, she belongs to the Order."

"Not as long as she's assigned to me."

"Still, you should be careful, like I said. Erekon—"

"Many men look at her with envy or even lust, because of what she is. Demi is a Handmaiden."

Adam cocked his head, studying Jarron. "Tell you true, but you shouldn't forget she's somewhat else, as well. Somewhat far more important."

"What's that?"

"She's a woman, too," Adam said and again closed the lid on the bowl.

# Chapter 17

The gardens, when in bloom, would be delightful. Demi looked forward to seeing them flowering. She hoped she'd have the chance.

She was failing miserably in her duties. Not on the surface. To all appearances, she brewed the tea, swept the floor, laid out the clothes, and took her patron to bed in all the ways he wished. She made him happy, he'd said so.

Happiness was not solace.

Not that either emotion could be so specifically cataloged or identified. In some cases they fit together like puzzle pieces, one impossible without the other. But they were not the same.

For the first time since stepping out of the carriage here, Demi felt . . . lonely. Jarron was locked away in his War Room, hammering away at his ministers. He came back to his rooms late and exhausted, ready to fall into bed, where he made love to her with such a fierceness she was left sore into the next day. He took care to make sure she had her pleasure, too—he was not a selfish lover, just a preoccupied one. Her function was more important now than ever, yet she felt her failure in every action.

He didn't forbid her to leave his rooms, though to find entertainment in the social hall without him felt awkward. The lords and ladies of Jarron's court were happy to friend her. There'd be a few generous souls who'd like her for who she was, but the rest would do it to get somehow closer to the king. She didn't avoid the social hall alone for that reason, but for the old one. The longer she went without telling Jarron she'd once been his subject, the more important it became to not have anyone else know it.

The garden had no hedge maze, no place into which lovers could duck to pitch their woo unseen. Only raised beds through which curving white-stone paths had been laid. Her boots crunched on the gravel now, and Demi tucked her hands into the pockets of her cloak. Jarron had given her the cloak, lined with fur. It would be too heavy to wear soon, as the weather changed, and Demi hoped she'd be here long enough for him to buy her another.

She went to the pond, a pretty little man-made decoration, deep enough for a few gape-mouthed copperfish but not much else. She'd brought a stale loaf with her, wrapped in a cloth, to feed them. But first, there on the far side of the garden where nobody walked on this chilly morning, Demi Waited.

Not the way she did for Jarron, with her buttocks resting on her heels and her hands folded, one inside the other, in her lap. Waiting had five positions, and that one was Waiting, Readiness. She did that when she attended him, or while she went through her meditations when he was otherwise occupied. She Waited in Readiness quite a bit and for many different reasons, but none of them suited now.

Instead, she ignored the bite of gravel into her knees through the layers of her gown and cloak. She settled onto her knees, heels resting on her behind, but put her hands flat in front of her on the ground. Head bowed. This was Waiting, Remorse, and though she had naught for which to apologize, she had much to regret.

The Mothers-in-Service ought to have called her Ridiculous and not Redemption, she thought, eyes closed. She'd been such a fool.

Full of pride at how well she'd perform her duties when the reality was she'd been thinking only of herself. What she wanted. Craved.

"Invisible Mother, grant me serenity enough to share, for there is no greater pleasure than absolute solace," Demi murmured into the brown and brittle grass under her palms. "Grant me patience enough to share, for true patience is its own reward. Grant me beauty enough to share, for a flower is made more beautiful by its thorns. And Invisible Mother, please, grant me generosity enough to share, for woman I begin and woman I shall end."

"Very nice."

The voice startled her, and Demi jerked up her head. "Erekon."

"Don't let me stop you. It was very nice, I said. Hearing you do . . . that. Whatever it was."

She got to her feet with less grace than her norm, her dress snagging her, making her clumsy. Mayhap it was him. He'd ever had a way of making her doubt herself, even in somewhat as simple as a step.

"I was meditating."

"Don't stop on my account."

"It's meant to be done in private," she told him coldly. "Did you follow me?"

He smiled. The wind blew his hair back from his face. Dark as ink, black as night. She could still recall the feeling of it against her face from before time had spun it with threads of silver.

"I did."

"You should go back. Leave me alone." She turned her back on him to look out over the pond.

"I thought mayhap it would be in my best interest to make sure the king's whore stayed safe."

Demi spat at his boot and instantly regretted it. That was the action of a whore. Not a Handmaiden.

"Notsah. I plead your mercy." He sounded sincere. "I shouldn't have said that."

She looked at him. "I don't need your protection, Erekon. Nobody's here but me, and at any rate, who wants to harm me? A jealous potential wife?"

"You never know." He turned to look out across the water. "Unease is carried on the wind, Notsah. Just because you don't believe you could be in danger doesn't mean you can't."

"That's the case in every event, but you chose here, where I'm alone, to find me and tell me so. You, yourself. Why not send one of your cubs? Surely they could do as well protecting me as you can. Better, even, for they're younger."

If her words stung him, Erekon didn't show it. Again, shame pricked her. She wasn't behaving in accordance with the Order's teachings. He'd rattled her. She pulled the loaf from her cloak and unbound it from the cloth, then broke off a palmful of crumbs to scatter in the water.

His laugh turned her face toward him. He gestured at the bread in her hand. "Again?"

She looked at the loaf, brow furrowed, for half a breath before she understood that he was referring to her last and final crime, the one that had sent her away for good. "You're such a bastard."

Erekon didn't look offended. If anything, her insult seemed to set him further toward good humor. He winked. She turned away, not smiling.

"Ahh, Notsah. Your mercy. You never used to have so little humor."

"Just because I laughed at your jests doesn't mean I thought them merry."

She tossed another handful of crumbs into the pond and watched the fish swallow them. The small, thin shape of an eel darted toward the surface and was gone so fast she couldn't be sure she saw it at all. She broke a larger hunk from the loaf and tossed it, too, to watch the fish swarm.

"Consider me put in my place," Erekon said finally.

She looked at him. "That would be a first."

"A goodly amount of time has passed, Notsah. You'd be surprised at how much has changed."

"My name is no longer Notsah."

"Redemption. Or Demi, if you give me the honor of calling you by the name he uses for you." Erekon's smile dipped on one side. "I promise I won't tell. But then I suppose, neither will you."

"I will tell him, if it becomes necessary. It hasn't."

"Worry not, your secret is safe with me. For now, at least. I've no stake in whatever game you're playing."

"No?" She faced him. "What game are you playing at, then? Following me, making veiled threats? Trying to convince me I should mold my patron to your bidding, when that is as far from my purpose here as we are to the sun."

"Would it occur to you I might actually be trying to help him?"

"By promoting this unification business?" Demi shook her head and tossed the rest of the bread into the water, then dusted her hands together to rid them of the last of the crumbs. "First, I've no interest in politics."

"You might, if it means your patron's happiness."

"I'm not responsible for his . . . happiness," she said after a pause.

Erekon snorted lightly. "Ah, no? Is that the truth, then? I suppose I thought all that business with the tea and fucking was meant to make him happy."

"That's only part of it."

"Notsah . . . Demi," he amended at once, "whatever your purpose, surely it includes making certain your patron is safe?"

"Do you threaten him, as well?" She kept herself from spitting again at his boot and satisfied herself with a scowl.

"I think our melek spent so much of his youth avoiding people he's had little enough experience in understanding them. Do I think he's a bad man? No. Jarron's ever been generous and just, so far as I've ever had chance to see. You'd know that firsthand, wouldn't you?"

"Is that what this is about? That he let me go back then? Or that I wanted to go?"

"It might surprise you," Erekon said dryly, "to learn this isn't all about you."

Demi drew herself up, intending to take an offense, but that was the woman she'd been when she knew him. Not the woman she was now. She relaxed her stance. "Point taken."

"I've been in the Shomer Melek since I was not yet twenty seasons old. That's a long damn time to work for a family. I might be an arrogant, vicious bastard, but I'm not disloyal."

Her own words flew back at her as fresh and stinging as they'd been ten seasons before. Demi had the grace to flush. "What, then? Why all this intrigue? Why not go to Jarron yourself, recommend to him that he consider this unification nonsense seriously?"

"Think you he'd take my counsel? I'm a soldier. True, I served his father and he trusts me with my duties. But the lad will scarce listen to the men of his council, men with more experience than I have. He'll scarce listen to his longtime friend, that posy."

"Adam Delano? Adam speaks in favor of unification?"

"Tell you true, but he's the one pushing your lover to take the throne for himself. Be king of all."

"And you think him incapable?"

"I think . . ." Erekon paused, studying her. "I think he is young. I think he is a little foolish upon occasion, but what man is not, when it comes to drugs and drink and cunny?"

"Yet you want me to push him to consider it. You'd have me convince him to join his lands with the other provinces, but not make play to name the Second Province the seat of government?"

"We can't win," Erekon said flatly. "We haven't the size or strength, even with recruiting every ruffian off the streets to serve the king's bidding. The Second hasn't had a true army in generations, haven't needed one. To raise one now would break this country. And we'd lose. Badly."

Her mind whirled with the thoughts of all this. "I can dance. I can sing. I can paint a landscape, compose a poem, knit a pair of socks. I can speak intelligently on any number of subjects. But I cannot, Erekon . . . I cannot fathom what it is you're trying to do."

"I'm trying to keep this province alive. That's my game. I would rather see this land kept together, unburned. Not destroyed. I would rather see our pretty little melek sit as governor than lead him into a war he cannot win."

"He is a good king! Why should he not be equally as skilled with more lands to command?"

"He's a fine king. But not a great one. He's a good man, but he's flawed, Demi."

"And who is not?" she demanded, advancing on him smartly enough to force him back a step. She poked his chest with her finger, hard. "Who among us in this whole great world is not flawed? You are. I am. Why should Jarron's flaws make him any less a man?"

Erekon captured her hand and squeezed it. Held it tight. "I never said it made him less a man. It makes him less a king, that's all. I suppose I shouldn't expect you to understand, with your pretty little poems and needlepoint. I thought Handmaidens were meant to be more than dolls."

"We are! I am!" She jerked her hand from him. "But you speak of what takes people a long time to learn as though I should understand without question, when what you really want, simply put, is for me to accept what you say. Without question."

Emotion flickered in his gaze, and he looked out at the pond. "You never did before, why ought I expect you to do so now?"

"You shouldn't. You want me to woo my patron into somewhat I don't understand or believe, and you want me to do it because you think he trusts me better than he might you. Or Adam. Or his Ministers of Advice. And you may be right, Erekon. Jarron might take my word, follow my urging. Because I'm supposed to be leading him toward solace. But I can't do that. I can't use that bond for any reason but what it's meant to be."

"So noble."

"Void take you," Demi said flatly. "I care naught of what you think about me. I'm not here for you."

"I know that."

"Then stop trying to use me!" She kicked at the gravel, sending a spray of grit toward him.

Erekon didn't move. "The former queen is moving against her son."

"What?" Too much. This was all too much. Her head whirled with it. "His mother?"

Erekon nodded.

Demi scrubbed at her face with both hands. "You jest. The queen, his own mother. She loves him. Overmuch, I'd say. Why would she set herself against him?"

"Because she's a fool. Because she's a spoiled, vain, vapid, and self-centered woman who views anyone close to her as a pawn in her own personal games, useful in providing her what she wants and naught else. Because her son refuses to be the social gadabout she'd like him to be, as she made his father be in his time and which he is no longer."

"You're suggesting she's what . . . setting up a revolution that she might have a merrier time in the social hall?"

"I suggest that she's setting up someone who will bend to her whim with rather more grace than her son has proven to be interested in providing."

"Adzo." Demi thought of the young man the former queen had introduced as her nephew. "He was in her quarters the day she sent for me. He seemed most . . ."

"Obsequious? Pandering? Ambitious?"

"Fond of her, is what I meant to say." Demi twisted the toe of her boot on the ground, crunching.

Erekon shrugged. "It's as the same."

"It's not!"

"You said yourself you don't understand these things."

She frowned. "Might it be so difficult to understand the man simply dotes upon his grandmother? As I recall, you were ever fond of your own mother."

"My mother, Invisible Mother bless her, was not a queen."

Demi refused to smile. "She thought you a prince."

"Don't most mothers think that of their sons?" Erekon narrowed his eyes, looking her over. "You'd think it of your own, if ever you had one."

"Handmaidens do not bear children."

"That's why he keeps you, aye?" Erekon asked softly. Gently.

It was Demi's turn to narrow her eyes. "Part of it."

"You think you can bring solace to a man so filled with self-loathing he refuses even to create a child? Pass on his lineage? Think a man like that could possibly be king of all?"

"It's not my place to judge."

"No, I suppose not. But you should think on all of this, Demi, I tell you true. Because whether or not you want to understand this, whether or not you wish to play at being your patron's counsel, all of this is coming. Jarron cannot ignore what the other four provinces are moving toward. Therefore, as his Handmaiden, neither can you."

Demi looked for a long time at the water, rippling in late winter breezes. "The Order of Solace does not involve itself in the politics of individual provinces. We serve anyone. I would be going against my Sisters-in-Service if I were to choose loyalty to one province or country or king, queen or premier over another. I can't do that. I won't."

"Not even for him?"

She looked at him then. "You say that as though he were different than any patron I've ever had."

"Isn't he?" Erekon faced the breeze to shake the hair from his forehead. "I've seen how you look at him."

"I look at him as I would look at any patron."

"You look at him the way you used to look at me," Erekon said.

Demi couldn't find the words to deny him, because what he said was truth. Once upon a time she'd believed she would spend her life with the man in front of her, before he'd made it all too clear he had no room for a wife. Before they'd both become fools bent on hurting each other to prove how little they loved one another. Erekon had taught her how to love and hate in equal measures. Her mouth opened and all that came forth was a sigh.

Erekon shrugged. He bent and picked up a handful of small stones, tossing them into the water, where they sank and left behind ever-widening ripples that broke against those caused by the breeze. "It was a long time ago."

"And he isn't you."

"No. I'd daresay he is not." He shot a glance at her, his hands empty. He turned to her with them palms-up before putting them at his sides.

"I can't do what you want. Not simply on your word alone. I need more information." Demi swallowed the sour taste of bile. "I need to know more about what the provinces are planning, how it might affect the Second. I need to know who is against him, Erekon. Including you."

"I can give you that information. Any you need. I can teach you what you need to know."

"You could teach me whatever it is you wish me to know. That's not the same."

She thought he might argue with that, but he only nodded. "You were ever a sharp, untrusting little bitch."

"Your pet names won't sway me." Her lip curled, and to her surprise, Erekon put his hand over his heart.

"I plead your mercy. We ever brought out the worst in each other, aye?"

Demi lifted her chin and again swallowed bitterness. "It was long ago and far away. I'm not that girl anymore."

"Mayhap I am still that man."

"You should know," she said tightly as she turned on her heel to go. "I hate you for this, Erekon."

"Hate is not a particularly Handmaidenly trait."

She tossed her braid at him, moving down the path before he could taunt her into saying anything else.

"You should know," Erekon said after her, "that when I said this is not all about you . . ."

She stopped, back stiff, didn't look at him.

"I was only half a liar."

# Chapter 18

The crackle and warmth of the fire ought to have soothed him, along with the fragrant mug of brewed tea, the platter of sliced cheese and fruit. The woman at his feet. And still, Jarron wanted to pace, not sit.

He'd spent another long day in the War Room, which had finally begun to feel as though it earned its name. Naught had been accomplished but hard feelings. His head ached with it all. He'd sent out letters to his contemporaries in three of the other provinces, refusing to send a word to Queen Caramin. There was an advantage in silence upon occasion, though he well knew she'd hear of what he'd written to everyone else.

Now he rested a hand on Demi's hair, tightly bound the way she wore it every day. "Unbind your hair for me."

Her fingers tugged free the ribbon binding the bottom of her braid and she did as he requested. She shook it a little until the silver moonlight of her hair fell down over her shoulders.

"So beautiful," Jarron said.

"Thank you."

He loved the look of her, kneeling that way. Her gown, with its demure high throat, long sleeves and floor-length hem, ought not to have been as appealing as it was, not compared to the current fashion of low décolletage and slit skirts that revealed shapely ankles, calves, and thighs when their wearer spun. Yet somehow, the fact Demi was almost completely covered made the sight of her body that much more arousing.

"Do you remember when I asked you if you wanted me to give you pretty clothes?"

"Of course." She rested her chin on his knee. "What woman could forget such an offer?"

"I'm glad you didn't agree to it. I like you this way."

She lifted her head from his knee. "Do you?"

He nodded. "It suits you."

She laughed lightly. "It suits us all, Jarron. It's the uniform of the Handmaiden for a reason."

"Surely not all of the others look as lovely as you." He smiled to see her smile, too.

"I would offer that beauty is a matter of opinion more than anything else."

This time, he shook his head. "You are lovely. Beautiful. Perfect."

"Far from perfect," Demi said in a low voice. "Though it pleases me to have you think so, perfection is too great a burden to bear."

"Rubbish. Who'd not wish to be perfect?" Jarron lifted the cup to his mouth and took the last swallow. As he put the cup down, she was already reaching for the kettle hung by the fire.

"Many might wish it, but it's not possible. Besides, sweetheart, it's one of the tenets of my Order, 'a flower is made more beautiful by its thorns.' I can hardly agree with you on the subject of perfection."

She paused, kettle in hand, and re-hung it. "No more tea."

He'd have drunk some, had she poured it. "You see? You even know when I really don't want somewhat."

Demi laughed. "Jarron, you've had four cups of it. If you drink any more you'll float away."

"What do I need, then?" He sat back in his chair, watching her.

Demi rose gracefully, silhouetted in the firelight. She crossed to him on gliding feet and stood to look down at him. A faint smile played on that pretty mouth. She reached and smoothed his hair from his face in so gentle a touch it fair overwhelmed him with a sudden rush of emotion.

He caught her hand and kissed it. "What do I need, Demi?"

"You need to relax, I think," she murmured. "You've had a long day."

"Always." He sighed and pressed another kiss to her palm and held her hands to his cheek. "Much to discuss. Much to argue upon. Coming back here to my rooms, to you, to the quiet grants me such . . ."

He'd almost said solace before he stopped himself. A small panic pricked him. He looked at her.

"Peace," she suggested. "I'm happy to hear it."

"How will I know?" He'd asked her before but needed to hear the answer again. "If it happens? How will we know?"

She bent to kiss him, her mouth soft. She looked into his eyes. "We'll know it. I can't describe it, but you'll know it, Jarron. Most likely before I do. But I can promise you, sweetheart, you will know it."

"You won't just . . . tell me it's done. You wouldn't do that, would you?" He pulled her onto his lap, her gown a tangle.

"Hush. No. I'd never do such a thing. Why would I ever?"

"So you can leave."

Demi pressed her forehead to his. "Jarron, why would I do that?"

"Mayhap I'm a hopeless case." He tried to make it sound like a jest but failed.

"I don't have to lie to you in order to take my leave of you."

This didn't make him feel any better. Worse, in fact. "You can just leave anytime you want."

"Or you can dismiss me."

"I don't want to," he said.

She smiled at that. "I should hope not, for I'm not near ready to go."

He closed his eyes against another prick of emotion he hated because it made him feel so weak. He felt her breath on his face. Her mouth on his. He kissed her, tasting her.

She ran her fingers through his hair, loosing the cord binding it at the base of his neck. She kissed his mouth, his cheeks, both eyes. She whispered into his ear, "Come to bed, sweetheart. I'll take care of you."

He let her, though in truth he was certain he wanted the comfort of her body only in the way he always did—the way his body always reacted. He let her take him by the hand and lead him, let her lay him down and undress him, and though his cock stirred under her touch, he felt inadequate to the task of making love.

He watched as she slipped out of her gown and hung it alongside the others in the armoire big enough to hold all her belongings yet so small it could scarcely contain even a portion of his. Her hair unbound and streaming over her breasts, she closed the armoire doors and turned to face him on the bed.

When she went to the bedside table to pull out the chest of toys, somewhat a little darker stirred inside him, twitching his prick. Yet even the promise of those delights did little more than tempt his body—his mind remained awhirl with every distraction. Demi sorted through the body jewels he'd bade her wear for him more than once. The anal plug. The aphrodisiac cream. Then she withdrew the bottle of herb-infused oil and held it to the light of the gas lamp, turning it so the glass caught the light.

She set it on the table with a satisfied nod and dimmed the lights. She lit a scented candle. Then, she put a hand on his shoulder and one on his hip. "Turn onto your belly."

He did and buried his face into the pillows. Demi was ever willing to play at whatever game he'd devised, but she'd never begun one, herself. He was going to be sorry to disappoint her with his ennui.

When the first stroke of her oiled hands slid down his back, however, he sighed. Her hands kneaded and worked at muscles he hadn't known were sore and stiff until she began her work. He groaned aloud, the sound very like the noises he made during sexual release, and heard Demi's soft giggle. Jarron didn't laugh, though he did smile into the dark embrace of his pillow. She knew. She always knew just what he needed.

He felt her weight on the backs of his thighs. The brush of her pubic curls on his ass. His cock, pressed into the sheets, thickened, but he was still enjoying the massage too much to think of anything else. She bent to use what felt like her elbows into a particularly tense spot on his shoulder, and he groaned again.

"You carry your tension here. And here." She touched his other shoulder, then worked at the base of his neck. "You grit your jaw somewhat fierce, as well. It's why you get headaches."

She dug deep into the sore spots, making him yelp, but he didn't pull away. The pain felt good. It felt necessary.

She spent some time on his neck and shoulders, then moved to his back. His upper arms. She worked her way down his body, adding handfuls of warm oil every so often so her touch never dragged or caught. She worked at the backs of his thighs, easing tightness he didn't know existed, then down to his calves.

"To the Void," he muttered when her nimble fingers pinched at a particularly sore spot.

She laughed gently; he felt the nudge of her mouth against him and shivered. She didn't stop, though. Her hands worked a powerful magic on every inch of him, even down to his feet. She oiled them as well, working each toe and the soles until Jarron was limp and dazed with pleasure.

He was fair certain he couldn't have moved had an assassin burst through his door to cut him to bits. At any rate, he was content to sink into the bed while Demi hummed softly and ran softer hands up and over him. No longer digging and kneading, now her hands stroked in a smooth, steady rhythm up and down his back. Over his buttocks. His thighs, calves, feet. Up again.

She nudged his ankles apart, spreading his legs, but Jarron thought little of it. The bed dipped as she settled her weight between his calves. Drifting on the comfort of her massage, he didn't move.

When she ran her oil-slippery hands up the insides of his thighs, though, his muscles tensed again. Not in the painful way of before. More like . . . anticipation.

The feather breath of her gusted up his legs, over his ass. Her hands cupped his buttocks, caressing. His cock, half hard while she was massaging him, got longer and thicker, still pressed to the sheets.

Demi slid a hand beneath him to caress his sac. Jarron let out a long, shaky sigh. She murmured some endearment he didn't quite catch and ran a slick finger up the seam and along the crack of his ass. The whisper of her breath followed.

Jarron groaned and pressed his face harder into the pillow, fists clutching the sheets under him. He lifted his hips a little to give her better access. When her hand found him, stroking just once before making the same trip along his sac and ass, he pushed up a little higher.

He wanted her hand on his cock. Her mouth, too. He wanted the stroke of her fingers on his prick, but unlike all the other times when Demi had given him what he wanted without him having to say a word, this time she did not wrap her hand around him. She stroked, aye, up and down, then drew her fingers again along the same path.

This time, she parted his ass cheeks and let her fingertips press against him back there for half a breath. He had no time to protest before the hot gust of her exhale caressed him there, too. Jarron had gone stiff, hips lifted just slightly, knees digging into the bed, and he didn't move now.

Demi grasped his cock from behind him, just as he'd wanted, but she pushed against him at the same time, urging him without words to push up higher on his knees. Ass in the air, face in the pillow, hands still gripping the sheets. This was the position he'd had her in the day he'd used the plug on her, and if he hadn't been so bonelessly sated from her lengthy ministrations, he'd surely have protested. So he told himself, even as he closed his eyes and drew in a breath, tensed in expectation.

He couldn't see her and didn't want to. Her touch on him was more than enough. Her hand gripped and stroked his cock as her other stroked his balls and his ass, pausing to press just gently back there. Not too much. Just enough.

Her strokes became a little faster and he relaxed into the steady pattern of stroke, stroke, press. He pushed forward into her hand, losing himself into this pleasure that required naught from him but acceptance. He thought briefly of turning, pushing her back, entering her, but just for the moment this felt so good he didn't want to pull himself away.

He cried out when her tongue replaced the gentle pressure of her finger. He bucked into her hand, head lifting for a moment. "Land Above!"

Demi licked him again, then blew hot breath over the wetness left behind. She hadn't let go of his cock. Her other hand stroked his balls while her tongue made magic against him.

"Demi . . ."

She said naught, but he imagined her smile. Jarron bent back to the pillow, spreading his legs wider to give her access to whatever she wished. Gone were thoughts of fucking her, even of having her take his prick in her mouth. This pleasure was new, it was thrilling. And this . . . this giving up to her seemed as though it ought to have put him in the place he'd always preferred to give her, and yet there was power in this, as well. Always, no matter what games they played, he'd made sure to give Demi the same amount of delight she gave him. Knowing she did all this to please him without having to do anything in return somehow made all of this intensely more exciting.

He stopped thinking of anything. He concentrated on her grip, perfect on his cock. When she pushed at his hip to turn him onto his back, he moved at once. She kept her hands on him, using both now on his prick, one up and one down. Twisting. Palming the head while the other crept down to give that same exquisite stroke to his balls. His ass.

It was different than being inside her—silky smooth from the oil, her grip firmer than that of her cunny. Though she could work him delightfully with her internal muscles, her skilled fingers loosened and tightened in a way that sent him to the edge of delirium before pulling him back. He heard the sound of her breath getting faster, but he kept his eyes closed, one hand over them to block out even the dim light.

His feet flat on the bed, Jarron rolled his hips to fuck harder into her hands. She made no spoken command, but her hands slowed though he moved faster, until he thrust into empty air with a low cry of protest. She gripped him again, keeping the pace steady but slow when he'd have bucked and jerked.

It was maddening, it was delirious, it was incredible. Everything of his being strained toward release even as he yearned for this pleasure to never end. When her finger again pressed gently at his anus, Jarron muttered a curse.

He opened his eyes to look at her, kneeling so prettily between his legs. Her face and throat had flushed, and her nipples had gone tight. His tongue swept his lips at the sight, wanting very much to taste them. Taste her.

Her gaze met his without hesitation as she stroked him. Slower. Stopping for a breath, then up again. Twisting. Down. He couldn't speak, could scarcely breathe. His hips moved on their own, pushing his cock into her fist.

How many times had he imagined this in his youth, his own hand moving along his cock while he pretended it belonged to a woman? Yet he'd never finished this way with a girl. His lovers had stroked him to full erection and then he'd fucked them, or they'd used their mouths upon occasion, but this was so much like his adolescent fantasies and yet so far removed he could hardly compare them. Yet somewhat about this made him think of when he was younger. Of how he'd closed his eyes and stroked himself to orgasm thinking of this woman or that, and none had ever given him a second glance.

He would've stopped her, rolled her onto her back, and pushed up inside her, but it felt too good to stop even for those few moments it would take. And somewhat in this suited him just now. This selfishness, for that's what it was. He was taking without giving, and delighting in being so served.

Her tongue crept out to dent her bottom lip as she focused her gaze on her hands and his cock. Her head bent. Her hair fell down, made her faceless. She might've been any woman—any of the women he'd ever been with. And somehow, this more than anything else she'd done, sent him surging toward release.

Jarron gave himself up to it, no longer even trying to pretend to himself that he meant to make love to her properly, or even that she was gaining some sort of pleasure from this. He no longer cared about anything but her stroking hands and the desire building in his balls.

This time when he fucked upward, she quickened the pace to match him. The bed rocked. Jarron groaned, his back arching as he fisted a double handful of the sheets. He pumped into her hands and cried out when she again stroked his balls. His ass.

His mind filled with the faces of every woman he'd ever lusted for—young, old, a tutor, a schoolmate's sister, one of his mother's ladies-in-waiting. His first whore. They shifted, blurring, eyes and mouths, breasts and cunts. Soft skin, soft hair. The smell of them—perfume and the musky feminine scent of arousal. The woman between his legs, pumping his cock, had become all of them but better than any of them had ever been. Better than his own fist had ever been.

The gentle pressure on his anus increased as her stroking did, too. When she slipped just the tip of her finger into the tight ring of muscles, Jarron shouted, hoarse. His cock strained, balls insanely heavy. He opened his eyes and saw her. Demi. His.

He came so hard he saw stars flashing in front of his eyes. Heat splashed his belly, his chest, and even his throat. The smell of his seed filled his nostrils as he heard the sound of his shout. His body shook with climax and he gave himself up to it completely.

When he could finally open his eyes, Demi lay curled next to him on the pillow. She was smiling. Her hair had tumbled about her, and Jarron brushed it away from her face.

"Land Above," he said, uncertain until the words became sound that he'd be able to form them. "That was . . ."

"Hush," she told him. "Go to sleep."

And though he meant to say more, to tell her how wonderful she was, his eyes closed again. This time, he'd bent to her command.

# Chapter 19

*Letter to the Mothers-in-Service,*
*Order of Solace Motherhouse, Neaku*

*May the Invisible Mother bless you and keep you today and all your others,*

*I plead your mercy for the contents of this letter, but I'm sore in need of your counsel. I am pleased to report that my patron has shown every inclination of being open to my service and allowing me to help him attain absolute solace, in keeping with the purpose of our Order. Truth, Mothers, he is the most amenable patron I've ever had, and my fondness for him is great.*

*My trouble comes from several sources. The first is that returning to my homeland has been more difficult than I expected. My patron has no memory of ever meeting me before, and as it hasn't seemed important to his well-being, I've not spoken of our previous meeting. The longer I wait, the more like a lie this feels, yet I find myself unable to find a way to tell him now without it seeming as though I kept this information from him* apurpose. The second is that my former lover, the King's Lion, does remember me. If he'd revealed the truth early on I might've weathered it, but he's chosen to keep my "secret," as it were, and at a cost to myself.

Though the Order of Solace holds no political loyalty to province or country, I am being asked to speak on the behalf of one certain political movement in order to convince my patron of its superiority over the opposition. The Aryon Melek has approached me on more than one occasion to suggest I might better have the king's ear than any other. He may be right, but I'm not comfortable in that position. It's not a Handmaiden's place, nor that of the Order, to play at intrigue.

Yet I find myself compelled to discern if the Aryon is mayhap correct in his beliefs, and therefore, my possible role in the convincing of the king. It is my experience that the Aryon is a man of fierce loyalty and unstinting attention to whatever path he feels is most just. I fear he will not cease to advocate this movement against the king, and I'm unable to determine if his course is the best for my patron or not.

Is it not my duty to support my patron and lead him toward that which will bring him to absolute solace, no matter what it might be? Is it not my place to do what is necessary to be certain he is not only safe but satisfied? How am I to know where my place as Handmaiden begins and ends when matters of this sort compete with my duties to him as man . . . and as sovereign?

I send this letter by post with the hopes by the time your most gracious and wise reply reaches me that this situation will have resolved itself, either in the completion of my duties or in the matters of my patron's decisions having been made without my counsel being made necessary.

Mothers, I implore you to advise me in this matter just as I also beg you not to relieve me of my position here in the Second Province. The simple answer of leaving would be a failure of myself and, dare I say it, the Order. I've not yet fulfilled my purpose here; Mothers, I cannot yet leave him.

> Yours sincerely in the service of the Invisible Mother,
> Redemption

The letter had taken her the full length of one chime to write, and she'd scratched out many a word before settling on the ones she felt best suited to explain her situation. Handmaidens didn't seek the counsel of the Mothers-in-Service in this manner, at least not any Demi had ever known. By the time a novitiate was granted her first patron, she'd been determined to be capable of handling any situation without needing the advice of her superiors. While a Sister-in-Service might consult her fellow Sisters or the Mothers between patrons, it was unheard of that any might need the wisdom of others during a period of service.

If this meant failure, she was ready to accept it.

Demi folded the parchment sheets, taking the time to admire the smooth, expensive paper. She sealed it with wax and her own fingertip, lacking any sort of signet ring. She held it in her hands for some long moments before writing the address on the front, then sprinkling some of the fine, soft sand over the letters and blowing it free to dry the ink. Jarron had the finest stationery she'd ever used, but she wished fervently she'd never had to lift the pen.

She could not trust this missive to anyone here in House Bydelay. She didn't have to be well versed in political intrigue to know that—a letter from the king's Handmaiden to the Motherhouse would be of enough interest to any amount of curious readers just for the sake of it being a curiosity. Most people didn't even know where the Motherhouse was, and though it was no secret, neither were they encouraged to casually reveal its location.

Instead, she dressed carefully in the cloak Jarron had given her, along with gloves and a scarf against the chill. Her walking boots. Her plainest gown, which might still attract attention should anyone get a close enough glance, but wasn't obvious. She took the purse he'd left for her to spend—not that she'd had any use for it so far.

She passed a few lords and ladies in the halls, curtsied and gave them cheery smiles but kept going with little more than a greeting. The maids and servants she ignored, as they expected her to, though

Demi had no trouble remembering the days when she'd been in their place and would've given them a kind smile at the very least, had she been doing her best to go without causing any kind of notice.

Jarron had never told her she might not have use of his carriage or horses, or that she might not travel outside the palace grounds. She suspected he wouldn't have forbidden it, and more likely gone with her, the way he'd done the night they went to the pub. However, this was an errand she needed to do alone and was grateful for the fact he was once more locked away with his Ministers of Advice.

She walked to town not only for the enjoyment of the exercise, which she'd had too little of over the past few months, but also because asking for the carriage or other transportation would have called attention to her journey. And frankly, she had no idea who to trust or not, to what depths the intrigue had gone. She suspected, at the very least, Erekon had men watching her. She knew him well enough to believe that.

She gained barely a curious glance in town as she went from shop to shop, taking the time to look in the windows. She had coin ample enough to buy whatever she wished, but baubles and trinkets didn't amuse her. She didn't need clothes or food. She did, however, intend to look for a gift for Jarron—that would be her reason for coming to town, should she need one.

It felt again like a lie, and it turned her mouth's corners down as she walked. Lies and more lies. This wasn't right. This wasn't her purpose, and her belly clenched as she thought of how she needed to get out from under the weight of these deceits.

In the stationer's shop, she kissed the letter and sent up a plea to the Invisible Mother for its safe sending, then paid the man behind the counter a few coins to assure its delivery. He glanced at the letter's address, then at her over the top of his spectacles. His brows lifted.

"Don't see this every day."

"I daresay you don't," she said. "But the letter on your wall says you're taken an oath to deliver letters and packages swiftly, no matter the circumstance. I shall hold you to it, sir."

He laughed. "Tell you true, I've signed the oath. Not so many care about it, of course, which is why they'll send their letters with any careless service that claims they'll do it for half my cost."

"It's important that letter get to its destination with discretion and speed."

He nodded and tucked it into a bag hanging behind him. "Of course. On the Invisible Mother's business, we don't tarry."

His words warmed her a little. "May the Invisible Mother keep you."

"Today and all your others," he said. "We don't hear that much around here. Not many practice the Faith in these parts. You're an uncommon sight."

"Anyplace I go, I'm an uncommon sight."

He laughed again. "Tell you true, I suppose you're right. But a welcome one, at least to me. You're the king's, ain'tcha?"

"I am." There was no point in denying it. As he said, she was an uncommon sight. "Here to buy him somewhat special as a gift."

The old man looked at her shrewdly with barely a glance at the bag where he'd stored her letter. "Of course you are. A patron gift, true? Somewhat special."

She smiled. "He has a lovely writing set already."

"Fit for a king, I'd wager," muttered the man as he leaned on the counter. "What about a pen? Special made, like, for him to sign those decrees and whatnot?"

"That sounds lovely. When can you have it finished?"

"For a king," said the old man, "I'd imagine it will take at least a fortnight to craft it. Special, like."

"Of course it would. And I suppose the price is thrice the normal amount?" For his silence, not just the cost of the work. Mayhap she did know somewhat of intrigue, after all.

He showed her a case of pens so she could choose the type and convinced her to add a custom-carved inkpot as well. It cost more than the coins she'd brought, but she assured him she'd have the full payment upon delivery, and they made the deal without haggling.

Back out on the street, Demi drew in a breath of familiar scents. Heard the old sounds of horses' hooves clopping on the cobblestones, children shouting as they played in the alleys, the sound of bartering fishwives. She'd been one of these people once upon a time, though in those days she'd never have dared step through the doorway to the stationer's—goods too pricey for her pocket. She paused, though, drinking in the memories.

Her stomach reminded her she'd not eaten in a few hours, and that she had a brisk walk ahead of her. Because she'd not fully paid the stationer, she had a few coins left in her purse and the promise of a pot of tea and a plate of pastries called to her from the bakery shop next door. It was another place she'd never have entered before, for the same reason. She breathed deep as she entered and the small bell jingled at the door's opening. Fresh bread, cakes, muffins, scones, butter biscuits . . . her stomach rumbled again, loudly.

She ordered a small pot of tea and a thick slice of cake heavy with cream and slices of dried fruit, then took them to one of the small tables in the front of the shop. She took off her cloak and sat, arranging her skirts as she did and looking out the window as the pair of women at the table next to her whispered loudly.

A mother-daughter pair, by the looks of them, dressed nearly identically with great expense but little taste. Demi gave them a tight smile and a nod, then ignored them as best she could. She'd met their sort before. They'd been the kind to toss her coins in the street when she was a child, then whisper loudly about how shameful it was she be allowed to run around that way.

Not much had changed, only now the whispers were about how she was an unescorted woman, not a running-wild child. Demi didn't care much for what strangers thought of her—she'd learned long ago to put aside unimportant opinions. She did think, however, the women must be stupid to think she couldn't hear them, or that they didn't see she was a Handmaiden and therefore didn't need an escort to legitimize her existence.

She was so busy ignoring the two women who couldn't be bothered to grant her the same courtesy that she didn't notice the man standing over her until he cleared his throat. When she did look up, she expected a stranger she'd have to curtly dismiss—or at least politely discourage. But it was a familiar face greeting her, his smile somewhat sheepish and the hint of a blush on his cheeks.

"Nigel!"

"My lady Redemption." He made a half bow that set the women at the next table all atwitter. "Might I have the pleasure of joining you?"

"Certainly, please do. Sit." She pulled her plate toward her so he might have room to set down his own. "The pleasure is mine, I daresay."

He glanced over his shoulder at the women. "At the very least, I hope I shall be a shield of sorts."

She flicked a gaze over his shoulder and permitted the barest smile. "Some women do themselves no courtesy through their actions."

He laughed at that. "I'd have to agree with that. Some men, too."

"Why is it, however, that men behaving badly seem to be so much less . . . silly?" she asked with a sigh as a fresh round of titters reached her.

"Mayhap more men should be silly and more women blunt? Would that suit you better?" He broke off a piece of the biscuit from his plate but didn't eat it. He studied her.

She studied him, too. "It might. Or we could hope that everyone simply behave properly."

He laughed. "We could hope, but I fear we'd be sore disappointed. And frequently."

She shot him a real smile, then, ignoring the ladies behind him. "Tell me, Nigel, what brings you to the bakery on such a day? Surely the House Bydelay kitchens provide better fare than this, if not in the social hall at least at your demand."

"I could ask the same of you."

"I came to shop for a gift for Jarron."

"You might've had the shopkeeper come to you with samples," Nigel said mildly, though his tone was deceptive. His eyes flashed with somewhat that said he knew better.

"I wanted the walk. I find the fresh air and exercise invigorating. Aside from that, I'm unused to inactivity and with Jarron so secluded at his work, I find I grow . . . weary." This was true, if not her whole reason.

"What did you buy him?"

"A pen." She paused to sip some tea. "What did you buy Adam?"

It was charming when men blushed, and Nigel did, crimson from his cheeks to the tips of his ears. He ducked his head and plucked at the biscuit, which he did eat, then, mayhap so as to have a reason not to answer her. Demi could be patient.

"I thought to have a jacket made for him," Nigel said when it became clear she didn't mean to speak until he did. "I thought . . . well . . . he so often spends his time worrying about what others should wear, it might be nice for him to have somewhat new he didn't have to design himself."

"That's a very thoughtful gift. And you knew his size, aye?"

"I . . . he . . . wears much the same size as I do, and I arranged for the tailor to fit it to him after I give it to him. To make sure he likes it."

"It sounds like a lovely gift." Demi sipped more tea. "I don't know him overwell, but he seems to like clothes. It sounds like a very nice gift."

Nigel cleared his throat, still blushing. He toyed with the broken biscuit, scattering crumbs. He leaned forward a little bit to murmur, "We aren't lovers."

Demi carefully didn't laugh. "It's not my concern."

"I know people think we are."

"Do you care what people think?"

He gave her an almost defiant look. "No. Not really. It's just that

they do talk, you know. I haven't spent much time in court. It's hard
to get used to."

She smiled. "Adam is the social one. He encourages, nay, fair
demands Jarron be more like him. But he gains so little pleasure from
it that even though I agree with Adam, I can scarce encourage Jarron's
attendance myself. Mayhap you could spend your time with Adam
elsewhere, where such matters are of no concern to any but those who
attend them."

He had a nice, full laugh, and a smile to match. "I could, if he'd
go with me. I'm off soon for another trade mission."

"Think you he'll go with you?"

Nigel picked apart his biscuit. "I don't think so, actually. He has
much to occupy him here. And I haven't asked him."

Demi would never have been granted the title of Handmaiden if
she hadn't learned how to listen, and well. Nigel wasn't her patron,
but it caused harm to no one for her to take the time to hear him
speak. He clearly needed someone to talk to.

"Do you think you might?" she asked gently.

"I . . ."

Before he could answer, the shop bell tinkled and though it needn't
have drawn their attention, Nigel turned, mayhap in relief at the
interruption. The man who sauntered through the doorway didn't
look the sort to frequent a bakery, a pub a likelier venue for him to
spend his coin. He held a packet of thick and ragged-cut parch-
ments under his arm. He looked 'round the room and headed for their
table.

"A half arro for a newsprint," he said, sliding one onto the table.

"We don't want one," began Nigel, but Demi had caught sight of
some of the text.

*Unification.*

"I'll take one. But I've only a quarter arro; you'll have to take that."
She slid the coin across to the man, who snapped it up.

"For a pretty lady as yourself, I'll take it." He shot Nigel a dark look and headed for the next table, where he tried unsuccessfully to sell one to the women still seated there.

"Trash," Nigel said.

"Trash that people are reading." She ran a finger down the smeared and blurry printing. She looked up at Nigel. "Tell me somewhat. What do you think about this?"

"Unification?" He shrugged uncomfortably.

"Pretend I'm not Jarron's Handmaiden. Pretend I've no connections to him at all. What would you say then?"

Nigel still looked uncomfortable. His blush had faded, but now he frowned. "I like Jarron."

"I like him very much, too."

"I don't speak against him. I want to make that clear."

She nodded, noting that he'd lowered his voice. She leaned to listen better. Nigel leaned, too.

"It's going to happen," Nigel said.

"You are not the first to say so."

He shook his head. "It's treasonous to speak against one's king. My father would be fair shamed of me. But I have to tell the truth. Caramin has called for the symposium and all three of the other leaders have agreed to go, Jarron, too. The Five Provinces are going to join. The only question is, at what cost?"

"More than a pen or a jacket," Demi said.

# Chapter 20

Y ou'll go with me." Jarron said this from the tangle of sheets as he swung his legs over the bed and padded, naked, to the shelf where he pulled down a container of worm and the bowl from which to smoke it. "Of course you'll go."

Demi didn't say anything for so many moments he turned to look at her. She'd propped herself up on the pillows, her hair loose and streaming over her shoulders. She pulled her knees up to her chest and linked her arms around them.

"Demi?"

She smiled. "If it pleases you."

Her answer didn't sit right with him. Somewhat in her eyes didn't match the smile. He lifted the lid of the bowl and filled it with the herb and dropped the lid again, but though he carried it to the bed and settled it on the bedside table, he didn't light it.

"Does it please you?"

"Of course I shall go with you, wherever you like."

"So accommodating," Jarron said stiffly, looking down at her. "But then, I forget. You've seen much of the world. The Five Provinces are as naught to you, tell me true? Mayhap you've even been to the First already. Mayhap you've even had a patron from there. The queen herself?"

She said naught, just looked at him.

His gut twisted. "Tell me you haven't."

"I haven't."

"Tell me true," Jarron said, voice low because his throat had gone tight.

"I've been through the First several times, my lord, but no. I've never had a patron there, Queen Caramin or otherwise."

He didn't miss that she'd called him "my lord," rather than sweetheart or even by his name. "You don't like to talk about them. The others."

"If you were the others, would you like to know I'd be talking about you?"

Jarron lit the bowl. "I thought . . . you'd like to come. With me. I thought you'd like to be with me, seeing new places. I travel in luxury, you know. It's not a hardship. And there will be parties and banquets and all manner of social functions, along with the rest."

Demi's smile was smaller and somehow more real for all that. "Your favorite pastime. Parties and such."

"I need you, Demi."

"I know you do, sweetheart. I know you do."

She got up on her knees and opened her arms to him. Jarron got onto the bed and pulled her to him. Naked, they sprawled on the sheets, and she tucked herself up against him all along his body.

"Of course I will go with you, Jarron. But you know . . . I'm not your wife, nor your mistress. People will talk. I'll call attention to you. They'll . . . stare."

He knew they would. "Then they shall have to stare. I must go. And I need you with me."

Demi kissed his shoulder. "I will be with you, sweetheart."

"But you're not convinced it's what I need. For the first time since you came to me, I feel like you're agreeing to somewhat you don't believe will help me."

"I don't believe it will harm you," Demi said quietly.

This was far from being the same. He frowned, looking down at her. "Do you think I should stay here while my peers meet to discuss what will inevitably change all of our lives?"

Demi's shoulders lifted on a sigh, but she looked at him with frankness in her gaze. "Jarron. I know naught of politics. Truly. All I know is people."

"What do you think all the rest of them are?" He stroked her hair, holding her close, mind whirling with all that lay ahead of them. "People. Same as me."

"Not the same as you, love."

He kissed the soft fall of her hair and closed his eyes. "Adam says he doesn't see how any can stand apart from the others if most agree to the joining. I think he's right, Demi. The Five Provinces . . . individually, we're all so small. We're not like the rest of the world. We're locked away here in this valley, our lands full of riches and yet never quite enough to supply everything for every need."

"It sounds as though you've begun to think it a good idea."

"I don't know." He pushed away from her to light the bowl, take a long, deep draught. Then to pace beside the bed. "I've asked my father to weigh in, but he's of no use." He turned to her. "The only way for me to know what is truly best for the Second is to go there myself. But I tell you this, Demi. I don't care what Adam says. If all the rest stand together for this union and I still don't agree, I'll not sign up merely to placate them."

"You would stand alone?"

He nodded, thinking of all the seasons of strategy, the talk of war the Second had never seen. "I don't want to be the king who brings war to the Second Province. But neither will I be the one who ruins it by giving it up."

Demi got off the bed and took her own deep breath of the smoke.

She coughed a little. She leaned against him, and he took her warmth as his own.

"I worry for you," she said under her breath.

Jarron tipped her face until she looked at him. "Why?"

"All of this is a great strain. You sent for me to help you reach absolute solace and there is naught about anything in this venture that hints at making my purpose a possibility. But I don't mind that," she added hastily before he could reply. "I tell you true, I care not for the length of time or the amount of service you need from me."

"Then what?"

She cupped his face in her hands, her gaze searching his. "I fear for your health, Jarron."

He didn't want to think about that. Every day he took the foul-tasting, dried and powdered herb the physicians had long ago pre-scribed for him and which was supposed to prevent the pox's outbreak. He wasn't sure if taking it really kept it at bay, yet he wasn't willing to take the chance.

"I'm fine." He put his hands over hers. "No fevers. No pox."

"Not yet."

It seemed like a cruel statement for her to make and set him back a step. "You have so little faith?"

"I've a great amount of faith, Jarron, but in the matters of your health, faith will do little. It's an illness."

"Mayhap you could ask your Invisible Mother for her mercy. Or Sinder, for that matter; he might be more inclined."

Demi's mouth thinned. "You could ask for such mercies yourself."

"I think it more likely you'd have their ears," Jarron said and turned to take another breath of smoke from the bowl. It soothed him. Allowed him to forget the slight tingling in the soles of his feet, the itch beneath his tongue and pressure behind his eyes that so often signaled an outbreak. With enough herb, he could forget he even wor-ried of such a thing.

"Anxiety can trigger—"

"My life is anxiety and argument," he snapped. "My decisions affect the lives of thousands. Think you that would not cause some anxiety? I cannot avoid it."

"No, I don't suppose you can." Demi pulled a loose robe from the back of a chair and belted it around her.

"If it comes, it comes. I can't stop it. I've never been able to. I'll suffer with it the same as I always have." Jarron shrugged as though it were of little concern.

He didn't fool her. She took his hand and kissed his fingers. Then the palm.

"And I shall do my best to make certain you have as little anxiety, or at least the relief of it, that I can offer."

Jarron let out a long breath and pulled her to him. "Having you here is a great comfort."

She squeezed him in reply. "I'll begin preparing tomorrow."

"You'll have little enough to do," he said with a laugh. "In this instance, I have many who can and shall take the burden from you. Maids, footmen. My intent is to travel lightly, but even so . . ."

"You must needs travel as a king. I understand."

He let out a small groan. "Adam is going to be in his glory with all of this. He's insisted upon new clothes for me. And you. Says the Second can't be shamed by my lack of style. He's sending his tailors first thing in the morning and they'll work through the chimes to ready my wardrobe. Now's your chance, love, should you have changed your mind about having me dress you in somewhat other than your Handmaiden's outfit."

"I should imagine that you'll want me to attend you at the parties, so . . . aye."

"I can't think of you as ever lacking self-assurance," he told her. Keeping hold of her hand, he spun her out in an elegant dance step he'd been taught but had little enough experience performing.

Demi laughed and struck a pose. "Should you wish me to be at your side in a feedsack, I could find a way to maintain my composure."

He spun her in toward him. "And if I bid you kneel at my feet, naked but for a collar and a leash?"

She ducked beneath his arm to turn and dip. When she came up, her mouth smiled though her eyes were serious. "If I felt it would bring you to solace."

"Only then?" He pulled her close to him again. The silk of her gown rubbed his flesh, and though not even one chime had rung since they'd finished making love, his cock stirred at the sensation. "Not simply because I wanted it of you?"

"Think you I should simply give you whatever you want?" She stood on her tiptoes to put her arms 'round his neck and kiss him lightly.

"Should you not?" His hands slipped over her back to cup her buttocks.

"Such a practice rarely benefits children, and I can tell you it benefits men even less so."

He marveled at how she could speak to him so honestly, in a way so few were brave enough to do. He loved that about her, even when her comments stung. "But I like it when you kneel for me, clad in naught but your skin."

"Would you like me in a collar, as well? I've seen such." She touched the base of her throat. "Would you make me your pet, held to your belt by a golden chain? My nipples adorned with jewels and painted for your pleasure, my clit so decorated as well?"

"You've seen such a thing?"

"Tell you true," she murmured with a sly smile, "such things are not just stories."

"They say Queen Caramin keeps her consort in such a manner. Bound to her in some way. They say she keeps a court of decadence and luxury."

"From what I know of her, that might well be true. I suppose we'll find out." She wiggled against him.

"You . . . you're prepared for such games?" He pushed the silk from her shoulders to bare her breasts.

"Handmaidens are trained in all manner of service. It's not always required of us. Not even of all of us."

He thought of how amenable she'd been to anything he suggested. "Have you?"

"Been asked to partake of the . . . sharper pleasures?" She shook her head. "Not before you."

"Is that what you think I've asked of you? Are they sharp?"

Demi laughed softly and reached between them to take his erection in her hand. "No, love. Not overmuch."

"But you know of other tastes. Other things." He looked toward the box, the contents not yet fully plundered.

"I've heard of some. Just as have you." She too looked at the box, then back at him. "And if you'd like to test them in the privacy of your rooms, I'll abide. I daresay even enjoy most of them."

"But not in public?" The thought of her attending him, naked but for the golden chain she'd described, did make his cock twitch. Such ideas were often best in fantasy, however; he understood that much. Even so . . .

"It would be difficult for me to serve you in public in that way, Jarron. It would feel undignified, as though you were putting me in a place not meant for me. Even Handmaidens . . . mayhap most particularly Handmaidens . . . have their limits."

"Has any patron ever tested yours?"

"Every one of them, sweetheart," she said softly, with another of those lovely smiles. "No two in the same way."

"Have I?"

"Not so fiercely. Not yet."

He pushed the robe off her the rest of the way so they both stood bare again. "But you think I shall?"

She followed him when he took her back to the bed and let him pull her atop his chest as he settled against the pillows. "You might."

"Do you hope I don't?" He twirled a lock of her hair.

She laughed. "I've no opinion on the matter. Either you shall, or you shall not. I assure you, they're broad enough to accommodate quite a lot of testing."

"How did you decide to take this path, Demi? To put yourself ever at the whim of someone else in this way?"

She ran her fingertips over his chest, circling his nipple, before she answered. "I believe what I do is for the good of the world."

"Do you, true?" It was odd to him, this implicit faith. They'd spoken little of religion, and she'd never forced the rituals of her Faith upon him. He knew she had to practice some. "You've not attended a temple service in all the time you've been here."

"I don't need to go to the temple to pray. Though I might've gone just to give your poor priests the business." She laughed. "They're unlikely to get much here."

"No. I don't suppose they do. My parents didn't practice, so neither did their friends. And I don't . . . but you could, Demi. I'd never keep you from it."

"I can speak to the Invisible Mother in my own words. I don't need the priests." She snuggled closer to him.

"What do you say to her?"

She was silent for some moments, her breath warm against his flesh. "Whatever I have to."

"Does she answer?"

"Not in the form of a fountain flowing where before there was no water, no," she said, referring to one of the stories in the Book of the Faith. "But I feel she answers me, aye. Not in words but in how I feel when I've finished."

"She doesn't tell you what to do? Do you feel guilty when you make decisions without consulting her?"

"She's not that sort of mother."

Jarron didn't laugh, though she'd spoken lightly. "I envy you that faith."

"You could find it, you know. It's there for you, if you wish it."

"Believe that I've a part in filling the quiver of an unseen god?

That what I say and do here will determine if I join the Land Above after I die, or instead go to the Void?"

"You must believe at least a little of it, else you'd not have sent for me," she pointed out.

He didn't want to tell her it had naught to do with anything of faith, but of pure selfishness. What might she do if he said that not only did he not believe she'd ever bring him absolute solace but that such a thing didn't exist? And even if it did, it had no divine meaning or purpose.

"How did you find yours?" he asked her.

She moved to straddle him, her knees pressing his sides. Her hair hung down over her shoulders in a most fetching way. She put her hands flat on his belly. "You'll laugh."

"I won't, I swear to you by—"

"By the Quiver you don't believe in?"

He put his hands on her hips. "Aye. By that. Or by my word, which I do believe in."

"I had a vision."

He didn't want to laugh, but a small chuckle eeped out of him. "A vision? What sort? I've had visions, too, but they came from too much worm."

"Not that sort." She tweaked his nipples too fiercely for comfort, and he captured her hands even as the slight pain aroused him.

"What kind, then? I promise I'll not mock."

"I'd gone into the forest—"

"What for? By yourself? Why would you? Where?"

She shook a finger at him the way a schoolmistress might to a naughty schoolboy. "Do you want to hear my story or does the sound of your own voice please you so overwell mine isn't important?"

Chastened, he sat back, her hands still in his. "Your mercy."

"I was by myself, aye, and the forest was in the Third Province."

"What were you doing there?"

She gave him a long, quiet look. "I was in domestic service there to a very large family with a great many children who were allowed to run wild. The only place I could find any time to myself was in the woods bordering their estate, and I took myself there as often as I could."

She had the finest breasts, and Jarron cupped them as she spoke. He thumbed her nipples, captivated by the way they tightened at his touch. "And you had a vision there."

"I did. When you asked if the Invisible Mother spoke to me, that is one time I can tell you that aye, she did, quite loudly."

He bent forward to take one nipple in his mouth, sucking gently as he rocked her a little against his cock. "And what did she say?"

Demi ran her fingers through his hair, tugging just enough so that he'd look up at her. "The story can wait."

Jarron grinned, already shifting so that she might slide onto his prick. "Are you sure?"

"I'm fair certain you're not listening," Demi said against his mouth as she kissed him.

And, lost inside her heat, Jarron didn't disagree.

# Chapter 21

Demi had traveled by foot, by horse, by cart, carriage, and train. She'd been rowed in a boat but had never gone a great distance in one. She'd thought herself to be a well-accomplished traveler.

That was before taking a king as a patron.

Of course he didn't travel alone, and of course those he chose to accompany him were all accustomed to traveling in comfort and style as well. What would've been a simple four days' journey for Demi by herself had become a grand affair estimated to take nigh on a sennight. It had taken that long to coordinate everyone involved; she had no doubts it would be as lengthy a time to actually make the trip.

She herself had, in place of her simple carpetbag, a full three trunks of gowns, shoes, undergarments, and jewels, along with another several bags of soaps, perfumes, and hair ointments. She'd refused a maid, insisting she was perfectly capable of taking care of herself, though Jarron had raised a brow and asked her flat out if dressing herself in the clothes Adam had designed for her would be as easy as slipping in and out of her Handmaiden's gown.

Jarron had even more luggage. He'd spent hours with Adam,

sequestered while Demi read or brewed tea that went undrunk. He'd asked her opinion of every outfit, and she'd smiled and nodded with naught to say—Adam had done so fine a job there could be no criticism.

Adam was going along, of course. So was Nigel. Jarron's mother was staying behind, allegedly to care for her ailing husband but more so because Jarron hadn't asked her to come along. The court was atwitter with this gossip, since of course it was not the former queen's right to accompany her son on such a diplomatic mission, yet everyone knew she'd have insisted, particularly since Demi was going and the queen had made no secret of how she felt about the woman with whom her son had aligned his life. In addition there were several members of the court—chosen by what lottery Demi did not know—their maids, body servants, and all manner of seemingly random people.

Erekon was going, too.

Of all those Jarron had asked to come along, this one surprised Demi the most. She watched now from the window as he settled a pack onto the back of his horse and tested his saddles, stirrups, the harness. Erekon wouldn't travel with trunks and trunks of clothes, she knew that much.

"The Aryon Melek? Does he not have important work to do here?"

"He's supposed to guard me, Demi. Hence the title King's Lion," Jarron said from in front of the mirror where he'd been angling himself back and forth, trying to see himself from all sides.

"Of course." She looked out the window again. Erekon was talking to one of the ladies joining the group. She couldn't see his face but the woman looked prettily flushed and flirting. "How many cubs is he bringing with him?"

"Only two others, his best. And four out of uniform."

She turned, surprised. "Guards not in uniform? Really? Why?"

Jarron fussed with his jacket, slipping the buttons in and out of their slots. "They'll play the parts of lords in my court. Erekon says it doesn't do to show your full hand."

"You're not playing cards, you're going as a guest to someone's home. Someone who is of the same rank as you, for that matter. Surely diplomacy—"

"They'll all have them, I guarantee you. Nobody will be there with only a few guards, Demi. We're talking about changing our entire lives and the way our governments have operated for centuries."

"You anticipate needing protection?"

"I anticipate," Jarron said with an angry sigh as he jerked at the hem of his coat, "the possibility of conflict. I anticipate argument."

"I hope you're wrong."

"I've a great many hopes," Jarron said.

"Here." She stepped up to smooth his jacket and fix his cravat, which was narrower than what most men wore. She tucked it firmly into his waistcoat and tugged the jacket's hem. "Adam outdid himself."

"I'm fair certain he broke me with this," Jarron grumbled. "Or at least the treasure house."

She laughed. She laughed a lot with Jarron, and thanked the Invisible Mother for the humor they so often shared, even if at this moment it felt a bit forced. She tweaked his chin. "Did he not suggest a tax on this type of fabric? Once you've set this as fashion, sweetheart, everyone will be fighting to get it. The issues of your depleted coin will be solved."

Jarron looked again at his reflection. She could see his gaze take in his clothes from top to bottom, but it lingered on his face, which he turned from side to side slowly. He passed a hand over his mouth to cup his chin briefly before stroking it back over his hair, which Demi had clubbed tightly at the base of his neck.

"He's made me into quite the posy, aye?"

"Pretty clothes are not what make a man into a posy, Jarron. Besides, your best and boon companion, your brother of the heart—he's proudly claimed himself as such. You'd be in good company, aye?"

Jarron shrugged. He'd been tense for the past few days, muscles tight, fair vibrating with an anxiety he pretended didn't exist. Naught she did helped him, and every hour that passed without being able to soothe him made Demi feel ever more a failure.

Oh, she'd trained for it—inevitable failure. They all did. Absolute solace was an ideal, and the Mothers and Sisters-in-Service knew overwell how difficult it could be to achieve. But she'd never believed it would happen to her. During her novitiate training she'd excelled at all the minor details of bringing peace to someone's daily life. Now even those were eluding her.

Sex was not the answer, yet was the only thing that seemed to work to get his mind away from what was happening. It was taking more and more of an effort—more tricks, more toys, more of everything—to even rouse his interest. Jarron had not yet turned her away when she offered herself to him, but nor had he become impotent . . . yet.

"You look very handsome," she said when he didn't answer.

Jarron shivered.

Demi took his hand and found it overwarm, though all the fires had been let to die down in preparation for their leaving. She pressed it between both of hers, feeling the unusual heat, then lifted it to look carefully at it.

Jarron yanked it from her grasp. "I'm fine. There's naught there."

Indeed, the skin had been smooth beneath the excessive heat. Still, she took his hand again, gently. "We've a little more than a chime's time left before we leave. Sit. Let me make you some—"

"I don't want any of your Void's bedamned tea." Jarron went to the desk and poured himself a generous glass of worm, which he downed in several swallows.

"Very well." She watched him, her heart aching for his turmoil. "But at least sit. You've naught to do between now and then."

He looked at her. "There is always overmuch to do."

"And others, as you've said, to do it. Sit, Jarron. Have somewhat to eat. You've not yet broken your fast this morn, and the road ahead is long. We won't be stopping for meals."

He'd already told her the group would be pushing hard to make time, eating on the road and staying as guests in the houses of nobles who'd offered to put them up. Such hosting was considered an honor, though Demi knew it had to put severe financial strain on those who offered it. Jarron had decided against bringing his own chef, and a great bulk of the delicacies he'd ordered packed were meant as tribute gifts to Queen Caramin, meant to share out among the other monarchs gathering for the symposium. They'd be eating bread, dried meat, and cheese on the road, which was better than what she'd sometimes had for fare during her travels. Even so, it was a far cry from the sumptuous banquets or even the groaning table in the social hall.

"Not hungry."

"You'll feel better if you eat. I made some simplebread, and we've a crock of sweet butter and jam for it that I kept back from the kitchen." She tempted him with a smile he didn't return.

"Simpering doesn't suit you," Jarron said.

Demi went cold. Her back stiffened, her shoulders straightened. She lifted her chin. "Derision suits you even less."

Before he could answer, she turned and went into the bedroom to finish packing the last of her bags. Her own, this one, the simple carpetbag she'd filled with what she'd brought with her. A couple of pairs of knitted stockings for warmth, her favorite gown, a few ribbons, a leather-bound journal in which she kept track of the days. Naught of value to anyone but herself.

"You don't need that," Jarron said from the doorway. "I'm bound to provide for you, and by the Arrow, I've done so. Fully."

"These are my things," Demi told him calmly as she snapped the locks. "I want them with me."

He crossed the length of the room in four great strides and put a hand on the bag so she'd look up at him. "Why?"

"Do I need a reason to have my belongings with me? You're

traveling with half your estate. I should think it quite reasonable for me to carry a few of mine." The moment the words left her lips she regretted her tone.

Handmaidens did not snap. This was not to say they could not be angry. Not even to say they could never be cruel, for there were occasions when a patron needed fury or fear. But petty snappishness, petulance—those were not the qualities of a Handmaiden. She pressed her lips together before she could say anything more.

"Is it so you can be prepared to leave, no matter where you are?"

Demi blinked, startled at how he'd put into words what had not even been made active in her mind. "I hadn't thought of such a reason, but . . . aye, I suppose that is part of it. I've little enough to call mine own. I should hate to leave them behind and even more to lose them forever."

"You have much to call your own. Trunks and trunks of clothes I've commissioned for you. Tell me I'm not the first to provide such for you! It's part of your contract, isn't it? What do you do with all of it every time you leave someone?"

"Not everyone was able to be so generous as you, Jarron."

He frowned. "Even so. Does the Order require a vow of poverty from you? Do you leave it all behind?"

"No, the Order doesn't, though I've made it my practice, as do many of my Sisters, to donate much of what we're given by our patrons to the Motherhouse to cover the costs of feeding and housing us when we are not in service, or to repay the Order for such costs accrued during our novitiate time. And if I've little use for baubles and bangles or pretty dresses when in the service of a patron, I've even less when I'm not."

He looked at the carpetbag, worn and still dusty from her trip to House Bydelay. "I could give you somewhat better than that. For you to keep, always. Better quality, richer materials. Prettier than that."

"I happen to like my carpetbag."

"It has a hole in it."

"It has a patch," she corrected him. "Made from a piece of a cloak I particularly favored. The leather at the corners came from a pair of boots I'd worn through. Every bit of that bag is made from a memory, and everything in it holds the same sentimental value. It is not the bag's beauty that makes me hold it so dear, but every single one of what you see as flaws. My belongings may be poor in your eyes, Jarron, but they are not so to me."

"That business with the flower, again? Made prettier with its thorns, aye?"

"A flower is made more beautiful by its thorns. Aye." She gestured at the carpetbag. "A carpetbag is made lovelier by its patches."

"I'm not a flower. Or a carpetbag."

"No, I daresay you are not." She didn't move to touch him. She didn't smile. She met his gaze head-on, both of them grim, the air between them acrackle with a tension she knew not how to dispel.

"The woman by my side must needs promote a certain appearance."

"Do you really fear I won't? Are you worried I'll shame you in some manner?" Demi said, insulted. "Have I ever given you reason to doubt my manners? I've been trained in etiquettes you couldn't even name. I'm more than capable of behaving appropriately in any situation, in any place, with any people, and what's more, Jarron, I have the confidence to know it."

"A worn and tattered carpetbag is not appropriate for the companion of a king."

Stunned by his insistence, she said, "Who will even see it, aside from you and I? Who will even know? The matter of my bag is trifling, and I daresay, ridiculous."

His gaze flashed. She might have pushed him a bit too far. "I ask no more of you than I would ask a wife or mistress."

"But I am not a wife or mistress," Demi said. "I am your Handmaiden."

Jarron scowled. Demi refused to look away, no matter how her stomach twisted and churned. Jarron ran his hand over his hair again, mussing it.

"I want you to leave this behind."

"Why?" she challenged. "So you might have the pleasure of knowing I bent to your will?"

"Isn't that what you're supposed to do? Bend to my will? You've had no troubles with doing so before." He gave a pointed look at the bed, where the night before he'd used a length of ribbon to bind her to the headboard while he teased her with items from the chest.

"Molding myself for your pleasure is a far cry from bending to your will for the sake of doing so. I'm not a servant. Or a slave. I do what I do for you because I want to, Jarron. Trust me, there is a difference."

"I want you to leave this behind," he repeated.

"Why?" she asked again. "Because you fear that I might go all the way to the First Province with you, only to leave? Is that why you want me to leave this bag, so that you might feel more secure about keeping me?"

He said naught. Only stared. Tears pricked at her eyes.

"If you think so little of me that you believe a carpetbag is the only reason I might stay, I have naught to offer you but my refusal. I am taking this bag with me to the First, where I'll be at your side in any manner you desire. Where I'll be the woman you've chosen as companion in the place of wife or mistress. Where I will not shame you with any word or deed."

"Don't defy me, Demi."

"Don't you bully me!" she cried loud enough to send him back a step. "I deserve more respect than that."

Jarron blinked rapidly, his mouth opening but silent. He ducked his head. He turned on his heel. In the doorway, however, he paused to look back at her.

"I plead your mercy."

"You have it," she replied, though not warmly.

"I have a great many thorns. How lovely do you find me now?"

She was not ready to soften. "I have ever found you lovely to look upon. I have ever found you to be a good man."

"But not now?"

"Not just this moment, no," she said.

Jarron laughed softly and rubbed at his face. "Your mercy, Demi. Please, grant me your mercy. I am . . . weary. I am anxious. I speak without thinking. I've allowed my temper to grow too short, and you don't deserve it."

"I granted you my mercy moments ago. You still have it."

He gave her a curious look. "For how long? How many times shall you grant me forgiveness?"

"It depends on how often you plague me with your short temper," Demi said sternly, though with less heat.

He crossed to her then, to take her in his arms. "I need you to stand against me when I'm behaving in such a manner. Thank you for putting me in my place."

"I find it difficult to believe you could ever forget your place," she told him.

"I don't mean being king. I mean my place in your affections."

She thought on this before answering, choosing her words carefully. "My affections are not so easily lost."

He kissed her. "Still, I should not try so hard to lose them."

"You say that as though you want to."

Jarron rested his hands on her hips and looked down into her face. "There are times I am so convinced you will leave me it's all I can do not to tell you to go, simply so I will no longer have to wait."

"I told you before—"

"I know what you told me," he interrupted. "But in matters of the heart, what good are words? It's not what you say. It's how I feel. You cannot tell me that you'll never leave me. Not without lying, and you aren't a liar."

She wanted to agree, but that would've been as much a lie as the ones she'd already allowed to remain secret. He stopped her with a kiss before she could say a word. He held her closer.

"Don't you understand?" Jarron asked. "I want to tell you I love you, Demi. But I don't want you to say it in return."

She drew in a breath. "No. I don't understand."

"Because I know you won't mean it. How can you?"

"The better question is, how can I not?"

Jarron shook his head. "You said it yourself. You are not my wife. Nor my mistress. You are my Handmaiden."

"Do you think that means I cannot love you?"

"Not forever," Jarron said.

She kissed him, clinging to his neck. "But for long enough."

# Chapter 22

Days of travel and sleep in strange beds, strange foods, long hours spent in the saddle or rocking in the carriage had left Jarron with every bone aching and a pounding in his head greater than all the pains together. There was a small cry of delight when they rounded the curve on the road to see the palace of Queen Caramin in the distance, but all he could do was groan. If it would not have taken another day to reach it on foot, he'd have walked solely to get himself out of the stuffy carriage.

Demi opened the window, though he knew she was chilly. "It will feel good to be settled in one place for some time."

"I'll settle for a hot bath and a soft pillow, but Sinder knows when I'll have such. I'm sure Caramin will have a welcoming party with lots of pomp."

"If she's any sort of hostess, she'll make sure her guests are safely escorted to their rooms to refresh themselves before she requires anything from them."

He laughed softly, though it pained his head. "This isn't a brannigan, Demi. She has the advantage of her home territory, and she's a well-known strategist. I wouldn't be surprised if we weren't all welcomed straight into the ballroom for a round of dancing."

"You give her too much credit for cruelty, I think."

"Really?" He settled back against the cushions that had felt divinely soft on their first day and now might well have been stuffed with gravel for all the comfort they gave. "You've heard the stories of Caramin's court. Think you true that she's benevolent?"

"Games," Demi said.

Jarron lifted a brow, which hurt his head, so he rubbed it. "Games?"

"The sorts of stories I've heard about Caramin's court tell me of the games she likes to play. Her lords and ladies, too. But they are games, Jarron, no different than the sort you've been playing with me. On a grander scale, mayhap, and more public. You're joining her as an equal, not subordinate. I suspect she'll be sure to show you respect unless you prove yourself somehow unworthy of it."

"You've never met her."

Demi smiled. "Neither have you."

"But you know people," Jarron said thoughtfully. "Tell me what else you think of Caramin."

"Well, she's a woman, quite obviously, and the first to reign the First Province. Her people, by all accounts, adore her, despite the decadence and darker pleasures she condones, which tells me that no matter what goes on in her court—which is essentially her private home—she does know how to behave herself in a befitting manner when she addresses her subjects. Which tells me she is an intelligent woman and not prone to allowing her vices to overrun her virtues."

The sound of her voice did more to soothe him than the tea she'd insisted he drink that morning when they paused to allow the travel party a respite. "Tell me more."

"She must be a strong woman, as well."

"I daresay a woman who keeps her lover on a leash next to her on the throne would have to be strong enough to keep him there."

"A woman who keeps her lover on a leash is more likely to have chosen a lover who would stay at her feet with naught keeping him there. The chain is just for show."

He thought of how Demi knelt at his feet, unbound by anything but her desire to make him happy. "Can men be Handmaidens?"

She gave a startled chuckle, the first real laugh he'd heard from her in days, which he knew had been his fault. "What?"

"Can men be Handmaidens?"

"Of course they cannot."

"Why not?" Curious, Jarron leaned forward. "Surely there are men who would be just as skilled at providing solace."

"First of all, men of the Faith who wish to bring absolute solace to the world become temple priests, not Handmaidens."

"To the world as a whole. But not to individuals, the way you do. I find that a much stronger and more admirable vocation. One at a time, filling Sinder's Quiver, and at great personal effort."

"The priests serve their purpose, Jarron."

"What if he doesn't want to be a priest?"

She laughed again. "Are you thinking of joining the Order?"

Jarron shook his head. "No. I don't have the personality for it. But surely . . . surely there are men who might."

"They couldn't be Handmaidens. How could you call a man a maiden of anything?"

"They could have a different name." The carriage hit a bump, jostling him, and Jarron gritted his teeth at the fresh round of aches. It was too hot in here, even with the windows open.

"I've never heard of a man who became a Handmaiden. I don't think it's possible. For one thing, Handmaidens serve patrons without regard to gender."

"So?"

"Most men," she said dryly, "prefer their service to come in the feminine form."

"Wouldn't women then like it to be male?"

"Surprisingly, no."

Jarron rubbed at his forehead again. "Do you suggest men are incapable of serving others?"

"Oh . . ." She thought a moment. "No, I don't think that. But there's a great difference between a lover chained to a throne and what I do."

"I know that. I don't see why a man couldn't."

"Mayhap there are some who could, but I've never heard of one who even petitioned the Order. I think a story like that would be passed down, don't you? The Order of Solace has existed for hundreds of years."

"Mayhap it's simply not spoken of."

She was silent for another moment. "There are many things about the Order that aren't spoken of, and yet we still know them. I think a man seeking to become a . . . well, I suppose he'd be a Brother-in-Service . . . I think his story would be one oft repeated."

"What else do they speak of that you're not supposed to?"

"If I told you, I'd be speaking of it."

Jarron found a laugh. "Tell me anyway. It won't leave this carriage, and I daresay my head aches so badly I'd be unable to repeat it anyway, should I ever meet anyone who'd care."

"Oh, sweetheart. Let me rub it for you." Demi shifted across the seat to sit beside him. She pulled a small vial, gillyflower oil by the scent of it, from the purse at her belt. "Put your head in my lap." There was barely enough room to do so, but Jarron managed. He closed his eyes with a sigh as her fingers, slick with oil, began rubbing. "Tell me."

"Ah, well. Let's see. We're never supposed to speak of our Sisters who fail, though we all know who they are. It's not supposed to be dishonorable. Solace is simply not attainable for everyone. But if the Mothers-in-Service send a Sister to a patron, it's widely believed they have faith he or she is capable of it. To be sent away, or to leave without providing it . . . well, it's not supposed to be shameful, but it is."

He relaxed under her touch. "What happens to those Sisters who fail?"

"We are extra kind to them."

He cracked open one eye. "That's all?"

"They're not punished, if that's what you mean. Not by anyone but themselves."

"What if they fail more than once? A great many times? What if there is a Sister who never succeeds?"

"That's never happened."

"Ah, just like a man wanting to serve the Order."

She pressed into his temples in rhythmic circles, easing the pain and tension. "Never."

"It could, aye?"

"Anything is possible." She drew her fingers over his forehead lightly in smooth strokes, then moved back to his temples.

He drifted under her ministrations, the pain in his head fading even if the others did not. "What else?"

"We don't speak of the Sisters who leave the Order."

"No? Why not?"

"Why would we? They make a choice to reject everything we hold dear. What could be said about them that would be of any sort of kindness? Why would we waste our time with negative talk about someone who thought so little of what we do that she left it? There's no point."

"But . . . you're women," Jarron said.

Demi's stroking fingers ceased. "Tell you true, that we are. Beginning and ending, both."

"So you do talk about them."

She sighed. "Sometimes. We do."

"Why do they leave?" Incredibly, he was drifting to sleep under the sweetness of her touch.

"Some lose their faith. It can be difficult to do your best for patron after patron, succeeding for all of them and yet the Quiver doesn't fill. For some it becomes about the destination. Not the journey."

"For me it has become about the destination, true. I'm fair weary of the road."

"We'll be there soon enough. I can see the palace growing closer. We'll reach it before night."

"Not too soon." He yawned and pressed her fingers back to his temple. "More."

"Aye, my lord."

He heard the smile in her voice and smiled, too, though without opening his eyes. "Tell me what else you don't speak of."

"Haven't you learned enough?"

"Are they secrets?" He asked her, words a little slurred. Land Above, she had talented hands. His headache had nearly gone, and the rest of him felt better, too. "Will they toss you out of the Order for revealing them?"

"No. But I wonder at your interest."

"Everyone knows about the Order of Solace and nobody knows anything. I'd like to know about it."

"You want to be more clever than anyone else, that's what you want."

"I find naught wrong with that. So, tell me. Why else would a Sister leave? Do they get too old?"

"Sisters-in-Service are allowed to retire from service whenever they choose without ever leaving the Order. They always have a home in one of the Sisterhouses. But aye, at some point, we find ourselves of an age when service to a patron is no longer a realistic goal. Some Sisters leave, then. Most stay."

"Why else?"

"The most common reason for Sisters to leave the Order," Demi said after a hesitation, "is because they've fallen in love."

Jarron opened his eyes. "With their patrons?"

"With anyone," she told him. "But . . . most often, aye."

"People who send for Handmaidens are damaged, flawed, wounded, miserable. How can they fall in love with their patrons?" Jarron asked, mind blurred with sleep and whatever magic she'd used to chase away the pain. He looked at her, though the sight was as fuzzy as his brain.

Demi bent and kissed his forehead. "And I say, as I said before, how can they not?"

He might've made more sense of this had he not been so tired. "Do they always leave the Order?"

"Of course not."

"Why?"

She looked a little sad and traced his eyebrows with her fingertip. "Why would you imagine?"

"Because her patron didn't love her in return."

She nodded.

Jarron thought he should say somewhat meaningful. Tender. He thought he should take this moment and made somewhat of it . . . but he did not. His mouth was too clumsy, his mind too hazy just then to find the words.

"What else do you not speak of?" he asked instead.

Was that disappointment in her gaze? Did he want it to be? When had this gone from somewhat he understood to somewhat he could not begin to comprehend?

"Well . . ." If she'd hoped he'd say somewhat else, she shook it off to answer. "We don't speak of Blessings."

"But you say them all the time," he said, thinking of the five sayings she was so fond of chanting.

Demi laughed. "Those are the five principles. Not blessings."

"What do you mean, then?" He settled back into her lap, eyes closed, though no longer drifting to sleep with quite the comfort he'd had before.

"Blessings are the children born of Handmaidens in service to a patron."

The carriage lurched, nearly throwing him from the bench seat. Jarron sat, gripping at the door handle to keep himself in place. Demi slid across the seat, holding the cushions with both hands to keep herself upright. They hit another bump, tossing them both toward each other. He caught her, kept her from falling. The ride smoothed, but his heart was pounding heavily.

"We don't speak of them often. I shouldn't even speak of them to you," she said after a moment of silence. "But . . . you asked."

"How can a Handmaiden have a child?"

"The same way any woman does, sweetheart," Demi said fondly. "Don't tell me you need a lesson."

"No. No, I mean . . ." He sat back from her, somewhat like horror sinking his gut. "I mean how do Handmaidens have children? I thought you were all infertile."

She gave him a curious glance. "Sisters are no more infertile than any group of women. But aye, it's true, we don't get pregnant. We take an herb to prevent it. The longer you take it, the more potent it becomes. It's very rare for a Sister to get with child. That's why they're called Blessings, Jarron. Because those children are so special."

His throat went dry as nausea climbed up it to paint its bitter taste on his tongue. He swiped it over his teeth, trying to keep his gorge from rushing up. "You could get pregnant?"

Demi looked stricken. She moved toward him, but he moved back, away from her touch. His skin crawled, itching and stinging. Heat flushed over him. He broke out in a sweat and turned his face toward the window to let the chilly air wash away the sick feeling.

"I . . . I do not believe I could get with child, Jarron. No."

"But it's not impossible!"

"Naught," Demi said, "is impossible."

He looked at her. "You knew this whole time?"

"Jarron . . ." She sighed, scooting toward him but not reaching to touch him. "It is truly so rare. In all my time with the Order, I've never known one of my Sisters to bear a child. Nor have I ever met a Sister who knew a Sister who'd borne a child. It happens, aye, but I tell you true when I am fair certain it will not happen to me."

"What if you stop taking the powder?"

"I wouldn't!" she cried, seeming as shocked by his question as he was at the revelation that she might be able to bear his child . . . possibly one inflicted with the disease Jarron had sworn not to pass along.

"What if you forget?"

"I can't forget. I never forget. At any rate, even if I did forget for one day, I can take some the next without losing the effectiveness, which is built up over time. I've had a quiverful of doses of the herb, Jarron. I don't even have my flow."

"What if you run out? What if we go somewhere and you lose your supply?"

"I can send for more from the Order should I become desperate, but trust me, love, I've enough to keep me for a long, long time. I need take such a small amount. . . ."

"But it happens," he said, horror thickening his voice. "You said so. It happens often enough for it to have a name."

Demi's mouth turned down at the corners in an expression so sad it would've turned his heart had he not been so stunned by what she'd told him. "Oh, Jarron. I'm sorry I told you."

"Why?" he demanded. "Because now I know it's possible? The truth?"

"You say that as though I lied to you about it. I never did. You know what every patron knows—Handmaidens do not get pregnant. For ninety-nine times out of one hundred, that is the case. Even more than that."

"But it can happen."

She nodded again. This time when she reached for him, he didn't pull away. She put a hand to his forehead.

"You're hot."

He brushed her hand away and looked out the window again. He closed his eyes, bringing in breath after breath of fresh, night-falling air. He opened them to the shouts and clatter of hooves on gravel. A welcoming party had arrived to escort them the rest of the way to Caramin's palace.

"We're here," he said.

He didn't look at Demi again.

# Chapter 23

House Bydelay had been big enough to house a royal family and a few court members who didn't keep houses in town or in the grounds immediately surrounding the royal estate. Caramin's palace, on the other hand, was truly grand . . . grandiose, in fact. It rose from acres of gardens, some of them in bloom with truly unusual flowers and trees, others set with carefully placed rocks and beds of sand. It had pillars and arches, a brick-and-marble façade, hundreds of windows, no few of them of colored glass.

"Sinder's Balls," Jarron said as he got out of the carriage to look up the lane leading to what on another house might've been called a veranda but here was of such a vast scope Demi couldn't think how to name it. "It's a bloody city unto itself."

It was so big they hadn't even driven right up to the front, but instead been stopped farther down by the stables so that groomsmen could take the horses and carriages to be unloaded. The guests were to be taken up to the main house by pairs or quartets in small rigs of plaited straw drawn not by horses or ponies, nor even goats as Demi had seen a few times before.

By men.

Not men dressed as ponies, thank the Land Above, though Demi had heard whispered tales of such extravagence. No, these young men, though as well-matched as any set of ponies, wore dark trousers and white shirts. All of them blond. All of them so near to the same height as to be indistinguishable.

"Does she breed them that way?" Jarron muttered, watching as his company got into the rigs and set off while he stayed back to stretch a bit and eye the situation.

"I like it," Adam said. "I think you ought to start this fashion in the Second."

"Unlikely. I can't imagine they're much use beyond this sort of thing."

Adam laughed and linked his arm through Nigel's—Demi noticed the other man neither blushed nor pulled away, though he didn't quite lean into the embrace, either. "Who cares? That's a good enough use for them, I say."

"You would." Jarron rolled his neck on his shoulders and cracked his spine. He looked at her, and if he'd not yet recovered from his dismay, Demi could scarce see evidence of it. "Shall we?"

"Of course." She took the arm he offered, wishing but unable to forget that he'd been so upset. Later, she thought. Later she'd talk about it with him.

"Shall we go together?" Adam pointed at one of the bigger rigs, pulled by two men who looked alike enough to be twins unless one looked close enough to see that one had dark eyes, the other pale.

"Sirs? Madam?" One of the men stepped forward. In the light of the many lamps lining the lane, his blond hair gleamed. So did his smile, full of bright and even white teeth.

"Land Above," Jarron muttered, but stepped forward.

"My lord." The man who'd invited them bowed low, then lower. "I'm honored to be the one to take you to the house."

"Thank you," Jarron said so tightly both Demi and Adam gave him a curious look.

In the rig, settled neatly against him, Demi took his hand. The uncommon heat had abated, but she knew better than to feel his forehead. He didn't look as flushed as he had, but in this light it would be hard to see. At any rate, he wasn't sweating as much.

Nigel didn't take Adam's hand, though he did sit close enough that both their thighs touched. "Hold on. The ride's gentler than with horses but they start off at quite a clip."

He was right. Adam and Demi both laughed when the rig jerked. The man who'd greeted them looked over his shoulder with a grin, then put his face forward and with his companion really set to pulling. They didn't have far to go, but the hill was steep enough Demi was glad of the transportation.

"You've been here before?" Jarron asked Nigel.

"He's been everywhere." Adam said this as proudly as if he were the one bragging.

"Only once," Nigel said with a modest grin. "And never had an audience with her majesty. Got as far as her undersecretary, who took my samples and made the deal. Which is to be expected, of course. That's why you lot have ministers and secretaries and whatnot. To keep from having to visit with the likes of me."

"Not this time, dear one," Adam said. "This time, you'll be invited into court as nicely as any lord could ask."

Nigel didn't return the endearment, but didn't startle at it, either. Interesting, Demi thought, watching the pair of them. Jarron, however, had set his gaze around them to look up the hill.

"Land Above," he said under his breath. "What a place."

"The palace of the First Province is commonly described as the most beautiful capital building in all the Five," said the man pulling the rig who'd not yet spoken. He didn't even sound out of breath as they trotted up in front of the wide set of steps leading to the veranda. "Pleading your mercy of course, my lord, as I'm sure House Bydelay is also lovely."

"Not so grand as this, I'm not ashamed to say." Jarron waited until the rig came to a stop, then stepped out of it without waiting for a hand from the pullers. "We have what we have and are well satisfied with it."

"Of course, my lord." The men helped Demi down, then offered their hands to Adam, who allowed them to help. Then Nigel, who laughed but did as well. Then they both bowed low again and set off down the hill with the rig.

Erekon waited for them at the top of the stairs. He'd traveled the hardest of any of them, never taking rest in one of the carriages but always on horseback. The last to sleep at night and first to wake in the morning. Despite this and the dust covering his clothes, he looked bright-eyed.

"My lord king." He gave Jarron a half bow, added a nod for Adam and Nigel and let his gaze slide past Demi as though she didn't exist.

"What say you, Erekon? Shall we go in?" Jarron sounded as though he meant to make merry, but his voice was too weary for the jest to sound real.

"The queen awaits you eagerly, my lord. I'd not keep her waiting."

Somewhat seemed exchanged among the men without including her, and Demi pushed down a surge of irritation. She wanted to blame Erekon for the dismissal and grew more annoyed by her need to somehow make him the villain. That he mattered even that much.

The five of them were greeted by a somber-looking man clad all in black who bowed as low as the rig pullers had. Jarron looked down at him for a bit before realizing the man was waiting to be told he might rise. Jarron's lip curled, just faintly, but his eyes gleamed in a way Demi couldn't decipher.

"Rise you up."

She'd never heard him sound like that.

It was gone in an instant, though, because the man was leading them through a set of carved wooden doors and into a vault-ceilinged room. Beyond that, a long hallway with arched doorways on either side, leading to more grand rooms and halls. Voices rang around them and Demi saw a number of people, though none from their party.

"I'll need a basket of bread crumbs to find my way out of here," Adam said.

"I could assign you a guard," Erekon said offhandedly.

"I'm sure you could." Adam made a face only Demi seemed to notice.

The man—butler or whoever he was—took them through another archway, then through a smaller door and into a room that was normal-sized, though still as elegantly appointed as all the others. This one was set up like a drawing room, with small ornate tables and several couches and chairs placed artfully around in the best positions to encourage conversation. A fire crackled brightly in the fireplace overhung by a carved stone mantel. It was a social hall smaller than Jarron's, and Demi wondered what that meant.

"My lord Bydelay. Please, come in and be welcome."

The voice, light and trilling and sweet as any bird's song, came from the corner where a large overstuffed chair had been set some small ways from the others. The woman seated in it did not rise to greet them . . . but then, Demi supposed queens did not rise for anyone unless they chose.

"My lady Caramin." Jarron's tone had again changed as he turned.

Demi turned, too.

Queen Caramin might have spent her share of seasons upon this plane, but she looked no older than Demi herself. Younger, mayhap, with the tilt of her head and the gestures of her hands. Twisting, flitting fingers. Expressive hands that drew the eye somehow always to her face.

Which was lovely. Of course. Demi had heard the queen of the First Province was beautiful, but who would ever dare say a queen was ugly? She hadn't expected this vision, however. Hair so pale it looked like silver—and in fact, was, Demi saw when the queen leaned forward into the circle of light from the lamps as Jarron stepped forward.

Silver hair and black eyes beneath matching dark brows, thin and arched. Wide eyes that looked innocent until you noticed the gleam in them. Her skin was pale as marble but for her mouth, red and lush as berries. Queen Caramin was a fantasy made real, tiny as a doll.

She held out her hand, and Jarron took it to kiss the fingertips. Demi looked away. It was protocol. She didn't have to like it.

"And what have you brought me, my lord Bydelay? Your Minister of Fashion, I see. My lord Delano, your reputation has far preceded you. You must dress me while you're here, have the run of my wardrobe. I insist."

"It would be my honor." Adam made a leg.

"And Nigel Witherspoon . . . do you know I still have a bolt of that spidersilk you sold me so many seasons ago? It wears like iron and holds the color so well. You really must share your source with me—but ahh." She shook her head. "Soon enough we'll have all manner of discussions of that sort. Soon enough there will be no need to hide such things from one another so that we might use the knowledge as bargaining pieces, aye?"

"I suppose that's what we're here to talk about. All of us." Jarron looked 'round the room. "Surely I'm not the first to arrive."

"Oh my goodness, no. Henrik, Bander, Kenston are all here." She ticked them all off on her tiny, perfect fingers. "They'll be in the large social hall, I imagine. I thought for your first night here, after such a long trip, you'd wish to sup more simply than that before retiring to the rooms I've had prepared for you. First, somewhat to eat, aye? And then to your rooms. And what . . . what is this?"

Caramin had risen, finally, and took one step to the side to let her gaze flow up and down over Demi. It was a foolish question. None could mistake Demi, clad in her Handmaiden's gown, as anything but what she was. And surely the queen knew Jarron was bringing her. Which meant the question wasn't foolish, but pointed.

"Might I present Redemption, my Handmaiden." Jarron stepped back to allow Demi a full view of the other woman.

"I'd heard you'd taken one, but how delightful." Queen Caramin circled Demi slowly. She came only to her shoulder and walked without regard to anyone in her way, confident any obstacle would disappear.

Which of course it did, Adam and Nigel stepping quickly back and Jarron to the side as she looked at Demi from all sides before settling back in her chair.

"Lovely," the queen said.

"Thank you," Demi replied.

"She speaks!" The queen clapped her hands in delight.

As though Demi were a trained monki. A puppet. Demi didn't frown, her brow did not crease. She looked straight at the queen and kept her smile light and pleasant, her gaze flat.

"Of course I do."

"Demi—" Jarron began, but the queen cut him off with a wave of her hand.

"Demi? Is that what he calls you? How delightful. How lovely! What a pretty name. I am Caramin. You must call me that. None of this 'your majesty' nonsense, nor 'my lady,' nor 'mistress.'"

"Caramin," Demi said. The name bit her tongue.

Caramin knew it; Demi could see that in the other woman's smile. She put her hand on the arm of her chair, and her rings clinked on metal. The chain, Demi saw. Made of fine gold, no thicker than the width of a necklace.

Or a leash.

Caramin tugged on it and the bent figure Demi hadn't noticed behind her chair raised his head. He had a shock of blond hair and eyes outlined in some dark cosmetic that had smudged. He was naked but for a pair of soft black trousers hanging low on his hips, and he was kneeling, one hand resting inside the palm of the other.

He was Waiting.

Demi stifled her gasp and looked at Caramin to see the other woman's smile. The queen tugged on the golden leash, attached to a thin leather collar banded tight to the man's throat. He didn't move or make a sound, and the tug didn't even pull him, but Demi put a hand to her throat in sympathy anyway.

"Gailen. My companion," she said as though half-naked men in collars and attached by chains to a chair were common enough to be introduced to kings every day.

In the First Province, Demi thought, she supposed that was true.

Jarron had come great lengths beyond his social awkwardness, but this had set him back. He looked at Demi, who stepped at once to his side. Not that she could put words into his mouth, but she could be there for support.

"How do you do?" Jarron said to Gailen.

"Quite well, thank you very much. Did you have a pleasant journey?" Gailen had a low, husky voice and spoke without hesitation. Without shame.

Demi had answered similar questions from a similar position, lacking only the collar and leash. Her stomach twisted at this, thinking of it. She'd never been ashamed to have been seen in service to her patron. There was no reason to think Gailen would be, especially when Caramin so clearly expected them to treat him with the same respect required for any companion.

"Long and dry," Adam said.

"Then my gracious, goodness me," trilled Caramin. "Let us not delay in getting you somewhat to drink! Gailen, sweetling, serve our guests."

Gailen nodded and rose with a grace Demi recognized and appreciated, knowing how diffcult it could be to get off one's knees in such a manner. Without even looking at him and as he moved, their movements so coordinated it looked choreographed, Caramin unlinked the chain from its hook on the arm of her chair and Gailen wrapped it neatly into a coil on his wrist, leaving enough length that he might move freely.

"Wine? Chilled or warmed. We have worm, as well, if you require somewhat sharper. Or lemon water."

"Water, please," Demi said, fascinated.

Are there any male Handmaidens, Jarron had asked, and she'd been so amused by the question she'd laughed aloud. But watching Gailen serve them all drinks as they took their seats at the small but fully set table, Demi saw herself in the echo of his every movement. He was not a Handmaiden—the very idea of it ought to have set her laughing again, but Demi found herself not quite so amused by the notion as she'd been before.

True, Gailen moved like a Handmaiden, all silence and smoothness. He Waited like one, too, though not at the table. There he sat next to Caramin and made sure her cup and plate were filled without her having to even look at them. He cut her food for her in a way that had Jarron's eyes rounding and Adam pursing his lips, but Demi recognized. Not as somewhat she would do, but somewhat she'd been taught how to do.

Through it all, Caramin watched them looking. It amused her, Demi thought, watching with as much intensity but a bit more discretion than the queen showed. Caramin enjoyed her guests' discomfort. It would've been rude for any to make note of Gailen's behavior, not that it was out of line in any way, and she knew it. She also knew how it affected the men at her table.

She couldn't know how it made Demi feel, though, for Demi was uncertain of her own emotions on the matter. He was not of the Order, that much was clear. The Order of Solace, while it prepared its Handmaidens for all varieties of sexual interest, made it clear that no Handmaiden was ever to be servant to any but the Order itself. Games of dominance and submission, sharper pleasures, all were accepted, but a collar and a leash? No Handmaiden would allow such a thing.

But if not of the Order, what then? There were too many similiarities in his manner, even his way of speaking, for it to be coincidence. Jarron, Adam, and Nigel wouldn't know it, but Demi did. And Caramin knew she'd be able to tell.

The woman was either taunting her or teasing her, one or the

other, Demi thought as Caramin lingered overlong with a touch on
Jarron's hand. She smiled at him too sweetly, fluttered her thick dark
lashes at him too much. They might've been the only two at the table.
In other circumstances Demi might not have minded—after all,
when kings and queens from different provinces socialized, it was to
be expected they might spend more time in conversation with one
another than with the peons sharing their table.

This was different, however. Demi knew it. Adam knew it, too.
Jarron didn't seem to notice, but mayhap he was so taken with the
flirtation he didn't notice how the conversation flowed between them
while excluding the others. Or he didn't notice because he lacked the
social skills Caramin had so clearly cultivated.

Demi looked across the table at Gailen, but his attention was taken
up by his mistress. If he minded her lack of attention, he didn't show
it. Adam and Nigel had fallen into deep conversation at their end of
the table, lowered voices and sly grins.

Demi was the only one left without a partner. She concentrated on
her food, savoring the flavors and ignoring all else. It wasn't the first
time she'd been in such a position, but she didn't like it any better
than she ever had.

Later, dismissed with surprising swiftness by Caramin, Jarron and
Demi were shown to their rooms by another black-clad servant. A
maid this time. She was also blond.

"Caramin has a preference," Demi said when the door had closed
behind the maid.

"Don't we all?" Jarron pulled her closer, mouth already seeking
hers, his cock already hard through his trousers.

He was already lifting her skirts to find her flesh beneath, his fingers rubbing and stroking with such skill she responded quickly—
though not as fast as him. His breath was already harsh with desire
when he took her to the bed and stripped out of his clothes, helping
her do the same with a fervent, focused desire she welcomed after so
many days suffering from his inattention.

He fucked into her with his fingers, thumb pressing just so upon her clitoris until she shivered, ready for him. But he didn't enter her. Jarron curled her fingers around his prick, urging her to stroke him as he fucked into her fist, even as he used his fingers inside her. Faster, the pleasure building, he moved against her, and she gave up to it the way she always did in the matter of what he asked of her in the bedroom.

She came with a small cry and watched his face work as he pumped against her. He wet himself with the hand that had been inside her. He closed his eyes, brow furrowed, biting his lower lip. Sweat stood out on his forehead. He muttered her name.

She thought he would finish in a moment or two, but when he didn't, she moved to open her legs for him. Jarron opened his eyes, gave the barest shake of his head. He fucked against her faster, breathing hard.

But it wasn't until he put his other fingers to her throat, collaring her with his hand instead of a band of leather, that he finally climaxed.

# Chapter 24

Caramin was not a woman to waste time. She'd called all four of the other monarchs not into her equivalent of a War Room, but into her private chambers, where being the only female seemed not to fash her in the least. She served them honeyed mead and pastries and bade them sit in comfortable chairs while she lounged on a set of tufted cushions and drew smoke from a mouthpiece connected to a long tube attached to a bowl, though not like the ones Jarron was used to. She called it a hukah and had made available mouthpieces and tubes for every one of them, though so far none had partaken.

"I understand the hour is egregiously early, my lords, but there is much work to be done and much merriment to be had, and we must accomplish the first if we wish to indulge in the second." Caramin looked at Jarron. "My lord Bydelay, what a pleasure to have you joining us at last. There was some concern you'd stay away."

Jarron looked 'round the room at the other men whose names and faces he knew so overwell but whom he'd never actually met. "I thought about it."

"As did I," grumbled Henrik Toulosh, the portly, red-faced premier of the Fifth Province. "Nasty long journey to get here, wot? And for what, I ask you? So that we might argue over who's going to be the first to carry the bone in his mouth?"

"My dear Henrik—you don't mind if I call you Henrik, do you?" Caramin smiled so sweetly it might've been easy to miss the spark in her gaze.

"So long as I might call you Caramin." Henrik lifted his plate of pastries, all half eaten.

"I propose we all toss away the burden of our titles and address each other as the bosom companions I'm fair certain we shall become." Caramin offered this seriously as she leaned forward on her cushions and looked at every man in the room.

Henrik Toulosh of the Fifth. Bander Mezzinghast of the Third. Kenston Deporter from the Fourth. And finally, Jarron Bydelay of the Second. Caramin lingered overlong on him, Jarron thought, but he met her gaze without looking away. She smiled slightly, then addressed the room again.

"My friends, and I speak to you as friends because I am certain that's what we shall be before all of this is over. The time has come for the Five Provinces to join hands and stand beneath the wedding canopy, so to speak."

"I've already got two wives," said Bander with a nervous twist of his fingers in the front of his jacket. "I'll be fair broken if I take on another!"

Caramin trilled laughter, tossing back her head so the pale, sleek column of her throat worked. She sipped at more smoke before answering him, but when she did, she gave him the full force of her attention in such a manner he blushed fiercely. "My dear Bander. I speak not of a physical marriage, though in the company of such a fine set of gentlemen a lady does have inclination to imagination."

Again, she looked at Jarron. Heat rushed to his face. He understood how Bander felt. Jarron, however, didn't pluck nervously at his clothes or look away—if Caramin had a game at which she played, he was determined not to merely be a pawn.

Her smile quirked just so once more, and she again looked 'round the room. "No, I speak of a marriage of state. Of our lands and governments. It has long served us all to work together for trade, but as times changed and resources become scarce and new ones discovered, our previous arrangements must needs also come under the consideration of change. Yet all of us have found ourselves weighed by seasons of protocol and the advice of ministers, advisors, or secretaries whose duties are not to enhance our lives or those of our subjects, but to increase the amount of coin in our treasure rooms and, I daresay, in their own purses."

"And what's wrong with that, I ask?" This came from Henrik, who stabbed a pudgy finger into the air. "What is wrong with acquiring coin, wot? I say naught. I like my pretty things and so does my wife, my daughters . . . Sinder's Balls, woman, so do my people! The Fifth is a prosperous land. Why should we not continue to be so?"

Henrik should watch his tongue, Jarron thought, watching Caramin's face as the premier spoke. Woman she might be, but she didn't approve of the casual address. He couldn't blame her. Henrik was a bit of a pompous braggart.

"Not every person in your land prospers," Jarron said aloud.

All eyes turned to him. Heat flushed him again, and he tasted sweat when he licked his upper lip. Demi had woken before him this morning and encouraged him to drink some of her specially brewed tea—for calmness, she'd said. It didn't sit well with him now, but he kept his chin up anyway, refusing to let the others see that their inspection of him made him anxious.

"What's that?" Henrik leaned forward. "What say you, Bydelay?"

"I said that not every person in your land prospers as you do."

"Of course they don't. I'm the premier, wot? It's right for me to be above the others. My family's been on the throne in the Fifth for a quiverful of seasons. We own it. We deserve it."

"And your family took it long ago from those who owned it then. As did mine. Surely you're not suggesting that Caramin's suggestion of us joining together means that we give up the benefits and rights of our lineage." Of the others, Kenston Deporter was the only one Jarron had ever met. They'd gone to school together, though Kenston was older and had been there only for one twelvemonth when Jarron was just starting. Their fathers had been friendly, however, and Jarron had met Deporter's parents on several occasions.

"No. Not that. But I'm saying Henrik's assertion that his entire province is prosperous is fallacious. It has to be. Every one of our provinces has its poor. Some more than others." Jarron carefully didn't look at Bander, whose province was the largest but widely thought of as the poorest ruled.

"I'm not suggesting we give up our privileges, my goodness. No. What I am suggesting is a coming together." Caramin sent a slow smile around at all of them.

"Unification," Jarron said. "It's what they're calling it in the streets."

"They're calling it integration in the Fourth," Kenston said. "Some groups have been marching for it. Passing out leaflets. I've had no fewer than a dozen petitioners in the past month asking for audience to outline the reasons they're for it, and these aren't common street thugs, gentlemen. These are merchants and farmers who've been cut deeply by taxes. Taxes, I might add, that have not been raised since before my father ruled. Some of us might be concerned about living on a grand scale, but in the Fourth it's all we can do to collect enough to pay for repairs to the capital city. There's never enough to cover the costs of the other responsibilities we have—orphanages are in disrepair, our streets are full of holes, we can't even manage the upkeep on the train rails. I don't need to tell you how that affects our ability to send and receive the products we're supposed to be selling and buying in order for my people to pay the taxes that will provide the money to repair the train so that we can send and receive those products. . . ." Kenston paused for a breath and tossed out his hands. "I, for one, need to hear more of what Caramin is proposing. The Fourth Province needs help. We are a large province with much to offer, yet we're struggling."

Henrik shoved another pastry into his mouth. "You can scarcely blame the Fifth for the Fourth's unfortunate lack of prosperity."

For a moment, Jarron thought Kenston might get up and punch Henrik in the face, but Caramin's sweet laughter turned both men's heads toward her. She was somewhat of a witch, with her dark eyes and pale hair, that red mouth. A witch who knew what she wanted and how to get it, Jarron thought.

"And you, Bander," she coaxed. "What is your thought upon this joining I suggest?"

He gave her a nervous, twitching smile. "I don't like it."

Both of her brows arched. "Pray, do tell me why not?"

"I have enough to deal with on my own, without adding the troubles of you lot." He pointed at Henrik. "Your province is rich with luxuries that do us little good and would only set the mouths of my people watering. And you, Kenston. Your land's atrociously misman-aged, though I suppose it's not your fault as we know it was your grandfather who squandered so much of the Fourth's national coin on building all those railways."

"The railway system of Fourth is what allows the Third to gain access to any place other than its own borders," Kenston replied sol-idly, frowning. "You folks would still be packing yourself on mules if not for the trains my grandfather built."

Bander shrugged and pointed at Jarron. "And you . . . well . . . the Second is doing well enough, but we've all heard the stories about how little control you have over your subjects—how they're marching in the streets for this unification because it's the only way they can feel safe their province will continue. How they want the control of decid-ing who to join with, rather than simply being . . . taken over."

Jarron got on his feet at that, heart pounding. "Who says such a thing?"

The room was silent. He looked around at each of them. Caramin drew in a breath of smoke and let it out, her dark eyes holding his, but she said naught.

"It's rumor and gossip," Kenston said after a moment. "They say you've not taken a wife."

"Neither have you, I might point out."

Kenston smiled. "But I do have an official escort, and I've named his son as my heir."

"You, on the other hand, have taken a Handmaiden," said Bander. "Which is true, as we've all seen her with you."

"A Handmaiden and not a wife because you don't want a child," put in Henrik. "That's what we hear. If we hear it, surely the citizens of the Second hear it, too. And what worth is a king without a son to carry on after him?"

"Or a daughter," murmured Caramin almost lazily, though her gaze sparked once more.

"An heir," Bander said. "You don't have one and the word is you plan to never get one."

Jarron thought upon a great many replies to these words, which were not idle accusations but truth. He'd been a fool to think nobody would mutter about his sending for Demi. A fool to believe none of his peers in the Five Provinces would hear of it, too. He straightened his shoulders and ignored the sudden rush of tingling in the soles of his feet and his palms, the sudden scratchiness of his throat.

Now was not the time to fall ill.

"I've not yet named an heir, this is true. But I have a goodly number of sisters and a fair number of nephews as well, any of whom could be named my successor. I have time."

"Not if you die tomorrow," Bander said. "Then what would happen? The Second would fall into chaos, or perhaps even civil war. Provinces have been torn apart for lesser reason than being left without a leader."

"People covet being told what to do and how to act. They need assurances." Caramin said this in a low, silky voice that once more drew every man's attention, including Jarron's. She stood and looked him in the eye. "Most do, at any rate. There are so few true leaders in this world, Jarron. Surely you see that and can understand why what our friends are saying is true."

He swallowed against the itch in his throat. "I understand. But I'm here, am I not? I'm willing to discuss this . . . unification. Integration. Whatever it is you call it."

"You're not in favor of it. I can see that written as neatly in your eyes and the set of your mouth as though you'd taken a pen and ink and written it on your skin." Caramin stepped closer.

She smelled of sweet smoke, not herb but somewhat equally as intoxicating, and faintly of perfume. Entirely of woman. Jarron's breath hitched when she fixed him with her gaze, which was frank and unflinching and offered a promise he knew he had to be imagining.

She tilted her head the tiniest bit, looking utterly fetching though not at all as innocent as the gesture was meant to be. "Jarron, my dear friend. I understand your hesitation. I've not even completely outlined my plan for how this will all work. And you . . . you are a proud man, are you not? You don't want to give up your crown for another."

"Who does?" Henrik said loudly. "Sinder's Balls, woman, nobody in this room would willingly give up being the ruler of all!"

"I would." Kenston stood. "For the love of the Fourth Province, I would be willing to listen to what Caramin has to say. Of all the Five, the First is the most prosperous of all, despite its lack of natural resources."

"So . . . you'd just hand over your entire province to her? Make it part of the First?" Henrik shook his head, clearly flabbergasted.

Kenston gave them all equal, steady looks, then nodded at Caramin. "Not as casually as you make it sound. But aye. I think I would consider a union."

"But . . . but . . . she's a woman!" This from Bander, who'd turned crimson.

"So are all your wives," Caramin said with just the slightest curl of her lip, "and yet you seem to take their counsel quite to heart."

"And what of you, Jarron?" Kenston asked. "What say you? As of yet we are at two and two. You'd be the one who tips it."

Again, with all eyes upon him, Jarron fought the urge to run a hand over his cheeks to make sure they remained smooth. Unblemished. He forced himself to remember that they stared at him the way they'd looked at each other—not from pity or fascination. They looked at him as an equal, or if not an equal at least a peer. Even so, he had to clear his throat several times before he could answer, and when he did, he looked at Caramin.

"I've not yet decided. How can I? We've spoken of only the barest of ideas. Naught permanent. I don't disagree with you, Kenston, the First Province is an exceptionally prosperous and well-run province, due no doubt to Caramin's skilled . . . hand."

Her lips curved at that small hesitation, as though she'd read his mind. Her gaze fell briefly to the arm of the chair in which Jarron had been sitting, and the small hasp bored into the wood there. Just the thing for keeping a chain held tight, though of course it was empty now. He'd let his fingers rest on it and could still feel the cool metal.

"But you don't trust me?" she asked.

Jarron pulled in a slow breath, the way he did when breathing in the smoke from a bowl, though now he just tasted her. She still stood very, very close. He could have grabbed her without problem, though once he had her he was fair certain he'd be unsure of what to do with her. "I need to know more. That's all."

"You don't distrust me then. How lovely." She made it sound as though he'd offered her a lover's gift, somewhat pretty set upon a golden pillow. She looked at the others. "Gentlemen, it is not my intent to set this before you with an ultimatum. This symposium is meant for the purpose of intellectual discourse, so that we might all benefit from what is decided. I've no issue with being the one to become the official sovereign of the Five Provinces combined, but neither did I bring you here to slaughter you all so that I might take everything you own."

Henrik and Bander leaped to their feet at once, and Kenston put his hand to his side at the sound of her laughter. Only Jarron didn't move. Caramin waved a hand to keep her guards, who until now had remained silent in the shadows, back.

"Have I frightened you? I just said that was not my intent. But that you wouldn't have considered it yourself surprises me, my friends. Surprises me greatly indeed." She gave Jarron another assessing look. "You don't seem afraid."

"You'd be a madwoman to kill all of us, no matter how easy it might be for you. No matter what turmoil's happening in our provinces, I would say the loyals still outnumber those who are not. You'd need quite an army to march on each of the other four and take them without a great loss to yourself, along with everything you'd be willing to kill for."

"And you don't think me mad enough?"

He shook his head and found a smile for her that seemed to set her back a step. "No. Not quite. Determined and bold as fire, aye, but we know that well enough. Used to having your way, that as well. And smart? Land Above, Caramin Ahavat, have I ever met a sharper mind than yours?"

"You enjoy sharp things, Jarron Bydelay?" Caramin murmured.

For one moment, one heartbeat, one breath, one sigh, the room was empty but for the two of them.

"With statements like that, it's no wonder I'd not consider joining with you, much less bending over that you might impale me the way you do your companion!" Henrik sputtered, crumbs flying. "I'll keep my arse unbuggered, thank you very much."

Caramin turned her gaze from Jarron and laughed again so merrily it seemed impossible she might be angry . . . though Jarron thought she was. "Henrik, my friend. If I wanted to bugger your ass I'd have had it twice already, with you begging beneath my touch."

Henrik sputtered more, shaking a fist but seemingly unable to speak. Bander, however, let out a squeaking gasp and fumbled again at the front of his jacket. Kenston, on the other hand, looked amused and covered his mouth to hold back what Jarron suspected was a laugh.

"For the love of the Land Above, man, get hold of yourself," Jarron snapped. "If you've no mind to discuss any of this in a reasonable manner, then get you gone and find out what we choose when it happens."

"When an army comes knocking at my borders, you mean? Because that's what will happen should you refuse her!" Henrik shouted. "Don't think I don't know it. She wants what she wants, aye? Used to having it, is she? Well, I'm not going to give up everything I have in order to become this woman's puppet."

Caramin looked at him so calmly Jarron had to admire her. "I have an army. You have an army. We all do. Mine, of course, is bigger, better equipped, and I daresay, rather better trained than any of yours . . . but then you've all had the luxury and privilege of playing at the monarchy, while I've had to be prepared to fight for my crown since before I took it. That changes a person, gentlemen. My father did not name me as his heir and die conveniently just as I became of age."

Bander squeaked again. Henrik glowered. Kenston did naught.

"Nor did he train me from my childhood to replace him, then generously step down so that I might take over." She shot a glance at Jarron, then at all of them. "No. My father, Void take him, was a madman."

"A trait it seems he passed along," muttered Henrik.

Caramin ignored him. She fixed each man with a steady, hard gaze. "I took the throne from my father. And I have not a single doubt that I could do the same to all of you."

She held up a hand before any of them could speak, and though Jarron hadn't intended to say anything, he was surprised Henrik shut his mouth.

"However. I don't wish to take anything from you. I find service is ever so much more palatable when willingly given." Her sweet smile was entirely at odds with the speech she'd just given, yet Jarron had no trouble seeing exactly how she'd been able to raise an army against her own father. "Discussions are ended for the day. Go and enjoy my hospitality, my friends. We shall convene here tomorrow morning at the same time and talk about my plans for the Five. If you wish to leave my house before then, you'll find no opposition from me. Yet know that if you leave, you'll not be invited back. You'll have to stand against not only me but whoever stands with me. I'm willing to discuss all manner and combinations of how this unification might take place, and all the outcomes we might expect without pushing for my place to be at the head of the table . . . but I assure you, gentlemen, I am no wilting flower. Nor a buggerer, though I daresay, Henrik, you protest so mightily I must needs wonder if mayhap you don't have a secret longing for the act."

Silence. Kenston's eyes gleamed with admiration. Bander refused to look at anything but the floor, while Henrik fumed, mouth opening and closing without saying a word. Jarron looked at all of them in turn and when he turned to Caramin, found her staring at him.

"Go and enjoy my hospitality," she repeated in a lower voice, one that sent shivers up and down his spine. "I believe you will find it most satisfactory."

# Chapter 25

In House Bydelay Demi had been more than happy to wait for Jarron in his rooms, but here in Caramin's palace she'd had no such contentment. The guest rooms, while adequately and even luxuriously appointed, were not familiar. Demi spent more of her life than not acclimating to new places, and it disturbed her to be unable to do so now, but that was the truth of things. She felt out of place without Jarron, and so sought the company of others to help pass the time until he returned.

She wasn't alone, even if her reasons were her own. Caramin had a full and lively court of lords and ladies devoted to her amusement and service, along with a countless number of secretaries both male and female determined to advise her on any and all matters related to the running of the First Province. Demi knew this before the noontime chime had rung because of one particularly chatty courtier, a certain Lady Wendola Flannert, an early riser who enjoyed brisk exercise, strong chai, and dogs. She had two of them, tiny things that disappeared beneath her skirts to rustle alarmingly.

Demi had come across this good woman while seeking her breakfast. Apparently Wendola was somewhat of an oddity amongst the others of Queen Caramin's household, for though the queen herself had called for a meeting with the sun barely over the horizon, the rest of the company was still abed. So said Wendola, and Demi knew this only to be partly true—the lords, ladies, and guests might be still sleeping, but the servants were sure to have risen even before the light of day. Even so the halls were quiet, the pair of them the only ones breaking their fast, and as Wendola had a great deal to say about a great many people, Demi sat and listened attentively.

"You're King Jarron's Handmaiden, of course. He's the only one with one right now. I've seen others, aye, I have." Wendola nodded. "My third cousin on my mother's side, Edward his name is, oh, he lives so very far away. He had a Handmaiden once upon a time. And I'm fair certain Jillian Kentwith kept one for some months last summer, as she entirely disappeared from court and didn't even travel to the summer palace, can you imagine! But she looks ever so much happier now, so I suppose whatever went on helped her."

"That is our purpose," Demi said quietly, stirring her chai. She'd eaten half a buttered biscuit while Wendola had consumed an entire platter of hotcakes drenched in rich syrup.

"Tell you true, I know it, I do. I've heard all about you. The Order of Solace. Such a pleasant name. Of course, there's not much solace to be had around here." She giggled into her napkin and gave Demi a knowing look. "The queen isn't much one for it, if you know what I mean."

"I don't, I'm afraid. You mean she doesn't practice the Faith?"

"No, no. Well, she doesn't, at least not that I would know, and I would know, you know."

Demi blinked slowly. "Would you?"

"Tell you true, of course. I used to wait upon her myself, in my younger days, that was not so long ago of course, I'm not so old now. But now she has him, of course, her companion—"

"Gailen?"

"Aye, Gailen, indeed! Of course he takes care of everything she needs. She's sent away even her maids, you know, so that he might dress her and undress her. He does her hair. He applies her cosmetic, I'm told, and with such a light hand, ah, well, some of the ladies hereabouts could use some lessons from him, I daresay."

"It sounds as though he makes her quite happy."

Wendola chortled. "Tell you true, that is exactly it. Before he came along she was quite dissatisfied with her life, you know. What with her father and all. I mean, really, what young girl could survive such a thing without being at least a little upset, I ask you?"

Demi had heard only pieces of Queen Caramin's story, but they'd all been bad. "Yet she has managed to rule the First for a long time and is well beloved, aye? So it all worked to her favor."

"And to mine," whispered Wendola with a naughty giggle. "After all, I'd have been married off by now to some old man with bad breath and a bald head, had I not been taken in by the queen to serve her court."

"You didn't wish to be married?"

"Oh . . . Land Above, I suppose I'd like to be married someday, of course. It's good to be with someone, you know. To have children. Though I suspect my days for children are past time. But still, aye, I suppose I'd not mind to find a husband. If I could pick just one." She laughed again and dropped several bits of sausage to the floor by her hem, where they disappeared with only the slightest scuffle. "But fortunately, our lady queen does not insist upon matchmaking, nor does she promote unwanted monogamy."

Demi was a firm believer in behaving by the rules of whatever house in which she'd found herself—if Wendola sought to shock her, she'd be disappointed. "There are many places in which multiple spouses are considered commonplace, even expected. There are even interpretations of the Faith that promote it."

Wendola studied Demi for a moment, then tucked the last piece of hotcake into her mouth and chewed slowly. She swallowed and licked syrup from her lips. "What do you think about it?"

"Me? I've no opinion."

"Everyone has opinions."

Demi smiled. "I should imagine that if I were in a position to be wed, I would choose to join my life with someone who wanted only to be with me, as I would wish to be solely with him. But that is not to say that I believe there can be only one mate for each person—if I were to find myself faced with loving more than one person at the same time, I might change my mind."

"But you don't have to think about it," Wendola said.

"No."

"Because you're not going to get married."

"I might, someday, when my time with the Order has come to an end, though I've no prospects at the moment."

Wendola winked. "Not your handsome king, then, aye?"

Demi made to answer but saw a familiar figure across the room and found only the words to say, "No. I think not."

Wendola looked where Demi was looking. "He's the captain of the King's Guard, true? What d'you call him? The King's Lion?"

"Aye."

Wendola shivered. "I know some of the ladies eyed him up right away, but I'll tell you true. He gives me the quakes."

Erekon was looking over the sideboard buffet and pointing out his choices to the serving boy. He hadn't looked even once in Demi's direction, but she would be foolish to think he didn't know she was there. She looked at her own plate instead of him.

"Why is that?"

"It's no secret Queen Caramin's in favor of a great deal more openness than some might approve of her. She allows her personal tastes free rein of course, and that means the people who wish to attend her are often of the same inclinations, you know."

"I know," Demi murmured though Wendola's pattering conversation didn't truly seem to need an affirmation.

"Well, even for this house, that man looks a little stern."

Demi burst into a surprised chuckle, then covered her mouth with her fingertips. Too late, Erekon had turned. Seen them both. He looked without smiling.

"See what I mean?" Wendola hissed. "He looks as though he might bite you, not in loveplay, but because he wanted to eat you."

"He's very serious and very stern, aye, but that's his job."

"It's more than that. He'll find no shortage of ladies willing to bend to him I wager, but I'm not one of them."

"You like to be on the other side of the leash, is that it?" Demi murmured, watching Erekon move toward them but not really paying attention to Wendola.

"By the Arrow, no, but nor am I interested in pain!" Wendola shuddered and got to her feet. A small yip emerged from her skirts, but she ignored it and moved away from the table. "He looks to have a heavy hand."

"Not so heavy," Demi said under her breath, but Wendola had already scurried away, leaving an empty spot at the table.

Erekon set his plate down and took a seat without asking if she minded. He said naught to her, just dug into his plate of hotcakes. Lifting the fork to his mouth. Chewing. Swallowing.

Demi watched, half mesmerized by the movement of his lips, jaw, his throat as he swallowed. She tried to see him as Wendola did, as frightening. But though she'd done her share of hating him and running from him, Demi could not remember ever being afraid of him. Of what he might do, aye. Of what she knew he would do, certainly. But of the man himself? Never.

"I've not shaved and my hair's a mess, I know it true. You needn't stare."

"You look fine, Erekon."

He jerked his chin toward the door where Wendola had gone. "She didn't seem to think so."

"You've apparently garnered yourself a reputation that has preceded you . . . else you've been up to some hijinks in the short time we've been here."

"Not to my knowledge. I spent a very quiet night outside your door."

This startled her, though it shouldn't have. "You did?"

Erekon shrugged and dug back into his food. "Jarron might believe himself capable of defending himself, but here we are in another monarch's palace along with the leaders of the other provinces. Four leaders in one place at the invitation of one who seeks to join them all? My duty is to protect him. Of course I spent the night outside his door."

"You think she means to . . . kill them?" Demi lowered her voice quickly, though they were still alone but for the servant—but servants had ears, too.

"No. I don't believe she does. But she could. Or one of the others could." Erekon shrugged again.

Demi shuddered and pushed her plate aside, having no appetite now though she'd woken ravenous. "I don't trust her."

Erekon laughed, low. "Sheathe your claws, kitten. What Caramin wants, she shall have. She's a queen, love. And you? Not."

Demi's stomach knotted itself tighter. "You accuse me of jealousy?"

He shrugged in reply, which did not suit her.

"Handmaidens do not suffer jealousy."

"Bollocks."

She hissed and pushed away from the table, but before she could get out of her chair Erekon had snagged her wrist and kept her still. His voice low, he looked 'round the still-empty room and back at her with such a fierce gaze she didn't try to get away. Only when she'd returned to her seat did he let her go, and Demi wished she hadn't laughed at Wendola when she said Erekon looked like he enjoyed inflicting pain.

She rubbed her wrist. "You are insufferable."

"Suffer me the way you refuse to suffer jealousy." He drank from his mug and set it down, wiped the back of his hand across his mouth. "Have you done what I asked?"

"Convince him to agree to unification? You grant me too much power. Jarron will make up his own mind on such a matter. It's not up to me."

"You have more sway over him than you know."

She hesitated before replying. "I know what influence I have, Erekon. And I still say you flatter me in that regard. Jarron is his own man. You might not like him—"

"I like him very much. I never said I did not."

"I don't understand you," she said. "You say you like him. Your duty is to him, your loyalty. And yet . . . Erekon, do you wish Jarron to give up being king of the Second Province and let another take it? Whether it's Caramin or one of the others? Think you true he can do no better than any of them?"

"You never understood me. Why start now? Just do as I tell you."

"And I never did as you told me; why should you expect that to suddenly change?"

They both stared across the table at one another, until finally he smiled. He ducked his head, the gesture just for the moment so charming she could not forget that once it was as though he'd set the stars in their places just for her. It didn't last. She was smarter than that, had too many bad memories to replace the good.

"Besides, I won't know until he returns what they talked about this morn. If he even shares it with me, which he may not."

"Ask him just after you've fucked him senseless. He'll tell you anything you want to know then."

He said it so flatly it became an insult, and she took it as one. "Who's the jealous one now?"

His lip curled, but he didn't deny it. This didn't make Demi feel any better. She didn't want Erekon's jealousy. Matters were already complicated enough.

"He'll talk about it with you. Or he'll have you in attendance when he talks about it with Adam. Either way, listen closely. Because this isn't a game, Notsah."

"I know it's not." She looked him over. "You think . . . you think he would lose, do you not?"

"If it comes to war . . . aye. Against the First, most definitely. Caramin's army is renowned. The woman led it against her father, for Sinder's sake, when she was but ten-and-seven seasons old."

"She's a strong woman."

Erekon nodded. "She's never once made any threat against the other four provinces. Never once tested her borders, not even to tease. She's been on the throne for twenty seasons, and in all that time, not once has she given anyone reason to think she could wipe them all out. But she could. Her army is magnificent."

"Now you do sound jealous," Demi said.

Erekon didn't smile, didn't even blink. "She has the finest soldiers in all the Five. And they are loyal to her. Well rewarded. Superbly trained. And there are so many of them, by the Arrow . . . if she wants to march on the other four, she could own them all. It would be a bloodbath, but she would win. I've no doubts."

"Mayhap you should join her. There is likely a place for you here."

Now he smiled. "You'd like that, aye? Get me out of House Bydelay, away from Jarron. So I can't tell him the truth about you? Are you still afraid of that, Notsah, because if I'd wanted to do it, I'd have done so already."

"Why haven't you?" she asked, genuinely curious.

"Because you're good for him." Erekon said this as flatly as he'd spoken before, but this time she took no offense.

"It's my duty."

"As it is mine to protect him. If I can't do it with my sword or my fists, then I must try to do it with whatever weapons I have at my hand."

"I'm not a weapon, Erekon."

"Not a weapon, no. A tool, mayhap."

Demi frowned and picked at her biscuit, though even the thought of a single bite churned her stomach and sent bile nudging her throat. "A gift. I am a gift."

Erekon made no smart reply and she looked up, expecting to see his sneer. He caught her off guard again, his face solemn, dark eyes gleaming with an emotion she thought she could name if she were brave enough. Erekon shook his head, that dark hair streaked with silver falling over his face.

"I'm no great soldier. I've never had to be great. Just good enough. There's no place for me in Caramin's army, even if I should feel the need to change my loyalties, which I do not. I love the Second Province. Born and raised there, I'll die there, too. But I don't believe that naught can ever change. Things must change. Must move on. The world does not stay in one season, and nor can we. If one quarter is true of what the unification promoters are saying is part of Caramin's plan, then the Second will be in a much better place than it would be with a king who is so focused on himself that he can't do what's best for the rest of us."

"Because he won't have a child? Won't name an heir, is that it?"

"If a man will barely force himself to attend a game of cards because it so cripples him," Erekon said, "how is he going to lead an entire province?"

"Give him time. Truly you don't think a game of cards is the most important talent a king can have."

Erekon leaned forward. "Caramin wants to join the Five together, Notsah."

She didn't correct him about her name but leaned forward, too. "That might be the best thing. I don't know. I can't be the one to decide that. Enough people seem to think it is the best choice, aye?"

"It's not for me to decide, either, and I'll abide with what my king decides. But Caramin wants not only to join them, she expects to be named the leader of all. And I know in my heart that Jarron will not agree to that. And if he does not . . ."

"You would protect him by encouraging him to fail?"

"It's not failure to admit you're not the best man for the job. Or the best woman," Erekon said. "Surely you of all people should understand that very well."

Blinking against a sting in her eyes, Demi sat back. "I thought you said I was good for him."

Erekon didn't answer. He stared, which was worse. He'd ever been well skilled at allowing his silence to fill in all the words she imagined he might say—and which were always worse than anything he did.

She got up, scraping the chair legs on the tile floor. More people had drifted in while they spoke, and this time Erekon didn't grab her arm to keep her in place. Demi composed herself with him watching her. Wanting him to see how little he affected her.

"Caramin gets what she wants . . . Redemption." Erekon stood, too.

"Mayhap this time she will be disappointed."

"In all of this?" Erekon waved a hand, not caring that he drew attention to himself. "Mayhap. But what if she decides she wants Jarron, sweetheart? What then?"

Demi swallowed a surge of sickness that had left her sweating and dizzy. She clutched the back of the chair and lifted her chin. Met his gaze. "Then I shall step away and let her have him, of course. Of course."

Erekon laughed and leaned too close, to nuzzle at her ear. "You always were a very pretty liar."

And then he left her there in the midst of strangers, all of them who knew her name while she had no idea of any of theirs.

# Chapter 26

She'd been ill earlier, blaming Erekon for the nausea that had spun her head so fiercely she'd had to lie down with a damp cloth on her eyes until Jarron returned. Now, however, Demi felt fine. Starving, even. Her stomach rumbled and she put a hand over it, feeling the slightly unfamiliar slickness of satin and silk.

"Hungry?" Jarron asked from his place beside her. They were in line to be announced. He didn't look excited by the prospect of having his name shouted out in front of a crowd, but he wasn't sweating or shaking, either.

"I am. You?" She tucked her arm through his and leaned close to sneak a kiss, intending to keep his mind from the night ahead.

He kissed her quite thoroughly. "Very. Caramin keeps a good kitchen, if what she served us today is any indication."

"She keeps a very good everything." Demi said no more. False praise was as bad as a lie.

"I should warn you . . ."

He trailed off and she turned to him. "Aye? What?"

"Kenston told me that dinners here are . . . unusual. At least to our standards."

She already knew that. "If you mean the main courses served off the bodies of naked men and women, I already heard of it."

"You did? When? Where?"

From behind the curtain that fell across the carved wooden doors leading to the dining room came the name of the couple who'd been in line four ahead of them. Demi paused, but Jarron was paying attention to her, not to how close they were getting to the front of the line. She leaned in closer to keep their conversation private—and thought abruptly of the breakfast room, when she'd done the same with Erekon. Too much secrecy had left a bitter taste in her mouth, but there was no help for it here. They were the last guests to arrive and therefore the last in line, but there were those waiting ahead of them, and discretion was ever a Handmaiden's virtue.

"There are always stories. Exaggerated, many of them. I've traveled a bit, Jarron, stories do get passed along."

"About me? Had you heard any of me?"

She smiled. "Tell you true, there were many stories of the elusive, handsome Melek Gadol Shetaya. How well he sat upon a horse, how eloquent his speeches. How well learned he was."

He snorted softly, but his eyes gleamed. "How ravaged his face? How disgusting his appearance?"

"There were those, as well," she said so that she didn't have to lie. "But I ignored them."

He kissed her as the line moved up again. "Those were the true stories."

"Exaggerated. Just as I suspect much has been aggrandized about Caramin's court."

"I don't think so," Jarron said, but then it was their turn. He took a deep breath as the footman waved them beyond the curtains.

Concentrating on giving Jarron her comfort at what she knew

would be another trial, Demi at first took his sharp gasp for anxiety. Only when she turned to look at the room in front of them did she understand. The stories had not been exaggerated.

The dining hall was not overlarge, not the size of House Bydelay's ballroom, for example. A long table, set for at least twenty, stood in the center of the room, while a large fireplace crackled merrily at one end and the doors through which they'd just stepped at the other. Curtains hung in vast folds of rich material over floor-to-ceiling windows, and the same rich coverings adorned the walls. This room had gas lighting, dozens of fixtures, and a hanging chandelier over the center of the table lit with at least a hundred tiny flames. Heavy carved furniture hugged the walls—sideboards groaning with dishes ready to be served as well as every manner of bottled beverage Demi had ever seen. This, however, was no more than she'd expected and had ever seen in any of the grand houses in which she'd served.

What set this room apart from any of the others were the additional decorations. At first glance they appeared to be statues. Men and women, clad in robes so sheer they might well have been entirely nude, stood in staggered rows along the table's length, one for each guest. Jewels glittered in their hair, at their ears, in their navels and their nipples. All wore thick lines of black cosmetic around their eyes. All had pale hair in varying shades of blond.

"*Does* she breed them for this?" Demi murmured and bit her tongue at once, though Jarron seemed not to have heard.

"King Jarron Bydelay of House Bydelay, the Second Province," said the footman, and the conversation died down just long enough for the announcement before buzzing back to life.

A near-naked pair stepped up from either side to lead them to their places. Jarron to the right of Caramin, Demi two spaces to her left with her companion, Gailen, between them. Amused, Demi waited for her escort to pull out her chair before she sat. She could feel him over her shoulder, presumably waiting to serve her. It was not an accustomed feeling.

The man to her left smiled but turned away at once to speak to the woman on his other side. The couple across from her were engaged in their own conversation, and the large flower arrangement would have made discussion difficult, at any rate. She tried to catch Jarron's eyes, assuming he'd be anxious and in need of her, but his attention was taken by Caramin.

Of course it was, Demi thought. It would be. All of this would lead to him falling into bed with Caramin, or if not, yearning after her. It was what Erekon had suggested and Demi knew to be true.

"Hello."

She startled a bit and turned slightly to her right to smile at the queen's companion. "Gailen, aye?"

He laughed. "Aye. And you are Demi. Short for Redemption."

He wasn't naked. Not even bare-chested. Whatever point Caramin had intended to make upon their arrival, she wasn't intent on making it now. Gailen was as fashionably attired as any of the men here, though in understated tones of gray and black, the only amount of color a tiny brooch in the shape of a heart, scarlet with rubies, over his real heart. There was no sign of a collar or a leash . . . but then Caramin didn't really need one, Demi thought, watching as Gailen's gaze went regularly to his mistress.

The same as hers did to Jarron.

The first course was announced in silvery tones, in an accent Demi didn't recognize, by a petite blonde at the end of the table. This wasn't entirely shocking—many formal dinners had such announcements. But as with everything else about Caramin's house, this had a small twist. The girl describing the first course—of boiled quail's eggs tucked inside wrappings of savory dough and baked with a crust of shaved, tart cheese, did so while stepping up onto the table and walking down the center of it. Her bare toes pointed before each step. She walked as delicately as an acrobat.

Demi hadn't noticed before that where there would normally be candelabras or other decorations there was an empty space down the table's middle. That explained the extra width. Demi watched the girl take step by careful step as she described the food. The girl stopped in front of Caramin, where she curtsied deeply. This could be no surprise to any of Caramin's courtiers, nor to the guests who'd attended dinner the night before. Of all the people seated at the table, only Jarron and Demi hadn't seen this display before. And yet all conversation ceased.

"Thank you, Salindra," Caramin said, and the girl tiptoed her way back across the table, leaped lightly down, and took her place again in the line.

The buzz of talking began again. Demi tried to catch Jarron's gaze across the table, but he was staring entranced at Caramin, who must've been most amusing, since he laughed.

"She'll give him back to you when she's finished," Gailen said lightly and gestured for the man standing behind Demi to fill her glass with spiced wine.

"He's not mine to keep." She should've said naught, she thought as soon as the words left her mouth, but Gailen didn't seem to mind.

He laughed instead. "Nobody ever is, are they? You can't own a person."

"Really?" She gave him a pointed look, though he wore a cravat instead of a collar. "Do you think so?"

Gailen studied her frankly and sipped from his own glass. "I know it's true. So do you, Redemption. Mayhap you'd like it to be different?"

"No." She shook her head. "If you can own someone, you can then be owned."

She thought of Erekon, who'd set out to make her his. Mayhap he'd not put her in a collar but the ring he'd offered for her finger had been a tight enough fit and the shackles he'd threatened had been real enough. No. Owning was too much.

"It's a big responsibility for both sides," Gailen said.

Caramin's trilling laughter set Demi's teeth on edge, and she clenched her jaw. She washed away the bitterness with good spiced wine, found it didn't taste as good as she'd hoped, and asked for water, instead.

"You'll like this dish," Gailen promised as the servants brought it out. "It's one of my favorites."

Demi sat back from her plate as two of the male servants, each as graceful as Salindra, served the food from atop the table instead of beside it. Bending, dipping, almost in a dance, they made sure each guest had a full plate. Then, as the other woman had done, they leaped down and took their places back in the line, faces impassive.

"You get used to it," Gailen murmured into her ear.

His voice, so close, and the heat of his breath, surprised a shiver out of her. Demi turned to look at him. He was smiling.

Demi returned it without thinking about it. "Does she serve every meal this way?"

"No. Just the special ones. She knows the stories. People expect somewhat grand and rather more . . . intimate . . . than this display. But it pleases her to tease."

Demi looked to the end of the table, the queen there. "Does it?"

Gailen didn't turn to look at his mistress but kept his even gaze on Demi. He had dark eyes, she saw. Not like the others. Blond hair, but dark eyes. Jarron's opposite.

"Sometimes." He cut into his egg and lifted his fork. "Eat. You should try it."

The food was delicious, each course announced and served by the same scantily clad and acrobatic servants. It was no meal served upon the naked bodies of slaves, but vastly more entertaining than that. Demi wondered if the others were disappointed or relieved. Dessert came, flavored ice that was all the sweeter for being so rare.

"She has it shipped in from beyond the mountains," Gailen explained. "We have a vast storeroom carved into the rocks, with ice cut from the river. I could show you, if you like. Tomorrow."

"Would she approve?" Demi's voice snagged on the word *she*.

Gailen looked over his shoulder. Caramin was still completely involved in serious discussion with Jarron, their heads bent together. He looked back at Demi.

"I believe she'll be busy tomorrow. She prefers me to keep myself occupied rather than be idle. And she believes in providing her guests with hospitality. You're a guest."

"One of many."

Gailen smiled again and leaned close. This time, Demi didn't pull away. "The others don't look me in the eyes."

"They don't?" Demi looked down the table at the other guests. The leaders of the Five Provinces, their wives or companions, their atten-dants. "Not a one, true?"

"How many look into yours?"

"I've not had the pleasure of meeting all of them."

Gailen spooned some ice and savored it for a moment. "How many would you wager? Half? More than that? Dressed as you are they might be more inclined, but clad as you were when you arrived, how many would you think might see your face and not your function?"

She had no answer for that at first and so spooned some of her own ice.

"I'm not required to play the part of host," Gailen added, scraping the bottom of his cup. "I'm the queen's companion. Not her husband. But if you wanted a tour of the palace, I could give you one. Seeing as how you and I have much in common."

"You think so?" Demi couldn't finish her dessert, had only nibbled at portions of the dinner. There'd been so much and it was all so rich. She sipped cool water, instead.

Gailen nodded, his dark eyes looking liquid in the gas lights. "You don't agree?"

From down the table came a burst of familiar laughter. Adam, tell-ing stories, Nigel at his side and looking fond. Before Demi could answer, Caramin rose and clapped her hands for silence. Gailen turned at once, and though she knew it was foolish, Demi felt a bit snubbed.

"My friends. I hope you've all well satisfied your stomachs. Please avail yourselves of my library, my social hall, your own guest quarters. Those of you who choose to view my after-dinner entertainments, they'll begin in the drawing room shortly." She looked down the table with a smile so bright, so lovely, Demi found it difficult to imagine the woman as anything but innocent. Of course she knew better.

Gailen stood as the servant behind Demi helped with her chair. He offered his arm. Demi looked at once to see Jarron doing the same for Caramin. She took Gailen's arm with a murmur of thanks. It meant naught. She knew that. It was polite to escort other partners from dinner, especially if you'd been conversing with them.

"I presume we're going to join the after-dinner entertainments," she said.

Gailen laughed. "Tell you true. I should think so."

Only a few followed Caramin into the drawing room. The doors closed behind them. She turned, a twinkle in her gaze that seemed more in keeping of what Demi thought of the woman's personality.

"Ah, you brave souls." Caramin clasped her hands together, just below her breasts. "Welcome. I can assure you that no matter what you've heard, I do not run a brothel. Nor revel in debauchery."

"Pity, that," Adam said none too softly, and Caramin's eyes went to him at once.

"Enjoy," she said and held out her hand to Gailen. "Come, love. Sit by me."

He did but not before giving Demi a polite half bow. "It was my pleasure to attend you at dinner."

"And mine to be so attended," she answered instinctively.

Jarron was there to take her arm before Gailen had even left her. Demi didn't care overmuch for being passed like a bowl of herb, but when Jarron smiled down at her, she lost a bit of her unease. They settled together onto a comfortable settee and though he offered her a smoke from what Demi recognized as a hukah, she refused. The room already seemed overwarm, and there was a servant there at once with a glass of cooled water for her. She was grateful there was to be some sort of show, as she was in no mood for idle chatter.

She wasn't surprised when the dance began. Nor when it became somewhat more real. She was most certainly not shocked at how avidly the guests and members of Caramin's court watched the dancers fuck on the floor in front of them all in a writhing, moaning pile of flesh, or even when a few of the observers paired off in dark corners to act out their own fantasies.

In fact, when Jarron stood and held out his hand to help her up as well, Demi expected him to take her into the shadows and join them. She looked at the performers, lost in their desires, and then at her patron, who leaned to kiss her mouth. She closed her eyes at that kiss, waiting for him to tell her what he wanted.

"Go to bed," Jarron told her. "I'll be along later."

At that she nodded and offered him a curtsy of assent. She turned and made her way out the door and into the hall. In the bedroom she closed the door and stripped out of her clothes and bathed and slipped naked into the cool sheets, where she buried her face into the pillows and could no longer hold back her sobs.

Even with everything she knew of him and had ever known, this had surprised her.

# Chapter 27

We shall take a vote." Caramin said this elegantly and simply, as though she expected no dispute.

Likely she didn't, Jarron thought, but she would have one. From Henrik, in less than a moment. Perhaps from Bander, if he got up the courage. Jarron himself hadn't yet decided if he meant to go against her.

She was charming, that woman. Smart, by the Arrow, so smart it made him feel a bit of a dunce. And cunning. A triply threatening combination.

Jarron felt threatened. He'd not have admitted such, not even to Adam, who'd have understood. Not to Demi, who'd have tried to soothe him. He didn't have to admit it to Caramin herself. She could tell.

It amused her, he thought, watching as she set up the hukah and offered it around to the men in the room. She enjoyed knowing she'd set them on edge. She might have played them harder and for longer with her fluttering lashes and the graceful gestures she made with every word. She didn't. She laid everything on the table in front of them and dared them to defy her.

"A vote?" Henrik asked. "For what?"

"For who shall take the seat at the head of the table," Caramin said. "The table being the entire Five Provinces, of course. And on the title. I like *emperor*, myself. Because that's what we'll be making. An empire strong enough to rival any of the others."

"So you agree it shall be one of us," Bander said. "Emperor. Not empress."

Caramin took a breath of smoke and held it for a long moment before allowing it to seep from her mouth. "My dear Bander, I made no such agreement. I would be happy to be titled emperor, despite my gender."

"What good is a vote here?" demanded Henrik, refusing Caramin's offer of the hukah. "We'll all vote for ourselves, of course, and what good will that do?"

"We could draw lots, though I think you're the sort of man who'd insist upon redrawing should he get the wrong one." Caramin shrugged and leaned back against her cushions, languid but not lazy. "A vote, gentlemen, to end the day. I suggest it might be the only way we can move forward without violence. It will take but one of us to be unselfish enough to bend to another."

Jarron had spent a good portion of the night before in Caramin's company, listening to her outline her plans for joining the Five into one. How each would retain its borders, its customs, and its leadership, though each former monarch would report to the one who ruled over all, much the way his Ministers of Advice reported to him though each had their own duties and power within their realm. How taxes, trade, and commerce would be standardized, with monies from wealthier provinces disseminated into the poorer ones so that all would benefit. He'd listened, drunk more on her vision than the wine and smoke she'd offered, and had stumbled into his bed this morning as the sun crept over the horizon with all of it swirling his head into mush.

"Jarron?"

He turned at the sound of her voice, having drifted a bit from lack of sleep. "Caramin."

She laughed prettily. "What say you? A vote?"

He agreed with Henrik—a vote would do little good when it seemed most likely each ruler would vote on his or her own behalf. He nodded anyway. "Aye. I'll vote."

Caramin snapped and one of her manservants, thankfully dressed this morn in more than a sheer robe, stepped forward with a plain black wooden box. "Lovely. To do this equitably, I've provided each of you with a piece of paper and a pen. Please write the name of who you wish to become emperor of this newly formed empire and put it in the box."

Jarron scribbled his name, folded the paper, and passed it forward where the manservant put it in the box. All the others did the same. Caramin watched them all with a small smile before offering the box to Henrik.

"You read them," she offered.

He opened the lid and began removing the papers one at a time. "Jarron Bydelay. Henrik Toulosh. Bander Mezzinghast. Caramin Ahavat. And . . . curse you to the Void, Kenston! Another for Caramin! Sinder's Bloody Balls, man, what by the Void are you thinking?"

"It would seem," Caramin said as smugly as a cat licking cream, "that I have won the vote."

"No! I'll not have it!" Henrik stood and slammed the box onto the table so hard it cracked and broke apart.

Caramin made a sad noise and pulled the pieces of wood together. She looked genuinely distressed as she cradled them in her palms, then turned her gaze toward Henrik. "You broke my box."

"I'll break more than that, you bitch." Henrik spat. "I'll not agree to one bedamned word of any of this. No treaty. No union. No bloody fucking empire! If you want the Fifth Province, you'll have to send your army and take it from me, but I warn you, I'm no pox-addled madman like your daughter-fucking father!"

Silence thundered.

Caramin stood, her face white. Her voice low and shaking. "Get you gone from my house, sirrah."

"Everyone knows it. It's why you killed him, aye? Because he used to creep into your bed—"

"Enough!" Caramin cried, standing.

It shut Henrik up, for all his swagger, when her guards stepped from their places along the wall and pointed their swords at him. Henrik's guards, fewer in number and not nearly so well equipped, moved but too slow.

"I could have your head cut off for that," Caramin said.

"You'd start a war over an insult?" Henrik was sweating, but motionless.

Beside him, Bander turned pale. Kenston stayed still, too, his eyes on Caramin. Jarron looked across the room to nod at Erekon, who'd not yet moved or motioned to his men. The room could easily become an abattoir with one wrong step.

"You've already started a war, Henrik, by your refusal to join us. You, and I suppose your lapdog Bander, aye? Tell me somewhat, will the pair of you join forces against me? You might have a slightly bigger chance of surviving. But only," Caramin hissed, "slightly."

Bander squeaked and shook. "My lady Caramin, I . . . I am . . ."

"He can't even bear this minor conflict without pissing in his trousers. Is that who you want on your side, Henrik?"

Henrik turned to Jarron. "What of you, Bydelay? You didn't vote for her. Do you stand with her, or against her?"

"Caramin has a great many good ideas," Jarron said. "I've not yet decided for or against supporting her in this venture."

"Well, I have," Kenston said. "I've already said the Fourth is in dire need of help. My people are starving. Our crops have failed too many seasons in a row, our fields too overseeded. I will gladly take a lesser place in the overall portrait to save those who depend upon me to lead them. I stand with Caramin."

"Bander?" Henrik demanded.

Bander shuddered again, his pale cheeks blooming crimson. "I . . . I . . . she has a vast and accomplished army, Henrik! Everyone knows it. And the things she says do make sense. Joining together will be good for the Third, too. We've suffered too much competition from Sergo, across the mountains. There've been threats of them testing our borders, next. If they decide to come across the mountains, well . . . I know we won't be able to defend ourselves. Even with the wall. Not without help."

Henrik drew himself up straight, immense belly trembling with his outrage. "Two for you, Caramin. Even without Bydelay, you've won this debacle of a vote. But you haven't won me, nor the Fifth. Leave us out of it, or attack us if you want. I'll meet you on the battlefield and die on it before I give anything over to you."

Caramin cleared her throat, a soft sound greatly at odds with Henrik's angry shout. "I'd hoped there would be no battles. That we could all agree on the issues. But if that's how you want it, Henrik, then go. By all means, go."

"Do you bring me war?" he asked, his voice at last trembling, but his gaze never wavering.

"Etiquette between monarchs demands I give you full notice," Caramin said softly, "though as you've heard, I gave my father no warning."

She held up a hand before anyone could speak.

"My father deserved no warning. Henrik, I do not declare war on the Fifth. But know you this—once we've determined the extent of this new empire and its laws, its trade routes, all of this . . . you will be left out of it. I have no qualms about making an embargo on trade with you."

Henrik blinked rapidly. "We don't need you."

"I will ruin you," Caramin said. "And you know it."

Henrik turned on his heel, the leather of his boot squeaking on the polished tiles. He snapped for his guards, who followed him. The room was quiet when he'd gone, but for Bander's sniffling and Kenston's sigh of relief.

Jarron watched as Caramin sat. She feigned calm but her fingers trembled as she brought the mouthpiece of her hukah to her lips, and she didn't keep the smoke inside her for nearly as long. She blinked rapidly, then smiled at them all.

"My friends. It would seem we are to be four, rather than five. But one great empire, overall."

Bander quaffed the entire contents of his wineglass. "By the Arrow, I hope you're right."

Demi had spent the morning with Gailen, who'd proven to be as charming a host as he'd been a dinner companion. Away from Caramin it was easier to see him as a man in his own right, rather than as part of her.

". . . And these were woven from Alyrian silk," Gailen said, describing some of the tapestries hanging in a sunny music room on the top floor, but he stopped when he saw her. "Demi?"

"I'm listening," she said. "Very lovely."

"You look a little pale. Sit, and I'll ring for some wine."

The thought turned her stomach. She took a seat on the chaise lounge. "Just water, please."

"Water it is." Gailen went to the wall and tugged one of the silk-tasseled cords that would ring someplace in the servants' quarters. Then he sat beside her and chafed her hands.

The intimacy surprised her, and Demi gently extricated her grasp. "I'm all right."

"Tell you true, you don't look well at all." He didn't pursue his grip on her fingers, though, and when the maid showed up he barked out an order for water and biscuits without even looking at her.

His forcefulness was so unlike his placid demeanor she blinked. "It's the dress, I'm afraid. It requires stays, and . . ."

"Handmaidens don't wear stays."

"Not usually, no. But in this dress, I must. I'm having a hard time catching my breath, that's all. I'll be fine." She smiled to show him she meant it, even as the world tipped a little, as though she'd been spinning.

"Why wear it, then? You're not at a formal dinner or a party."

Demi wet her lips, hoping the water arrived quickly. She didn't want to tell Gailen that she'd dressed in this gown this morn so that she might not look the part of Handmaiden but of a woman. That she even wanted or needed to remind her patron of such a thing was shameful, not to be admitted, even if she thought he might be one to understand.

"You look beautiful," he assured her when she didn't answer. "I just thought a Handmaiden always felt more comfortable in her own gown."

"That would be true," she told him with a hand on her belly as she sipped at the air, trying to keep herself from fainting.

"Here." With matter-of-fact fingers he unlaced her bodice and the top laces of her stays then pulled the material of her gown closed so that no glimpse of her flesh showed. "That should be more comfortable for you."

He'd moved so fast and without hesitation that Demi couldn't even feel affronted. And it did feel better, not entirely, but enough that when the girl arrived with the pitcher and cups, Demi could sip the water and not gulp it. Gailen dismissed the maid and filled his own cup, though he let it sit on the table without drinking from it.

"You know a lot about Handmaidens, Gailen." The world was spinning a little less, but she sipped slowly, anyway.

He laughed softly. "I suppose I do. I ought to, as I was raised in the Sisterhouse in Delvingdon."

She'd have choked had she not been sipping so carefully. "What?"

Gailen leaned back against the chaise and crossed one leg over the other. He looked at her seriously. "I thought . . . I assumed you'd have guessed as much. I saw you looking at me. I thought you knew."

"How would I know?" Demi put her cup on the table and her hands in her lap.

Gailen shrugged. "It's not a secret, though I don't share it with just anyone. Most people wouldn't understand."

"But you thought I would?"

"Don't you?" He gave her a half smile. "You, of all the people here, should."

"You serve Caramin as I would a patron, is that what you're trying to say?" She shook her head. "It's not done. The Order would never—"

"The Order of Solace had everything to do with the man I have become and naught to do with what I do. My service to Caramin is . . . complicated."

"All service to every patron is complicated," Demi said flatly. Then, curiously, "Do you . . . love her?"

At this, Gailen sighed and leaned to lift his cup to his mouth. He drank it dry and turned the cup in his hands before setting it back. He looked at her. "I do. As you love him."

She didn't try to deny it. "I thought I loved him before I ever even became his Handmaiden."

"And now?" He didn't question the details.

"Now . . . I fear much is changing, due in no small part to your mistress."

"I told you, she'll give him back when she's finished."

"I don't want him back when she's finished," Demi snapped. "I don't want her to have him at all."

Gailen's smile shifted a bit. "Does he know how you feel about him? I mean, have you told him you don't think of him as a patron any longer?"

"Does it not affect you," she queried in return, "if you love her so much?"

"Caramin has her reasons for what she does, and I can assure you, Demi, they're good ones. And they need not affect her affections for me. Or mine for her."

She looked into her bodice and began tugging the inner laces tight again, fingers fumbling. "No. I haven't told him."

"You ought."

She looked at him as she worked on the laces of her bodice. "That would be utterly foolish of me. Not my place. Not my purpose."

"If you love him . . ."

"I loved him," she corrected. "I loved the man he was. I was foolish and I thought I knew what love was."

"And you don't love him anymore?" Gailen's head tipped, his brow furrowed. "I don't understand."

"I don't know what I feel for Jarron. I have a duty to him, to provide him with absolute solace. To try, at least. To do my best for him. As I've done with any patron."

"But he's not any patron."

"No." She shook her head and stood a little shakily. "Nor do I need your advice upon this matter, sir."

Gailen stood, looking chagrined. "I plead your mercy, Demi. I do. I spoke out of turn. I just thought . . . I thought you had to tell him. Especially considering your condition."

The floor slipped from under her feet and she reached, grasping. Gailen caught her. Cradled her as he eased her back onto the couch. Offered her water.

"How could you know," she gasped, "when I've not even thought of the possibility until just this very moment?"

Gailen held the cup to her lips and let her drink before answering. "I could tell right away."

"But . . . how?"

He laughed softly and smoothed her hair away from her sweating forehead. "Call it a gift. Those of us who are can usually know about those of us who will be."

Gobbledygook. Nonsense. She managed to catch her breath. "For the sake of the Invisible Mother, Gailen, tell me true. Are what? Will be what?"

"Blessings, of course," Gailen said as though she ought to have known. "I'm a Blessing."

# Chapter 28

Blessing. A child born to a Handmaiden in the service of a patron. They were rare, but not impossible. And Demi was going to bear one.

Gailen had helped her halfway back to her room before they came upon Erekon, stalking the halls with storm clouds in his gaze. He'd taken one look at them, Gailen's arm around Demi's waist, and glared so fiercely Gailen had actually moved them both back a few steps.

"Your queen will require your services," Erekon had snapped. "I'm to take this one to her king. Now."

Gailen had gone at once, though not without an encouraging whisper to Demi. Erekon hadn't taken the other man's place, had offered no helping hand. No support. He'd stared her up and down, lip curled. He'd said naught to her as he escorted her back to the rooms she'd shared with Jarron. Not until just outside the door. Then he'd gripped her by her upper arms so tight she'd bitten her lip to hold back a cry. He shook her as one does a naughty child.

"What game are you playing at?" He'd spat, fingers pinching. "By the Arrow, Notsah, what can you be thinking?"

She'd ever known him to be a jealous man, but now to be jealous on the behalf of the man who'd replaced him—Demi had jerked herself free of his grip. Lifted her chin, though she felt anything but brave. "You don't know what you're talking about!"

He'd stepped back, chest heaving, fists clenched. "I know naught. As always is the case with you. Your lover is waiting for you inside, Demi. You'd better tend to him."

"What happened?"

But Erekon had only shaken his head, opened the door, and pushed her, stumbling, through it, before closing the door behind her.

Now she stood, still not quite able to catch her breath, her head whirling. Jarron was pacing, his hair unbound and flowing over his shoulders. Her own jealousy stabbed her. Had Caramin loosed his braid?

He turned when she came in and strode to her with a laugh shocking in its triumphance. He kissed her, tongue stroking hers, hands roaming her body. Demi didn't have the strength to turn him away—not physically or in any other manner.

"Ah, love, I've so much to tell you," Jarron said into her mouth. "But . . . later. First, this."

He tugged the already loosened laces of her bodice, exposing her breasts slowly to his gaze. Demi's heart skipped and so did her breath. She waited for his comment upon her attire, but Jarron seemed not to have noticed how she'd dressed, making the effort worthless. What did it matter when he only took the clothes off her with swift and eager fingers to leave them crumpled on the floor? She might've been dressed in anything for all the attention he gave her garments.

When she stood naked before him, sudden shyness made her put a hand over her breasts, another covering her groin. Only for a moment, because she realized how foolish it was to hide herself from him. She took her hands away, watching his gaze grow ever more heated.

Would he see what Gailen had so miraculously deduced? What Demi herself had not even had time to contemplate? Would Jarron notice somewhat different in this body he'd spent so many hours learning?

But, as with her clothes, her nakedness made no new impression upon him. He sighed, looking at her, his crotch bulging. He swept his tongue over his lips. His eyes met hers.

"How fortunate a man I am, to have been granted such a gift."

She wanted to weep at his words but blinked away the tears before they could fall. "I've been equally as blessed to have the privilege of being yours."

Jarron shrugged out of his coat. Unbuttoned his waistcoat, loosed his cravat. Unlaced his breeches and stepped out of them, along with his hose and shoes. Then pulled his shirt over his head. When he stood naked in front of her, he took his thickening cock in his hand, stroking idly.

"I have somewhat for you. A gift of mine own."

Without the encumbrance of her stays and unaccustomed clothes, she felt lighter. She managed a smile. "Aye? What sort of gift do you have for me, sweetheart?"

"Come here, and I shall give it to you."

"Oh, it's a kiss," she said and went to him, standing on her tiptoes to offer her mouth. "I'm well pleased to receive such a present."

Jarron laughed, his hands settling on her hips. "No. Not a kiss, though I'll give you as many of those as you like. No. This is somewhat . . . different. Come with me."

He took her by the hand toward the bed. "Close your eyes."

She did, obediently. Her skin pricked into deadman's flesh in anticipation. With her eyes closed, every sense heightened. She could smell the faintest perfume—Caramin's—and frowned. She heard the creak of hinges. The clink of metal.

"Jarron—"

"Hush. Sit on the bed, here." He guided her to the edge and settled her on the mattress.

"Ah, so it's to be that sort of gift?"

"Patience. Spread your legs a little wider."

She did, back arching a little, mouth open in anticipation. She wasn't disappointed. Demi felt the rough wetness of a tongue against her clit, followed soon after by a pressure nudging at the opening to her cunt. She spread her legs; fingers entered her, fucking gently in time to the delicious licking.

The mouth left her. She sighed in protest. In the next moment, she felt again a gust of hot breath, but instead of a slick tongue against her, she felt the cool press of metal. Demi opened her eyes, twisting her hips, but Jarron muttered another "Hush! Still," and she lay back.

Eyes wide, staring at the ceiling, her heart pounding and throat closing on a gasp. Her fingers bunched the sheets. She felt Jarron's hair on her thighs as he leaned in. Somewhat hard pressed onto either side of her clit, squeezing it tenderly almost but not quite the way fingers would. This was somewhat else, and trembling, she lay back and waited for his permission to see.

"There." Jarron sounded proud. And aroused. "Look and see how I've adorned you."

Demi pushed onto her elbows to look down. Between her legs, nestled amongst her curls, a thin hook of gold clipped to her clitoris. Two tiny golden chains, heavy with jewels, dangled from it.

She shifted experimentally and looked at him. "What is this?"

"Jewelry. You don't wear earbobs, nor rings, nor bracelets. But this . . . this, I thought would suit you perfectly."

He looked so pleased with himself she didn't want to deny him the joy of his gift. Aside from that, the pressure of the gold clip on her clit was quite nice, though strange. She'd heard of such jewelry and had never worn a piece of it before.

"Stand up. Let me see it." Jarron pulled her to her feet and sat on the bed while she posed. "Open your legs. Let me see."

She did, feeling both a little silly and quite aroused herself. She watched his face, saw his reaction. That more than anything sent shivers of delight all through her.

"Turn," Jarron said in a thick voice.

Demi turned, slowly. The hanging jewels made the clip tug against her clit as she moved and also tapped at her folds. Teasing.

"I cannot decide if I wish to have you wear this beneath your gown and attend me at dinner tonight, or if I wish to keep you here naked with me and call for dinner to be brought here."

"Whatever you decide, I am happy to provide."

"I know you are," Jarron said, gaze fixed between her legs. "By the Arrow, Demi, you wear that beautifully."

She felt beautiful in front of him. She turned out one leg and tipped her hips to show off the jewels. Her nipples tightened, and she cupped her breasts, thumbing them. Did they seem extra sensitive because of Jarron's gift, because of his look, or because of the life she'd not yet confirmed growing inside her?

Jarron stroked his cock slowly. "Dinner here. Ring for it. Answer the door wearing that."

"To the maid?" It wasn't as though she'd never been naked in front of a stranger, but this was different.

"To the maid or whoever knocks," he told her in a dark voice. "Unless . . . you find yourself unable to comply?"

"No. Not at all." The jewels tugged her with every step, so that by the time she reached the cord to ring the bell for service, her knees were a trifle weak. She pulled the cord and imagined a far-off bell jangling in the servants' hall.

It couldn't have been that far off, because in the next few minutes a knock came at the door.

"Open it, Demi."

She took a breath or two, but did as he'd said. The petite blond maid who waited outside didn't seem surprised to be greeted by a naked woman, but Erekon, standing with his arms crossed on the other side of the hallway, did. Demi didn't look at him. Let him judge.

"Dinner for my lord Bydelay and myself, please. Served here."

The maid bobbed a curtsy. "Aye, miss. Right away."

Demi closed the door behind her and turned to see Jarron's grin. His hand still fisted his prick. He gestured and she went to stand between his spread legs.

"Tell me how that felt." He flicked the jewels so they tugged her again.

"How did you want it to feel?" Not the words she'd expected to say, though her thick and dreamy tone matched how she felt.

Jarron looked at her, brow creased. "I want to know how you felt when you opened the door, wearing naught but this gift. Not how you think I wanted you to feel. I want to know the truth."

"I don't know how I feel about it," she told him.

Her honesty seemed not to suit him. He frowned. His thumb caressed her clit, tapping the metal.

"How do *you* feel about it?" she asked him.

He said naught at first, then replied, "I like it very much when you do as I command. Without hesitation."

"Surely you've had your share of being obeyed. You're a king. Before that, a prince." She shifted her hips, pushing herself against his caressing hand. Her hand found his hair, and she sank her fingertips deep into it.

"It's different, with you. Everything is."

She tugged his hair until he looked up at her. She kissed him. She put her hand over his and moved it on her clitoris until her breath became ragged in her throat.

"I don't need jewelry or games to find pleasure in your touch," she murmured against his mouth. "It's just you, Jarron."

He groaned and slipped off the clip. The sudden release of pressure sent delirious swirls of desire through her, so fierce she had to put a hand on his shoulder to keep her knees from giving out. In the next instant, he slid a finger inside her. Then another. His thumb stayed on her clit, pressing and releasing as he ate her mouth with his kisses.

"Touch me," Jarron said into the kiss. "Use your hand."

She found his cock, so wonderfully thick in her hand. She put one knee on the bed next to his hip, moving to straddle him, but Jarron stopped her with a shake of his head. He pushed his hips, thrusting into her grip.

"No."

Already his touch had taken her close to the edge. There wasn't much room for rational thought with his fingers moving inside her, curling, finding that magic spot behind her pubis and stroking. They fell forward onto the bed, rolling until they faced each other with limbs tangled. He moved down her body with his mouth, shifting when he reached her cunt so that she could reach his cock with her mouth as he used his lips and tongue on her.

She took his cock down her throat, easier in this position, as he moved his tongue over her. Together, they rocked. She cupped his balls, stroking with her thumb the way he'd done to her earlier, and felt the throb of his blood beating there.

His cock pulsed on her tongue as he climaxed. The taste and smell of him filled her head, leaving little room for anything else except her own pleasure, reaching its peak. It washed over her, blotting out everything but the sensation of his mouth and hands on her, and passed just as quickly to leave her breathless and limp in its aftermath.

Jarron rolled onto his back, away from her. Demi did the same, their bodies touching though in strange places—her knee to his shoulder, his hand on her ankle. She relaxed into the soft bed, content for the moment.

When the door opened, she looked up expecting to see the maid coming in with the food, but instead was greeted by the sight of Caramin, Gailen trailing behind her, Erekon behind the both of them though he stopped in the doorway.

"Call off your dog," Caramin snapped at Jarron. "I've already promised not to murder you."

"My lord, I asked her to let me at least announce her—"

Caramin shut him up with a flick of her fingers that Demi would've admired under different circumstances. "Shut up. He knows who I am, and in case you hadn't noticed, this is my house. I'll go where I please, and when. Jarron, for the love of the Invisible Mother, finish your fucking and get out of bed."

Demi was already rolling off the mattress, not going for her own clothes, but for his. She snatched up his breeches, his shirt, but looked up to see Caramin studying her with a small smile.

"It's more important to you to cover him than yourself? Is that because you think he'd be more ashamed of his nakedness, or because you'd rather keep him from my sight?"

Demi straightened, Jarron's clothes in her fist. "My lady Caramin, I am my lord's comfort and his grace. I am what he needs before he knows he needs it. I would never have him shamed before anyone, no matter how rudely they behave."

Gailen laughed under his breath, but Jarron let out a low curse and got out of bed to stand beside her. Erekon looked stone-faced from his place in the doorway, then went out, closing the door.

Caramin did not laugh, nor did she smile, but her gaze took in all of Demi from head to toe. "You are quite a credit to your Order. However, I've business to discuss with your master—"

"He is not," Demi said evenly, "my master."

Caramin looked faintly surprised. Jarron let out a small groan. Demi handed him his breeches.

"Your patron, then. I've business with your patron. So do whatever it is you must do to make it . . . comfortable for him."

Demi held the other woman's gaze for a long moment before nodding. She turned to Jarron. "My lord. Let me help you dress."

She couldn't tell if he was angry at her display of temper, or impressed. Jarron nodded. That was all. And Demi did what she was there to do.

# Chapter 29

"Henrik is a fool," Caramin said without even waiting for Jarron to finish lacing his breeches.

Demi had offered only his breeches and shirt, but that was enough. Caramin herself wore a loose dressing gown, while her companion wore a pair of loose trousers and shirt. This was not meant to be a formal affair, then.

"Aye, he is that, but one with convictions." Jarron took the glass of wine Demi had pressed into his hand.

Caramin settled herself onto the settee, hand out to take the glass Gailen was giving her. She sipped, handed it back for Gailen to take. Jarron wondered if he should do the same with Demi, but using her as his personal table seemed . . . excessive.

"I know the stories that are told about me, Jarron. I know what you other four think of me. But I tell you this. I don't wish to bring war to the First, nor to any piece of the Five Provinces. But I meant what I said. If he will not join us, he will not benefit from our prosperity."

Jarron knew she meant it. "He seems determined not to. Bander joins only out of fear. Kenston is your ready helpmate in this venture."

"And you," Caramin said. "You, Jarron Bydelay. What have you decided?"

He shook his head. "You've set forth a great plan, Caramin. You make much sense, and I admire what you mean to do. But to give up being king . . ."

"Doesn't set right with you, does it?" She laughed. "Oh, my dear, I understand. Think you I'd be so sweet if someone had come to me suggesting I give up my seat for another?"

"I daresay you wouldn't."

"Of course not!" She took the cup again from Gailen's hand and sipped more slowly this time.

Demi had dressed quietly while Caramin spoke. Now she nudged Jarron's elbow gently until he moved toward the armchair across from the settee. She took the cup from his hand, settled it onto the low table between them. When he sat, she folded herself gracefully next to him. Waiting.

Jarron saw Caramin's gaze flicker that direction but couldn't read it. Gailen didn't kneel. Caramin leaned forward.

"Bander cannot be expected to take it up. Kenston has already agreed I am better suited for the task. And Henrik . . . he will either change his mind or his province will suffer for his stubbornness. Tell me, Jarron. What would you have for the Second?"

He could not answer. Heat rushed through him, not sexual. Feverish. His palms tingled, and he rubbed them on his thighs to scratch.

"I've not yet decided."

Caramin sighed extravagantly. "Because I am a woman? Because you feel better prepared than I to take on the duties associated with such a venture? Because you're a greedy bastard? Why?"

"Because no matter how much I might agree with everything you've said, I can't just step aside."

Caramin studied him, eyes narrowed. "What if you didn't have to?"

"A governorship or whatever you're calling it is not the same as being king of mine own province, nor is it anything close to being emperor," Jarron said.

The room was overwarm. He got up to pace. He felt their eyes on him, their bedamned eyes. Void take them for staring.

"I'm not talking about that. Somewhat greater than that. Land Above, stop your pacing, Jarron, it's highly distracting, ultimately irritating, and quite rude. You'll make me quite fractious should you continue."

He turned on his heel to face her. "What, then?"

Caramin rose from her chair and crossed to him with gliding steps. She was so tiny she had to tip her head quite far to look up at him, but she managed to make him feel small. She smiled. She ran a hand along his shoulder, down his arm, to his hand, but she didn't take it.

"Marry me."

Jarron heard Demi gasp, but it was Gailen's face he saw. Impassive. Unmoved. He looked at Demi then. She'd gone pale, her lips pressed together, her hands no longer folded easily in her lap but clutched tight against her. He looked down and down into Caramin's eyes.

"You would have me as your husband?"

"Don't sound so surprised. You come from good enough stock . . . aside from that unfortunate wee affliction that plagues you."

His palms itched again and he rubbed them together. He needed a drink with a desperation he didn't want to show, and Demi had not moved from her spot. She looked stricken, an expression Jarron thought he should understand but could not, at that moment, take the time to think upon.

"Trystan's Pox is not merely an unfortunate affliction. It's hereditary. It's passed from father to son."

"I know what it is," Caramin said. "I know what it does. It makes you quite ill, does it not? It could kill you, should you be already sick with somewhat else, aye, or should you contract somewhat else while suffering an outbreak? Men have died from it, tell me true."

"They have. I don't intend to be one of them. Nor one who passes it . . . passes it along." His throat went tight. He snapped, "Demi."

She got up at once and brought his cup. Her fingers were cool on his, the wine cooler when it splashed on his hands. Not from her trembling touch, but from his. Jarron breathed deep to gain control.

Caramin held out her hand and Gailen pressed her cup into it. "I find you attractive enough, in your own way, though you're a bit too . . . bold for my usual tastes. But alliances have been made for less than that."

He breathed again, the cool wine easing his distress. Slow breaths. In through the nose, out through the mouth. He ignored the itching in his feet and hands.

"I know about your wee vow, by the by." Caramin took a drink, watching him from over the rim of her cup. "Very noble. I approve."

"So you'd find a marriage without possibility of an heir acceptable? Most women wouldn't."

"I'm not most women. But what you're really asking me is if I find the idea of a marriage without the possibility of fucking bearable. Why not just say it?"

Jarron gritted his jaw. "Somehow, I think you already have an answer to that."

Caramin smiled. Not the sweet smile he'd grown used to, nor the slightly smirking grin he'd seen upon her face several times before. This smile looked genuine. It softened her. She looked at Gailen, then at Demi.

"I think we both know," she said, "that neither of us would suffer for lack of bedmates."

"And what of him? What of you, Gailen? Can you speak for yourself, or must your mistress ever speak on your behalf? What say you? Should I marry her?" Jarron stopped himself from stuttering the words only by great effort. "How would you feel about that?"

Gailen looked solemn. "As my lady said, alliances were made for less reason than what she offers you."

"And you don't care? It matters not to you that your lady would take my troth, wear my ring, take my name—"

"Oh, not that," Caramin laughed. "No, my dear. I'll keep my name, thank you. And my place would ever be next to you, not beneath. I could suffer to be co-regent with you, though we both know I'd be the one doing all the hard work—"

"You make a mockery of me!" Jarron shouted.

Caramin stepped back, eyes wide. He was pleased to think he'd shocked her into silence. He imagined few had ever done so.

"You treat everyone around you like puppets, dancing naked for your whim. You set yourself so far above everyone else there is no possibility of you ever accepting someone as an equal, Caramin. Your idea of an empire is a good one, but tell me true. Is it really for the benefit of the Second and the people who were loyal to you even when you rose up against their sovereign, your own father, who by all accounts was slaughtered in his bed in a manner not befitting his position?"

Caramin blinked rapidly. Surely that was not a sheen of tears? She swallowed, hard, but waved away Gailen's offer of her cup. Instead, she cupped her elbows in her opposite hands, a gesture that made her look much younger.

"I had his cock cut off and stuffed in his mouth, is that what you want to hear? How merry a jest should I make it, Jarron, my father's murder?"

"Is it true?" His stomach turned at the thought of it. "You did that to your own father?"

"Better than someone else's, aye?" She laughed bitterly. "Ask me again and I'll tell you true, but know that once knowing you cannot unknow it."

"Tell me, then," he said. "True."

"My father had no sons. No other daughters. He had a wife he loved to distraction. My mother. His queen, who died when I was just past ten and six. He went so mad in his grief they say the sky went dark for three days while he raged and cursed it. He tried several times to take his own life. Would that he had, for he might have spared us all a great deal of trouble."

Jarron felt Demi's presence behind him and took comfort from it. She put her hand on the small of his back, not intruding, but her touch helped him straighten and square his shoulders. It left him able to listen without speaking.

"I'd always known I looked very much like my mother, but my father in his madness began to believe I was actually my mother. The young woman with whom he'd fallen so passionately in love. There was no dissuading him. I like to believe my mother loved him as much as he loved her. I also like to believe that had she refused his advances the way I did, he'd have taken her refusal as a gentleman would and not forced his attentions upon her the way he did to me. Mayhap that is simply a pretty story I told myself when I was trying so fiercely to blame my father's madness and not my father, himself."

"So you killed him."

"What would you have done?" Caramin retorted. "He was incapable of leading this province, incapable of anything but his own delusions!"

"How old were you?"

From behind him, Demi sighed softly. "Does it matter?"

He didn't turn to look at her. "How old, Caramin?"

"Ten and seven."

"You lasted a twelvemonth then." He looked her over. "That's a long time to suffer."

She inclined her head just slightly. She didn't look ashamed. She didn't look sad. He admired her for that. Unapologetic.

"Why marry me, then? What good will it do you, when you could take your army and simply force me to give up?"

"As I told Henrik, I'd rather not. I've had enough bloodshed in my lifetime, and I've no mind to destroy what I'd care to own."

This amused him, but his laughter startled him as sounding as though it came from someone else. Someone far away. "That's only answer to half the question."

"If I don't take a husband, like you, I will be left without an heir. Women, no matter how high we might rise, cannot claim their bastards as their heirs. Even the Invisible Mother herself learned that, did she not, when she fell pregnant with some other man's spawn?"

Demi let out a hiss from behind him but didn't interject. Jarron looked at her, though. She was pale and serious, and he reached for her. She held his hand tightly.

"Jarron, you should sit. You don't look well," she said.

"I'm well enough." He turned to Caramin. "So marry your companion."

Laughter twisted her mouth, but she still could not look ugly. "Gailen? He's a bastard himself. Certainly not husband material. He'll make fine babies, of that I have no doubt, but they should carry your name even if I will not."

Jarron flinched. "You would have me wed you and claim this man's children as mine own?"

Caramin sighed. "Jarron. Listen to me. I would welcome the opportunity to share the burden of leadership with someone else. Someone I could trust not to try and rule over me as much as he does his lands. I cannot marry Gailen—my citizens have accepted much from me, but in that I doubt they'd see clear. Add to that the turmoil creating this empire will take, how much I will have to struggle for control . . . aye, it would be nice to have a helpmate. One who might accept me as a partner and a wife in name only. To get a child with you, one that might be stricken with the pox? No. I did not mock you when I said I thought your vow was noble."

"And of my part in this? What can I expect? To share with you what was once solely mine?"

Caramin gave him a curious look. "Your Handmaiden is correct. You don't look well. You should sit. Have a drink."

"I'm not thirsty. Answer me."

"You'd be sharing with me what was never yours, and would never have been. Will never be. You have the chance here to join with me and grow stronger. Stay by yourself . . ." She paused to let her gaze sweep him up and down. "You will be naught but weaker. Think on this. I tell you true, I want what's best for the First Province, but what is best for us will be good for all of you. I will make it so."

"And what you want, you get." Jarron shook his head, refusing to sit though by now the world had gone a little hazy around the edges. "And if I tell you I will make a play to be the one who holds it all?"

"You'll be like the man holding the edges of a cloth with a handful of coins in the center. You can't grab the coins without letting go of the cloth, and what happens when you do? You spill them." She traced a fingertip along his cheek, a touch from which he pulled away. "Don't spill the gold, foolish man. Gailen. Come."

Jarron half expected her to turn in the doorway and offer some final biting words, somewhat meant to poke at him, but Caramin swept through without a second look. Only then did he sink into a seat and put his head into his hands. He shook all over. Fever. He knew it. The itching, too. Soon enough the first blisters would break out on him. If he were lucky—and it didn't feel as though he would be, not this time, they would cluster in small groups, easily healed or even hidden by his clothes.

"Demi. Get Erekon. Have him make the carriages ready. We leave tonight."

She pressed a cool hand to his forehead. "I think you need a medicus."

"Tonight." He bit down to keep his teeth from chattering. "I want to be home before . . . before."

She nodded and pressed her lips to his temple. Then she left him in the chair while the world spun, and Jarron closed his eyes against it. He needed to get home.

# Chapter 30

"Hello, sweetheart." Demi kept her voice low, so as not to startle him when he woke. She put the back of her hand to his forehead, but it was cool. The fever had broken the night before, but he'd only just now seemed to know where he was.

Jarron pushed up on his elbow. "How long?"

"Just three days."

"Three days is long enough," he said bitterly, but lay back on the pillows at once.

He turned his face from her when she tried to replace the damp cloth she had for his forehead, and she didn't insist. "You must be hungry. I have some broth for you. You should eat it slowly. . . ."

"I've been through this before," Jarron told her without looking at her. "A hundred times, if once. My stomach is fine. Get me the broth and some bread. I can feed myself. I don't need you to mother me."

"I won't, then. Your own mother can do that well enough, and she's been waiting just outside the door to do just that." Demi stood, despite his mutter of protest, and went to the door of his bedroom.

No matter what Jarron might think of his mother, or his mother might think of Demi, the woman had been sick with worry. It hadn't mattered that she'd been through this as many times as Jarron, she'd sent for the finest mediculses and made certain to stay close by at all times. She had not, however, offered to nurse him herself. That she'd left to Demi with the grudging admittance that she might be better suited to it, and that her son might prefer a Handmaiden to a mother.

Now, though, Demi motioned her inside and left her there to weep on his coverlet. Demi needed a bit of a rest, herself. The past few days had been a terrific strain.

Adam slept on the couch in Jarron's library, his mouth open, arm flung over his head. Nigel sat on the chair across from him, not asleep. Just watching. When Demi came through the door, he looked up and put a finger to his lips.

"Though if he could sleep through the queen mother's incessant chatter, I think he can most likely suffer through yours," Nigel said with a small smile. "He's exhausted with worry."

"Jarron's awake," Demi said in a low voice and poured a glass of water from the pitcher. She took some broth for herself, as well, though she wasn't hungry. She had to eat to keep up her strength, and the more she kept in her stomach the less likely it seemed she would empty it.

Three days had never seemed so long as the last three had.

"How is he?"

"His fever's gone. The pox broke out on his body and face, though his limbs are mostly clear. The medicus says it could've been worse. That it has been worse. At any rate, he's awake and complaining, which I suppose says somewhat of his condition."

"You should sit and rest. Go to bed, if you can. You look exhausted, too."

At this, Adam stirred and scrubbed at his face, sitting up abruptly. "Demi. How is he?"

"Awake and grouchy. His mother's with him now, which I fear won't improve his mood." She dipped a hunk of bread into the bowl and ate it quickly, her hands shaky.

"Sit." Adam got up and urged her toward the couch he'd vacated.

At that moment, the door opened and Jarron's mother bustled out, nose in the air, her skirts rustling. "He's impossible! I blame you."

She pointed at Adam, who looked affronted. Then at Demi, who sighed but said naught, and finally, after a hesitation, at Nigel. He blinked and shrugged.

"All of you! You're supposed to keep him from getting upset, aren't you? What use are you as friends or . . . whatever it is you are," she said with a sniff in Demi's direction, "if you can't keep him from getting upset? It's strain that brings it out in him, you know. And it's not easy for me, either. And with his father failing, I might imagine you'd take more pity on me than this, but no! What do you do? You let him gambol off to the First Province and let him cavort with that woman there. Don't think I don't know what goes on in that place."

"You've no idea," Adam said under his breath, hand on the back of his neck.

"I've every idea," said Jarron's mother. She fixed them each with a stern look that left Demi with a sense of unease she couldn't pass off as a result of being with child.

Without another word, Yewdit swept from the room, making sure to slam the door behind her. From the bedroom, Jarron called Adam's name, and he gave Nigel a quick squeeze as he passed. Then he paused and stepped back. Kissed Nigel on the cheek, near enough to his lips that the distance scarce made a difference.

Nigel was quiet as Adam left the room, closing the bedroom door behind him. Then he laughed, ducking his head. He gave Demi a sheepish grin.

Her stomach had settled with the food, and she found a smile for him but no words. There were none to be said. Whatever had changed between Adam and Nigel, it was obviously making them both happy.

"I'll go. Tell Adam I'll see him in his rooms. He needs some time with his friend, and you, my lady, need to get some sleep."

"I will. I promise." She spooned more broth, ate more bread. She was suddenly ravenous, though careful not to overindulge. She'd learned the consequences of that the hard way.

Erekon came in as Nigel went out. Demi paused in her meal at the sight of him but then kept on. He wouldn't be there to see her. She was wrong.

"He's awake?"

She nodded. "Adam is with him."

"What are you going to tell him to do?"

"Who, Adam? I don't believe I'm in any position to tell him anything."

Erekon shook his head. Demi sighed and put aside her bowl. She licked her lips, tasting salt. She knew what Erekon meant.

"I will . . . convince him," she said in a low voice. "I will advise him, as you've encouraged. I see now that he does need my counsel, no matter how ill-informed it might be. Or how out of place I am to give it."

Erekon nodded and let out a slow breath. He closed his eyes briefly and rubbed them. She knew that look. He'd ever suffered headaches that little could cure but sleep.

"You'll tell him to agree to Caramin's terms?"

"Her terms?" Demi's laugh was not low, nor modulated, nor in fact at all humorous. She hadn't heard herself sound that caustic in a long time. Erekon would recognize the tone. "If you call proposing marriage to him a term . . ."

"Think of it, Demi. Your goal is to do what is best for him. What could be better than having him join with her, not just the provinces but as rulers?" Erekon laughed and punched a fist into his other hand. "I never thought, of course, that she would make such an offer."

Demi said naught.

Erekon looked at her. "You will convince him, aye? Oh, it will take some work. This change. Work for me and my sort, I tell you true."

"Soldiers." Demi watched him carefully. "Even if there is no war, there will be a battle or two."

"So you will convince him?"

"I will try," Demi told him.

Jarron held up the letter that had come on a swift rider just that morn. "She knows I fell ill. If Caramin knows, I've no doubts the news has spread far and wide. Such gossip. The king of the Second Province, felled once more by the pox. Have you seen the fence around the estate?"

Demi, who'd been looking out the window, shook her head. "No. What's on the fence, love?"

"Hanna flowers." He crumpled the letter and tossed it to the ground. "For healing."

"They're your people. They love you. They want you to be well, of course."

"Folklore and legend and nonsense." He softened his tone. None of this was her fault, but wasn't she supposed to make him feel better than this? Make this somehow more bearable?

She turned to him. "Your mother is setting your nephew Adzo to take your place."

"I know that," Jarron said. "I've known it for a long time. But she hasn't yet. And if she does, I'll be ready to stand against her. And him."

She looked out the window again. "I should have known you'd be aware of any intrigue far better than I might be."

Jarron came to stand beside her. Even the window's faint reflection sickened him, showing as it did the remains of the pox only just now healing. He wanted to lean against her. To bury his face in the curve of her neck, to lose himself in the pleasure of her body. But when he put an arm around her, she stiffened and didn't melt against him as she had every time since the first he'd touched her.

He disgusted her. Oh, she would bed him, he was fair certain of that. She would do whatever it was that he wished. But she'd do it out of duty, not desire.

"If I marry Caramin, my mother will have no tapestry in which to weave her designs. She can run this court however she pleases in my stead, and I will pass my time in between House Bydelay and the First Province." Jarron said this steadily. He'd been thinking of this a lot during his recovery. He'd asked the advice of his best friend. Of his most trusted ministers. Of his father, though the old man could say little and understood less. But to the one person to whom his decision might make the most difference, he'd said naught until now. "Tell me, Demi. Should I do it?"

She faced him then, her eyes red. She'd been a faithful nurse to him during his illness, but though he'd been well on the mend for a sennight, Demi still remained pale with strain. She didn't sleep well, he knew that, for she got up in the night often and still rose before him every morn.

Now she drew a shuddering breath. She clasped her hands together, just below her breast. Surprising him, she went to her knees in front of him, but though she Waited, it was not the same as she'd ever done before. She didn't sit upright, but placed her hands flat on the ground, her head bent. Her shoulders heaved.

"No." The single word rose, as heavy with emotion as his had been without. "No, Jarron. Please, for the love of the Holy Family. Please, please do not marry her."

Jarron had never made a habit of kneeling but he went to his knees now to pull her upright. He took her hands. They were cold, though two bright spots of color burned high in her cheeks.

"Give me reason why I shouldn't," he said quietly.

"If you marry her, she will not make you send me away. She would gladly allow you to keep me with you, the way she will keep Gailen. She would not even take my place in any manner, for I cannot imagine Caramin Ahavat ever doing anything to serve you, even if you were her husband. But even so, Jarron. If you marry her, I will have to leave you."

"Because you believe a marriage to her would ruin any chance I had of ever achieving absolute solace," he said, convinced that was her reason and knowing she was right.

"No, oh no." Demi shook her head. Her fingers twisted in his. Tears glistened in her eyes. "No, Jarron."

"Why, then?" he asked, stupid with the hope she might have a different reason.

"Because I love you," Demi told him. Silver tears streaked her cheeks and her voice shook, raw, but he understood her every word. "Because I cannot bear for you to take another woman to wife. Because if you marry Caramin, I will have to leave you else my heart break."

If he'd been standing he might have staggered, so vast was his relief. Jarron closed his eyes though, to say what must be said. "Would you have me stand against her, then? Or do you ask me to step down, take the place she offered to the rest of the Five? Would you have me be less than what I am . . . for you?"

Demi wiped her face with trembling fingertips. "I would have you do what is right for you. If that is taking your country to war . . . then I would support you."

"You would be the only one," Jarron said.

"But might I not be the one who matters most?" she asked in a voice so small and unlike any he'd ever heard from her, Jarron could not bear it.

He pulled her to him, and this time she did melt into his embrace. She met his kiss eagerly, her hands linking behind his head beneath his hair. She pressed her body to his. His prick responded at once, fickle thing. His mind, on the other hand, took a little longer.

Jarron broke the kiss to look at her. "Demi. What you're asking . . . what you're saying . . . you would leave the Order for me? You'd become one of those Sisters about whom the others do not speak?"

Her lips parted, a sigh came out. She blinked rapidly and another pair of tears slipped over her cheeks. This time, he was the one who wiped them away.

"I would. I am. I will be, for you, Jarron. I love you. I have loved you for so long. Tell you true, I could not imagine going back to the Order after knowing you. Even if you don't want me."

"How could you think I don't want you?" He pulled her to her feet, then lifted her against his chest. The bed was but a few steps away but she clung to him with a cry, her face against his chest. Together they tumbled onto the bed's softness. He kissed her, long and soft and slow. Sweet. The heat between them built.

If he thought there to be any hesitation between them because of his illness, Demi proved him wrong. She undressed him, following each bit of bared flesh with her mouth. She kissed all of him, sparing no scar, and when she at last met his mouth with hers, he tasted the salt of her tears.

She made love to him with her mouth and hands, and for the first time since she had come to him, Jarron gave himself up to her. Completely. Demi set the pace, the rhythm, the length of the stroke. She moved her mouth to his nipples, one then the other, circling them with the tip of her tongue until his back arched. She did the same to his prick, sucking and licking, even nibbling at the flesh of his sac until he thought he might go mad from the bliss of it.

But when she straddled him to take him, he sat up. "No. Not that."

She closed her eyes and sighed, but made no protest. She slid down his body and took him again into her mouth, working him with lips and teeth and tongue until he could no longer hold back the thrust of his hips. His groan. His cry. With her name on his lips, Jarron's seed boiled out of him in a rushing jet of ecstasy.

"I love you," he said when the mindlessness had passed and he once again could speak coherently. "Enough to keep you."

Enough to go to war.

# Chapter 31

Jarron rose before her and took his leave before she'd even opened her eyes. Demi woke, stretching, feeling for him beside her but he'd gone. She sat, scrubbing at her eyes. The sunlight shafting through the window told her she'd slept very late, but for the first time in many days she didn't feel the surge and roil of nausea in her gut. She felt rested. Content.

Loved.

She took her time in the bath, luxuriating in the warm water and scented soap. She hummed under her breath, thinking of naught but her comfort and of how she would greet Jarron when he returned. She looked up when the door opened, a welcoming smile on her face, ready to take him into the bath with her—but it was not Jarron who stood there.

"Erekon! Get out!" She reached for a drying cloth, but he'd already grabbed her by the wrist to pull her out.

Slippery in his grasp, Demi yanked free. The water sloshed, wetting his boots, but Erekon didn't even glance at them. He grabbed her again, this time by her upper arm, pinching, and pulled her out of the water.

"What have you done? Curse you to the Void, you stupid, witless wench, what have you done?"

Her feet slipped on the wet tiles and she went to her knees. Demi bit back a cry of pain as she fumbled again for the cloth. She held it in front of her. She looked up at him.

"You said you would convince him to do what is right," Erekon said, voice a growling rasp.

"I did." She got to her feet, her knees aching from hitting the floor and her arms sore from his grasp.

"He speaks of war, Notsah! War on the First Province! Against Caramin Ahavat and her army? Did you listen to naught I told you? Beyond what is your duty as a Handmaiden, I thought you cared for him!"

"I love him!" She tossed the words at him.

Erekon flinched. His mouth thinned and his nostrils flared. "Tell you true, I forgot how well you . . . love."

Demi tucked the drying cloth around her, her gown too far out of reach. She wasn't going to put herself within his grasp again. "I love him, Erekon. I will leave the Order for him. I will stand by him if he chooses to wage war, or if he chooses to take a lesser role."

"Selfish is the heart that thinks first of itself. Is that not one of your principles? How selfish are you being? Thousands will die because of your love." His lips twisted on the word. "You leaving the Order means naught, can you not understand that? You mean naught. This is greater than you and him. This isn't about love. It's about so much more."

She shook with chill but faced him squarely. "I could not counsel him to marry that woman."

"Why? He could still have kept you!" Erekon raked a hand through his hair, tugging lose a bunch of strands that fell forward. He kicked at the puddle on the floor. "Now he will try to raise an army. He might succeed. But even if he does . . ."

"Mayhap you ought to have more faith in him."

"And mayhap you," Erekon said, "should have less."

Demi's skin had humped into deadman's flesh. "I carry his child, Erekon."

The color drained from his face. He staggered one step toward her, and Demi had no place for retreat. She stood her ground.

When he got onto his knees in front of her, Demi's first thought was that she'd somehow killed him. Alarmed, she reached for him, found his shoulder. He looked up at her, dark eyes wide. He put his hands on her hips below the edge of the towel.

"Marry me, instead."

"What? No!" Pinned between Erekon and the bathtub, she had no place to go and didn't even struggle.

"I will claim your child as mine. Let Jarron wed Caramin. Let him make an empire."

"Erekon . . ." Her voice softened. Her hand found his hair and smoothed the silky texture. She could remember without much effort how that hair had felt on her bare skin. She swallowed, hard.

"You have ever held my heart, Notsah. All these seasons I've longed for your forgiveness for whatever it was that drove you away."

"You have it," she told him. "You had it long ago."

He pressed his face to her belly with the cloth a thin, ineffective barrier between them. She could still feel his heat on her. Her fingers tightened in his hair.

"He won't allow you to bear his child. You know it."

"I didn't get pregnant on purpose. This child is a Blessing. A true miracle. Surely Jarron will—"

With a cruel laugh, Erekon got to his feet. "He will make you get rid of it."

"He won't." She shook her head, conscious of how the weight of her wet hair hung down her back. "He can't."

"You haven't told him yet."

"No." She pushed past him, careful not to slip on the floor, and grabbed up her clothes. She tossed the towel away, there being no point in modesty with him, and stepped into her shift, and then the gown. Her fingers fumbled on the buttons.

"You'd better do it soon. He'll guess himself, otherwise, and wonder why you lied."

"I haven't lied!" she cried, advancing on him.

Erekon held her back with one hand put to her shoulder but didn't grab her again. "All you've done to him is lie."

She bit back a sob. "No. I've done what is necessary to provide him with comfort. With peace."

"But not with absolute solace, aye?" Another cruel laugh, this one tinged with bitterness. "In that you've failed."

"There is no time limit on how long it can take."

"You're leaving the Order. What do you care?"

"I care," Demi said.

"I will ask you again. Once more. Marry me instead of him. Let me raise your child as mine own, afflicted or no—"

"You truly think," Demi said, "that if I bear a child afflicted with Trystan's Pox, none will guess who fathered him?"

Erekon drew himself up. "You speak of love, and I know well how hard it can bite, for I've found myself half slaughtered by it already. But I speak to you of duty, Notsah. My duty is to protect my king and my province. Yours is to do much the same to your patron. We have the same goal. But what you want will thwart what I must do. What I know is right, and what Jarron would see was right if he were not so blinded by what you offer him in the name of love. If you really love him, you will . . ."

"What? Let him go? Let him marry another? How could I have him give himself to another woman, even in name only?" she cried.

Erekon's gaze didn't waver from hers. "Believe me, I know the pain of it. But if you truly loved him, you would see him safe. Not just happy."

"I was happy with you," she whispered, hating old wounds that simply never healed. "But I was never, ever safe."

"No," Erekon said, "and I will ever plead your mercy for the fool I was."

"We cannot keep playing this between us. I beg of you, Erekon. Let this go. Let me go." She held herself back from touching him, afraid what might happen if she did. "Please."

He shook his head, stepping back. "This is beyond us, now. And I can't let it go. You've made your choice. Now live with the consequences."

His words sent uncertainty skittering through her, but Erekon had ever been skilled at making her doubt. "I will ask him to choose a governership instead of war. He will listen to reason."

"You should hope he does," Erekon said, "because if he does not, he will be taken down."

"You speak of treason," she breathed. "And what would happen if I told Jarron you stand against him? His own Lion?"

"He will be disappointed. He will be wounded. And," Erekon added, "he will be imprisoned, if not killed outright."

She gasped, sick at the thought, but Erekon cut her off with a wave of his hand.

"I'm what stands between him and revolution. A word from me and it goes either way, Notsah." He paused, no longer looking so cruel but merely resigned. Older and tired, too. "Be what the Mothers-in-Service named you. You have this chance. Be Jarron's Redemption."

I f you wanted a man to give you somewhat you wanted, you had to give him somewhat he wanted, first. So Notsah's mother had taught her, and so had the Order of Solace. Their reasons were as different as glass is from snow, but the methods were much the same.

Handmaidens were trained to be what their patrons needed, and Demi had gone to the Order already well skilled in the application of cosmetic, hair styling, how to wear clothes that best emphasized her feminine attributes. The Order had taught her many skills, but she'd learned most of how to please a man from her time as a whore.

She'd not thought of herself in such a manner for a quiverful of seasons, though when she outlined her mouth with crimson and her eyes with Void-black cosmetic, she realized part of her had never stopped.

"Woman I begin and woman I shall end," she said to her reflection. "A flower is made more beautiful by its thorns."

The words gave her no comfort, true as they might be. She smoothed her hair into an intricate braid. She applied perfume oil. She adorned herself with the jewels Jarron had given her.

She made a display of herself, and she Waited.

Kneeling, body upright, buttocks resting upon her heels as usual, but her hands clasped behind her neck. This was Waiting, Submission, and she intended to submit. She'd done this in practice. Never for a patron. She would do it for Jarron, because she meant to do whatever it took.

Erekon was right. She'd been selfish. She had failed utterly in her duty. She had put aside the needs of her patron to fulfill her own.

She could not be the reason Jarron took the Second Province to war. If that meant urging him to step down or watching him wed another woman, then that was what she must do. Her place was not politics. It was solace, of which Jarron was still as sorely in need as ever.

She found a place inside herself as she Waited. Memories. It might've seemed dispresectful to be thinking of a previous lover while she Waited for another, but without Erekon she would never have known Jarron at all. She'd never have sought his mercy when on the run, and she would not be here in this room, now, had Erekon not made her see how necessary she had become.

If not for Erekon, Demi would never have loved Jarron.

For that, if no other reason, she would always be grateful to the King's Lion. Not beholden or indebted, and her love for him had long

ago had burned away . . . but it cost her naught to understand his part
in her life and the woman she had become. To credit him for it. She
hoped someday he might understand the same of her.

The door opened, Jarron already calling for her. She heard his
boots sound on the floor, muffled for a moment as he crossed the carpet. The clink of glass as he poured himself a glass of worm.

She Waited.

"Demi, sweetheart, you should hear what we've been . . . Demi?"

She opened her eyes but did not move.

Jarron finished the worm and put the glass aside. "What is this?"

She knew the picture she made, because she could see it reflected
in the looking glass on the wall. A naked woman, breasts and clitoris
sparkling with the jeweled metal clips. Her nipples painted crimson
to match her lips, her eyes thickly lined. The glitter of gold powder on
her skin. It was a sight at which most men would pause, but she knew
that was not what had stopped him.

It was the position.

It spoke of surrender. Yielding. Submission. The giving up of power.

Jarron wiped a hand across his mouth. He loosed his cravat and
tugged it free. Tossed it to the floor. His fingers worked at the buttons
of his jacket, then waistcoat. He took them off. Unlaced his trousers.

He was already half hard as he circled her. He tugged one of the
jewels on her nipple; Demi hissed out a sigh. She closed her eyes again.
She did this for him, but couldn't stop herself from gaining her own
pleasure from it, too.

"Stand up," he ordered.

She did. Jarron's gaze heated when he saw the jewelry on her clit.
He tugged that, too, earning a moan for his efforts. He smiled. His
fingers slid inside her, found her wet.

"You do this for me."

She looked at him, her heart aching. "For us both."

He took her to the bed, then. Kissed her mouth. Worked at her cunt with his tongue until she cried out her desire, and then he moved between her breasts, his cock thick and hard as he stroked against her flesh. His brow furrowed and he bit his lower lip.

"Jarron, I would have you inside me. Please."

"No." He eased off, his cock against her belly now. Still hard, though he no longer thrust against her. He looked into her eyes. "I can't, Demi."

She took his face in her hands. "I promise you, I cannot get with child tonight."

He shivered as she moved against him, rolling her hips. "I can't."

She reached a hand between them, stroking. "I promise you."

He groaned and buried his face into her neck. He shifted. His cock pressed at her entrance. She opened for him. He pushed inside with a shudder, pausing to catch a breath before moving.

He'd already sent her into climax, but this, the pressure of him inside her after so long, sent desire spiraling inside her. More than that, it was his surrender to her. He yielded this time, and more than ever Demi understood why he so loved the exchange of power.

After, she curled into the strength of his arms as he drifted toward sleep. She knew by the slow in and out of his breath, the rhythm of his heartbeat. She kissed his bare chest, a leg flung over his.

"Jarron."

"Aye." He sounded sated and content, the best time to ask any man a question.

"Could you not love a child?"

"It's not a matter of love. It's because I would love a son too much to ever see him suffer." He pulled her a little closer.

"If I were to carry your child . . ."

He looked at her, no longer so sleepy. "But you won't, aye? Tell me true, Demi. You promised you wouldn't get with child tonight."

"And if I did?"

Jarron looked at her with eyes of stone. "I wouldn't allow it."

"You would have me end it in the womb?" She could barely say the words aloud, hearing them in Erekon's voice.

"Better its soul have a chance at life in a body untainted by illness."

"What if you knew there was a chance it could be . . . cured?"

"There is no cure for Trystan's Pox."

She curled closer, her face hidden against him. "Not after the child is born, no. But there is a treatment for when it's in the womb. It's dangerous, though. It can kill both mother and child."

His fingers tightened on her. "I'd never risk your life to save that of another."

It was the sentiment she'd hoped for, even as it broke her. "Never?"

"No. Never." Jarron kissed her.

"Do you swear such a thing?"

"By the Arrow, I swear it." He smiled. "What is this?"

"Do not go to war." She pushed herself up to look at him. "Take the governorship or marry Caramin and take equal rule of the combined provinces. But do not go to war."

"What is this, now?" Frowning, he pushed away from her. "First you tell me not to wed her, that you'll support me—"

"It is certain defeat. There are those poised to rise against you should you take the Second Province into battle just so you can stay its king."

Jarron scowled. "Where do you hear this? Who is against me, other than my foolish, vapid mother and her toy, my nephew? That is not—"

"Erekon told me. He says there is already a revolution ready to brew. If you don't join the Second Province to the others, or if you fight for your place as ruler of all, they will rise up against you. You won't have an army supporting you against Caramin. You will lose. You will . . . he says you may be killed." She burst into tears and clutched at him. "I could lose you to another woman, Jarron, but not to death. Promise me you will step down, one way or another. I beg of you. If you love me, do this."

He pushed away her touch as though it were made of fire. He got out of bed. "I cannot believe you'd say this to me."

"I love you. This is the truth. All of it."

"How long have you known?"

Demi hesitated, not wanting to hurt him but knowing her answer would wound. "He has been telling me since I arrived that I should lead you toward agreeing to the unification. I didn't want to be involved this way, Jarron, but he convinced me he's right."

He looked so stricken she got out of bed to put her arms around him. He allowed her touch, but didn't return it. His heart had begun beating furiously, and she put her hand flat over it.

"It is because they think me incapable, tell me true. Because of the pox. The Void-bedamned pox, aye?"

"That is a large part of it. Those whose voices ring loudest fear you will succumb too often to illness, that you could be taken advantage of while you are sick."

"And Erekon is one of those voices?"

"Erekon has told me his duty is to protect you," she told him honestly. "I believe he means it."

"And he believes he protects me by taking me off the throne."

She nodded. "Aye."

"And you, Demi. You believe he's right? I should step down, that I might better serve my province? And you."

She took longer to reply this time but had to answer with truth. "I do."

He put her from him gently but firmly. "Get dressed. Take what things you need. I will have a room prepared for you."

The floor fell out from beneath her. "You're sending me away?"

Jarron's gaze was flat, unreadable. "I need you away from me that I might think. If you wish to leave entirely, go back to the Order—"

"No!"

"Then give me time to think on this."

She nodded stiffly, made cold by the lack of emotion in his look. "If it pleases you."

Jarron turned his back to her. "I cannot think of anything that pleases me less and yet is made so necessary by what you have said."

There were no more words. Demi gathered her gown, her shift, her carpetbag, which had her few belongings. She did as he'd commanded.

She left.

# Chapter 32

M en were marching outside the gates of House Bydelay. Posters demanding the rights of the people to have a say in the future of the Second Province had replaced the white flowers and healing tokens that had only days before been tucked amongst the bars. It wasn't quite a mob—not yet. But Erekon had added guards all along the borders of the estate, and the atmosphere inside the house was subdued. Even frightened.

Though she'd not made it her habit upon first arriving to visit the social hall, Demi had spent many hours there since Jarron had put her out. She didn't pretend to herself or anyone else that she wasn't hoping to see him, but no matter what progress he'd made with her help, he was totally ignoring the social hall now.

The lords and ladies of his court were kinder to her than she had a right to expect, and she understood of course this was in large part to the desire of many to be the first to gain the gossip. There were many, however, who asked her to join them at their tables without pressuring her for details, and Demi was grateful for that. She caught glimpses of

Adam on his way to or from the War Room, but she didn't have the chance to ask him for news.

Everyone, it seemed, waited for news.

Never in the current memory of anyone at court had the Second Province hovered so close to war of any sort, and now there were two possiblitilies in the making. Either the country would be split in its loyalty to their liege, or they would be taken into battle against what the news runners were reporting as the new empire Caramin had promised. The First, Third, and Fourth Provinces had declared themselves as one, with the Fifth banned from all commerce.

All that waited was what Jarron would decide for the Second.

*Invisible Mother,* Demi thought, *grant me the patience to understand what I cannot control, for true patience is its own reward.*

She couldn't concentrate on the cards in front of her and was so startled when the page slipped a note into her hand she dropped her hand. Cards scattered. She didn't bother to pick them up.

The Mothers had come in answer to her letter. They waited for her in the foyer. Demi had never heard of such a thing—Mothers-in-Service coming to attend a Handmaiden. She had no time to dress or tidy herself. She couldn't keep them waiting.

Three of them faced her when she entered the foyer. She knew them, of course. Mothers Sympathy, Empathetica, and Considerata. They didn't even look travel worn, but Demi snapped for a servant to bring them tea and refreshments served in the small parlor close off the hall.

"Redemption," Sympathy said as she settled into her chair. "My dear child. Word of your distress reached us none too soon. We've come to bring you home. This is no place for you."

"I can't leave, Mother." Demi couldn't drink the tea she'd carefully poured. She put the cup down to look at each of them. "I've not yet fulfilled my purpose."

"And I daresay you never shall." This came from Empathetica, who looked over the rims of her spectacles with a frown. "A man set on war will never achieve any moment of solace, no matter how fleeting."

Considerata, the youngest Mother, leaned forward. "Take no shame in this, Redemption; there are some patrons who are incapable of it."

"I am shamed of much," Demi said to each of them. "I have failed. Not just in this. But in many things. I cannot leave him."

"Oh, my dear." Sympathy sighed. She looked closer. "Oh, oh, my dear."

"I thought as much," said Empathetica with a sniff and sat back in her seat. "At any rate, you've no choice. You must return with us."

"Has . . . has Jarron dismissed me?" The thought sickened her.

"No, my dear. But nevertheless, you must come away." Considerata reached for Demi's hand. "It's the law of the Order."

"What? That a Handmaiden must abandon her patron simply because of political upheaval?" Demi took her hand away, looking at each of them. "Now more than ever, he needs me."

"Not because of that. Think you we cannot tell when one of our own has gotten herself with child? Redemption, it's evident in every inch of you. The Invisible Mother has blessed you. And Blessings belong to us."

Demi put her hands on her belly, protective. "My child belongs to me."

"You'd not deny the Invisible Mother her claim, would you?" Considerata asked this seriously. "You would bring a child into this house of conflict?"

Demi closed her eyes against tears. "I cannot leave him."

"But you shall," said Sympathy. "My dear Kosem, please escort our Sister to the carriage."

Demi's eyes snapped open. Erekon looked solemn but not sorry as he stood beside the Mothers on their couch. Demi got to her feet.

"I've not even gathered my belongings."

"You can leave behind whatever he gave you. Take only what you brought with you." Empathetica pulled a pastry toward her and took a huge bite. "But hurry. We want to make time before dark."

She got to the door before Erekon's voice came behind her.

"You know she's not going to come with you."

"Don't be ridiculous," answered Sympathy.

But Demi was already running.

Jarron, head hazy from the hours of discussion and planning along with no small amount of worm, slouched in his chair. He didn't feel even the tickle of a fever or any sign the pox meant to strike him again, but he was well aware that it could. Anytime, for the rest of his life.

At least it wouldn't leave him a drooling idiot like his father, he thought. What a double bladed knife. Clear head or clear face. He hated the pox with everything he had, but he couldn't deny he'd been granted the better portion.

He'd written a dozen letters to Caramin. Everything from a proposal of marriage to a declaration of secession, that the Second would take the stance of the Fifth and remove itself from all commerce with the new empire. That he would take her governorship. That he would fight her for control. None of them had been easy. None had felt right.

Exhausted, hand cramping, eyes blurred, he dozed.

He missed Demi. She'd have brought him a drink and rubbed his shoulders. She'd have teased him into a smile. She'd have taken him to bed and made him forget all of this, if only for a little while.

Land Above, how he loved her. If not for her, he might've just marched into battle without a thought for anything but his need to be the one to have it all. Denied so much for so long, he'd lost sight of what it was like to give and take. Not until her.

Yet he couldn't deny he thought more clearly with her gone from him. Without her by his side, he felt her presence so keenly he knew how important it was for him to make the best choice. The right choice. Not for him, but for everyone.

For her.

When his door flung open so fiercely it hit the wall and shook the shelves of books, he startled but didn't get out of his seat. He was still a little too fuzzy for quick response. When Demi ran across the floor to him and went to her knees in front of him, somewhat inside him shifted. A memory.

"Jarron. Please. Listen to me, I haven't much time." She sounded desperate, her eyes bright and voice thick with tears, though none spilled over her cheeks. "They are going to make me leave with them."

"Who, love?" He touched her cheek, her hair, drunkenly but with love.

"The Mothers-in-Service have come for me. I thought it was because of a letter I'd written asking for their counsel, but it seems the news of what is happening here in the Five Provinces reached the Motherhouse. They've come to take me home."

"They cannot. I've paid them a fair enormous amount of coin for the keeping of you, love." He smiled. "I've not yet had my solace."

Demi didn't smile. She pressed her face to his knees. Her shoulders shook with sobs.

Alarmed, Jarron put his hand upon her hair again. "Demi, look at me. They cannot take you away from me. I won't allow it."

"You will," she said against his leg, then lifted her face to him. "I fear you will."

"Never."

She shook her head. "I carry your child, Jarron. A Blessing. I know I swore to you I couldn't get pregnant, and I believed it when I said it. But it happened."

He took his hand away, his gut clenching as though she'd punched him in it. She was saying more, though, her words tumbling out of her mouth so fast his worm-addled brain could scarce keep up.

"I must tell you somewhat else."

Before she could, the door banged open again. Erekon. Demi shuddered, looking up at Jarron, her gaze pleading.

And he remembered.

"You," he said. "You . . . that day . . . it was you?"

How could he not have known her? The length of her hair, her demeanor had changed, but her face surely had not. How had he been with her this long, and so intimately, without remembering her as the whore who'd been in just this place in such a different time?

"It was me." She squeezed his knees, holding tight. "When they sent me to you, I considered it a happy fate, a gift from the Invisible Mother."

"Notsah. It's time to go."

Notsah. He'd not known her by that name, or any, and she would ever be Redemption to him. What a jest. Jarron had believed her to be just that, his redemption, only now to see she was never anything of the sort.

He pushed her hands away. "Get you gone."

"Jarron, please. I should've told you, I know that. But I was not that woman any longer. You not that man. I came to you to be what you needed—"

"And you are this, instead? A liar? A betrayer?" The worm roiled in his guts, and he swallowed the sour taste of bile.

"It's time for you to go," Erekon said.

Her gaze pleaded with him, as did her words. "You gave me mercy then. Please. Do the same now. Tell them to go. They'll have to listen. Tell them I'm to stay with you. As yours."

He shook his head, mind aspin. He remembered granting her mercy in the past. But now he found he could not.

# Chapter 33

There is never a journey so long as leaving someone you love.

"You'll be fine, my dear." Considerata patted Demi's hand as the carriage jerked on rutted roads. "The Invisible Mother will take care of you, and we will, too."

It was not the same as the first time, when they'd taken her from Jarron's room in chains, sent her to gaol. Then she'd had no choice. It only felt like she had no choice now.

She'd thrown herself on his mercy and he'd refused. She supposed she could not blame him. Now she looked out the window at the countryside passing by and turned to the Mothers across from her.

"What will happen to my child?"

"Your child is a Blessing, welcome in any Motherhouse or Sister-house for his or her entire life. It will be raised and educated with all the wealth and privilege the Order can offer."

"By someone else?"

"Only if you choose to go into service. Demi," said Considerata, "do you really think we keep the children from their mothers? The Invisible Mother herself would not be kept from her son, even when his father tried to take him from her. We will raise your child if you are unable or unwilling, but we won't steal it from you."

"And my place in the Order, should I decide not to return to service?"

"That is a subject of subtler discussion." Sympathy shifted on the carriage's soft cushions, for though Handmaidens most oft went to their patrons by whatever transportation they could manage, the Mothers-in-Service traveled in rather more luxury.

"We have a rather long journey ahead of us," Demi said. "I think we have time to discuss it."

Empathetica sniffed. "Ours is not an Order of command, not in that way. No matter what lengths to which we might send ourselves in service to our patrons, it is not the place of the Mothers to dictate how any Sister chooses to spend her days. If you do not choose to return to service, you shall not. If you choose to retire from the Order you shall ever have a place within our houses, though of course you'd be expected to earn your keep in some manner."

"You could be a teacher," offered Considerata.

"Or a scullery maid," said Empathetica. "We've not much use for whores, I'm afraid."

Demi did not allow the other woman to rattle her. She drew in a deep breath and put her hands on her belly, then looked at each of them, in turn. "My child is heir to a king."

"Only for the moment. Who knows, by the end of this sennight he may no longer be a king at all." Sympathy spoke calmly, without the acerbic bite of Empathetica's tone, but nonetheless, her words stung.

Demi lifted her chin. Stared them all down. "My child might also be sick. And I know you can cure him."

The Mothers exchanged looks, but Sympathy was the one who spoke. "You can't know—"

"I know." She'd known for a long time, since her first days in the Order, spending long hours in the libraries researching the myriad descriptions of Trystan's Pox. Back then it had simply been from curiosity, a way to keep her memories of the Second Province's prince fresh. Now it seemed like fate.

"It's too dangerous," cut in Considerata. "We can't allow it."

"With all due respect, Mothers," Demi said, "it's not for you to decide."

J arron had no choice but to return to the First Province—leaving Caramin to decide the fate of the Four Provinces along with Bander and Kenston felt in Jarron's mind to be naught but a recipe for disaster. She welcomed him with an embrace and appropriate cooing over his fading scars that surprisingly did not irritate him, for though he had no doubt Caramin might have been able to make him feel embarrassed about his illness, she seemed genuinely concerned.

The second symposium met for a sennight, this time without the dancing shows or meals being served on the backs of naked servants. Caramin, for all her deviant charms, turned out to be serious in her plans to reunite what had once been one. Long days and nights of planning, however, urged Jarron no closer to agreeing to give her the title and take for himself a lower position.

Caramin, on the other hand, made no secret of the army she was building to even greater strengths. She didn't threaten—but then, she didn't have to. With what she could pull from the Third and Fourth Provinces attached to her own already considerable resources, if she'd wanted to march across the mountains to take the provinces on the other side, Jarron had no doubts she could conquer them, too.

"You must decide," Caramin told him one night after Kenston and Bander had taken themselves wearily off to bed, leaving Jarron to smoke the hukah with her. "I want you to decide for yourself, Jarron, not have the choice made for you. Believe me, I would far rather have you by my side than against me."

"Don't you mean beneath you?" The smoke tasted sweeter this way than smoked from a bowl, and Jarron took less joy from it.

Caramin laughed. "If I thought you might like it . . ."

"I wouldn't."

She looked sober. "I know you would not. But that doesn't change the fact that you must decide to take your place in this new government or fight me for what you know you can't have. I've been gracious enough, have I not?"

He had to admit she had. It didn't change his loathing for stepping aside, for giving his province and its people into the hands of another, even if in reality he would remain their liege in every way but his title. "Your grace isn't in question."

"Just everything else." She laughed and drew in the smoke, holding it deep before letting it sift out of her. She regarded him through narrowed eyes. "Where's your Handmaiden? She might advise you. Or at the very least, soothe you in your decision."

To that, Jarron only shook his head. Demi had been taken away by the Mothers-in-Service, and he had let her go. Pushed her to go.

"Where's yours?" he asked instead, indicating the spot where Gailen generally sat. All that remained was the hasp and the golden chain, unattached to anything but air.

Caramin gaze flickered as she drew more smoke. "The time came to give up substitutes."

"And replace them with what?" Jarron asked, weary but too curious not to ask.

At that, Caramin rose and pressed an entirely chaste kiss to his temple. She squeezed his shoulder. "With whatever will suffice."

"And if naught will?"

She gave him only a smile as an answer and left him there to sit while the lamps burned down and the hukah's flame burned out.

Jarron needed to think. He could trust no counsel, not even Adam, whom he loved as a brother. But it was just that sort of love that would betray him, Jarron thought as he filled his glass with worm and drank it back, grimacing at the taste. He could not rely on love to guide him now.

He sent for Erekon, instead.

"My lord king." Erekon stood without bowing or making a leg, his hand on the dagger at his waist.

"If I called for war," Jarron said without preamble, "would you be with me? Or against me?"

Erekon didn't look surprised at the question. "I cannot support you in this. Even if I wanted to, I would still be only one man amongst many who would not."

"So you'd betray your loyalty to me and my house to save your own skin?"

Erekon smiled. "Not only that. Because . . . my lord king, I tell you true, I think it's your best choice. The right choice. Not the easiest and not the one that would make you feel the best. But the one that would best serve the Second Province and its people. Your people."

Jarron studied him. "It's true, then. Revolution?"

"There are always those who speak out against those in power. Sometimes they're more easily quieted than others. This talk of unification has caused a lot of talk."

"And fear."

"And that, aye. Fear. Which can lead to dissent. Revolt. Civil war, certainly."

"Not in the Second Province," Jarron said grimly. "I'll not be the man who brings that."

"But you'd bring war with the others?"

Somehow, Jarron found humor. "I suppose I put too much faith in you, Erekon. I thought you capable of raising me an army."

"That's not what you want."

Jarron paused, looking him over. "No?"

Erekon shook his head. "No."

"Tell me, my Lion. What do I want?"

"You want her."

Jarron's throat burned, and he gave the other man his back. "You've no idea."

"Tell you true, I have more an idea than ever you could imagine," said the King's Lion in a low voice thick with grief. "But I made my mistakes. And have paid for them. Have learned little, I'm not shamed to admit. But what I know is this . . . if you love her, my lord, you should not let her run so far from you that you cannot catch up to her."

Jarron's shoulders slumped, but he didn't turn. "She's not who I thought she was, Erekon."

Erekon laughed, the sound brittle and rasping. "Of course she is. She's your Redemption."

But was that enough?

W hy are you doing this?" Pindy, one of the novitiates, bent over Demi to rub her back in slow circles. "Why do this to yourself?"

Demi heaved up naught but air and a bitter strand of saliva, then sat back against the headboard. Every part of her ached, fever-wracked, but the solid lump of her belly beneath the loose gown comforted her. "So that my child will never have to."

Pindy sat gingerly on the edge of the bed and pulled a pot of salve from the nightstand to rub into the blisters breaking out on Demi's arms and cheeks. They were worse than she'd ever seen on Jarron, breaking and oozing, the scabs bleeding and more blisters cropping up on top of them. The fever, instead of breaking as she knew it usually did during the first few days of an outbreak, continued to rise and fall, never abating. It was accompanied by nausea and a headache so fierce she felt it would split her head and fair prayed it might, just so that the pain might end.

"You might have a daughter," Pindy murmured, "who would never suffer this at all."

"Or a son who could."

"Never so bad as this," Pindy said as she capped the salve and laid a cool cloth upon Demi's forehead. "It's never so bad for any of them as this."

Demi closed her eyes against the light that seemed too bright and tried to draw in a deep breath, though even her lungs burned with fever. The medicus who attended her had said he had no idea how long this would last. Or if it would ever end in anything but perhaps her death. He prescribed treatment, but that was the best he could do.

There was no cure, just an illness that needed to run its course.

It would all be worth it, she thought as another round of agony split her skull and more blisters broke out on the roof of her mouth and soles of her feet, itching and burning. Everything would be worth it if it meant her baby would be born healthy.


There was someone else who might understand the difficulty of the choices set before him, but Jarron went to see his father with little hope the old man would be able to help him. His father had never suffered from any outbreaks of the pox, but it had taken his mind, and every day that passed stole a few more memories from him.

Bedridden, incapable even of feeding himself, Zevon Bydelay nonetheless looked up with a smile when Jarron entered his chamber. "Are you here to read to me?"

"No, Father."

The old man's brow creased. "Father?"

Jarron swallowed against the emotion that rose in his throat no matter how often he visited, how accustomed he ought to be to this sight. "Zevvie. No, I'm sorry, I'm not here to read to you today. I've somewhat to ask you, and I hope you'll be able to answer me."

Jarron's father looked confused as Jarron sat, taking his hand. "What do you have to ask me?"

Jarron held his father's hand tightly, noting how the old man's age-spotted fingers matched the length of his own. This man had spent his adult life ruling the Second Province as justly as he'd been able, and he'd taught his son to do the same. He'd stepped down when it was time, without any apparent regrets, though it must've been unimaginably difficult for him to make the decision.

"Which is more important," Jarron asked quietly. "Love of yourself, or love for someone else?"

The old man squeezed Jarron's hand and said naught for a long, long time. Jarron didn't ask again. He sat and waited patiently for the words to form in his father's mind and make their way onto his tongue. Outside the window, the gardens had begun to bloom. Two months had passed since Demi had left him, and the world had continued to spin even though there were many times Jarron had hoped it would cease.

"If you don't love yourself," Zevon finally said, "how can you love anyone else?"

Jarron clasped his father's hand gently, watching the old man's face twist in thought. "I love you, Zevvie."

The old man laughed, showing the spaces where his teeth had once been. "I love you, laddie-bright. You read to me. What did you bring to read to me today?"

"I'm sorry, I didn't bring anything to read."

"Oh, well," Jarron's father said. "I suppose we can just sit here together for a while. Won't that be merry?"

"Most merry indeed," Jarron said quietly.

And that's what they did, until at last Jarron's father closed his eyes and began to snore gently. Then Jarron laid his hand gently on the coverlet and made to leave. His father's voice stopped him before he'd taken two steps.

"Sometimes, giving somewhat away is the best way to keep it close to you."

Jarron turned, throat again tight with emotion, to find his father's gaze clear and bright—at least for the span of a breath or two. "Father."

"Your mother could never learn that. But you're not just her son, are you?" The old man blew out a breath, already drifting back into sleep. "You're mine, too."

Though Jarron stayed another few moments watching him, he said no more after that.

# Chapter 34

The Second Province did not go to war. News could travel on swift wings or plodding hooves, depending on what it was and who'd requested it, and here in the Motherhouse in Neaku, Demi was in no position or condition to demand anything but scraps of stories carried from mouth to mouth by new novitiates or Sisters returning from service. Still, news of a war would've somehow found its way to her, of that she was certain, if for no other reason than any requests for Handmaidens made from any of the Five Provinces would've been affected by political unrest.

She clung to life though every day brought her naught but suffering, determined as she was to bring forth this child no matter what it cost her. The days seemed ever long as she lay abed, sometimes feeling well enough to knit or embroider upon impossibly tiny clothes, other times barely able to move her head from the pillow. She ate and drank despite her lack of appetite, because it was necessary for her baby. She slept when she could and simply closed her eyes when she could not. She read when the pain in her head allowed it, and gratefully accepted the comfort of another reading to her to pass the time when her eyes refused to focus.

Then came a day when she was certain she would not last.

The pain in every limb, the burn of fever in her cheeks and throat, the splitting agony in her head all conspired to leave her sobbing into her pillow with eyes unable even to shed tears. She couldn't even resist the gentle hand that placed a damp cloth on the back of her neck, the fingers that worked at the pain of her cramping calves and soles. Nobody had thought to do such a thing for her before, and Demi roused herself enough to see what ministering savior had arrived to soothe her.

It seemed impossible it could be him, after so long. His hair had grown long, and he'd ceased shaving for long enough that the shadow of a beard obscured any hint of scars. He looked rough and travel worn, a man who'd slept on the sides of the road or mayhap not slept at all. He smiled, though, when he saw her looking at him.

"Hello, sweetheart," Jarron said quietly as his strong fingers worked away the sting in her muscles.

She wanted to cover her face, hide away the blisters she knew he'd too well recognize, but all she could do was relax into the relief his hands were bringing.

"This always made me feel so much better," Jarron said. "The blisters scab over and can be ignored, but the muscle cramps seem so much worse because they affect everything else."

Demi licked her lips, found them cracked and dry, and managed to breathe out the dual syllable of his name but no more.

"Hush, love," he said and bent to kiss her pox-riddled cheek, not shying away from the ugliness of it. "I'm here."

When at last Demi slept, Jarron crept from her room to take long, slow breaths that kept him from losing himself in his grief. She was dying, and why? To cure their child—the baby he'd so callously told her over and over he didn't want. Couldn't love. Wouldn't have.

The Mothers-in-Service had wanted to turn him away when he showed up, but he'd refused to go. At last they'd taken pity upon him after the fourth night he'd spent on their front doorstep without moving; they'd taken him inside and insisted he at least eat before they would take him to see Demi. They'd told him then about what she'd done—dosed herself with a virulent serum designed to infect her with Trystan's Pox even though traditionally women didn't contract the disease.

She had, though. Violently. Breathing deep now to keep himself from crying out, Jarron strode the halls of the Motherhouse, ignoring the nervous novitiates in their headscarves as they dove out of his way. He slammed open the door to the Mother's office without caring how it banged so fiercely into the wall it rattled the portraits hung there.

"How could you let her do this?"

The Mother seated behind the desk looked up at him. A small portly woman with gray hair and a pair of tiny spectacles perched on her nose, she didn't look the least bit frightened of him. "Jarron Bydelay. Sit yourself and get composed."

He didn't want to sit, nor get composed, but somewhat in her manner made him obey. "She's going to die."

"She won't die, my lad. She's simply quite ill, and I might add, she chose that path. Ought we to have tied her down so that she might not take the poison when she was so intent upon it?"

"Why not?" he demanded. "If you knew how ill she would fall, if you knew it might kill her! Would you not stop one of your Sisters from drinking a different sort of poison?"

"No." The Mother shook her head and favored him with a gentle smile.

Jarron's throat worked and he gripped the arms of the chair. "She could die."

"She won't die."

"You can't know that."

She inclined her head and sat back in her chair to study him. "Actually, you are correct. We all die, eventually."

The breath soughed out of him, and his shoulders slumped. His head hung. The floor swam in front of him as tears he'd been forcing away blurred his vision. "She cannot die."

"She did this to save your child. She did it for love. If naught beyond that, you should credit her for being unselfish. That was ever her virtue. And mayhap a vice, too," the Mother said with a small chuckle that had Jarron scowling at her. "Ah, don't look at me with such a fierce face. She went to you because we sent her, and you needed her. But do you not think we chose her for you because she might have had need of you, as well?"

"I don't know. I don't care. I just want her to be safe and well."

"And of the child?"

Somewhat twisted inside him, wrenching and tearing. Jarron put the heels of his hands to his eyes, pressing away the tears. "I will love it, of course. Raise it. I will cherish the child because of the sacrifice Demi made for it, and because we made it together in love. What more do you want me to say? Think you I came here to tell you I would rather she live and it die? Is there any way a man could say such a thing and mean it, true in his heart? I cannot find a way to wish for that, no matter how I might have forced myself to think I didn't want to become a father."

He looked at the woman across the desk. "I vowed I would not become a father, but Demi told me what those children are called. Blessings, true?"

"Oh and aye, they're called Blessings true enough. For that's what they are." The Mother studied him. "And what of the rest? You'd think us isolated, so far away from where you came from, but the fact is that we know much of what's been happening in the Five. Or the Four, as it may be."

"Then you know what I've done."

She nodded slowly.

"You know why I couldn't come sooner."

Again, she nodded.

Jarron's shoulders slumped again. "My father passed. My mother made her play to set my nephew in my place, and surprised she was when I stepped aside to let him take it without struggle. He's now the governor of the Second Province in the empire that doesn't yet have a name. And I wish him the best."

"And you, Jarron Bydelay? What of you?"

He suspected she already knew. "I am in service to the Emperor Caramin, serving as her delegate. When and if I should be of a sound mind and body to do so. Which I am not, just now. Won't be, until I know Demi is all right."

"The child will be born some months from now. Think you to stay here until then?"

"I'll take her someplace where she can have the best of care—" He stopped to stare at her. "You've given her that, I wager."

"Oh, yes. Indeed. Better than even a king could provide. But of course, there is somewhat here that is lacking we cannot provide."

Jarron gave her a weary look. Before making it here, he'd traveled much, between the First and Second Provinces, then out of their protected valley and across the mountains, a long journey overland to here. He was exhausted. "What's that?"

The Mother smiled. "You, my dear lad. We cannot give her you."


D emi did not wake for quite some time. She dreamed of floating in a warm and salted sea, her hair unbound and streaming around her like seaweed. She dreamed of voices urging her to . . . to do somewhat, she was uncertain what, exactly, they wanted her to do. To speak? To sit?

To wake.

But, cradled in the softness of her dreams, a place where pain didn't touch her, Demi didn't want to wake. She felt hands upon her, lifting. The rock and shift of the world beneath her. A carriage? A train? She didn't know. She didn't care.

She heard a voice, low and deep. Singing to her. Felt the touch of firm and gentle hands massaging her in all the places she ached. And she knew, somehow, this was what she ought to be reaching for, if only she could force her body to respond.

She began to try.

It was difficult, for she'd gone down very deep, away from anything that might've brought her back to the surface. But she tried. She swam. She floated. She sank and drifted and swam again.

And eventually . . .

She woke.

"Push," said the woman in the white robe standing next to the bed, her hand gripping Demi's. "Push hard now, love, wot the baby's on its way."

If she'd thought there was pain before now, Demi had been foolish. The splitting agony in her head, the ache in her limbs, had been naught compared to this. This pain went soul deep, slicing at her from the inside out. Her womb contracted as though someone had sliced her in half.

She screamed.

And he was there, her Jarron, holding her other hand, his face pale but for the hectic spots of red on his cheeks. He leaned in close to murmur soothing words into her ear, and Demi calmed as the pain faded, leaving her panting. She blinked, coming back to herself and the world.

"Jarron?"

"Love, I'm here."

"But . . ."

"Get ready," said the woman in white. "'Ere comes another."

This time, Demi couldn't even muster the breath for a scream. She'd known childbirth would hurt. She'd known it would take a great effort. She had never imagined that it might be so agonizing, so difficult, that she would not make it through.

"She's losing a lot of blood," said a voice from her feet.

Demi looked down to see another woman in white settled between

her knees, her face grim and freckled with spots of what Demi realized with some alarm was her own blood. The woman looked up at
her, all seriousness. Demi felt a building pressure inside her and an
answering push against her privates.

"Push," said the woman between her legs. "The baby is coming
now."

The baby was coming. Somehow, no matter what it took, Demi
had to do this. She looked at Jarron, his face as serious as ever she'd
seen it. She gripped his hand.

He kissed her. "I'm here, love. Do what the midwife says. We're all
here."

She had no voice to tell him she loved him. She had naught but the
pain building again, and the sudden inescapable urge to bear down
and push. Demi focused. She found a breath. She pushed, hard and
long, straining with the effort.

She pushed again.

She'd felt her child move inside her but it was nothing like what
happened now. The huge and undeniable shift of somewhat inside her
that did not belong there permanently. Her muscles contracted, her
body tensed. She pushed. The baby moved. It tore at her, but the pain
was no worse than any she'd had so far, and it was made better by
knowing that in a few moments more she'd hold her baby in her arms.

*Invisible Mother*, she thought as the world threatened to go gray on
her, *please, please let me have at least those few moments with him before
you take me.*

*Please.*

She had ever been a determined and stubborn wench, according to
Erekon, and she was ever more determined to remain so now when
those qualities could only help her. Demi pushed. She screamed. She
pushed again.

And then, a great and gaping emptiness filled her.

The baby was born.

And Demi looked to the man she loved, trying desperately to

focus on his face before she was swept away again by darkness. Jarron wept, his gaze not upon her but at the foot of the bed. In the next moment, the midwife who'd been holding her hand placed a loose-wrapped bundle on Demi's chest.

"It's a boy," said the midwife.

"Get ready to push again," came the other midwife's voice from the foot of the bed, her tone surprised. "There's another!"

The second was easier, slipping from her without so much as an extra effort from her. In moments Demi's arms were full of wriggling, warm infants. Two of them. Red-faced, squalling, and so beautiful it hurt her heart to look at them more than anything else she'd undergone.

"They're perfect," she managed to say.

Jarron laid a hand on each of their heads, his face twisted with awe. "Two? We have . . . two?"

"A girl and a boy! Double the blessing," said the midwife who'd been holding Demi's hand before she went to the foot of the bed to assist the other.

"Blessings," Jarron said as he pressed a kiss to Demi's forehead. "They truly are."

# Epilogue

Before you know it, you'll have a set of your own," Jarron said to Caramin, who snorted lightly but chucked the infant boy beneath his chin and cast Demi an eye-rolling glance.

"Don't rush me," Caramin said. "I'm a bit busy with running an empire at the moment."

Demi wanted to get up and out of the wheeled chair Jarron insisted she use so that she might not grow overtired by walking. It had been nearly two months since the babies' birth, and every medicus Jarron had hired—and there had been nigh on a dozen of the best sent to tend her—had said she would recover. Slowly, but she would.

More important, her children did not carry Trystan's Pox.

"As if you couldn't be both a mother and an emperor," said Erekon from his place standing behind Caramin.

He sounded admiring, not scornful, and Demi watched him carefully, noting what mayhap none other would, not even Erekon himself. But that was naught of her concern she reminded herself as she watched her husband dandle his daughter upon his knee as proudly as any father ever had. She watched the woman who might've been her rival admire her son. And she watched the man she'd once loved more than anything in the world stand over them all to protect them with everything he had.

"Are you tired, love? Shall I take you back for a rest?" Jarron, their daughter, Galya, under his arm, bent to kiss Demi softly. "Gideon's probably ready for his nap, too. They both are."

"And I must steal your husband for a few chimes' worth of time," said Caramin, handing Demi her son with a final kiss to the baby's cheek. "Though I swear to you, I'll send him back to you before the night grows too late."

"Promises, promises," Demi said with a laugh and squeezed her boy to her. "I know better than that, don't I?"

Caramin straightened, her glance going so swiftly in Erekon's direction only the most attentive observer would have noticed. "I mean it this time. Even I've got to sleep upon occasion."

"I'll walk back with you, help you settle the babies, then come back." Jarron waved a hand at Caramin before she could protest. "Ring for supper; if I'm to be working late the least you could do is feed me."

Laughing, she agreed, and Jarron settled Galya onto her mother's lap, then wheeled them all down the halls and into the chambers they shared while Caramin's guests. Then, with as much grace as he'd ever had playing any sport, he insisted on changing both sets of nappies and settling the babies into bed with their mother, one at each breast and both suckling contentedly.

"You've the ribbon to ring for the nursemaid when they've finished," he said. "And for the maid. And your pitcher of water is just here. . . ."

"Go," Demi said. "I'll be fine."

Jarron left off his fussing and sat next to her, his gaze falling to their children nursing. He touched each small head with reverent fingertips, then looked at her. "Our double blessing."

Demi smiled at him, this man she loved so much. "And I've the pleasure of yet a third."

He laughed at that and kissed her. "So have I. Aren't we a fortunate pair? I love you," Jarron whispered against her mouth, careful not to dislodge the babies, who would certainly have protested being interrupted in their feeding.

Demi kissed him back. She ran a hand through his hair, then down his cheek to cup the scruff of his chin before pulling him close to kiss him again harder. "I love you, too."

There was much to be done in the world—an empire to build. Children to raise and love. A marriage she still could not believe was real to foster and grow. Beautifully, they had all the time to do it.

And that was the true blessing.